EVERYBODY'S SUSPECT IN GEORGIA

EVERYBODY'S SUSPECT IN GEORGIA

THREE ROMANCE MYSTERIES

CECIL MURPHEY

BARBOUR
PUBLISHING

ISBN 978-1-60260-411-7

Cover thumbnails:
Design by Kirk DouPonce, DogEared Design
Illustration by Jody Williams

Published by Barbour Publishing, Inc., P.O. Box 719, Uhrichsville, OH 44683, www.barbourbooks.com

Our mission is to publish and distribute inspirational products offering exceptional value and biblical encouragement to the masses.

Member of the
Evangelical Christian
Publishers Association

Printed in the United States of America.

EVERYBODY LOVED ROGER HARDEN

ACKNOWLEDGEMENTS:

Thanks to members of the Bible Discovery Class and to my wonderful agents, Steve Laube and Deidre Knight. Most of all, my love and thanks to Shirley.

1

When I agreed to attend Roger Harden's dinner party, how could I have known the terrible events that would take place on Palm Island and especially what would happen to Roger himself? I also had no idea that anyone would find out about my past. Roger knew, of course, but imagine—me *voluntarily* telling everyone my long-held secret.

Sorry, there I go again. I'm getting ahead of myself. I do that a lot. I start telling a story and jump ahead to the best parts. I'll try not to do that again. I've promised myself that I would write everything down exactly as it happened. So I can't reveal anything about what took place on Palm Island before I reached Roger's house, can I?

I'm Julie West, and I decided to write down all the strange occurrences on Palm Island so that I don't forget anything. There's one part that Burton needs to explain because I wasn't there. I asked him to note those events, exactly as I'm trying to do.

So here is how it happened. I had barely reached the dockside, and it was exactly 7:51. It was late June, and the breeze along the Georgia coast made the evenings cool enough for a sweater or light jacket. I had worn a windbreaker and slacks, so I was all right. Sure, my hair was a mess, but everyone expected that. Because I keep my titian-colored hair short and it's naturally curly, a comb was all I'd need anyway.

I was more concerned about the time than my hair. When Roger said eight o'clock for dinner, he meant everyone was to be present, seated, hands in their laps, and silent—totally silent—when the large hall clock struck the hour. I knew the ritual: I'd been to dinner there three times previously.

If anyone was late, Roger never said anything. He didn't need to. His pale blue eyes glared in a way that made words unnecessary. Each time, I felt like a fourth grader on my first day of school when the teacher's roving eyes intimidated me.

I would have arrived at the dock at least fifteen minutes earlier if it hadn't been for the heavy traffic along I-95. There must have been an accident near Savannah. Although I never saw the collision, I got jammed up in the snarled, stop-and-start trail of automobiles.

When I finally arrived at the dock and caught sight of the boat, I sighed with relief, knowing I could reach the island in time. After I shut off the car engine at the dockside, I hurried around to the trunk of my Honda hybrid.

A man I didn't recognize struggled to get his suitcase wedged into the specially built hold on Roger Harden's prized Boston Whaler. Alongside him, Simon Presswood, Roger's handyman, pulled the bag from the man's hand and deftly twisted the bulky suitcase so it slid with ease into the special compartment.

"I need a little help over here," I called to Simon.

He got out of the Boston Whaler and came over to me. When he reached my car, he shrugged.

I shrugged in return, but Simon ignored me. He walked directly to my opened car trunk and picked up the heaviest of my bags. He then offered his arm to help me into the Whaler.

This time Roger hadn't come along, which was unusual. He loved to give his guests such a detailed explanation of his boat, it almost sounded as if he had designed and built the craft himself. For someone like me, it was more fun to observe his excitement than it was to listen to him talk about a two-hundred-horsepower Mercury Verado four-cycle engine. He hated it when anyone called it a motor—as if the person had used profane language.

At the beginning of my two previous trips, Roger had lectured us as he pointed out the remarkable features of the boat. "It will still float, even if ten people are inside and it's filled with water." (I refrained from asking him why ten people would stay inside a water-filled boat. Why wouldn't they bail with their life jackets on?) Both times I cringed when he pointed out that the boat could withstand a thousand rounds of automatic weapon fire. That statement always puzzled me. Unless, of course, he expected South American terrorists to pursue him.

The Boston Whaler was about eight feet wide, big enough to keep us dry, and it had an engine that worked well. Okay, it was nice to look at, and the boat shouted quality and money, but to me, a boat is a boat. On my previous trips, during Roger's lectures, I'd stared at the ocean vessels streaming across the Atlantic while he droned on. Or I'd gazed at the sea oats along the sand dunes. Only about six inches tall (with roots as long as five feet), the sea oats not only protect the dunes from erosion, but I like to think they wave at me.

I thought it was funny when Roger condescended and treated us like idiots, so I referred to the Whaler as a "rowboat with a motor."

Roger didn't have a great sense of humor. He reminded me that the Whaler was "very stable, very dry, and very comfortable." He clasped his hands behind his back. "And it has an engine, *not* a motor."

On my first trip, another passenger added, "It's a quality boat for the obscenely rich."

Roger loved that remark, indicated by the swell of his chest. "Quite right," he'd say. Yes, Roger liked to give his guests the best.

But today Roger wasn't present, and Simon was ready to leave. He had tied the Whaler to the small dock so no one had to get wet climbing inside.

Without going into details of the boring introduction, the stranger's name was Dr. James Burton, the minister at a church in Riverdale in Clayton County on Atlanta's Southside—about ten minutes' drive from my office. He told me he had arrived at the dock in Brunswick at 7:20—the time I was supposed to have gotten there. He mentioned that I was the last to arrive.

If I had driven in by 7:20, that would have given us plenty of time to board the Whaler and arrive on Palm Island long before 8:00.

I didn't blame the minister for being irritated, though he didn't say anything overtly negative. His frown told me he wasn't happy at being delayed.

I thanked Simon for helping me. He's tall—about half a foot over six feet—and always keeps his head shaved. I never could figure out why, because he doesn't have that slick bald scalp that most men do who shave their heads. He has a large, barely visible scar on the left side of his face, running from his temple to the top of his lip. Simon would make a frightening appearance with his broad shoulders, dark coloring, and huge eyebrows—except for his soft brown eyes. When he looked at me, I felt as if he were like a small boy trapped inside a huge body. He never revealed anything about himself and always ignored any personal questions. I assumed he didn't understand English well because he rarely spoke. Mostly he shrugged or answered in terse statements.

"Are all the others here?" I asked.

Simon nodded.

"How many are on the island?"

He shrugged. "Nine. Also Mrs. Harden. Jason." (Jason was Roger's stepson).

"He go," Simon said, his chin jutted out to point to the man already seated in the red boat.

Dr. Burton, or as he informed us with a grin that showed a set of teeth a Hollywood movie star would envy, said, "Just call me Burton. Everyone does."

"I'm sorry I'm late." I laughed self-consciously and said, "Just like a woman, huh?"

"You want to blame your whole gender because you're late?"

"Just trying to make it a joke," I said. "Traffic problem around Savannah."

"Hmm," he said.

"Or maybe I should blame it on the way we women drive or—"

"Or that you could have started earlier."

"Tide soon full. Wait no longer." Simon shrugged.

It was my turn to shrug. This time his back was to me and he didn't see my action. I like doing that with Simon. Sometimes he smiles when I imitate his gestures, especially the way he uses his chin to point at an object. It's better than using fingers, I guess. I love that chin thing; it's his best gesture.

"We're ready," I said to Simon and smiled at Burton. I knew it wouldn't do any good to smile at Simon.

Burton sat on the far right side of the Whaler as if he wanted to give me three-fourths of the seat. I moved to the far left and figured a third person and perhaps a fourth could have sat between us. Instead, we both put our life jackets in the empty space even though we knew we were supposed to wear them.

I could write another couple of pages about Dr. James Burton. I knew he was irritated—and as I was to learn, that wasn't typical of him. He certainly had a right to be upset. I was upset at myself for being so late.

Besides his perfect teeth, Burton is all-around good-looking. I'm five ten in my sneakers, and he was maybe less than an inch shorter. He wasn't wearing a wedding ring, and that made him look even better. I liked his dark eyes and those fabulous dark curls. He had two short ringlets right in the middle of his forehead. He was trim, and his arms made him look like a weight lifter. He didn't have that football belly I'd seen in so many men his age—around thirty, I figured—and I liked that about him.

Burton tried to talk to Simon as the engine caught hold and the Whaler pulled away from the shore. The ride was noisy, of course, but I could hear Burton's questions easily enough. The answers came back with shrugs, nods, or shaking of the head. Simon was, well, just Simon.

—

Palm Island was originally an isthmus, but billionaire Roger Harden had the land dug away from the mainland because he wanted isolation, and he got it. The gossip I heard said that isolation had cost him somewhere around twelve million dollars. I don't know what power he had to exert to make the isthmus an island, but he did, and I assume part of those millions was to influence the right officials and politicians. Roger told me that once he separated it from the mainland, he had to give it a name, and he called it Palm Island. He laughed and said, "I planted three palm trees."

In the late 1990s, he had spent more money—a lot more money—to install an underground land telephone line. The telephone worked about 60 percent of the time.

"Any Internet access from here?" Burton asked. "I brought my laptop. I thought I might use it."

"If the phone works."

"If the phone doesn't?"

Simon shrugged. "In two weeks, Wi-Fi."

"Cell phones? They work here?"

This time I laughed. "About 1 percent of the time. Roger tried to explain it to me once, but I never understood the reason. Right, Simon?"

Simon shrugged.

Just then, Simon nosed the Whaler expertly to the small dock at the island, turned off the engine, and jumped out. He held up his hand for Burton to remain seated. Simon was barefooted and wore loose, pale green shorts and a brown shirt that hung almost to the bottom of his shorts. From the side of the boat, he leaned forward, grabbed a rope from the dock, and effortlessly pulled the Whaler the last few feet. "Out," he said. "Suitcases I bring."

The tide was rising fast, and I realized there was almost no beach left. Now I understood what Simon had meant about no time. In a few minutes, the fierce waves would have made it impossible to settle at the small dock, a T-shaped walkway.

Simon jumped out and reached down to give me a hand. Once out of the Whaler, I hurried across the ten-foot walkway and up the steps. From the top, I paused to look into the west. I loved to watch the sun move slowly toward the horizon. I'm not one of those nature freaks, but sights at the coast dazzle me. Bright steams of red and gold sneaked across the sky as if they wanted to make an announcement of sunset. Dark clouds appeared in the east as if to promise rain before morning.

I looked at my watch. It was 7:58. "Hurry. Roger hates it when anyone is late."

Behind me, Burton stumbled, so I grabbed his hand, and we raced toward the front entrance.

"If I was rude to you," he yelled, "I'm sorry."

"You were rude, but it's all right because I didn't hear you," I yelled back to him as we raced ahead. I love it when I can give smart-mouthed answers.

I didn't knock but pushed the door open. We hurried through the foyer and straight toward the dining room, which was perhaps thirty feet and to the left. The minute hand on the large antique clock showed 7:59. I sighed and released Burton's hand. We paused, and I smiled at him as he stepped back and I walked sedately into the room. I liked the feel of his hand—smooth but strong. Very masculine. I caught the barest whiff of his cologne—a strong, manly fragrance.

Several people attempted to smile at us—or perhaps they only grimaced. I didn't know anyone except Amanda Harden and her son, Jason. She indicated the place for me on her right, which left one space for Burton directly across the table and next to Jason. I liked that because I could look at Burton without being rude.

The host's chair, of course, was empty.

"Hello, everyone," I said as my gaze swept around the table. "I'm Julie West from Atlanta."

Across from me and down one on my right, a heavyset man smiled at me. "Hi there! Welcome to Palm Island! I'm Lenny Goss. This is my first time to meet with such a fun group of people." He laughed as he lifted his hand in a kind of handshaking gesture. He looked around, but no one responded to his "fun group of people." His smile melted into a small pout.

No one else spoke or acknowledged me, but I wasn't surprised. After all, this was Roger Harden's house, and he knew exactly what he wanted. Obviously, the others—except Lenny—had been well trained. None of us could see the large clock in the hallway, but I knew everyone strained to hear its ticking. Like most of them, I had been to Palm Island before, so I understood Roger's odd behavior. It was simple: He did not want to hear any talking when he made his grand entrance into the immense dining room. I thought it was a bit eccentric but decided that when a man's net worth is somewhere in the low billions, he could act as nutty as he wanted.

The absolute silence seemed a bit weird and silly, but it was his house and we were his guests.

No one else said a word. Just then the wind began to huff at the windows, and somewhere a loose shutter banged. I had checked the weather on the Internet before I left; the experts predicted rain before midnight along the coast.

Burton started to say something to the middle-aged woman on his right. But she put her long, red-nailed index finger to her lips.

Lenny's eyes darted toward a tall bottle-blond across from him. She looked vaguely familiar. Her thick hair had fallen across one eye. She pushed it away with her tapered and perfectly formed fingers. They were natural nails and painted a light pink. She wore a pink cotton-blend blouse and a dark blue Chanel suit, and her nails matched the shade of her blouse. *Nice touch*, I thought.

Without trying to be obvious, I looked closely at Amanda, one of the most strikingly beautiful women I'd ever seen. She wore tight-fitting gold silk pants and a matching low-cut, cowl-neck, satin blouse that probably cost more than I earned in a month. Her shoulder-length golden earrings and heavy gold chain seemed a little overdone, even for Roger's house. About a year ago she started dyeing her hair—and it looked great—into a slightly lighter shade of ash blond than her natural color. I couldn't detect one bit of gray. Amanda had always been trim and beautiful, although I noticed the seams of her silk pants now strained when she shifted her weight. She must have added ten pounds since I'd seen her last. She smiled at me, but it seemed slightly forced.

While the other guests waited in silence, Burton looked across at me and arched his right brow. I shrugged in a perfect Simon-like gesture. He returned the Simon shrug—not quite perfect, but he'd get it right before we left.

I put my napkin on my lap and imitated everyone by sitting with my hands folded. The seconds ticked away. We had fourteen seconds to go. I sighed in relief. I had made it on time.

As we waited, I tried not to look around, because I never liked Roger's taste in furniture. Everything in the house was done in the rococo style. While Roger thought it exuded delicacy and lightness—which I suppose it did—I thought it was too elaborately ornamented with shell motifs, serpentine curves, and cabriole legs, and not particularly comfortable. Finely done needlepoint of floral designs cushioned the seats and chair backs. I used to tell him I'd rather look at his chairs than sit on them. He didn't like that part of my humor, either.

The grandfather clock began its first clang.

No one moved. I closed my eyes so that I didn't laugh. We were all adults, all sitting in stiff obedience like kids in a military school. But then, that was Roger's way.

Silently I counted the gongs. Surreptitiously, I looked around at the other guests. Across the table from me sat a fiftyish-looking woman whose lips moved silently as she also counted. She had one of those severe hairstyles—hair pulled back into a bun—and she wore thick, dark-framed glasses. Later I learned her name was Tonya Borders, Roger's longtime lawyer. She looked like a woman who had forgotten how to smile. But then, I reasoned, maybe the poor woman had nothing to smile about.

The clock finished chiming.

Our eyes automatically turned toward the open door, which was only feet from Roger's office. This was the moment for his appearance—just as the clock struck its eighth and final gong.

Roger didn't come into the room.

For several seconds, no one spoke a word, but all of us turned toward Amanda as if on cue.

"Where is Roger?" she asked no one in particular. "He is never late." She rang the small bell beside her plate.

A tall, rail-thin woman in a maid's uniform appeared immediately. She carried a soup tureen. "Where is Mr. Harden?" Amanda asked.

"I do not know, mum. I'll go check on him."

Her name was Elaine Wright, and she had been with the Hardens for about four years. Elaine turned back into the kitchen with the soup. We could hear her set it on the stove or a ledge, and seconds later, she crossed the room and left by the other door. She wore a type of backless shoe that made every footstep echo through the dining room. She knocked on the door of Roger's study.

A few seconds later, we heard her knock again. More like pounding the door this time. "Mr. Harden? Are you in there, sir?" Her tone was a notch below panicked.

"Sir? I'm coming in now." Apparently, she then opened the office door. She screamed.

2

After Mrs. Wright's scream, we all hurried out of the dining room, rushed into the hall, and turned left. Elaine Wright stood at the door and pointed. "Mr. Harden—he is—he is—something has happened to Mr. Harden!"

Burton pushed past her and entered the office, and the rest of us followed. Roger lay on his back on the floor behind his desk. A pool of blood stained his face and his shirt, and blood had dripped onto the floor.

Burton squatted then pressed two fingers to Roger's neck. "No pulse," he said. "I'm no expert, but I'd say that looks as if he's been shot." He pointed to what was obviously a gunshot wound in his temple.

Amanda brushed past me. She didn't kneel—not in those form-fitting silk pants—but she bent over, and it was obvious she was genuinely shocked. "Shot? Who would want to do that?" She turned around and stared at us. "Who would—who would want to kill him? Why would any of you—?"

Although all of us had hurried toward the office, I was the last one to enter. Just then, Simon walked into the house with our luggage. I turned around and heard the thump of our suitcases. He raced past me and pushed several people out of the way. "No! No!"

The next few minutes remain jumbled in my mind while we tried to adjust to the shock of Roger's death. Somebody screamed, and I heard wails of "It can't be! It can't be!"

"He was my best friend, my best friend," moaned a balding man in glasses. He put his right hand under his glasses to wipe his eyes. I couldn't be sure, because I couldn't see clearly from where I stood, but I don't think he actually shed tears even though he made a big show of wiping his face.

There was so much noise and talking and groaning, I don't remember anything else distinctly until Simon hurried out of the office and down the hallway. Seconds later he returned with two dark blankets. "Go," he said and covered the body without moving it. It was only an impression I had, but the gentleness with which he covered Harden's body appeared more genuine and heartfelt than any other response I had observed.

The one exception was Jason Harden. I wasn't sure, but he seemed to show genuine grief. He made no noise, but tears slid silently down his cheeks.

Burton took over and quietly got us all back into the dining room. I don't remember how he did that, but he had obviously taken charge.

I stood by the door and didn't move until everyone was gone. Simon remained by Roger's body. He came out last.

"Lock door," he said and pulled a key from his pocket. He turned and put the key into the lock.

The others whispered to each other, but I heard more than one person say, "Why? Everybody loved Roger Harden."

"What reason would anyone have to kill dear Roger?" one of the women asked.

Once we had returned to the dining room, we stood around awkwardly. No one seemed to want to sit at the table.

"If he was shot, surely one of you heard the noise," Burton said. He pointed to me. "Julie and I arrived with Simon less than a minute before the clock began to chime. The rest of you were here." He turned to Mrs. Wright and asked, "Is there anyone else on the island?"

"Just the eleven of you, as well as Simon and me."

"His body is still warm, so it must have happened recently."

They began to stare at each other, raise eyebrows, and make quiet protestations as if they didn't want poor Roger to hear them discuss details.

"I would never hurt Roger." I don't remember who said that, but it was one of the men.

Burton turned to the maid and said, "Uh, sorry, I don't know your name, but—"

"My name is Elaine Wright."

"Okay, Elaine, please—"

"Mrs. Wright, if you please."

"Sorry. Mrs. Wright, will you call the police?"

"I shall use the extension in the kitchen." She left the dining room.

"While we wait, I wonder if anyone has any information about Roger that would shed light on this."

"Everybody loved Roger Harden," said a woman in her midthirties who identified herself as Paulette White. She was overdressed in a black poufy dress and overjeweled with three strands of pearls. Her bouffant hair seemed as if it had been glued to her scalp. "No one would ever want to harm him. Why, he's such a kind man, and he's done so much good for the community, and—"

"The phone is out again," Mrs. Wright announced from the doorway.

"How long has it been out?" Burton asked. "Do you have any idea?"

"Phone rang two hours ago," Simon said.

"Yes, that is correct," the maid answered. "It rang just a couple of minutes before or after 6:00. I was clearing up the last of the tea dishes. By the time I reached the kitchen, Mr. Harden had picked up the phone in his office."

"Did you overhear what Mr. Harden said?" Burton asked.

"Certainly not," she replied. "I would not do such a thing." She stared at Burton as if she dared him to challenge her.

"If I offended you, I apologize," Burton said. "I assume you heard his voice when he first spoke to the other person."

"It was a man on the other end, and he said, 'All right.' Then Mr. Harden said something to the effect that it was not an appropriate time to call. I hung up the phone in the kitchen."

"So that means he must have been killed some time after 6:15."

"He was alive at 7:00," said a man with a deep voice. He was paunchy, probably about sixty, with blotchy skin. He might have been handsome once, but that could only have been before his second birthday. He had a bulbous nose, large ears, and deep-set brown eyes. He wore those old-fashioned tortoise-colored glasses that made him look as if he had worn the same pair since about 1970.

"And who are you?" Burton asked. "I don't know any of you except Jason and Amanda."

"My name is Wayne Holmestead," he said in a low, deep voice that probably scared employees. "I have known that kind, generous, and wonderful man for nearly forty years."

"You were good friends, then?"

"Good friends? We were extremely close. I am—I was—also Roger's partner in real estate and especially along the coastal area from Savannah to the Florida line. He owned a number of businesses, as you probably know." Wayne paused to remove his glasses and rub his eyes. He wore an expensive navy pinstriped suit with a vest. Everything about him said either that he had a lot of money or he wanted us to think he did. He was balding and carried a football-sized paunch. "He's—he was—my best friend for more than twenty years. I loved him like—like a brother—perhaps more than a brother."

He took out his handkerchief and wiped his eyes. I stood close enough to see that there were no tears.

"He was my best friend," Wayne said in what was supposed to sound like a blubbery voice.

"Probably *your* only friend," Jason said and stared at him. "Besides that, you weren't *his* friend." Jason was twenty, but as I stared at the peach fuzz on his cheeks, I would have lowered his age by at least three years. Like his mother, Jason had that excellent bone structure and those high cheekbones that would keep him looking young long after he had said good-bye to middle life.

"That was absolutely uncalled for!" Holmestead said loudly. He stared at the boy and pulled his vest down over his paunch. "You have no right to talk to me like that."

"I do when I know what I'm saying. You hated him."

"Look who says such words," Wayne said. "I wonder if I could count the times I heard you scream, 'I hate you! I hate you!' and now you try to accuse me of not—"

"I know what I know!"

"Tell us what you know," Burton said. He turned and draped his arm around Jason's shoulder. It was obvious they knew each other well.

"I heard him just before teatime. I wanted to talk to Dad—and yeah, we had problems in the past." He stared at Burton. "You know about—"

"Yes, I know."

"But—but he and I—well, we got everything straightened out. Uh, well, sort of." He smiled at Burton. "You were the biggest reason—and I guess that's why Dad wanted you to be here tonight. He wanted to thank you. At least, I assume that's why."

"It seems rather easy for you to talk like that, Jason," Wayne said, "but I know he planned to cut you out of his will. You would receive absolutely nothing. Not a penny." He lifted his chin as if to say, "See, I've bested you on that."

"That was true three weeks ago, but we got our differences straightened out," Jason said. "Besides, that's got nothing to do with me. I heard how you talked to him and I heard the names you called him—"

"How dare you attempt to sully my name with such—"

Burton put up his hand. "Let Jason tell us what he knows, and then you can speak."

"I was outside Dad's office door, and Mr. Holmestead said, 'You're a despicable tyrant. Everyone thinks you're a man of compassion. You can't do this to me! You can't!' That's when Dad looked up, saw me, and said we'd talk after dinner. So I left."

"I said no such thing!"

"Sure you did. You also swore at him—words my mother doesn't want me to use."

"You have a powerful imagination."

"Then ask Simon. He stood at the hall closet. He was supposed to be adding clothes hangers and making space, but he listened. I know he did."

Everyone turned and stared at Simon, who had moved toward the back of the group.

He shrugged. "Maybe."

"Let's get back to the timing," I interrupted. "Can't we narrow this down? Wayne, you saw him at seven o'clock, you say. How did you know it was seven?"

"The evening news had barely started. I spotted Roger on the steps and started to talk to him, but he waved me away, went into his office, and closed the door."

"I saw Wayne when he entered the room," said Paulette White, the woman dressed in black.

"Yes, I saw them at the door as I started to descend the staircase." We had to stop then and listen to the speaker tell us all about himself. Dr. Jeffery Mark Dunn taught biology and other first-year science courses at Clayton University on Atlanta's Southside. I knew who he was. In fact, years ago I had signed up for one of his courses, but he was so boring and monotoned, I knew I'd never stay awake.

I dropped the class after the first day. He still wore the same cheap toupee. It was solid black, and the hair that stuck out below was gray. His glasses were now a little thicker, but the voice hadn't changed. He was tall and extremely thin—I guessed about six four—with sharp, bony features. He looked even skinnier than he had when I tried his class eight years earlier.

I probably ought to thank Dr. Dunn. Until I sampled his class, I had planned to go into medicine. He was the major reason I changed my mind. I'm now a psychologist. I've received my doctoral degree from Georgia State, and I'm in private practice.

For the next half hour, Burton made everyone sit down and tell us what he or she was doing before coming to the table.

Just as we started the informal interrogation, Jason said he was hungry, but Mrs. Wright refused to serve anyone. "I am far too upset to think about food. It is in the kitchen. You may help yourself if you choose." She stared down Amanda's stern gaze. "I cannot—I cannot." Crying, she sat down in a corner of the room.

Most of them said they didn't want anything to eat. I think they lied because they assumed that it was the right thing to say. Roger, the man they all claimed to love, had just been murdered. As I gazed around the room, I figured that most of them would move toward the kitchen within minutes.

One by one we all sat down at the table. Lenny, the short, slightly rotund, carrot-headed man, pulled his chair back against the wall and balanced it on two legs.

"Do not do that," Mrs. Wright said with no sign that she'd been crying.

"Okeydokey," he said and grinned. "You're the boss."

"I am *not* the boss. I am merely an employee."

"Is there a Mr. Wright?"

"When was the last time a woman dumped you?" she asked.

"That's irrelevant," he said.

"You are exactly right," she said and turned her back to him.

Lenny Goss stared at her before his face lit up. "Hey, that's great. You're a great comedian—straight face and all! You rock, mama!" He roared with laughter and turned to me. "Isn't she a hoot?"

"If you say so," I said and tried to give him enough of a smile that he didn't feel offended but not enough that he'd keep talking.

Lenny had enough sense to shut up. He pulled a toothpick out of his jacket pocket and started to pick his teeth. He was about five feet five with elevated heels that brought him to about five seven. He was chubby—that's the kindest word I can use—not quite obese, but he was well on his way. He had that awful carrot-red hair, pale green eyes, and skin pocked with acne scars from his teen years.

"Please eat," Amanda said. She sat at the table twisting a gold lace handkerchief that matched her outfit. As I watched her hands, I sensed that she tried to project a stronger image of the grieving widow than she felt.

It also struck me that no one had walked over to her to express sympathy. Jason was seated next to her and patted her hand a few times. I wasn't sure about his emotions. He had been volatile toward Wayne Holmestead, but now he seemed sad. Was that genuine? I wasn't sure.

"I'm hungry," I said. I got up and walked toward the kitchen. My action seemed to give permission to the others. Jason followed me, and immediately behind him was Reginald Ford. I had met him once—briefly—at Roger's house. If I remember correctly, he is the head of the largest construction firm along the Georgia coast.

He wasn't a particularly good-looking man, but he wasn't ugly. About six feet tall. His prematurely white hair probably made him look older, but as I studied his face, I pegged him for mid- to late thirties. Reginald had an athletic build and wore a tailored shirt that emphasized his muscular arms. But there was something about him I didn't like. I've learned to rely on my instincts, and I felt he wasn't a man I could trust.

Next to him stood the bottle-blond with what I call a plastic smile. Maybe I think of her that way because she was so beautiful. She was probably one of those girls who never had to squeeze a pimple in her life. She wore thin, spiked Charles Jourdan shoes that made her nearly three inches taller than Reginald. She carried a sleek, cornflower blue Hermes shoulder bag that looked perfect with her Chanel suit. Her pale blue scarf probably cost her more than my entire wardrobe.

"Your face looks slightly familiar," I said, "but I don't think we've met."

"Everybody knows me," she said and flashed her plastic smile. She posed with her right arm in the air as though she held a pointer in her hand.

"The weather girl! Beth Wilson! That's who you are!" Lenny said.

"Yes, of course," she said, twirled, and bowed slightly—just the way she performed at the end of each of her weathercasts. She had one of those naturally thin bodies most of us women hate because we know we can't be like her.

"Then you'll want something to eat," I said, unaware of my non sequitur until the words popped out of my mouth. Embarrassed, I turned and led the line back to the kitchen. I'm fairly thin—not Beth Wilson thin—yet when I get nervous, eating calms me down. After all, someone had just been killed. Or maybe I just use that as an excuse. Besides, I know that Mrs. Wright's squid tastes like no one else on the planet can cook it. Okay, Roger insisted we call it calamari, but it's still squid to me.

Eventually we all sat down at the dining room table. The calamari was excellent, and the vegetables tasted as if they had been cooked at a five-star hotel. The now-lukewarm fish consommé still rated better than at any restaurant I've visited. Amanda didn't appear to have moved from her chair. Lenny had finished his soup, returned to the kitchen, and come back to the table with two bowls for himself.

"You really like that consommé, do you?" I asked.

Lenny had been so busy shoveling it into his mouth, it took two seconds for the message to get through.

"Yeah! Great soup," he said. "It's a little fishy, but great."

"It's supposed to have a fish flavor," Reginald said, "but how would you know the difference?"

Lenny didn't respond but finished off the first bowl, shoved it aside, and spooned out the second. I assumed he could have been eating canned tomato soup and would have said, "Great soup."

Burton had stayed in the dining room. He picked up a glass of water from his place, but he didn't sit down. He moved around as if he were Hercule Poirot or maybe a better dressed and more graceful Columbo.

Without going through a lot of who-cares details about who said what, it came down to this. Except for Burton and me, everyone else had arrived in time for tea that began promptly at 5:00. He and I had been invited for tea—an English high tea, complete with cucumber sandwiches—but both of us had sent our regrets. I had to see a patient at 2:00, and I couldn't have made the trip from Atlanta in less than four hours. I don't remember why Burton couldn't get there in time.

Everyone agreed they all took tea in the "drawing room" (a term that seems a bit pretentious to me), and Roger left them about 6:25, as far as anyone could remember. He went up to change clothes—something he always did. He had come to tea dressed informally—slacks, loafers, and polo shirt. For dinner, he always put on a dark business suit. He was wearing a pinstriped, dark gray suit when we found his body.

EVERYBODY'S SUSPECT IN GEORGIA

They all had alibis to account for their whereabouts and thus prove their innocence.

My instincts shouted, *They're lying*.

I never doubted my intuition.

In the next few hours, I learned that my instincts had been correct.

All the guests claimed to have gone upstairs a few minutes after Roger left them. Simon said that when he picked up the last of the tea dishes at 6:50, no one was in the dining room or the drawing room. He had helped Mrs. Wright set the table.

Beth Wilson said she was the first one to come downstairs, and when she did, she turned on the TV. She wanted to see how well her substitute did. "It was a man," she said in a disgusted tone. She said it was about ten minutes to seven, because she endured the last portion of the dull local news and three minutes before the weather.

"Wayne and I came in immediately behind Beth," Paulette said. "We met at the top of the stairs and came down together."

Jason and his mother were the last ones. They said they had been together in Jason's room.

No one heard anything unusual.

Except for Jason and Amanda, who arrived about 7:20, the other guests claimed to have been in the drawing room from 7:00 until 7:30 for the evening news on CBS. Reginald remembered Beth's weather commentary. Beth had pointed out all the wrong moves made by her substitute—a man with the beginning of male-pattern baldness, which she verbalized three times. "I taught him—or tried to—but he's simply not very good at it."

At 7:30 Wayne Holmestead had turned the TV to CNN and they had watched *Headline News* until a few minutes before eight when they headed into the dining room.

"Why the TV in the drawing room?" Burton asked. "Didn't any of you watch TV in your rooms?"

"TV here only," Simon said as he came back into the dining room.

Burton arched a brow. "One TV set for a house this large?"

"It's the only place where we can get decent reception," Amanda said. "Roger has arranged for a satellite system hookup or whatever they call it, but it won't be in effect for another couple of weeks."

"Still no phone service?" Burton asked Simon.

Simon shook his head.

"Could someone have cut the phone lines?"

He shook his head a second time. "Checked."

"We have only two phones in this house," Amanda said. "One is in Roger's office, and the other is in the kitchen."

"Couldn't you have installed more?" I asked.

"Roger liked it that way," she said and looked away.

That seemed odd to me. The flicker in Burton's eyes said he agreed.

"We have had trouble with the telephone most of the week," Mrs. Wright said. She shrugged, probably an unconscious imitation of Simon. "We are used to it. If the phone works, we use it. If it does not, we wait for one or two days."

Something about Mrs. Wright seemed odd. Her language carried a stiffness to it. I decided to watch her more closely, although I'm not certain why.

"Stay from office," said Simon as if we hadn't remembered. "Locked until police." He held up a key and then put it inside his pants pocket. I assumed that was the only key.

"Good idea," I said, and several others nodded. I couldn't think of a reason why anyone would want to go into a room containing a dead body.

Wayne Holmestead insisted he had spent most of the newscast time writing e-mails on his BlackBerry, even though he hadn't been able to send them. He held out his BlackBerry for Burton to examine.

I liked the way Burton went around the room. His manner was so gentle that no one seemed to feel he interrogated them. I wondered why he had wasted his time to become a minister. He would have made an excellent therapist. I would have hired him, and I'm a good judge of people.

"This must be difficult for you," Burton said and made direct eye contact with Amanda. "If you want to talk about it now, it might make it easier for you later on when the police come."

Tears glistened in her eyes, and she brushed them away with her hand. She wore clear nail polish, and it looked perfect on her. I wished I were as graceful or had beautiful hands like hers.

"Jason and I came downstairs. The news had been on perhaps ten minutes, but it might have been longer. I sat in the chair at the far side of the room and stayed there until Mrs. Wright announced it was time for dinner."

"That's right, and I sat next to her," Jason said. "Just like I'm sitting next to her right now. So that means neither of us could have hurt Dad."

"Or both of you did it," Beth said. Then she smiled.

"How dare you say that!" Jason said. "That was totally out of line."

"Of course. You're right. I apologize." The smile pattern was so firmly in place that it seemed to me as if she couldn't talk without the smile. That's always something serious to watch. No normal person smiles all the time.

Each of the guests claimed to have been in the drawing room. It was a high-ceilinged room about forty by thirty feet with no windows. The house was amazingly large, with ten bedrooms on the second floor and five on the third. Roger had it decorated with commissioned paintings and busts from artists he liked. I liked the paintings but didn't think much of the sculptures. They might have been artistic masterpieces, but they all had a kind of sameness to them. Their drabness didn't do anything to accentuate the rosewood rococo furniture.

While Burton asked routine questions, I gazed at the paintings on the walls. I don't know anything about art, but these particular pieces had a cold gloominess about them. For example, I recognized the lighthouse at St. Simon's Island—which was located less than twenty miles away. The artist painted it at dusk with fog moving in, and I could see a tiny light at the top. Aside from the light, the colors ran from light gray to black.

"And no one left the room until after Mrs. Wright called you to dinner. Is that correct?"

"Oh, but yes, I did get up at one time," Tonya Borders said. "Just once."

Tonya spoke with a slight Slavic accent—at least most of the time. I have a fairly good ear for accents, and she confused me. Sometimes she sounded like she was from Eastern Europe or Russia and at other times like she was from the Deep South. That accent made me decide to watch her more carefully. She tried to smile but wasn't very good at it and could have taken lessons from Weather Girl.

She patted her silvery-brown bun and smoothed out her hair. "I, uh, went to the little girls' room." She leaned forward as if she wanted Burton to have her undivided attention. "A commercial had just begun, and the news was just coming back on when I returned."

Why, that old prune is flirting with Burton, I thought.

"So that gave you a good two minutes," Paulette said. "And it would have been so easy for you to make a detour to Roger's office." She turned to Burton and said, "She would have had to walk past his office to get to the only restroom on this floor."

"Yes, I did pass his office," Tonya said, "but I must assure you that I did not stop and shoot him on the way. I loved Roger. I truly loved that gentleman." The Slavic accent was really thick. "I owe him so much for my career and have always had such deep personal feelings for him." She made another attempt to smile at Burton after she spoke the last words.

"Yes, dear, we all loved Roger," Amanda said to Tonya in a tone that wasn't quite convincing. She leaned over and patted Tonya's hand. "And, Burton, although I realize someone here killed my husband, I find it nearly impossible to believe that any of the people in this room would want to hurt him. These were his friends. They all loved him—at least as far as I know—and he had helped each one of them. They weren't just his friends, but close friends."

"I wasn't a close friend," I blurted out.

"Yes, but he had deep regard for you. Very deep," Wayne said. "He told me so."

"Really?" I asked.

"I would never hurt him in any way, let alone kill him," Tonya said. "Death is, well, so. . .so final. And so very, very sad." Now her voice sounded like an imitation of Katharine Hepburn with a Slavic accent.

"I also left the room once," Jeffery Dunn said. "My doctor has me on a prescription antibiotic, and I take one with each meal. I had forgotten to bring down a pill, so I went upstairs." He turned to Amanda. "I walked right past you."

"Perhaps you did," she said. "I honestly don't remember. My mind was on the news."

"Yes, I remember seeing the good Dr. Dunn get up," Wayne Holmestead said.

"How long was he gone?" I asked.

"I'm not sure. It did seem like several minutes, maybe as long as ten minutes."

"It was nine minutes. You see, I could not find my medication. I had to search through my luggage."

"Did you find it?" I asked.

"Yes, I did." He went into a lengthy and boring-as-usual explanation that he couldn't find the medicine but remembered having packed it. He took us through every step of his search through his luggage. He explained that he always made a list of everything he needed for the trip and had checked every item to indicate that it was inside one of his two suitcases. His antibiotic was the seventeenth item on the list. So he knew he had to search until he found it. He found the pills finally, because the container, which was only one inch high and three inches long and made of clear plastic, had slipped inside one of his folded shirts. He also unpacked everything while he was there. "I was gone exactly nine minutes. I have a habit of timing myself when I do things like that."

"Very thorough," Burton said, and I wondered if that was sarcasm in his voice. Probably not from him.

I had listened to everyone talk, but something bothered me. Perhaps it was the therapist part of me at work. I turned to Weather Girl, the smile lady. "Did you like Roger—I mean really like him?"

"Didn't I say I did?" She did her facial thing before she added, "I adored

26

him, simply, simply adored him. He was so much older, of course, so there was no romantic involvement." She paused, and another plastic smile filled her face before she spoke again. "I assure you, I owed him so much. He was, uh, like a dear uncle or an older brother." This time she smiled at Burton.

Doesn't he get it? That yucky every-second smile—she's such a phony, I thought. Maybe Burton isn't as sharp as I thought he was.

I turned to Jeffery and asked, "Did you like Roger?"

"Like him? What a strange and positively absurd question. I was his guest, his friend, and he was someone I'd known and liked," he said. "We'd been close for many years." He started to explain how they had met and where, but Burton interrupted and thanked him.

I winked at Burton for doing that. Had Jeffery been allowed to continue, I'm sure we would have had to hear what he ate for lunch the day the two men met, and he may even have taken us on an endless journey back to his childhood days.

Burton's eyes caught mine and locked for perhaps one second. I was sure he sensed what I was feeling. Maybe he did catch on to Beth's one facial expression.

"Hey, I'm the most unlikely one to have shot old Rog," Lenny said, "but that would probably make me the most likely suspect."

He laughed at his little joke. Or what I assumed was a joke.

"Really! I meant that. Don't you people watch TV? It's always the one—"

"You never left the room?" I asked.

"Hey, babe, exactly right," he said and winked, "but I would have left the room with you anytime!"

"You are rather crude, you know," Reginald Ford said. Before Lenny answered, he looked at me. "I apologize for him. He's not my friend, merely an acquaintance. We rode together from the mainland, and he assumes we are now chums or buddies or at least that I like him. I assure you he's equally offensive to everyone."

Lenny burst out laughing. "I love this guy. What a sense of humor. He absolutely kills me." As he heard his own last words, he had enough sensitivity to blush and mumble, "Sorry."

"But to answer your question before you ask," Reginald said, "I did not leave the room. Neither did Lenny, so I can vouch for him. I tried to watch the news, and his mouth ran the whole time."

"Hey, Reggie boy, are you trying to insult me or something?" Lenny yelled and laughed.

"I gave up trying. You're immune." He cleared his throat and said, "I am not Reggie and I am not Reg. My name is Reginald. Please—for at least the tenth time."

Lenny laughed again. "You got it, Reggie boy! From now on it's only Reginald."

Reginald raised his hands in defeat. He got up from the table, took his chair, and moved to the end farthest from Lenny.

"Why don't I pour everyone a glass of sweet tea?" Amanda said and got up. Her hands were shaking. She tried to pick up the tall pitcher in front of her but couldn't seem to coordinate. "Jason, come and help me."

As soon as Burton looked at me again, I motioned my head toward the door. He caught on immediately, and we both left. So that no one would overhear us, I didn't say a word until after I led him outside the house and we stood on the antebellum-style porch. It had four large columns that were probably supposed to look as if it had come from *Gone with the Wind*. The porch encircled the entire front of the house.

Storm clouds flooded the sky, and within seconds they had hidden the moon. The heavens became black and forbidding. The wind felt damp; rain was certainly on its way.

"Everyone keeps saying how much he or she loved Roger," I said.

"It doesn't ring true, does it?"

"That's exactly the way I felt. What do you think is going on?"

"You're the therapist," Burton said.

"And that weather girl—" Okay, that was catty of me, but the words came out anyway.

Burton laughed.

"Why are you laughing?"

"Why are you jealous of her?" he asked. "She's as self-closed as you are open."

I smiled—no, I grinned. I had to revise my opinion of him once again. This man was really bright.

The first raindrops landed softly on the window next to me. Enough light came through from the hallway that I could see his warm smile. I felt it was genuine—the first truly genuine smile I had seen since coming into the house.

"You're leading this investigation," I said, "so you tell me."

"They're lying. I mean, really lying," he said. "They loathed Roger."

"That's a bit strong—"

"Yes, but it's true—"

"I absolutely agree," I said, "but I wonder why. Why would they hate him? If they hated him, why would they come here? Roger hasn't made it easy to visit—being on an island."

"Why did *you* dislike him? If I could understand that, maybe I could understand why the others didn't like him."

His words shocked me. I thought I had covered my feelings well. After all, I'm a therapist, and we're careful to remain objective and not to show our emotions. I wonder how he had discerned that I didn't like Roger.

"What do you mean?" I asked trying to equivocate while I figured out how to answer.

Burton wouldn't play my game; he waited for me to respond.

"I didn't want to see him dead. It wasn't that kind of dislike."

"What kind of dislike was it?"

"My dislike had nothing to do with his death or with any of the others. It was, uh, a personal thing with Roger."

"Do you think his murder was impersonal?"

This man was good. Maybe he should have been on the police force. "Of course, it was personal," I said. Burton had started to move in a direction I didn't want him to go. "I didn't kill him—*as you know*. My feelings were— well, something I choose not to discuss. Because you know I'm innocent, I'm sure you won't push me."

"That's an excellent answer, and you've also set the limits on how far I can go with you," he said, and I saw his dimples up close. He could pose for a toothpaste ad on TV.

"Good," I said.

"However, just this—you're sure it has nothing to do with his death? Really sure?"

"Positive."

And I was sure.

At least I was then.

4

Before Burton and I went back inside the house, we agreed on a strategy. He would ask questions, and I would listen. He laughed and added, "You know that's what we preachers do—we talk—and you therapists listen."

Frankly, that juvenile attempt at humor didn't deserve a smile, but I gave him one anyway because I liked the man. "I reserve the right to change my mind or to interrupt."

He shrugged exactly like Simon, so perfectly it was as if he had taken lessons. Then I really smiled.

"Would you like to reverse roles?" he asked.

"I'll let you know if you're not doing an adequate job," I said. Okay, I gave him a third smile, and this time it was to deflect any offense my smart remark may have caused.

His face showed me that he hadn't been offended. I liked this guy even better. He could be direct, but he wasn't offensive or defensive. He didn't have that fragile male ego that jumped at every careless word. I wish he had been one of my blind dates instead of some of those vain, self-centered, over-the-hill jocks I had dated.

Back inside the drawing room, Burton asked everyone to sit down. Three people came from the dining room with plates of food. Lenny had his plate so full I hoped he could balance everything until he sat down. No matter how fancy the meal, Roger always had Mrs. Wright cook a few Southern dishes, such as collard greens. Half of one plate contained the watery greens. I've been in the South all my life, but collard greens are far from my favorite food, and I hate the smell. I was glad I wasn't near Lenny.

Lenny sat on a straight-backed chair—as straight as those rococo chairs can be—and dug away without dropping a single pea or a tiny shard of lettuce. To his credit, he didn't drip any of the vinegar water from the collards. I'll say this for him—he sure knew how to handle his food.

I thought it was odd that not everyone ate in the dining room, but now they came into the drawing room with mounds of food on their plates—even those who had already eaten. Roger never would have allowed them to do that. I wondered if that was the reason they did so now.

They joined the others who sat and ate casually. Everyone seemed to have dropped the pretense. No one any longer made a show of being overcome by grief.

I looked around and counted. We were eleven people. Everyone was in the room except Simon Presswood and Elaine Wright.

I watched the way they ate. Dr. Dunn attacked his food as if it would run away from him. Wayne took dainty bites as if large ones would be too much to chew. Tonya Borders sat quite still, bent slightly forward as if she would repel anyone who tried to taste her food. Paulette White had a plate half filled with food, but she had made no attempt to eat anything. Reginald Ford was the only one who seemed to eat normally.

It still seemed bizarre to me. Other than Jason and Amanda, they seemed untouched by the death of the man they all claimed to have loved. Occasionally, Amanda shed a few tears and Jason wrapped his arm around her to comfort her. He spoke softly, and I couldn't hear what he said.

"Thank you, dear," she murmured several times.

I was sure Burton would want to stop and get himself something to eat, but he didn't. In fact, I'm not sure he ate all night. I had eaten plenty, but I went back to the kitchen for a large bowl of ambrosia—another dream from our superb cook. She used fruit and coconut, but she added some special ingredient that made me realize why my grandmother used to call it the food of the Greek gods.

Even though I ate an immense amount of ambrosia, it still wasn't enough. Gnawing hunger pains—or what I perceived as hunger pains—grabbed at my stomach. I had an energy bar in my pocket. I pulled it out and nibbled on it. I thought of going to the kitchen for more food, but I didn't want to miss out on anything, and who knows what might happen while I was out of the room. I felt my other pocket and found three pieces of peppermint candy. I would be fine.

Just then, Tonya Borders put her plate on the table. She took off her glasses and put her head in her hands. I sensed she posed as a picture of grief more than she felt the emotion. Of course, Burton was directly in front of her, and I suspected she made the gesture for his benefit. She didn't go into the grief act until Burton looked her way. As I watched, I thought, *Honey, I doubt you ever feel any true emotion.*

Burton waited until she finished her melodramatic pose and had summoned a tear or two. She held a handkerchief in her right hand and gently wiped her eyes.

"As each of you has talked about where you were and your relationship to Roger," Burton said, and his gaze moved from face to face, "you made a point of saying how much you loved Roger."

"And of course we did, and I certainly do, and I'll say it as often as you wish to hear the words," Wayne spoke up. "He was my dearest friend, my closest associate, and—"

"Excellent. Suppose we start with you. Tell us about your relationship with Roger."

Burton's soft voice and smile would put anyone at ease. *Burton, old boy, you are amazing,* I thought. *You make it clear what you want, but there's something about the way you interact so that people don't feel offended or intimidated.*

"To begin with," Wayne said and paused to clear his throat. "I owed that wonderful man so much for his help through the years. In fact, many, many people owed Roger a great deal, you know, especially here in Glynn County."

"And why is that?" I asked.

"I'll tell you," Beth interrupted. "More than anyone else, Roger has given so much to so many." She sounded as if she were reading from a prompter. "For example, he invested millions to improve the coastal area, and it has attracted more than twenty new businesses in the past two years."

"That's correct," Wayne said. "Another example is tourism. Because of his endeavors, tourism is on the rise by nearly 30 percent this year. He planned to bring in a regional opera company to attract tourists from November until March."

Whenever Wayne spoke, he pulled down on his vest. Maybe he thought it would hide his paunch. Although I had observed Wayne do that before, I now realized that was one of his frequent mannerisms.

"In what way did he help business? What did he do?" Burton asked. As I watched, I knew he didn't care about the answer. He simply wanted to keep Wayne Holmestead talking.

"For one thing, he brought in a fish-canning factory. The experts said it couldn't be done and there wouldn't be enough business—"

"But he proved them wrong," Paulette said. "That was typical of his brilliance. And he was brilliant, you know. He made that factory profitable within the first year." She dabbed her mouth gently with her napkin. "In case you are unaware, that was quite a financial achievement for such a short span of time."

"That's not all," Wayne said. "If you go down to the beach along the coast—anywhere south of Savannah—you'll be amazed at how pristine the beaches are. He cleaned them up—every inch—and paid for everything himself. Jekyll Island and St. Simon's Island used to get all the tourists because the beaches around Brunswick were dirty. The odor of dead fish repelled people."

"He was very shrewd, you know," Beth Wilson said.

"Beth is right," Wayne said. "He had that uncanny sense of what would work. People had stopped visiting here more than thirty years ago. Roger changed that mind-set." He paused and licked his lips, and it was obvious to me that this was also part of a well-rehearsed presentation. "There is also the matter of the—"

"And you have been part of those projects, haven't you?" Burton asked. He smiled and patted Wayne on the shoulder.

"We were partners in the ventures. We wanted to help others and worked to benefit the people. We wanted unemployment to be less than 1 percent—perhaps that was not possible to achieve, but it was our goal. We cared about—"

"Commendable. That's truly humanitarian," I said with some sarcasm in my voice.

"We believed in serving others." He either hadn't gotten my sarcasm or ignored it.

"Surely you made a few dollars," Burton said. "Even with great humanitarian projects, there must have been opportunities for financial reward."

Good old Burton. He knows how to do it. I began to wonder if we were going to play good cop, bad cop.

"Oh, well, of course, I've, uh, made money—not a great deal—but uh, I made money on my investments. That's one incentive, but—"

"He means he's made a fortune, a very, very big fortune, by buying property along the coast," Jason said. "As soon as he knew Dad was going to clean up the beaches, he bought everything he could, held them until after the cleanup, and resold them at exorbitant prices—"

"That is not entirely accurate," Wayne said. "I did buy property. Any astute businessman would. I—uh, had started to buy before—"

"Stop lying!" Jason said. "That was part of what Dad got angry about. He had just learned that you bought all those properties near the ocean through some offshore corporation. You took advantage of local people until after—"

"You were obviously eavesdropping. You nasty—"

"Yeah, I was." Jason gave him the full-mouth grin. His light brown eyes lit up, and he raised his chin as if to say, "So hit me."

"This—this vile boy grossly exaggerates—"

"Perhaps we can change the tone of this interrogation or whatever it is," Tonya said. "While I want to go on record"—she stared at Burton and then at me—"that is, if there is a record, I loved Roger. He trusted me and opened many doors of opportunity for my career. It would have been stupid of me to want to get rid of him." She paused as if to make certain we understood. "I've been one of Roger's lawyers—his most trusted lawyer—for nearly twenty years." Her Slavic accent had disappeared somewhere after she said she wanted to go on record.

I leaned forward, looked directly at Tonya, and said, "I think you wanted to tell us something before you launched into the matter of your close relationship with Roger."

Her stare might have frozen an adversary in litigation proceedings, but she didn't intimidate me.

"Uh, yes, I suppose you are correct." She glared at me and took a deep breath. "All right, I shall tell you the truth: I came because I had no choice." Her accent was extremely noticeable again. "I received a *summons* to attend."

"That is being a bit harsh," Jeffery Dunn said. "I will not have my good friend's reputation besmirched—"

"You are a hypocrite," she said softly, but her dark eyes expressed her venom. "Yes, it was an invitation—a *written* invitation, mind you—something I had never received in all my years of dealing with Roger, but still—"

"We all received such an *invitation*." Jeffery overcame his monotone to emphasize the last word.

"You are too much, Jeffery. I am quite certain Dr. Burton will discover the truth, so we might as well speak up." Tonya actually batted her eyes twice as she looked at Burton. "I shall then say it more plainly. I have worked for Roger for many years—as I have already stated. He did a great deal for my career, and I assume that's true of the others. But through all those years, he treated us like indentured servants. I observed that he treated Simon and Elaine better than he did us."

"That information surprises me," Burton said, "although I scarcely knew him."

"It's true," Amanda said. Jason had brought her a plate, although she had not eaten more than one or two bites. "He did treat us all rather shabbily."

"So you came because you were afraid of Roger?" I asked. "All of you?"

"Of course they did!" Jason said. "They knew Dad could make them or break them financially. They may have despised him in their hearts, but if Dad had told them to, they would have crawled into the house on their knees."

"You are a rude child," Beth said, but her face expressed nothing but sweetness. Was she some kind of *Stepford Wives* clone?

"That is not exactly true, Jason. There was a reason we came—and just the eleven of us—and no one else," Tonya said. "Roger had an announcement to make. It was something that involved all of us."

"How do you know that?" Amanda asked.

"He added a handwritten note on my *summons*." Tonya glared at Jeffery. "The message said, 'I have something important to tell you and the others.' Just that."

"A summons?" I asked.

Her face hardened. "I would hardly call it anything else. Or perhaps you would prefer the word *demand*."

A summons?" I repeated Tonya's words. "Or a demand?"

"What was the nature of the announcement?" Burton asked.

"I have no idea," she said.

"Roger didn't write warm, sweet notes," Beth said. "So I assumed it was something—something ominous." She said the handwritten note on her invitation read, "I plan to make an important announcement, and I want you here. It affects you."

"You mean you expected some kind of exposure?" I asked.

Without changing a facial muscle, Beth said, "If you choose to say it that way."

"Did the rest of you receive a personal note with your invitation?" Burton asked.

"I thought it was just a big joke," Lenny said and laughed. But his laughter didn't sound genuine.

"Roger never joked about such things," Reginald said. "In fact, I don't think our dear, departed Roger ever joked about anything. And yes, I received a handwritten note in which he said he had an important announcement that would affect my life."

"I did, too," I said.

"So did I," Burton said. "It seemed slightly odd to me. You know, I'd met the man only once before. Do any of you know anything more about the announcement?"

One way or another, everyone murmured that they didn't know or said, "Nothing."

"That's strange," I said. "When I received my *invitation*" (and I emphasized that word), "I assumed it had something to do with a personal thing— something Roger and I had spoken about before. Obviously I was mistaken. Mine said he had something *important* to talk to me about, but it didn't sound ominous. Apparently, it was something that affected all of us."

"Yes, strange," said Lenny. "And I thought I was special and that he liked me the most!" He started to laugh, but even he realized it wasn't funny.

"Amanda, what about you?" I asked. "You're his wife, so surely—"

"I don't know." Tears slid down her cheeks. "I had no idea. I didn't get such a note. I mean, I'm his wife and—"

Burton and I momentarily locked eyes. We realized Amanda had almost blurted out something and then censored herself.

"He must have confided something to you, Amanda," Jeffery said.

She shook her head. "Nothing."

"Leave her alone." Jason handed her his white handkerchief, and she wiped her eyes. "Don't you have any respect for her grief?"

"It's all right, dear," she said. "I had no idea because I have not lived in this house for three weeks. Roger and I had a rather nasty row, and I moved to Savannah—"

"That's certainly news to me," Paulette White said. "Dear Roger never said a word to me."

"And it's none of your business, either, because—"

Amanda held out her hand to silence her son. "I had already started divorce proceedings."

Paulette gasped.

"I've never spoken about this to anyone—except to Jason, of course."

"And Roger hadn't been much of a father to me—I mean, most of the time," Jason said and turned to Burton.

"It's okay, son," he said and wrapped his arm around the boy's shoulder.

"I'm ready to talk, and I'd like to talk. That may help me sort out things." Amanda leaned her head back and closed her eyes. "I might as well start down the line of truth. I want to tell you I had an extremely miserable life with Roger. For years, I've been careful to maintain a charade and mask my unhappiness."

"Yes, it must have been miserable counting all those millions!" Lenny said.

"You really are obnoxious," Reginald said.

Lenny received enough glares that he mumbled, "Sorry," and shut up.

"He exerted a strange kind of control. I had to give him a reason every time I left the island. I had to account for everything I did." She started twisting Jason's handkerchief the way she had her own at the table. "He didn't mind my spending money—he actually encouraged me—and I was allowed to buy whatever I wanted." She paused and opened her eyes. "I wonder if you heard what I just said?"

"Heard every word," Beth said. "Poor rich woman."

"You still don't get it, do you? I'll make myself clearer. Spending his money was never an issue. What made my life so miserable was that I had to inform him first. Roger said *inform*, but he meant ask for permission and explain what I planned to do."

"I'm sure you're just overwrought," Paulette said, "and overstating—"

"No, I'm not." She glared at Paulette. "Did you know that I had to tell him which car I wanted to drive? He bought two cars for my use. We keep both at our private garage at dockside. They were his gift to me, he said, and for my use. *My use.* I was the only one who drove them, *but*—"

"How sad, how very sad for you," Tonya said, and this time she truly sounded like Greta Garbo. "I have seen your severe punishment. Your Aston Martin V12 and your Mercedes-Benz 30082 Roadster. Both of them, I believe, cost more than most people earn in a single year."

"I think you've missed the point, Tonya," I said. "Let Amanda explain."

"Roger did provide those cars. He urged me to buy a Ferrari when I told him I was leaving. He thought material things mattered—as if another car would make me less miserable."

"I get the picture," I said, "but I'm not sure everyone understands."

"It's quite simple. I could have the best of anything, but I had to let him know which one I chose. *Every time.* Worse than that, he provided a palm pad with some kind of mini spreadsheet, and I had to list every place I stopped and jot down the mileage each time. When I left the car, the figures I wrote down had to match the mileage the car showed. I felt like a prisoner."

"Oh, my dear, dear Amanda. I had no idea," Wayne said. "I'm sorry—"

"Liar! You knew!" Jason said.

"Do you realize what it's like?" Amanda said, as if she had not been interrupted. "At the end of each month, I had to account for every cent I spent—and I mean to the penny—or he would give me no allowance for the next month."

"I had no idea." Wayne knelt in front of her and patted her hand.

Hmm, I thought, *I wonder if that idiot is trying to nuzzle up to the widow.*

She pushed him away. "You may have been Roger's best friend—I don't know about that—but you are not mine. I don't want your false display of sympathy."

I wanted to shout hoorah for Amanda.

She stood up, turned her back to everyone for perhaps a full minute, and then spun around and faced us. "The rest of you may have loved Roger Harden, but I didn't. Perhaps at one time, in the beginning, I loved him. I'm not even sure now, because there have been so many miserable years since then. I married Roger, as most of you know, after my first husband died and left me with a two-year-old son. Roger's first wife divorced him. Do you know why she left him? She left him because of his constant attempt to control her life."

"He was a bit demanding," Paulette said. "I'll admit that, but—"

"A bit?" Tears raced rapidly down Amanda's cheeks. "I'll say it better then. Roger Harden was a power-hungry, totally controlling monster, and I detested him."

"I'm sorry your life has been that bad, Amanda, but that's the most honest thing anyone has said this evening," I added.

"Then why did you come, Amanda?" Burton asked.

I hadn't thought to ask that question. I was so caught up in genuine sympathy for Amanda. I walked over and draped my arms around her. She was about five inches shorter than I was, and she laid her head against my shoulder and cried.

Burton held up his hand for silence, and no one said anything until Amanda stopped crying. She used Jason's handkerchief to wipe her eyes.

"Why did you come back to the island?" Burton softly asked again.

"He called me. Yesterday."

"True," Simon said. "I heard. Phone."

"He did call, and it was rather strange. He *asked* me to come. It wasn't a summons. He said, 'Will you come? Please.' In eighteen years, Roger had never *asked* me for anything, and I didn't know the word *please* was in his vocabulary. I'm not sure what was going on with him, but I knew it was something significant."

"Did he say why he wanted you here?" I asked.

She shook her head slowly. "I asked—twice—but he was evasive. He said at least three times, 'I have something significant—something I have to tell you and the others. I want to make my announcement once and to all of you at the same time.' That was the most I could get out of him."

"Is there anything else you can tell us?" I asked. "Are you holding back? I don't know why, but I sense that there's something you're not telling us. Is there?"

"Tell them, Mom," Jason said.

"It's not something I can readily explain. It was—it was as if he was different. His voice was softer. . .kinder perhaps. That may not mean anything to the rest of you, but I had lived with him for eighteen years. Just before we hung up, I asked, 'What has happened to you?' "

"And what did he say?"

" 'I've made an important decision, and I want a special group of people here. It affects them.' I asked him about the decision, but he refused to say."

"But you admit you hated him?" Paulette asked.

"Yes. But I came anyway because—well, because I hoped—I truly hoped he had changed for the better. I have prayed for him every day, and on the phone he begged—"

"And, of course, you didn't want him to cut you off financially," Paulette said. "He would have, you know. Roger was capable of such acts."

"You are despicable," Amanda lashed out.

Paulette smiled as if she had won a victory in the courtroom.

"Money? That had nothing to do with Mom's decision," Jason said. "I won't have you talk that way to her."

Amanda held up her hand to silence her son. "That's sweet of you, darling." She faced Paulette and said, "I didn't need Roger's money. I have enough—more than enough without him."

"I doubt that," Lenny said. "No woman ever has enough." He laughed loudly, and everyone ignored him.

"I have money. When my first husband died, I received a large insurance settlement. My parents were well off. They left me enough money that I could have lived comfortably for the rest of my life. So you see, I didn't need Roger's money."

"That's true," Wayne said. "I can vouch for that."

"So what about you, dear Paulette," Beth purred. "Maybe your motive wasn't so pure."

"I can tell all of you this much," Paulette said, "I resented Roger at times, but I didn't hate him."

"Not true," Simon said. "Lie."

We stared at Simon, but he would say nothing more.

"If you know something, please tell us," I pleaded.

"Truth will come," he said. He took his plate of half-eaten food and returned to the kitchen.

I got up and started to go after him, but Burton shook his head. I gave him a splendid Simon shrug and sat down.

"Is there a gun in the house?" Burton asked. "I don't know why I didn't ask earlier."

"Yes, Mr. Harden kept a gun in his office. It's in the bottom drawer of his desk, and he keeps the drawer unlocked." Elaine Wright said to Burton, "Follow me and I'll show you."

"I think the rest of us should stay here," I said.

Wayne Holmestead immediately attacked his food again as if he hadn't eaten in days. Tonya stared into space and sipped whatever was in her cup.

Within a minute, Burton and Mrs. Wright returned. Before he spoke, I could tell from the expression on his face what he was going to say.

"The gun is gone."

6

"Whoever shot poor Roger must have stolen the gun," Reginald said and then blushed. "I suppose that's obvious, isn't it?"

Lenny opened his mouth, but this time he had enough sense to close it in silence.

For several minutes, we discussed the possibility of searching every room to find the missing gun—which we assumed was the weapon that had killed Roger—but it was a large house, and the hiding-place possibilities were endless.

Mrs. Wright went to try the telephone. She came back to say it was still out. "Perhaps by morning we shall have service again," she said.

"I don't know about anyone else, but I intend to go to my room," Jeffery said. "I have several important lectures that I plan to give as a guest speaker next month, and I need to prepare." He turned and left us.

I had to stuff my hand in my mouth not to burst out laughing. He taught the basic biology course and three other basic science courses. Everyone at the university knew he hadn't changed a word in his lectures in years—whether in the classroom or as a guest at an outside venue. I had no idea what he needed to do, but it wasn't to prepare lectures.

"I am too upset to serve anyone or to wash the dishes," Mrs. Wright said. "The kitchen is open. Do what you want." She started for the door, paused, and looked back. "I did not hate Mr. Harden, and I cannot stand to listen to the rest of you lie about how you feel."

"Did you love him?" Burton asked.

"I did not. Furthermore, he did not treat me well, but I—I owed him a debt. He promised me that I would have the debt paid by the end of this year."

"What kind of debt?" Burton asked.

"That, sir, is none of your business. I did not hate him. I did not and would not kill him. There are people in this room who had reasons to kill him, but I am not one of them."

"Please explain, would you?" Burton said.

Her gaze shifted across the room, and then she stared at her feet. "Those who have things to hide know who they are. I have nothing to hide. I know what I have seen with my own eyes." She left the drawing room.

I didn't understand what was going on. I heard her words, but I sensed she was giving someone some kind of message. A warning perhaps?

Burton looked my way. It was uncanny, but I knew he had picked up the same vibration.

One by one the others left the room. Jason and Amanda sat in a corner and whispered to one another for several minutes. At one point, Jason put his arm around her shoulder. "Let's go upstairs," he said. Without waiting for a response, he led his mother from the room.

Soon everyone was gone except Burton and me.

If Burton's eyes said what I thought they did, he had caught everything. In fact, he may have been ahead of me.

"What do you think?" he asked me.

I started to do the Simon shrug and stopped. "What do *you* think?"

"Two things. First, Mrs. Wright was intentionally being cryptic, and I have no idea why. I knew it would do no good to push."

"I agree. And the second?"

"Rather obvious, I suppose, but Amanda isn't the only person who didn't love Roger. In fact, no one at the table tonight even liked him. Jason used to hate him—I can safely tell you that much. I have no idea what's accounted for the change, but his hatred is gone."

"What about Simon? We know he didn't kill Roger. At least if he did, he had to do it before he made his final trip to pick us up. Is that possible?"

"I hadn't thought of that," Burton said.

Just then Simon walked into the dining room. He quietly picked up the dirty dishes.

"I have a question for you," Burton said to him. "You were on the dock to meet us, but you didn't arrive until ten minutes after seven and—"

"Good logic, but not kill."

"Did anyone see you?" I asked.

He nodded. "Four trips first." He held up his fingers. "Put on different pants. Served tea. Never alone. Talked to Mr. Goss five minutes before seven. Follow me to dock." He shook his head. "That man. Many words. I wait mainland from 7:04."

"You're amazing, Simon," I said. "You use the minimum number of words, but I always figure out what you mean."

As I expected, he shrugged. But he did something else. Before he turned to leave, he winked at me. This time I didn't know what he meant.

"That eliminates him," Burton said. "Agreed?"

Burton hadn't seen the wink, and I didn't think that was the time to discuss it. Besides, I had something else I wanted to ask. "Why did you get an invitation?" I asked. "You don't seem to fit with these people."

"I assume it was because of Jason. At least that's the primary reason I came. He was quite a troubled teen when we met. He was a student at Clayton U. He and some of his classmates played basketball in our church gym, and we got to know each other. After a few weeks, he asked to talk to me. We met regularly, and he got better."

"He was troubled? In what way?"

He gave me that handsome-hunk grin, but he didn't say a word.

"Okay," I said. "It was worth a try to ask. It was a good test to see if you ministers talked about your parishioners."

"I can't speak for all ministers. I can, however, speak for myself."

"You just did. You're good. You know that?"

He shrugged. "See, I can imitate Simon, too." Then he turned on that fabulous smile before he asked, "So why did you get an invitation?"

"As you probably know, Roger lived in Clayton County for a number of years. He was a kind of benefactor to me."

"Kind of?"

"I'm a therapist. At the time, I hadn't finished my doctoral program and did only private counseling. Roger intervened, and I became the head of Clayton County Special Services."

"Intervened? How did he do that?"

"The way he influences most people in the state." I laughed, but Burton didn't get it. "Okay, his influence is called money. He gives money, lots and lots of money, to the right causes and at the right time—"

"The causes where he can be in control?"

"Something like that. But I honestly thought my record and my work had gained me the position. It might have anyway. As Roger put it, he was my insurance."

A peal of thunder punctuated my last few words. It reverberated in the window glass. The rainstorm was on the way.

"This is unusual—the weather I mean," I said. "This is June. It's too early for this kind of storm."

Blasts of thunder rolled like great broken wheels of stone across the sky. A strong, gusty wind pummeled the roof.

Burton seemed hardly aware of the weather or my comment. He stared into space for a long time before he said, "I'm not sure where to go next, and you obviously don't want to go down the path we've started. One thing bothers me about those last words of Mrs. Wright. I have a niggling feeling—"

"That she knows more than she's willing to tell? Or that maybe she meant her words as a message to someone?"

"Exactly that. You sensed it, too? I felt as if she answered me but was talking to someone else."

"Let's go find her," I said.

We walked into the dining room, which was empty, and into the kitchen, but she wasn't there, either. Simon sat at the kitchen table with his back to us. In front of him was a steaming cup of tea with the string of the bag hanging over the side.

When I asked Simon which room was hers, he used his chin to point toward the kitchen door, "Number one."

That seemed like an odd response, or it would have if it had come from someone else. We went through the door and walked down the hall. The first room had the number one on it. Burton and I looked at each other and smiled, and I said, "Elementary, my dear Dr. Watson."

Burton knocked, but no one answered. He knocked a second time and leaned close to the door to detect movement inside. He shook his head and turned to walk away.

"Let me knock," I said. I knocked with one hand, and with the other I turned the knob. Her door opened. I walked inside and turned on the light, and it was obvious she wasn't there. I had assumed number one meant a tiny room, but it was a small apartment. I stood in what resembled a den, complete with a sofa and an easy chair. The furniture certainly didn't match the rest of the house. This looked as if it had come from Sears—sturdy, usable, but not expensive.

She had her own kitchen—which I could see from the doorway. I took a few steps inside. The bathroom was on my left. I gave it a cursory look and turned to her bedroom on my right. I saw nothing special about the furniture there, either. Then it hit me. "This could be anyone's room. It looks more like a hotel suite."

"I thought the same thing." He pointed out that there were no pictures on the walls. "It's more like a place where she lives temporarily."

"No books. No magazines," I said. "Not even a newspaper."

"Nothing out of place, either," he said.

"She's not in her room," I said and realized how stupid the words sounded.

"So where would she be?" he asked.

When we returned to the kitchen, Simon seemed not to have moved.

We returned to the dining room, which was still empty. We assumed she hadn't gone upstairs, so that meant she must have gone outside. Just then Simon came in from the kitchen.

"Mrs. Wright isn't in her room," I said. "Do you have any idea where she is?"

He turned his face toward the back door and lifted his chin with his pointing gesture.

Tonya Borders strolled into the dining room just then. "She sometimes walks along the cliff," she said. She turned to Simon. "Is there more coffee?"

The shrug.

"Because she never leaves the island, the walk along the cliff is her only way to get away from the house," Tonya said without accent. "There is a nice little trail around the backside of the house. Have you been out there?"

After both of us said no, she said, "It's a circle of exactly three-tenths of a mile of paving stones." The Slavic accent miraculously reappeared. "When I was here in March, she told me that every morning, and again in the evening, she completes the circle three times."

Tonya went on to describe the area. Roger had a variety of azaleas—the kind that bloom in the spring and again in the fall. She rambled on about plants such as coreopsis (whatever they were), varieties of lobelia whose colors varied from white to carmine. She raved about the hybrid camellias and the highly improved impatiens. She described the poisonous Jerusalem cherry, nine varieties of ajuga, and at least a dozen types of hosta.

I tried not to yawn. I buy trays of flowers from Home Depot, and they live about three weeks before they die of thirst or starvation. I always forget about them.

"Roger wants to make sure something blooms all year long." I thought the flora lecture had reached the near torturous, but I was wrong. She had progressed to the fourteen varieties of trees on the island. Although I didn't pay much attention to what she said, it fascinated me to listen to her. I loved the accent that came and went.

"You have an interesting accent," I said. "Slavic?"

"Very good. Polish. I was born in what is now Gdansk."

"That's near the German border, isn't it?" I asked.

"Germany borders Poland on the west, of course. Gdansk is on the Baltic Sea and at the mouth of the River Wilsa. Do you have more test questions, or must I sing to you in Polish? I came to America when I was sixteen. I have worked very, very hard to get rid of my accent, but sometimes it pops out. Is that what bothers you? I shall be glad to answer any serious questions if you doubt me."

"Yes, and I apologize," I said.

"You enjoy nature and working in the garden, do you?" Burton asked and rescued me so I could silently castigate myself.

"As a matter of fact, Roger asked me to supervise this when he had the area landscaped."

"He used you in all kinds of ways, didn't he?" I asked.

"I resent that," she snapped. She turned and walked away.

Burton and I stared at each other. "I think we need to talk to her after we come back in," I said.

"You are direct," he said. "Very direct."

"Is that bad?"

"Different. I'm not used to that. Some people might not like it—"

"Does Burton like it?"

He seemed to ponder the question for several seconds before he said, "I think so."

"Okay," I said. "And back to Tonya: She's suddenly quite sensitive about something."

We descended the four steps from the back door and started down the gravel path. Immediately I smelled the sage plant. I wish I could have seen the spices Roger or Tonya planted. Even though I couldn't see anything, my nose told me. I can't cook, but for some odd reason, I can identify spices. I recognized the peppery scent of savory and the fragrance of sweet marjoram. Strong breezes from the ocean seemed to fill the air with those fragrances. I paused and breathed deeply.

Aware that I had stopped, I apologized, and we started down the path. The path was a good three feet wide, so there was plenty of space for us to walk side by side.

The stars were dimmed by broken clouds, and they shrouded the moon. The smell of rain was heavy in the air, but none had yet fallen. The night clouds were at least one shade darker than when we had been out earlier.

We had gone perhaps thirty feet when I stumbled and fell into Burton. He grabbed my arm, "Hey, steady there." He took my hand and led me.

"Thank you," I said and smiled in the dark. Apparently I had done a good job on the tripping. I had decided to play it like the helpless damsel and would have worried if he hadn't responded. I liked the feel of his hand. He had stumbled at the beach, so I thought this was a good trade-off. I had perfected that tripping trick by age sixteen. In those days, I breathed deeply, sighed, stared into the boy's face, and said, "You're so strong." That line no longer seemed appropriate.

What also didn't seem appropriate was that he held my hand as he would that of anyone in distress. So far he hadn't succumbed to my charms. That was okay. I decided I'd give him another chance before we left Palm Island.

As we walked closer to the cliff, the harsh waves and the heavy wind meant we had to lean close to each other to hear. I liked that. I had to put my lips about five inches from his face. He had a faint, masculine smell, and it took me another minute to identify it. Mennen Skin Bracer. That's what my older brother used. He always said he hated the smell, but it was all he could afford. I figured Burton liked it even though he could afford better. That fragrance seemed right on him.

Despite having been on the island three times in the past, I had never been to the backside of the island and wished I could have had a daylight view. On my previous trips, I arrived from Atlanta at night. I left the next morning before daylight so I could avoid the heavy traffic going north on I-95.

I spotted a copse of oaks with Spanish moss swaying in the breeze. I counted three stunted palm trees in a sheltered area behind the oaks—just as Roger had said. We made the complete circle of the small island, but we still saw no sign of Mrs. Wright.

An involuntary shiver came over me.

7

"Let's follow the path one more time," Burton said as he started out. This time he held my elbow. I felt as if I were a tottering eighty-year-old and my grandson led me forward.

We stopped and moved into the shelter of the oaks. I didn't want to hurry back, even though I did want to talk to Mrs. Wright. In the shelter, we could hear each other without shouting. He let go of my arm.

"So, you're a reverend," I said, "and that means?"

"Pastor. Or rector or preacher—whichever feels better."

"You have a large church? I mean are there a lot of people?"

He shook his head. "I'm a shepherd, not a rancher."

"I don't get the difference. You mean you handle sheep and not horses?"

He laughed. I love it when I play ignorant and it pays off.

"I used to be the pastor of a large church in Oklahoma. It started small—just a little more than sixty people. But it grew and grew, and after four years, we had nearly three thousand. That's when I left."

"But why? Isn't that the kind of thing most rever—I mean preachers—dream of?"

"Some might. They think that having a big church means getting more things done. I found I left more things undone."

"Didn't you have assistant priests?" (I used *priests* to show my ignorance.)

"Oh, I had four assistants, and they were fine, but that meant they got to do all the human-interest things. I conducted weddings and funerals and made a few hospital visits. You see, I'm a shepherd. For me, that means I like to know everyone by name, know where they live and what they like. When I became a rancher, I knew the names of maybe a few hundred. The rest were just people who shook my hand and called one of my assistants when they had problems."

"I suppose that gives you more time for your family."

"I don't have a family; I'm not married; I have never been married—almost got married once." He laughed. "Why is it that every time I meet an attractive woman, the first thing she wants to know is whether I'm married?"

(He said I was attractive. I liked that.) "I didn't ask if you were married."

"That would have been your next question, right?"

"You're just too quick for me," I said. I resisted batting my lashes.

"Look, you're too bright to play college-age games. I like being with you. I like you. You're bright and funny, but there's one thing we need to face right now."

"Oh, oh. You said *but*, and that's always a giveaway word."

"I like you, *but* I don't think we have a future ahead of us."

"Is something wrong with me?"

"That's not the way I'd say it."

"Oh, you can say it so it's less offensive or—?"

"Wait—wait. I want to make sure you understand. Give me a chance, please."

"Okay, try it again." I didn't like the direction of this conversation. By now, I wanted him to be falling all over me.

"I find you attractive, and we seem to have some kind of mutual insight—some kind of connection with what's going on around here."

"So that's wrong?" I asked, now really puzzled.

"Okay, I'll say it like this. First, I'm a—well, I call myself a serious, committed Christian."

"You mean you can't listen to jokes?"

He laughed. "No, I mean I'm serious about my faith in Jesus Christ and that He's the Savior—"

"Hey, I went to Sunday school—well, maybe six times. I actually know that stuff."

"You may know about what I believe, but—"

"So, I don't believe—at least not the way you do. Is that bad?"

Burton took a slow, deep breath. I wasn't going to make it easy for him. "That's not the way I want to say it. You keep bringing in judgmental words—like bad or wrong. I'd prefer to say it this way: You and I live in different worlds." He held up his hand so I wouldn't interrupt. "Julie, forgive me if I've misled you in any way. Jesus Christ is the most important thing in the world to me. I couldn't—not ever—get serious about anyone who didn't share my beliefs."

"Oh, I see," I said. "Yeah, I guess that is bad, because I don't—I mean, I don't *not* believe exactly. It's more—more that I just never saw much use in God. You know, calling on God when you face a problem instead of handling it yourself, and then ignoring Him—or her—or it—when things go well."

"That's not the kind of Christianity I believe in," Burton said. "I don't want to tell you my life history—"

"I don't mind listening," I said.

"I don't want to tell it all, but I'll say this. I didn't grow up in the church and didn't turn to the Lord—to Jesus Christ—until I was in a pretty hopeless place in my life. I wasn't looking for a crutch as much as I needed help—

ongoing help. I needed something—Someone—to guide my life. I had sure made a mess of it. I came to God out of an intense search for meaning—for purpose in living. And that's what I found."

"Is this where you tell me about how sinful you were so that I can open up and tell you what a terrible sinner I am?"

"Hey, you have been around."

I nodded. "You know why I like you, James Burton? You're different. All the other Christians—preachers, boyfriends, or my girlfriends' boyfriends—eventually got to this point and told me about burning in hell and—"

"I'd prefer to talk to you about a God who loves you—really, truly loves you," he said. "And before you interrupt again, I want to say this: I like myself. I enjoy my life. I have peace I never had before."

His sincerity sneaked through my line of defense. Okay, so I melted a little. "All right, I admit it: You're different."

"Will you think about this?" he asked. "I'd like to talk to you some more—a lot more—about the God who loves you very much."

I didn't know what to say, and without realizing it, I began to cry. "No one—no one has ever talked to me that way before."

"I didn't mean to hurt your feelings—"

I shook my head and sniffed several times. "You didn't offend me."

"I wouldn't want to hurt you. That's why I want to be clear about where I stand—where we stand."

"Let's find Mrs. Wright," I said and rubbed my tear-stained face. "I'm not ready to talk about God."

"Let's do that."

Again we circled the back side of the island, but we couldn't find her. "She might have gone back at any point, and we missed her," Burton said.

We walked back to the house. "Just one thing, James Burton. I do like you. I don't understand your brand of Christianity—it's certainly different from the kind I'm familiar with. All anyone wanted to do was get me to the altar so I would confess all my sins."

"If you ever believe," he said so softly I had to strain to hear him, "no one should ever try to force you to do anything like that. You'll do whatever you need to do. I'm more concerned about your faith than I am about getting you inside some church building."

I took his hand, patted it, and released it. "That's why you're different. You're the first Christian who—who made me feel, well, that you care, and that maybe God truly loves me."

"I do care," he said, "and I'll tell you something else. While we were walking along, I decided that I will pray for you—every day." He turned and rested both his arms on my shoulders. "I feel we have some kind of—call it mental connection or whatever—but I will pray for you every single day. That's my promise to you. I won't bug you about Jesus Christ, but I'll always be open to talk to you about the Lord."

"I'm not sure how much I like you, James Burton, but at least you've passed the tolerance test. Not many preacher types do."

He leaned close and kissed my forehead. "You know something? For a shrink type, you're okay, too. Just one thing—" and he laughed. "Okay, I promised I wouldn't push. I won't."

"That's the second thing I like about you." No one had ever talked to me like that before. I didn't know how to respond.

I wanted it to be clear that if I ever believed or turned to God or however they say it—I wanted it to be genuine and not just a means to get closer to Burton.

Once inside the house, we saw Wayne, Paulette, Reginald, Beth, and Tonya in the midst of some tête-à-tête in the drawing room. "Have you seen Mrs. Wright?"

All five shook their heads or mumbled negatives. They made it obvious they didn't want us to join their group. Lenny sat in a corner by himself. He looked up at us, smiled, and was ready to say something—something stupidly unfunny I'm sure—but we both hurried back out of the room and into the dining room.

We knocked again at Mrs. Wright's door, but there was no response.

"The kitchen?" Burton said, and we went there.

Simon sat on a stool and looked as if he had guarded a now-cold cup of tea for the past half hour. He shook his head before we could ask.

"But we couldn't find her out there," I said. "Come on, Simon, help us." I looked at my watch. We had gone out just before 9:20, and it was now slightly past 9:45.

"Come," he said. He left his stool, stopped at a kitchen counter, and pulled a large flashlight from the bottom shelf. "Likes walk. Stands near tree."

We followed him outside. The wind had picked up even more. Thin, sharp drops of rain struck me. I tried to say something to Burton, but he wouldn't have been able to hear me. He did take my hand, and I allowed him to lead me. So there was some compensation.

"There!" Simon shouted and pointed to a large, sprawling oak. He flashed his light on the tree. We walked up to the spot, and Burton dropped my hand. He leaned forward to examine the tree. It was fairly low, and someone had nailed four steps into the tree. I assumed Mrs. Wright climbed those steps and sat on the large, lower branch.

"Not here! Something wrong! Come!"

Simon grabbed my hand and pulled me down toward the path, and we kept going. After maybe ten more feet, we reached the precipice. "Careful!" he said and released my hand. He stood in one spot and flashed the beam downward. I don't know much about tides, but I assumed the full tide had come and was now on its way out. Below I could see the tips of huge stones. I assumed they were there to retard the washing away of the land. I realized that we were on the high end of the island and the beach—what little existed— must have been at least fifty feet below.

For perhaps forty seconds, none of us said anything, but our eyes followed the slow, methodical sweep of the light. "See!" Simon said.

At first I saw nothing, and then I stared at the light more carefully. Burton saw where Simon pointed.

"Oh no," Burton said.

Then I saw it, too. An arm stuck out from the rocks and waves rushed over it. As the next wave receded, I saw the body.

"Come!" Simon walked rapidly another dozen feet along the cliff and pointed to a narrow, uneven path that led down. "Stay!" he said to me and started down the uneven terrain.

I didn't answer him, but I was miffed. I wasn't some heroine in a 1950s film who stood and screamed for five minutes. I jumped in front of Burton and followed right behind Simon. I didn't misstep anywhere.

As soon as he reached the rocks and had his feet firmly placed, Simon grabbed the protruding arm, reached under the cold water, found a leg, and dragged the body to the sand. Elaine Wright's body lay face down. We knelt beside her, even though the waves trickled upward and touched my feet.

The back of her head was bashed in. The sea had obviously washed away the blood, but it wasn't a pretty sight.

"Fall maybe?" Simon asked.

Burton shook his head. "I think she was hit on the head and pushed." He pointed out that she was on her stomach. Simon tried to keep the light off her head and focused on her body so we could see bruises and cuts on her arms and legs. Even though the light wasn't directly on the top of her body, I agreed with Burton. Someone had bashed in the back of her head.

"Murdered," I said softly. "A second one."

"Go. Move her higher," Simon said and made the motions of wrapping her. "Tarp. Police." He said enough that both of us understood.

"Just don't disturb any evidence," I said.

"I careful." Disdain filled his voice.

"Go on. Both of you," Burton yelled. "Simon, I'll stay beside the body until you get back."

Simon handed me the flashlight.

"I'll wait with you," I said to Burton.

"No, I want to stay here. *Alone.*"

"It's safe. After all, who would come back and—"

"I want to stay here *and pray.*"

"But she's dead. You're not going to pray for—"

"I want to pray *for the others.* For guidance. For the murderer or murderers. I need a few minutes alone."

"Sure, I guess if it helps. That's what we expect clergy types to do."

"Laypeople also pray."

By now Simon had reached the top and disappeared from view.

"I want to be alone, please," he said softly, turned away from me, and faced the ocean.

I did the Simon shrug and turned around. I made my way up the path. The sprinkling was just heavy enough to make the path slightly slippery. I shined the light at my feet and pondered what he had said. I thought about the death of Roger. Now Mrs. Wright. I agreed with Burton that someone had bashed in her head and then pushed her over the cliff. But why? What message had she tried to give someone in the room? Was it because she knew something or had seen something?

Just as I pulled myself to my feet, a lightninglike thought struck me: *Murdered.* At least one person inside the house killed two people.

A murderer? Who? Why?

I shuddered as I asked the next question aloud. "Who will be next?"

8

A killer is on the island, I thought. *No, a murderer is staying in the same house as I am.* I walked over to the oak, climbed the four steps, and sat down. I turned off the flashlight. I wanted to be away from everyone and think for a few minutes. The wind intensified, and more fat drops of rain struck my face, but I didn't care. I thought about each of the people inside the house and asked myself, *Who would do this? Who would hate someone enough to kill?*

Amanda said she hated her husband, and Jason didn't seem to like him, either—or said he hadn't in the past. They could have done it, or one could cover for the other. One thing for sure, all the suspects were still on the island.

Wayne Holmestead was a snake. I wouldn't put anything past him. Okay, just because I didn't like him didn't make him a killer. Dr. Jeffery Dunn might be the one, but he was so boring—or maybe he did do it. What about Paulette White or Tonya Borders? I obviously didn't like Beth Wilson, but I didn't have any feelings about her as the murderer. I sensed the carrot-headed Lenny Goss, who seemed to have a joke for everything, might be the most malevolent of them all. Reginald Ford seemed harmless enough. But then, I didn't know much about him. Maybe I simply didn't want him to be the killer.

We could eliminate Simon. He accounted for his time before he left the island to meet us, and he was with us when Roger died. Also, I'm sure he didn't leave the house while we were gone, so he couldn't have killed Mrs. Wright. I couldn't prove that, but I just couldn't believe Simon was the bad guy. I kept thinking about that wink from him. I wondered what that meant.

I pulled my thoughts back to the guests in the house. We had ten suspects. The phone wouldn't work. The storm was approaching, and it wouldn't be safe to leave the island before morning. Would there be yet another murder?

I became aware that the temperature had dropped and I felt chilled. The wind had also increased. Hard spikes of cold rain struck with such sharpness that I felt as though they would nail me to the tree. I didn't care. I'd been wet before. Nearby rosebushes that had been twined around support stakes drooped, soggy and heavy with the rain.

I stayed by the tree with my thoughts until Simon returned with the tarp. I don't think he saw me; at least he didn't acknowledge me. I had the flashlight turned off. I'm not positive, but I think he was crying. He wiped his eyes just before he started down. He might have wiped away the rain, but my intuition said it was tears.

Why would Simon cry for Mrs. Wright? Or was he crying for Roger? Or both? Simon crying? That seemed odd.

I had finally had enough of the torrential downpour, so I raced toward the house. I heard footsteps behind me, looked around, and Burton was about ten feet behind me, running faster than I had.

I hurried inside and held the door open for him. "Where's Simon?" I asked.

"He'll be along."

We both stared at our wet clothes. "We need to change," Burton said.

I turned and headed toward the front of the house.

The first people we saw were Paulette White and Wayne Holmestead standing outside the drawing room. "Would you call the others into the drawing room?" Burton asked Paulette. "This is quite important."

"Are you ordering me?" Paulette asked.

"I apologize. I didn't realize I had ordered you," Burton said. "It's just that—that we have a new development, and everyone needs to know."

"Oh, that's different then." Her voice softened, and I assumed that was as close to an apology as Paulette would give anyone.

"We're both going to change clothes," I added as if that wasn't obvious. My hair felt plastered against my face, but it would dry. I have enough curl in it that I don't have to worry about doing anything with it after it's wet.

"We can use the room intercom from the kitchen," Wayne Holmestead stepped forward and said. "I'll do it."

"What is going on?" Tonya Borders asked. She had just reached the foot of the stairs. "You have no right to take over and order us around. That is the job for the police, is it not?"

"He wants us all here so you can give us a weather report and tell us that it's raining?" Paulette asked.

Burton and I rushed up the stairs. He gallantly grabbed my hand, smiled, and said, "I don't want you to trip." He laughed.

I giggled and said, "How can I when such a strong man guides me?"

His room was across the hall from mine. We hadn't been up there, but we knew our rooms because Simon had left our luggage outside our doors. That made it simple.

I hurriedly changed and was back down in less than five minutes and went into the drawing room. Even though Wayne wanted to know what was going on, I said, "Burton will tell you."

Just then Burton came into the room. He looked around and said, "Let's wait until we're all here."

Amanda and Jason hurried into the room. Lenny hadn't gone anywhere. Paulette and Reginald stood together, speaking in whispers. With a lot of hip swinging, Beth vamped into the room. She carried a cup of tea. I suspected that Professor Dunn had waited in the dark someplace until everyone had entered. He walked inside, looked around, and slammed the door behind him.

Beth, startled, spilled her tea, but no one paid any attention. The rest of us turned and stared at Jeffery. He breathed faster than I'd ever noticed before, so that was probably meant to be a dramatic entrance.

Burton held up his hand and motioned to indicate he wanted everyone to sit down. Simon came into the room through the doorway from the dining room. He had changed his shirt, but his shorts were soaked and he was barefooted. He must have wiped his feet, because I saw no prints on the hardwood floor.

I looked around. All twelve of us were present. Then I thought, that means if we eliminate Simon, Burton, and me, any of the remaining nine people could be the killer.

"Somebody murdered Roger Harden nearly three hours ago," Burton said, and his gaze seemed to take in everyone. "Now someone has killed Elaine Wright."

"Oh no, no," Amanda cried out. "Why? Why would anyone want to hurt her?"

"Why would anyone want to hurt Roger?" Burton asked.

"For Roger there was plenty of motive," Simon said. "All of them hated him. For Mrs. Wright, there is no motive that we know of."

"You—you spoke in full sentences!" I shrieked.

9

I stared at Simon. Was no one on the island what they seemed?

"Simon, I didn't know you knew enough English to—"

"That was part of Roger Harden's strategy. People assumed I didn't know much English, so they spoke freely. Sometimes too freely."

"Is there something you want to tell us?" Burton asked.

He shook his head. "Not yet. But if the others don't speak up and tell the truth about themselves, I may have to do some accusing."

"Would you check the phone line again?" Burton asked.

"Still dead," he said. "I checked on my way in here."

Burton nodded his thanks to Simon. "Each of you, please, tell me again about Roger and your relationship with him. Yes, this is a matter for the police, but all of you are suspects. Only Simon, Julie, and I were on our way when Roger's death occurred. We've now had a second death. We can only assume they are connected."

For several seconds, no one said anything and no one looked around. It was a strange atmosphere, almost as if no one wanted to speak, and yet everyone had something to say.

Even though we were in the windowless drawing room, we heard rain pounding against the dining room windows with increased fury. Torrents cascaded through the confines of the aluminum downspouts.

"I'll go first," Wayne Holmestead said. He attempted to look pleasant as he pulled his vest down over his stomach. "Jason and Simon haven't been kind in what they've said about me."

"Let's hear your version," Burton said.

"I agree Roger was, uh, well, controlling at times, but he was a good man. He was certainly an honest man. He was the best friend I ever had, and I loved him."

"I can say exactly the same things," Paulette White said. "Dear Roger was like a father to me. I'm only thirty-five—which is quite young to be one of four vice presidents—"

"Or perhaps not so unusual for a woman of your, uh, abilities," Amanda said.

"If you imply there was anything between Roger and me—other than business—I assure you and everyone else that is not true. I had absolutely no romantic interest in Roger. It would be like—like having an affair with my father. That is what he was like. He was my mentor and my father figure. I owed him so much. So very, very much. And I truly loved him."

"Roger planned to help me move out of weather reporting into hard news," Beth said. "He assured me that within three years, I would become an anchor in one of the major cities." She paused and looked around at us. "That certainly ought to eliminate me as a suspect."

"Unless he told you he had changed his mind," I said.

Before she could respond, Tonya Borders stood up and surveyed all of us. "I do not speak easily of emotions, but if in my heart there is any love, it was for Roger Harden."

Oh no, I groaned. This performance has to be something straight from the early talkies. Or maybe it was just a bad imitation of Greta Garbo from around 1930.

"We met—that is Roger and I—after my husband died, which was followed by the loss of my lovely daughter a few days later. Both because of an automobile accident. I did not want to live. I wanted to take my own life, but Roger came to me. He helped me want to live. He was my friend. He was my *only* friend."

The entire time she spoke, she never looked directly at any of us. For the first time I realized that she didn't make eye contact with anyone. I needed to watch that one. Something wasn't stacked right on her shelves.

"I suppose it is my turn," Dr. Jeffery Dunn said. "I teach biology classes at Clayton State University. I am tenured and have taught there for thirty years." He rambled on about his achievements and told us all about the articles he had written and the two books he had authored and that both of them had sold nearly fifty thousand copies, which was considerable for a textbook. I was half afraid he was going to pull out one of his mind-numbing articles and read it to us.

I snickered when he called himself an author. I knew the woman who had ghostwritten both of them. She told me that he handed her his lecture notes and she did an immense amount of research, updated his material, and wrote both of his four-hundred-page books. He paid her well and, in fact, more than she normally would have received. The extra money was to make certain she told no one. She told me only because I was her therapist. Naturally, her work under his name became the required texts for his classes.

He rambled on and on about his achievements and finally mentioned that Roger Harden had admired his intellect and had invited him several times to visit him in his large Clayton County estates. "Five times since he moved to the island I have been privileged to have been his guest. I can only assume he respected me highly in a professional capacity, as well as regarded me as an adviser and perhaps even a close friend—"

"Uh, excuse me," Burton said. "Thank you for all the background, but tell us about your *relationship* with Roger—especially when he invited you to the island."

"I was almost to that point—"

"Get directly to the point," I said, "before we all fall asleep." That was rude of me, but he didn't seem to take offense.

"As you like." He took a deep breath. "Intimate friend may be too strong a word, but I was certainly his confidant in many matters—matters which I cannot divulge here. I don't easily employ the word *love*, and I daresay it's not quite accurate, but it is as close as any other word for the affection I felt toward him."

He started to elaborate on his emotions, but Burton thanked him and turned away from him. He faced Lenny Goss. "Why don't you tell us about your relationship."

"*Moi?* Moi?" He grinned. "I think he liked me because of my jokes."

"Doubtless," Reginald said with such venom in his voice that even Lenny couldn't have missed his meaning.

"I want you to do something, *Reggie*," he said and grinned. "When we break up here and you go to your room, I have a small task for you. Just before you hop into your bed, I'd like you to get on your knees, close your eyes, and ponder how little your opinion means to me." He laughed and slapped his thigh. "Hey, wasn't that a good one?"

Reginald shook his head, rolled his eyes, and looked away.

"Please tell us, Lenny," Burton said. "But save the jokes, will you? We're talking about two murders."

The smile evaporated. "Yes, of course. All right, here's my story, and I'll keep it short."

"Excellent," Tonya said and smiled as if to deflect the sharpness of her tone.

"I was a literary agent when I first met Roger Harden. One of his cronies, state senator William Rice, became a client, and I represented his book. Unfortunately, I was unable to sell the book, although I sent it to fourteen publishers." He listed them by name, which impressed me that he had bothered to memorize them. "Through the Honorable Mr. Rice is how we became acquainted."

"This is the short version?" Reginald asked.

"I could go into more detail, but I'll spare you." By now it was obvious that the big jokester wasn't always a bundle of laughs.

"And your relationship with Roger?"

"Oh, it was excellent. I did all right as a literary agent, you understand, but Roger gave me one of those offers I couldn't refuse."

"What kind of offer was that? Not to turn you over to the police?" Simon said.

He glared at Simon and said, "He *invited* me to give up my agency and to work for him. He liked me, and I liked him very, very much. He felt I was—in his words—a born salesman. I'm now regional sales manager for Harden Homes in the states of Georgia, Florida, and the Carolinas. And I might add," he said and stared at Simon, "my sales have been impressive and the commissions extremely impressive."

"Even negative figures are impressive," Reginald said.

"Okay, Reginald," Burton said, "suppose you tell us about your relationship with Roger."

"Quite simple. I own a construction company. We are, uh, one of the largest in the Southeast. We build upper-scale homes—nothing less than ten thousand square feet." He smiled and said, "Much higher quality, of course, than those pedaled by Lenny."

"Okay, boys," I said. "You two don't like each other very much, but let's stay on the subject of Roger."

"Yes, yes, of course. Roger befriended me—as he did many others. He helped me out when I was, well, in a rough spot—that was years ago. I've been absolutely grateful. To show my appreciation, I have made several trips to other states on his behalf—you know, as a favor."

"A favor? Yeah, I'll bet," Jason said. "I'll bet you resented those trips."

"You seem to guess so much," Reginald said, "but you know so little."

"Jason, how about you?" Burton asked.

The boy shrugged—a gesture quite different from Simon's. He held out his hands, palms upward. "It was no secret the way I felt about Dad—my stepfather really—but that began to change almost a week ago. I don't want to talk about the details, but we had a reconciliation of sorts. I can tell you this: I used to hate him; now I love him."

"That's quite an abrupt change," Wayne said. "Perhaps too abrupt to be believable—especially when we're trying to figure out who killed my dear friend."

"Dear friend?" Jason snorted.

"Amanda, is there anything else you wish to add?"

She shook her head.

"What do you think, Simon?" I asked. Although I tried to observe everyone in the room, my gaze continued to return to him. His eyes were alert, as if he had just awakened. Brightness glowed in those soft brown eyes—as if he had just decided to join the party.

"Lies. All of you are lying." Simon stood up and shook his head. One at a time, he pointed his finger at Wayne, Paulette, Tonya, Lenny, Reginald, Beth, and Jeffery. "Why do you keep saying such things? You did not love him. You detested him. But I think I know why you insist that you loved him. You feel you should have loved him and—"

"How dare you speak such words to me," Tonya snapped. "That is most insulting."

"I told you the truth," Paulette said.

"I am deeply and personally offended. Furthermore, I resent such a blatant, repulsive, and—"

"Be quiet, Dr. Dunn," Simon said. "I know things. I can speak up if I must."

"You—you—you—," Jeffery sputtered.

I smiled. He *could* raise his voice a full octave. I didn't know he was capable of that much inflection.

"You detested him. Every one of you hated him. At least Jason admitted it. The rest of you are first-class hypocrites."

"How dare you!" Paulette said. "You weasel, you. You think that because you acted like a dunce around here that excludes you from suspicion? How dare you say I lie?"

"Yes, I agree," Wayne said.

"You are, after all, only a servant," Reginald said, "and your whole demeanor has been a fabrication. So why should we believe you?"

"For myself, I have spoken only the truth," Tonya said as she crossed her arms in front of her and turned her gaze downward. That was the strongest accent so far.

"Hey, knock me all you want, guy," Lenny said and gave him the benefit of the defenseless grin. "I was his friend. He was mine. It's that simple."

"I certainly had no reason not to like him," Jeffery said. "He did marvelous things for my career. He helped me gain tenure a year earlier than normal and opened publication doors and—"

"Will you shut up?" Wayne said. "I can't decide if I want to fall asleep or vomit when you go into one of your long, boring speeches."

Simon shook his head but said nothing.

"Simon, you said with certainty in your voice that they hated Roger," Burton said. "You wouldn't make outlandish charges like that unless you knew something."

"That's totally correct."

"Tell us then. Tell us anything you can that you think will help."

"You ask them. I tell you they have been lying. For now I will not say anything more." He turned and started toward the door.

"Simon, please—"

The handyman stopped and turned around. "Very well. I will tell you this much. You think Elaine Wright loved Roger? Here is the truth: She hated him." He stared at Amanda. "You thought he was kind to her?"

"I never saw him treat her badly," Amanda said. "I lived in this house, too."

"Yes, when you were around, he seemed kind, but when you were not, he was despicable. He raged over little things. He screamed one day that the clock was one minute slow as if she had slowed it down herself. Another time he went into a rampage because she served him filet of flounder when he wanted sole. He called her stupid, incompetent, and slow-witted."

"Why didn't she quit?" I asked. "She was an excellent cook and easily could have found work elsewhere."

"I can answer that in one word: *blackmail.*"

"What are you saying?" Wayne stood and walked over to him. He stopped in front of Simon and shook his finger in the man's face. "You dare to speak such things about my best friend?"

Simon took the man's finger and bent it downward. "Even now you're lying. He was not your best friend. Sit down or I may have to tell them about you."

"What? What do you mean by—"

"That's a good idea, Wayne. Please sit down, and let's allow Simon to tell us." Burton stood between the two men. He took Wayne's arm and led him to a chair.

Simon came farther into the room and stood near the fireplace so he could face everyone. "I will tell you the truth. Elaine was a criminal. If she had displeased Roger, he would have made certain that her next place to live would be a prison cell, and for a very long time."

10

"Surely you're mistaken," Amanda said. "I can't possibly believe that Elaine would be some kind of criminal."

"It's true though," Jason said. "Dad told me this earlier today—a little bit anyway."

Stunned looks filled several faces. Burton didn't appear surprised.

The room had a slight chill. Or maybe it was just something I felt. I sensed that we were moving into a new phase of the investigation—a deeper level or something. Thunder rumbled in the distance. We could no longer hear the pounding on the roof. The rain had already moved on.

"Please tell us about Mrs. Wright," Burton said. "You can't hurt her now."

"I'll tell you what I know, but I never learned the entire story," Simon said. "She told me parts of it at different times, but I know a few details."

For several minutes, Simon related a story about an armed robbery that had taken place in Brunswick, the nearest city from Palm Island. "A man robbed a bank and walked away from the counter with a large sum of money. A woman customer tried to stop him. He shot and killed her. He raced from the bank and jumped into a waiting car. The car sped off. The driver wore a dark hood, so no one knew who it was."

"Elaine Wright was the driver?" asked Paulette.

He nodded. "They caught her brother several days later. They recovered less than half of the money, but he refused to name the driver or divulge the whereabouts of the rest. Somehow Roger found out that Mrs. Wright was the driver."

"I know how Dad found out," Jason said. "Mrs. Wright's brother is Doug Burns, and he worked in the cannery. He needed the money for an expensive procedure for his daughter. She had some rare form of cancer, and there was an experimental treatment available. He hadn't worked in the cannery long enough to have insurance, and there was also something about a preexisting condition."

Between Simon and Jason, we learned that the police tracked down Burns before he could send the money to his former wife. "When they caught Burns, he turned over every cent he had."

"You mean they didn't recover all of the money?" I asked.

Simon shrugged. "He gave Mrs. Wright several thousand dollars. She never told me the amount. The prosecution threatened the death penalty unless he revealed the name of the driver—who would also be charged with murder and armed robbery."

"In desperation, he pleaded with his lawyer to contact Dad for him," Jason said. "Dad went to see him."

"And what did Roger do?" I asked.

"He paid for the medical procedures—some kind of transplant—it was successful, and the daughter is doing well. As for Burns," Simon said, "he received a death sentence, and Roger either couldn't do anything about it or wouldn't. He's still alive and, so far, he's lost every appeal. The governor definitely will not commute his sentence to life in prison." Simon paused and cleared his throat. He brushed his arm across his face, but not before I saw the moistness of his eyes.

He liked Elaine—I could see that. I wondered if he had been in love with her. Simon would never answer, even if I asked, but there was one question I could ask. "He said Mrs. Wright. Is there a Mr. Wright somewhere?"

"No. They divorced. She had been a highly successful chef with an impressive business in Savannah."

"That explains why she was such a fabulous cook," I said.

"She was a hard woman—really tough," Simon said. "But she had begun to thaw. Not a lot, but some. I think we were friends. At least, I tried to be her friend."

Yes, I believed that he loved her—or at least liked her a lot. The tone of his voice made it obvious to me. I glanced at Burton, and the slight raising of his eyebrow made it clear that he caught it, too. That Burton is uncanny; he should have been a therapist.

"If Burns had informed them of the identity of the driver, they probably would have commuted the sentence." Simon shook his head. "He refused and said he would never tell. Roger told Elaine he would give her a job, and he expected her to serve him well for four years. At the end of that time, he promised to return all the documentation of her guilt, help her establish a new identity, and move to another part of the country."

"But that wasn't right," I said. "She *was* a criminal."

"Yes, she was."

"Hey, that's like TV, isn't it?" Lenny said. "You know, the criminal escapes punishment for the crime and dies in another. . . Oh, I . . . Sorry."

Reginald shook his head. "You're not only despicable, but you're also an idiot."

"Now you understand why Elaine never would have quit, no matter how harsh he became. Besides," Simon said, "she had less than five months on her sentence. Her Harden sentence. That's how she spoke to me about it."

"So she wouldn't have killed him, would she?" I asked. "If she had stayed with Roger that long—"

"And he promised to turn over the evidence to her," Simon said. "I don't know what that evidence was. Elaine never told me, but she did say he had shown it to her. But I think I know."

"Then tell us," Amanda said.

"I think it was a confession written by Doug Burns, in which he detailed everything."

"Why would he do—?"

"In return for the money for the surgery," Wayne said. "That sounds like one of Roger's methods. Humanitarian—at a price."

"So the obvious inference is that she knew something about Roger's death," Burton said. "Perhaps she saw the murderer. Is that possible?"

For what seemed like minutes, no one said a word. Simon cleared his throat and said, "I know one thing that none of you knows. And this may help move things along. I know why Mr. Harden invited each of you. I know why it was just the twelve of you."

"I've wondered about that," Burton said. "Why was it just us? Why us together? Why not others?"

"Each of you has something to hide. Each of you has a secret—a secret known only to Roger Harden."

"A secret?" Amanda asked. "What kind of secret? Do you mean blackmail or something like that? If you do, then surely—oh, you can't be serious."

"I know what I know," Simon said.

"I think that's true," Jason said. "I don't know for certain, but Dad as much as hinted at something like that. He said that for years he had enjoyed pulling the strings and making all of you his puppets."

"What did he mean by that?" asked Wayne.

"Suppose you tell us which strings he pulled in *your* life," Jason said.

"I resent that statement."

"You may resent it, Mr. Holmestead, but it's still true."

"It is *not* true. At least it is not true in my case."

"I suspect that it is true for each one of us," Jeffery said. "It is true in my life. He certainly pulled my strings. Okay, here is the truth, and I'm ready to confess. Besides, I'm sure that one way or another, it will come out: I can honestly say I'm not the least bit saddened because he is dead. I detested Roger Harden."

Even with that last sentence, Jeffery said the words with no inflection, and I almost missed the meaning. "Detested?" I heard myself ask.

"I'll say it another way then: I hated the man. I'm delighted someone finally got rid of him. Am I clearer now?"

11

"You say you hated Roger—and you say that as casually as if you were saying there will be rain tomorrow or—" Amanda choked and couldn't finish. Jason hugged her and soothed her.

"Why don't you explain?" Burton interjected. He sat next to Jeffery Dunn and stared into the passive face.

"For thirty years he blackmailed me. Can you understand my feelings—thirty years? Thirty years ago, Roger came to see me at the university. He held my dissertation in his hand."

"And that means?"

"He had learned that it was—uh, that it was not original." His hand felt around his toupee and gave it an unnecessary tug. That must have been a nervous habit.

"You mean you copied from someone?"

"Absolutely not. It was original research; however, Roger knew I had paid someone else to write it for me." He hung his head. "I was quite busily involved in private research, you see, and I didn't have time to do both, so—"

"Yeah, right!" Jason said. "The truth is you paid someone to write it for you because you weren't smart enough to—"

"That is a malicious lie! You are a detestable boy, you know." He shook his head. "But it is true that I hired someone to write it for me. I have no idea why, but she informed Roger, and he confronted me. And I have paid for my indiscretion every day of my life. Oh, not at first. No no no. He said he wanted to help me, and I agreed. But first, of course, he insisted that I sign a confession—a signed confession that he had prepared and that he promised to destroy if I 'lived a satisfactory life.' Those are the words he used—a satisfactory life—but he meant he wanted to hold the confession over me."

Tears filled his eyes. He reached up once again to straighten his toupee. "He was a deceptive man. That's what makes him so evil. At first, he was kind and I thought he was a great friend. He used his influence, and after my second year of teaching—which is unheard of at our university—he arranged for me to get tenure."

"And you liked that?" Simon said.

"I confess that I did. But I had no idea what a price I would have to pay. I became a servant to that man. If I didn't do everything he asked—everything, even trivial things—he said he would expose me."

"What did he ask you to do?" Burton asked.

"Mostly meaningless things. I frequently came in answer to a summons to his home in Clayton County and later, after he moved permanently, to this island. Five times he asked me to break into the university's computer system—which I did. He never asked me to change anything. He simply wanted to know confidential data. I supplied him with information about the university staff and, well, about anyone else I heard about. Eight times he had me break into the president's personal e-mail. I became his personal messenger to pass on gossip or any kind of private, sensitive communication. He was detestable."

"Which would give you a strong motive to kill him," I said.

He shook his head. "Absolutely not. I came here to confront him—but not to kill him."

"We have only your word for that," Wayne said. "I think you need to give us more convincing information—some proof of what you say."

We waited while Jeffery cleared his throat and shifted his skeletal weight several times. "I am fifty-nine-years-old, and at the end of this school term, six weeks ago, I became eligible for retirement."

"So you thought you could make Roger back off?" I asked.

"No, not that. You see, I went to the president just before the end of the term. I confessed to him what I had done—about the dissertation, I mean. He doesn't know about anything else. I certainly never told him about Roger's extortion."

"And the result?" Burton asked.

"The president said I could retire and there would be no repercussions. I had to endure a stern lecture by him. I think he was glad to get rid of me. He has never liked me very much, and it was an easy way to push me out of the system without any problems for him. I accepted Roger's invitation so I could spit in his evil face."

"Did Roger know why you agreed to come?"

"No, although I whispered to him during teatime that I wanted—that I *needed*—to talk to him privately."

"I heard him say that," Amanda said. "Roger said he would see him after dinner."

"It was a little more than that," Jeffery said. "In fact, it was rather—how shall I say? Cryptic. He said that he had a significant announcement to make at the end of dinner. If I still wanted to talk to him, I could do so after that. I wondered if he meant he would expose me—"

"So that would have given you a motive," Paulette said.

"*Au contraire.* It absolves me. I had nothing more to fear from him. I was ready to confront him, yes, and tell him how despicable he was. In fact, I looked forward to telling that old devil that I was no longer his slave."

His words were powerful, but typical of the man, they were spoken in such a monotone he might have discussed a feature he had seen on TV.

"I did not kill him," he said, and then he raised his voice and emphasized each word: "*I did not kill him.*"

"Thank you," Burton said. "Dr. Dunn, I appreciate your honesty." He patted Jeffery on the shoulder as he might gently touch a child. Burton looked around at the rest of us. "Is there anyone else who wants to speak?"

"I'll tell you," Beth said. "It's all written down someplace. And if someone has that information, I suppose it will come out." She told about her life before she got on television. She had never been married, and she had used recreational drugs regularly. Because of her drug use—and she insisted she had never been addicted or been in rehab—she had served a year in prison for "selling myself," as she put it.

She changed her name to Beth Wilson with forged documents. "Roger found out, and I have no idea how he learned the truth. That was nearly a year ago. Since then, he has controlled my life."

As I listened, I felt sorry for her. Maybe I had been jealous of her gorgeous hair and smooth skin. As I listened, I realized that she hid a lot of pain behind that constant smile.

Burton thanked her for being honest with all of us.

"You might as well speak up," I said. "You all have something you're holding back."

"Okay, you might as well hear my story now," Lenny said. "I'm not proud of what I've done, but it's over, and I didn't kill Roger."

"Make us believe that," Reginald said.

12

"Tell us your story," Burton prompted Lenny.

He looked around at us, dipped his chin, and said, "I told you earlier that I was a literary agent, and that's true. Or perhaps it's better to say that's what I called myself in those days. I had an office in Savannah and a post office box and even a toll-free number."

He put his hands together, palm against palm, held them up to his chin, almost as if he were a child at prayer. His green eyes looked so sad. For the first time, I felt sorry for him, and I didn't even know what he had done.

"I called myself a literary agent. I worked mostly through the Internet. I paid for those huge pop-up ads that told people I could help them publish their book. Very slick, very professional looking. Why wouldn't they be? I paid plenty for them to look first class. I used the ploy that everyone has at least one book inside them. You probably saw the ads."

Because none of us seemed to know about them, I think that disappointed Lenny.

"Uh, well, I actually ran a scam," he said. "Yes, it's true: I did. I cheated people."

I stared at him. Did he think we wouldn't believe him capable of such a thing?

"It worked like this. They read my ads that said I would get their manuscripts to a publisher and help them get published. They paid me five hundred dollars to read the material, because I assured them that's how I'd know how and where to sell it."

"I know how the rest of that goes," Reginald said.

"Maybe you do." Lenny explained that even without reading a story—he never looked at any—he told every want-to-be writer that his or her manuscript still needed work. "I told them they had great ideas but the book wasn't publishable as it was. I made a big point of saying that the material had great potential but it still needed professional fine-tuning." He stopped and smiled at all of us as if he expected us to applaud his brilliant scheme.

No one responded.

Lenny sent each one a personalized letter (meaning he inserted a personal note here and there on his form letter) and said he worked closely with an editing service. He was in Savannah and the editing service was supposedly in New York. That was the come-on, because the material was sent to a Manhattan post office box and then forwarded to Lenny's sister, who also lived in Savannah.

"My sister did edit—a little—before she returned the manuscripts in large packages to her friend who picked them up at the same Manhattan post office. Each of them was addressed, stamped, and mailed from New York. We wanted to make sure the clients could see a Manhattan postmark on the envelope. Clever, right?"

Again, no one responded, and once again he looked deflated.

Lenny wrote the client and said he had received an edited copy from the editing service and made the clients an offer. For a thousand dollars, he would send their manuscripts to twenty publishers; for twenty-five hundred dollars, he would send it to fifty.

He laughed. "Most of them wanted fifty publishers to see it."

"And no editor ever saw the manuscripts," Burton said.

"Correct. This is the beauty of the scheme. We sent them rejection slips—maybe five or ten at a time, and from our office. They looked exactly like stationery from bona fide publishers." He grinned and slapped his knee. "It was a great system. You see, I had sent manuscripts to each of the publishers, received rejections, and made new stationery from their letterheads." He paused, I suppose, for us to absorb his brilliant scheme. "I thought that was an excellent touch. Most scams wouldn't go that far. Perhaps that's why I was so successful."

"How did Roger find out?" I asked.

"Earlier this evening, I mentioned that one of my clients had been William Rice, a state senator. One day he boasted to Roger that he expected a contract for his memoirs from a New York publisher."

"And Roger didn't believe it?"

"Believe it!" Lenny slapped his knee again. "That idiot Rice couldn't write five grammatical sentences. My sister thought it was one of the worst manuscripts we'd ever received."

Lenny said that Roger tracked him down and informed him that he had violated federal law because he used the postal service. Of course, Lenny knew he had violated federal laws. "I thought I had everything covered so that no one could detect any wrong—okay, any fraud."

Roger threatened to expose him and then offered his silence for a price.

"So what was your slave contract with him?" Jeffery asked.

Lenny said that Roger hired a ghostwriter to revise the manuscript and induced a regional publishing house to accept William Rice's book. "Rice got his book, loved it, and never learned how it came about. It sold well. He pushed all his friends to buy a copy—I think he sold something like twelve thousand copies. And for a lousy book like that, anything more than fifty copies would have been remarkable."

"But what price did you pay? What did Roger demand of you?" I asked. "There always seemed to be a price for his generosity."

"Total control. That's all. I gave up the literary business and went to work for him. I also, uh, spied on other employees, and I let him know anything I heard about his competitors in other areas. I did a little industrial espionage for him. You know, I'd find out what products a corporation planned to produce and someone—I don't know who—either stole or copied the information and allowed one of Roger's companies to beat the competition. That kind of thing."

"And you hated doing that?" I asked.

"Not at first. For a year or so, it was fun—really—but I realized that Roger was never going to let me go. The more I did for him, the more evidence he stacked against me."

"Sounds like a good motive for murder," Jeffery said.

"Maybe, except that I didn't kill him. I hated him, but I liked the work—the real work—the sales. I make good money, even if he forced me to do a few, let's say, unsavory things."

"What about the rest of you?" I asked.

"Go ahead and tell him, Reggie, old boy," Lenny said. "I can and I will if you don't. You see, I know your story—or at least enough to embarrass you if you don't speak up."

In that moment, it became obvious why the two men disliked each other. Not only did Lenny know, but he had made sure Reginald was aware of what information he had.

"I suppose I should. If I don't, this loud mouth will tell you and intentionally distort everything."

"Then let's hear your version," Burton said.

Reginald reminded us that he owned a prestigious construction firm. He had figured out a way to skim a few dollars off so that the government wouldn't know. He also bilked a few wealthy clients. He banked the extra profits in the Cayman Islands.

"How few dollars?" I asked.

Reginald ran his hand through his prematurely white hair. "Uh, quite a lot as a matter of fact."

"About sixteen million dollars?" Lenny said.

"That's quite untrue. It was less than half that amount."

"Sixteen," Lenny insisted.

"All right, let's *say* sixteen million, but—"

"How did Roger find out?" Simon asked.

"I told him."

That statement surprised all of us.

"I told him because I was desperate. You see, I had three accounts set up, but they were actually bogus." He went into a lengthy explanation that was almost as dull and circuitous as listening to Dr. Dunn. It was getting late, I had had a long day, and (to be truthful) my mind wandered. But I did get the final pitch.

Auditors uncovered the fact that two million dollars was missing from one client. Reginald said he had the money in a safe-deposit box. He gave some kind of explanation to the auditors about his reasoning that was supposed to make sense, but they were skeptical—naturally. It was something to the effect that the client was paranoid and might demand the money in cash at any time, and Reginald felt he needed to keep the account liquid. As crazy as that sounded, the auditors said they would come the next day to collect the fund and deposit it properly. He asked them to come after three o'clock and he'd have the money.

"I called Roger and pleaded with him. I said I had to have two million dollars in cash before three o'clock tomorrow." Reginald smiled momentarily. "He said that although it would be a little inconvenient to get that amount of money in cash, he could do it and would have it delivered to my office by noon. He was true to his word. Messengers brought the money in five briefcases, mostly in hundred-dollar bills. They went with me to my bank where I deposited the money."

Reginald went on to tell us that the auditors threatened to report him for such a business practice. That would mean a jail sentence and a huge fine. "I called Roger again, and he came through a second time. I don't know what he said to them or what transpired. I know only that one of the auditors phoned me the next day and said they were satisfied and would not make any complaint."

After that Roger called Reginald regularly—sometimes as often as once a week—and asked him to make trips for him. "Can you believe that one time he made me travel all the way to Seattle to bring back a shipment of fresh salmon? He could have had them shipped faster than it took me to go there, collect them, and bring them back."

"Control," Wayne said. "That was his forte all right. Just control."

"And you speak from experience?" I asked.

He shook his head. "I knew of several people. That's all."

"Are you sure it's only other people you know about?"

"I told you, I was Roger's friend—maybe his best friend."

"Or his best puppet," said Jason.

"Do you have anything to tell us?" Burton asked.

"I do not."

Neither did anyone else.

"Suppose we adjourn for the night?" Burton asked. "Is there anyone who's afraid?"

"All the bedroom doors can be locked from the inside," Amanda said. "Jason has a connecting room next to mine. He and I will get up and have breakfast by 7:30. By then, we hope the phone will work."

Within two minutes, everyone had left except Burton and me.

"I'm not sure what is going on," I told him, "but I'm grateful to Roger Harden. He has been tremendously helpful to me personally and to my career."

"Really?"

"Absolutely. That's why I wanted to come. I wanted to thank him." I told Burton about three specific programs Roger had started before I went into private practice, and how he helped me establish two humanitarian programs afterward. One of them was to give special tutoring to children of poor families that needed help. The other was his privately funded program where women could learn retailing or simple office work and be paid while they learned.

Burton listened without a word. I liked that. As I talked, I kept thinking, he actively listens just by the use of his eyes. Something about the intensity of his gaze made me know he heard every word.

He also had that rare ability to invite intimacy—I don't mean sexual intimacy—something deeper, more personal. He didn't blink or look away. It was almost as if his dark eyes bored into mine and invited me to open myself to him. I wish I had that ability. If I had, I suppose it would become a technique or a gimmick. The interesting thing about James Burton was that he didn't seem to know what a gift he had.

"Very interesting," he said. "But what about the other kind of help he gave you?"

I stared at him in confusion. "What do you mean?"

"The blackmail. The threat of exposure. He held it over the others. What about you?"

"What about you? You tell me first. Why did you come to the island?"

"I have no idea what he wanted," Burton said. "Roger phoned me a week before I received the invitation. He said he wanted to thank me for being a friend to Jason. The three of us had planned to go snorkeling tomorrow."

I focused on his eyes; I didn't think he was lying.

"So what about you?" he asked. "You don't have to tell me, but there is something—something he held over you, isn't there?"

I felt my eyes widen. "How do you know that?"

"I'm not sure," he said and gave me that full-teeth grin that melted me.

"You're not going to say that God told you about all my past sins, are you?" I laughed. "That would at least be a good line. No one ever used that one on me."

"Call it intuition. Call it experience, I honestly don't know. I'm a pastor and I do a little counseling. You know, people come to see me all the time. I listen, and over the years I've developed what I call my truth antennae. I often seem to know when people lie—not all the time—but usually when they try hard to make me believe something that's a definite fabrication."

"Okay, so what about Dr. Dunn? What he told us, do you think that was true?"

"Most of it. I believe Roger blackmailed him. I suspect there is more to it than what he told us—something a little less tasteful."

"I agree with you there. Do you want to know what I think? I think he stole his dissertation. He stole it from somebody, made a few cosmetic changes, and passed it off as his own."

"I agree. I can't tell you how I knew, but I was sure he didn't buy it."

"You're very good, Burton."

"So are you, especially when you want to evade an answer."

"Was I that obvious?"

"You're very good at evasion. I'll bet that's how you hold people off when they try to pry. You throw a question at them."

"Is that what you think?"

Burton laughed. It was a good full laugh, and I enjoyed watching him. There was nothing pretentious about it. He was quick, and he didn't miss anything.

"It's a long story," I said.

"It's a long night." He leaned back into the sofa and patted it for me to sit at the other end. "I assure you that I won't fall asleep while you talk."

"I'm innocent of murder, and you're my alibi. That's obvious, isn't it?"

"Simon is your alibi, too," he said. "But you're saying then, that you're guilty of something but not of murder. Is that correct?"

"Yes."

"Of what are you guilty?"

"It doesn't matter. Not now," I said. "Why do you want to know?"

"Ah, evasion again. Good! Wait a minute. Are you saying that you had a motive for killing him?"

"Absolutely."

13

I said it was a long story." That was another evasion, but I should have known Burton wouldn't be put off.

"I like long stories." Burton leaned just slightly forward. "Please trust me, Julie. Anything you say, I promise to hold in absolute confidence."

"Isn't that what we say to clients when they're skittish?"

He didn't respond to my evasion. I stared at him for several seconds, although it seemed like minutes. I wanted to tell him because I had never told anyone before, and it was a burden I had carried too long. Most of all, I was too ashamed to tell the truth.

As if reading my mind, he said softly, "Sometimes we let fear or shame hold us back. And as long as we hold it inside, we're never free." He got up from the sofa and said, "I'm going to get iced tea or whatever there is to drink in the kitchen. May I bring you something?"

I nodded because I didn't trust my voice. I wanted to tell him. *But what if he doesn't like me afterward?* I thought. *What if he thinks I'm a terrible person?* As I heard those words inside my head, I thought of my own counseling situations. If clients said those words—and they sometimes did—I would have answered much like Burton, and I would have urged them to expel their demons by talking.

I picked up two pillows, pulled them in front of me, and huddled against the sofa. *Can I tell him? Can I trust him? Will he understand?* I wanted to explain everything to Burton, but I wasn't sure I had the courage.

He brought in two glasses of iced tea, pulled up a small table, and set mine down. He sipped his tea but said nothing.

I still wrestled with my inner voice. I opened my mouth, and once the words started, it became remarkably easy to talk to him.

"I was married once," I said. "I married when I was barely eighteen, and my husband was twelve years older than I was. I loved him—or perhaps I should say I loved the man I thought he was. He seemed sweet, charming, and thoughtful. I never detected who he really was until we had been married two months."

I paused and stared at Burton.

"As I've already said, I like long stories," he said.

Julie had met Dana Macie during her first year of college. It had been one of those whirlwind romances and marriages. Dana came from a moneyed family. He told her he was a freelance businessman, but he never explained exactly what he did. She knew only that he always had money and didn't seem to have regular business hours. He was sometimes gone for two or three days at a time, and when she asked, all he said was, "It's just business."

She was young, impressionable, and very romantic. He was six five, blond, with a broad chest and narrow waist and hips—almost like a man with a sculptured body. Her girlfriends all but swooned whenever Dana came around. When she looked back, she realized that the reaction of other women had been a strong motivation for accepting his attention and saying yes when he asked her for dates. Other women envied her, and she liked that.

Julie had grown up in Villa Hills, Kentucky, a small town near Cincinnati, and gone to college in Georgia to get away from an unhappy home situation—a dominating stepmother and a docile father.

She and Dana met in late November, dated most of December, and married in January. No one in her family attended the wedding. Her stepmother wrote, "This is a most inconvenient time for a wedding, so we shall not attend." Just that note and nothing else. Not a phone call or e-mail. They didn't send a gift.

Dana tried to comfort Julie and promised he would be all the family she ever needed. She believed him because she wanted to believe he could wrap his arms around her and take away her rejection and hurt.

One thing about Dana bothered Julie: He drank—not much, but regularly. It was as if he had to have at least one (and usually it was two or three) drinks every night.

After they married, his drinking increased. He drank an expensive brand of scotch and grumbled if she didn't restock before he needed more. At first, she ignored the liquor. Then she tried to be subtle and asked him to cut down. He laughed and said, "I'll think about it." After that, his drinking increased.

The crisis came at an afternoon cocktail party in early April. His friends had decided to throw a belated party to celebrate their wedding. To please her husband, Julie drank half a glass of chardonnay, but she didn't enjoy it. He insisted on a second, so she let him pour her one. After she took a sip, he kissed her on the forehead and walked away. An hour later, Dana realized the glass was still full. "You haven't touched your wine." He stood in front of her and said, "Cheers and bottoms up."

She took a tiny sip.

He smiled and leaned toward her. "Bottoms up."

"I've had my limit."

"Drink it. *Now.*" The smile was gone and a hard look filled his face. Dana had never spoken to her in such a tone before.

She gulped down the second drink, even though she had to force it. She set the empty wine glass on the table. "It's—I guess I just don't like this. You know, I'm not used to drinking."

Dana left and returned almost immediately with a bottle. "This is mavrodaphne, a sweet Greek wine and difficult to find in most parts of the country." He opened the chilled bottled and filled her glass. "I have a special source, and I share this vino with few people."

"I really don't—"

"*Just drink it.*" He touched her hand, and his voice became gentle again. "You'll like it."

She brought the glass to her lips and held it there as she tried to think of an excuse not to drink it.

"*Just drink it.*"

"But, darling—"

Dana said nothing. He stood in front of her until she drained the glass.

"It's sweet, but I don't really like—"

"You can learn to like it." His voice had a slight edge to it. As soon as she finished it, he poured her another.

"No, that's really enough," she said. She forced a laugh. "You don't want to carry me out of here."

"It's not enough. You're still too uptight."

Julie had never been drunk. She had learned a number of tricks over the few months of their marriage to avoid taking more than a few sips. One was to pour the wine into a nearby receptacle or stroll outside and pour it over the balcony. A few times she dumped the drink into the toilet, flushed it down, and sprayed the room with air freshener.

This time Dana stayed only a few feet away and watched her. He insisted she finish each glass. It was as if he made it a personal crusade to get her drunk. While he watched, he drank at least ten glasses of scotch.

"I don't want any more," she said after the fourth drink. "Please, Dana. My head is spinning."

"It's not spinning enough," he said. "I know your tricks to avoid having a good time. I like to drink, and I want to share all the good things in my life. I enjoy living this good life and—"

"You call this enjoying life?"

"It used to be fun."

"Used to be?"

"Yeah, it was until I married you."

"I didn't force you to marry me," she said. She set her drink on a table and staggered from the room. She had to get outside and into the air. The room, filled with people, loud music, billows of cigarette smoke, loud talking and laughing, made her feel trapped.

She walked over to the patio door, and she had to hold on to the building to retain her balance. The early evening sky had changed from gold to apricot and orange. As she watched, shards of gray streaked through the flaming colors as if to say, "The night has almost come." She watched the clear lines of the hills fade away. The landscape seemed ready to sleep. She inhaled the fragrance from the nearby magnolia tree. If she could stay outside long enough, perhaps the dizziness would go away.

She had no idea how long she stayed on the patio. She closed her eyes and tried to shut out everything. After what seemed like a few minutes, although it may have been longer, she heard someone come up behind her; she didn't turn around.

"Don't be that way, darling." Dana stood behind her and ran his fingers across the back of her hand. "I'm sorry. Sometimes I do dumb things."

Julie didn't move or say anything.

He wrapped his arms around her. She wanted to lean back and let him hold her as he'd done so many times, but something was different. Perhaps it was the way he held her. Then she realized what it was: He also tapped one foot.

Afterward when she thought about it, the moment seemed ludicrous. While he begged her to forgive him, he tapped his foot impatiently as if to ask, "How long is this going to take?"

Without turning around, she asked "What's wrong?"

"Nothing you can't change," he said gruffly. "Just loosen up. This is party time. We're supposed to be the guests of honor. This is a party my friends set up for us—to celebrate our wedding. Get it? To celebrate? That's what we're trying to do, and you desert everyone."

"I doubt that anyone has noticed—"

"*I* noticed. That's what counts, isn't it?"

"How can you change so quickly from warm to cold?"

Dana laughed. "Maybe that's part of my charm." He kissed the back of her neck. "Now I want you to take my arm and smile, and let's go back inside and I'll give you a fresh drink."

"I've had enough," she said.

He whirled her around so that she faced him. He gripped her left arm. "Listen to me and listen with your full attention. I've put up with you for a long time. I'll tell you when to stop drinking. You want to spoil every party and every fun time. No more, babe. No more. Got that?"

"You're hurting me," she said.

He tightened his grip, grabbed her other arm, and squashed her against his massive chest. "I'll hurt you more unless you do what I say." He pulled tighter.

She tried to push away, but he pinned her arms to her side. She could hardly breathe.

"Will you do what I ask?" He pulled her tighter still.

She nodded as she gasped for breath.

Slowly he released her, and she took several deep gulps of air. She tried to look into his face, but it was too dark on the patio to see his features. "What is going on? This isn't the Dana I married, or is this the real Dana?"

"Just shut up. Get back inside. I expect you to enjoy yourself as much as I do. Got that?"

He turned and walked back into the party. A full minute later, one of their hosts came out with a glass of red wine for her. "Dana told me to bring you a drink. Here it is. Nice and chilled." She handed it to Julie and added, "If you want anything stronger, let me know."

Julie grabbed the glass and drank the contents in one long swallow and handed back the glass.

She brushed past the woman, went inside, and drank another.

Julie could think only of oblivion. She didn't want to see the people or hear their mindless chatter or cough whenever someone blew cigarette smoke her way. A distinct odor drifted her way. At first she thought it was some kind of spice, but it wasn't one she recognized. It had a strong, sweetish aroma. She'd never used marijuana, but she spotted four people in the far corner. They smoked, and she heard words such as *toke*, *hit*, and *joint*. Classmates in college had used those words, so now she knew.

What are we doing at a party like this? Who is this man I married? What is going on? He's never been this way before. Is it because he's drunk?

A moment of reality slipped through the haziness. She dropped into a nearby sofa and closed her eyes. *No, this is the real Dana Macie. The man I dated was an actor, an imposter.* She closed her eyes. *How blind could I have been?*

"Wake up!"

Rough hands shook her, and Julie opened her eyes. Immediately she felt dizzy. Dana pulled her to her feet, and she held on to him so she could stand. "The party's over and it's time to leave."

"Leave?" she asked numbly. "Where am—? Oh, the party."

Dana pulled away from her and headed toward the front door. She tripped over an empty bottle and upturned an ashtray. She stumbled into a crystal serving tray, and glasses fell to the floor and shattered. A few feet away, a man lay on the floor, a stupid grin on his face, and he sang to himself.

Julie's body felt fully relaxed, and she only wanted to sleep. But she had to move—and to keep on moving. She had to tell herself, move your right foot. Move your left. After what seemed like minutes, she reached the door. Dana had left it open, and a cool breeze struck her face.

"Ah!" She inhaled the blowing air. Not only did she detect the magnolia, but a scent of honeysuckle filled her nostrils. Ordinarily the cloying odors were too much for her, but tonight it rallied her senses. She stood straight and willed away the dizziness. She walked slowly down the five steps to the driveway. Dana had pulled their Mercedes convertible fairly close. Although she felt light-headed, she was able to walk.

The day had been warm but overcast, and now fog crept along the street. She felt as if it had thickened while she watched. She peered at the street lights that seemed to compete with the gathering murkiness. They were in Henry County, about forty-five miles from their house, in a low-lying area where they often received heavy fog before and after rain. She felt a few drops of moisture on her hand.

"Will you hurry up?" Dana abruptly got out and came around to where she stood. He thrust the key into her hands. "You drive. I'm too mellowed out."

"I'm not fit to—"

He grabbed her by the throat. His fingers dug deeply into her skin. "Maybe you didn't hear me. You drive!"

"Okay," she said. She threw her purse into the backseat of their convertible and drove off. They had at least an hour's drive to reach the southeast side of Atlanta.

Dana fell asleep almost as soon as he got back into the car. He snored gently from his side. After they passed the vast houses in the wealthy community where they had partied, she drove along a long stretch of highway that would eventually lead to I-75. The fog grew denser as she drove. With her lights on, she could see only a short distance ahead of her and rarely more than twenty feet. She had started out at fifty-five but slowed to forty miles an hour. She eased up on the gas pedal until the speedometer registered thirty. Her hands gripped the wheel, and she felt the strain from leaning forward.

Her stomach roiled, and bile snaked its way to her throat. Several times she wondered if she would have to stop and vomit. Her palms sweat, and she wiped them on her skirt. Sweat trickled out of her armpits and down her sides. The rope of nausea in her stomach knotted tighter.

Julie slowed to twenty. At that speed her headlights barely illuminated the yellow lines ahead. For the next nine miles, the road curved badly. The yellow diamond-shaped sign showed the snake icon and said thirty miles an hour. That was the speed limit for good weather.

She feared that she would run into a ditch. Another mile, and she realized that rain had come and gone in that area. The roads were shrouded with a thick mist, and the highway was silvery wet. Even going twenty-five, she misjudged and the right tire went off the pavement. She jerked the car back onto the road.

Dana awakened, rubbed his eyes, and blinked at the speedometer until he could read the numbers. "I told you to drive, not *coast* down the road." He scooted toward her until his foot reached the gas pedal. He kicked her foot aside and pressed on the accelerator. The car spun forward. She tried to stay in the middle of the road, but the fog was too heavy for her to judge properly. She crossed the double yellow lines on every curve.

"Please take your foot off—" she yelled and realized that was a mistake. Dana pressed harder. "Don't tell me what to do. I tell you. Now drive and shut your mouth." He closed his eyes and swore at her.

Julie leaned forward and tried to peer through the massive clouds of fog. She had no idea how long she drove. Three times the right front wheel went off the road. So far they hadn't encountered any cars coming toward them.

She had no idea where they were, and Dana's foot didn't let up on the pedal. They were down to less than a quarter tank of gas, and she hoped they'd run out of gas. But a quarter tank would probably take them all the way home.

She may have fallen asleep; she may have only blinked. Julie would never know which. A sudden crash, and the next thing she knew, she lay on the ground outside the car. It took her a few seconds before she was aware enough to get up. Nothing seemed broken, but whenever she moved, her body ached in a new spot. She crawled to the front of the car and slowly pulled herself upright.

To her surprise, the car lights still worked. The vehicle had climbed nearly three feet up a magnolia tree and hung there. Because of the impact, the tree leaned backward. She hobbled to the driver's door. Dana's body had fallen over on her side, the door was open, and he hung face down. His face was covered with blood.

She felt for a pulse.

There was none.

14

Julie didn't know what do. It must have been close to three o'clock in the morning by then. The fog slowly drifted away, and she could finally see the road. Ahead she spotted a sign that pointed Macon to the left and Stockbridge to the right. At least she knew where she was.

She found her purse on the floor in the backseat and pulled out her cell phone. They were less than three miles from Roger Harden's massive estate—it was huge, several hundred acres. Roger and her dad had been good friends when they were young and were classmates through high school. As a favor to her Dad, she had called Roger when she first enrolled at Clayton University. Roger visited her several times, took her to dinner, and insisted she keep his number. "If you ever need anything—anything—just call me," he said.

Julie fumbled through the address book in her purse until she located his number. She didn't know what else to do except call Roger. Her hands shook so badly she had trouble dialing and had to start over.

Dana's dead, her mind said. *You killed him. He's dead.*

"Noooo," she cried and finally punched in the right number for Roger Harden.

"I killed him! I killed my husband—I was driving and he put his foot on the pedal and I couldn't see and—"

"Calm down," Roger said in a soothing voice. "Please relax. Tell me where you are." He talked for at least two minutes, and she did calm down.

"I'll be there. Don't do anything; don't touch anything."

Roger arrived at the crash within ten minutes. Julie walked around slightly dazed, afraid that if she stopped moving, she'd lie down and go to sleep. Roger walked up—held up his hand, and said, "Let me look it over." He stood at the side of the car and carefully took in everything. Finally, he said, "Dana was driving."

"No, I was—I told you—"

He came up close and stared into her eyes. "Listen to me, Julie. Dana was driving. He was drunk, but he insisted on driving. Is that correct?" She tried to explain what Dana had done about the gas pedal, but he motioned for her to stop talking.

"You have not been listening," Roger said.

He pulled Dana's body over so it was fully in the driver's seat. He opened

81

the passenger door, applied pressure, and bent it so it wouldn't close. He grabbed her purse and threw it on the ground on the passenger side. "Stand over here when the police arrive," he said. Then he dialed 911.

—

"So that's the horrible story," I said. "Roger covered it up for me. I was charged with nothing. I might have been acquitted anyway, but I don't think so. I was driving under the influence, and Dana died. That is a crime.

"Roger has held that accident over my head for the past seven years. He never wanted money—Roger wasn't that kind of extortionist. He wanted power—he had to have control in my life. I didn't realize until I got here that I wasn't his only victim."

"I'm sorry," Burton said.

"In case you wonder, I've never had a drink since. And I have no desire for one—I didn't before, but I drank just to please him. After Dana's death, I learned a number of things about him."

"Such as?"

"I learned he was into drugs—really into them. I found them hidden all through the house. He had more than fifty bottles of Ecstasy. I found several pounds—I guess you call them kilos—of marijuana. He had nineteen bottles of prescription drugs—all of them some kind of speed." She laughed self-consciously. "I was so naive, I had to look the drugs up on the Internet to know what they were."

"What did you do with them?"

"I flushed them down the toilet. It took me exactly nine flushes to get rid of everything."

"You had no idea about his other life?"

I shook my head. "None. I also began to receive phone calls—on his cell. People wanted a fix, or usually they'd say they wanted a little help. I told them to hang up or I'd call the police. After a few weeks, they stopped calling."

"I went back to my maiden name of West to get away from that whole scene and especially from Dana's friends or customers or whatever they were."

"And Roger took care of everything with the police?" Burton asked.

"Everything. He took over, and I have to say I was glad. He told the police he had been driving by, heard the crash, and rushed to our aid. He said he knew Dana, which he didn't, and he also told them he had heard that my husband drank a lot, and he said that he had even observed him drunk once in public. In Georgia, the legal limit is .08. Dana's was twice that amount. Worse, they found he had several prescription painkillers in his bloodstream as well as marijuana.

"After Roger spoke to the police, no one ever questioned me. Roger brought me to his house. I stayed in shock for most of the next week. That's when I met Amanda and Jason, and they were extremely kind to me. Eventually the police chief came to Roger's house to see me. 'Sorry, ma'am, that you had to be involved, but the world is better off without him.' That was it. I never had anyone ask me anything else."

—

I filled in a few more details, but Burton had already figured it out. "Roger had taken pictures before he moved Dana's body. He threatened to show the pictures to the police if I ever gave him any problems. 'Murder has no statute of limitations,' he reminded me.

"'But it wasn't murder,'" I insisted.

"'It will be if you cross me,' he said. He also told me that he could 'enlist half a dozen people' to testify to our fights and arguments and that I'd threatened to kill Dana on more than one occasion.

"'But there were no fights,'" I protested. "'I never threatened him—not ever.'

"'Perhaps,' Roger said, 'but I can assure you that no one will believe you.' That's when I realized he would do anything to keep me under his control."

"And what did he ask you to do?"

I couldn't look at him, because I was embarrassed to admit it. "I was a spy—like Dr. Dunn. He had someone show me how to break into the county mental health files. He also showed me how to gain undetectable access to the files of eight psychiatrists."

"And you reported—?"

"Only information that he demanded. I never volunteered. Roger didn't know it, but I held back as much information as I could," I said. "But yes, I did a totally unethical thing. I was one of Roger's robots."

After I finished my confession, Burton and I stared at each other. I felt the sympathy pour from him, but he didn't say anything. Finally, he took my hand, patted it, and said, "Please forgive me. I had no idea—"

"It's all right. I've held it in all these years, and I truly needed to tell someone. Thank you for being that someone."

Burton hugged me then. No kiss. No magic moment. Just a hug. But it was warm and tender, the kind given when we want to comfort someone who hurts. I've been out with enough men to know the difference. I felt as if he cared about *me*. I could have been a woman of seventy or a boy of fourteen and the hug would have been the same.

As he held me, I realized that the demons of shame and embarrassment were—if not gone—at least greatly diminished.

We sat next to each other on the sofa like that until my tears began. I had no idea they were coming, but it was like an unexpected eruption. I cried with a lack of self-consciousness and control that I hadn't experienced since I had been a child.

Burton released me, and I stared at his moist eyes. He had felt my pain. That brought even more comfort. No one had ever felt my pain before.

Then the convulsive sobs began. I have no idea where they came from, but I couldn't stop them. More tears came—tears I had not shed at Mom's funeral, at Dana's, or at any other time in my life. It felt as if everything came together at once. My body shook, and I wept until I thought I would never stop shaking with the sobs and the grief—and especially from the guilt. Wisely, Burton didn't touch me; he didn't need to. He provided a safe environment for me to focus on my pain.

I couldn't stop the tears. They kept coming. Burton handed me his handkerchief and whispered, "It's okay. Sometimes they're good tears and they need to be freed."

15

How could I have figured out what happened next? I want to be sure and get all the details right.

I was ready to say good night to Burton, go upstairs, and try to get some sleep. Shortly after I had opened up to Burton, the clock struck eleven.

"Are you sure you'll be all right?" he asked as we started out of the drawing room.

Before I could answer, we heard a gunshot followed by a scream. Both of us raced toward the stairway where the shot had come from. I didn't think of it then, but I outran him on the steps.

By the time I reached the landing, and Burton was two steps behind me, the others had come out of their rooms and stood in the hallway.

"I heard a shot!"

"And a scream."

"Is anyone hurt?"

I don't remember who said what, because everyone seemed to talk at once. All of them looked as if they had just jumped out of bed. Jason was the only one without a robe. He stood in jeans, bare feet, and bare chest.

Just then Wayne Holmestead poked his head out of his room, and the light was on behind him. His was the room at the end of the hallway.

When he saw us, he stumbled out of the room. He visibly shook. His glasses were askew. He slumped against the wall as if he feared he might fall. He seemed unable to move or to say anything.

Within seconds everyone focused on Wayne. He opened his mouth several times before words came out. "Somebody shot at me! I could—I could have been killed."

"Who shot at you?" Burton asked.

"I don't know."

He straightened his glasses and pushed himself away from the wall. He wore a robe over pajamas, and he tightened the belt. Those minor actions seemed to put him back in control. He stepped forward. "I had gone down the hallway and visited Paulette—perfectly innocent—just to borrow a Percodan—which I know she takes. I hadn't thought to bring any. I have an old football injury, and sometimes my sciatica acts up and the pain is excruciating. She gave me two pills, and I was returning to my room."

"There are the pills!" Lenny said, pointing. "So scared he dropped them, huh?"

We stared at the floor, and they were both on the carpet, about four feet apart from each other.

"Look! The door! Isn't that a bullet hole?" asked Reginald. He walked past Burton to the frame of the door. Embedded in the door was a bullet.

No one seemed to know enough about bullets to give any opinion about what kind of gun had been used.

Just then, Jason stepped forward and looked at the bullet lodged in the wood. Paulette hurriedly explained what had happened. Beth walked down to where Burton, Wayne, and I stood. She stared closely at the hole and the casing. "Beretta—.32 caliber," she said.

"How did you know that?" I asked.

"I know things like that."

"That's probably right," Jason said. "Because I think it's the gun from Dad's desk—we presume the one that killed him."

It took several seconds for all of us to absorb that information. I realized not only did we have two murders, but now we had an attempted third. What was going on here?

"Hey, sounds like the old Agatha Christie novel, *And Then There Were None*." Lenny laughed. "You know the story? There were ten people on an island or an estate. One by one, they all died or something like that."

"Except the murderer killed himself, which made the last couple of people mistrust themselves and they killed each other," said Reginald. "*Or something like that.*"

"That's so—so horrid," said Amanda. "Please. That's not something to joke about."

"I wasn't joking. Not this time," Lenny said and laughed. "Or maybe I was."

"Or maybe you have the gun?" Jeffery asked.

"Search me. Search my room," Lenny said. "Stay for tea in the morning."

"What do you think is going on?" I asked Burton. I kept my voice low, and most of them didn't hear me. By then, a gaggle of voices repeated to each other what they had heard, and most of them insisted they had been sleeping soundly.

"Are you afraid to be in your room alone?" Burton asked Wayne.

He shook his head. "I'm safe now, and I'll lock the door. I won't come out again until I hear others moving around in the hallway."

"I'll ring your room from the kitchen for breakfast," Amanda said. "As I said earlier, I'll have some kind of breakfast ready by 7:30."

Burton didn't tell anyone not to touch the bullet. In the TV shows, the

86

hero always says that, and it always sounds stupid to me. Why would anyone want to touch it? Who wanted to feel a spent bullet in the door frame?

"Let's all go back to bed," Burton said. "Go inside, lock your doors. You'll be safe tonight."

"Aren't we going to search everyone's room?" asked Lenny. "That could be fun. I'd love to know what people brought into their rooms."

"Good night, Lenny," I said. "We'll leave that kind of thing to the police."

"Good night, everyone," Burton said. "I'll stand out in the hallway until everyone is locked inside."

The others turned and went into their rooms. That is everyone except me. I had been ready for bed, but now I was wide awake. I stared at Burton.

"I'm awake, too," he said. "You want to find some sweet tea or something downstairs?"

"I'd prefer a snack. If I eat something, that relaxes me."

We walked downstairs to the kitchen. Burton made himself an instant hot chocolate, and I found a box of Oreos. I planned to eat two but finished off eight without a pause. Burton just watched and smiled.

"I think I'm ready to head toward bed now," Burton said.

"Sounds like a good idea."

We left the kitchen and walked down the hallway. Just as we approached Roger Harden's office, I heard a soft brushing noise—as if someone moved something inside the room. Burton paused. Our eyes met, and he put his index finger to his lips.

Burton turned the knob slowly and pushed open the door.

The lamp on Roger's desk was on. Paulette's back was to us, but she was rummaging through his desk. She was so focused on her search she didn't see or hear us. She lifted a pile of file folders from the right-hand drawer and skimmed them as if she wanted one particular paper.

"What are you searching for?" Burton asked.

Paulette jumped and gasped. Her hand went to her breast. "Oh, you startled me."

"You were so intent on your search, you never heard us," I said. "And obviously you haven't yet found what you want."

"So what papers are you looking for?" Burton asked. "They must be important to you."

"Yes, they are."

"How did you get in here?"

"Roger kept a spare key over the door ledge. He locked his office only when he had a party because he didn't want guests to wander in here accidentally." She forced herself to smile—and it was obvious it was forced—and added,

"You know how it is with powerful men like Roger. They constantly fear someone will steal from them."

Burton held out his hand. "Why don't you give me the key? We can lock it behind us when we leave."

She handed him the key.

"What did you hope to find?" I asked.

"I'm not clever enough to think up a safe or evasive answer, so I think it's wiser if I say nothing." She pulled the top of her heavy hot-pink robe tighter around her neck. She may have been dressed for bed, but she hadn't taken off her makeup. I wondered what she wore under that robe.

"It might help us believe you didn't kill Roger if you tell us," Burton said as he walked closer to her. "If you don't tell us, it becomes easy to believe you killed him because he had something you wanted and wouldn't give it to you, so you shot him, and you came back to find it when you thought everyone had gone back to bed."

I walked over and pulled open her robe. She still wore the same black dress from earlier in the evening. "You haven't been to bed, have you?" I asked. I noticed her purse on the corner of the desk and decided to see if she had already taken anything.

She saw what I was going to do, and her hand reached the purse before I could touch it. "You may choose to believe whatever you wish." She opened her purse, fumbled around, and closed it angrily. "I forgot. I quit smoking two weeks ago." She laughed—a bit forced from my observation—and said, "Grabbing a cigarette was a nice way to give me a few seconds to collect my thoughts." She opened the purse again and shoved it toward me so I could look inside before she snapped it shut. "Satisfied?"

"Want to try a stick of gum instead?" Burton held out a pack.

She shook her head.

I couldn't understand how she could search through Roger's desk when his body lay on the floor less than two feet away. *What kind of woman is she?* I wondered.

From behind the desk she had carelessly tossed file folders around. Burton came around on one side of the desk to face her, and I came around from the other—the side away from the covered corpse. Without discussing it, I sensed both of us wanted her to feel intimidated by our presence.

She stared at me and then at Burton but said nothing. She sat down in Roger's chair. Her face was a mask, and she wasn't going to reveal anything.

"You disliked Roger, didn't you?" I asked.

"Disliked him? I *loathed* him." She laughed. "But I'm not a murderer, even though I'm glad someone took care of him."

"Why did you loathe him?" Burton asked.

"Let's just leave the statement at that, shall we? You're not a police officer, so I don't have to answer, do I?"

Burton sat on the edge of the desk, and he invaded her space just enough to intimidate her. "You're right, of course; however, I'd like to leave this office believing that you're not the cold-blooded killer who's already taken two lives. You don't have to say anything."

"Do you think I killed Roger? Do you honestly believe that?"

"What do you want me to think?" As Burton talked to her, his voice softened and took on a kind of intimate confidentiality. An act or not, if Burton had talked to me like that, I would have spilled every secret I had ever learned.

"Let's just say I had no love for him or even that I detested him. Now that he's gone, I haven't shed any tears, and I won't. I think the world is better without Roger. I feel sad about Elaine. I didn't particularly like her, but she didn't deserve to die."

"And you have some way to know who deserves death?" I asked. "You are some kind of judge?"

"No, I didn't mean—"

"What did you mean?" I reached down, pulled the chair around so she faced me. I grabbed her shoulders. Burton had tried the let's-be-sweet approach. Now I would try mine. I shook her twice. "Don't try to play games with us. Someone has killed two people and shot at a third. If you didn't kill them, I would expect you to do everything you can to turn suspicion away from yourself."

"Take your hands off me."

Her words lacked conviction. I didn't shake her again, but I didn't let go. I had suspected that, although she was cool on the outside, she was fragile on the inside. "Then tell us."

"I want to be able to believe you," Burton said in his still-soft voice.

"Is this some kind of good-cop-bad-cop deal?" Her voice shook as she asked.

I knew we had her.

"I wouldn't play games with you," Burton said. If anyone else had used those words, I would have cried, "Yuck," but they came across with sincerity. "Please."

I released her and stepped back. I pushed the file drawers back into place and sat down on the other side of the desk.

Paulette swiveled her chair back so that she faced Burton. She closed her eyes and leaned her head back in the chair. "I'm too ashamed to talk about it."

"Please tell us," Burton said. "We're both professionals, and we'll respect your confidence."

Paulette opened her deep blue eyes. "Is that a promise?" She didn't look at me. Her full concentration was on Burton. I suspected that was part of her charm in the business world. She stared at him as if he were the only person in the room.

This time I was smart enough to keep my mouth closed. Burton was doing a good job, and I was willing to let him do it.

16

R oger Harden was my mentor," Paulette said without looking at either of us.

"And you loved him and he was your best friend," I said. "We read that novel. Now let's try a little nonfiction."

She nodded two or three times as if trying to decide where to start. "We met when I was nineteen years old and struggling to finish my degree in business at the University of Tennessee—in Knoxville—and I worked full-time at Faces."

"What's Faces?" Burton asked.

"It was a high-level cosmetics firm. It was fairly small by industry standards, but they made only quality products—not the kind you find in Walgreens or Kmart. I was in sales. I mean, I spoke only to top buyers—Macy's, Nordstrom—that kind of place. We had a few independent stores, but mostly it was the upper-end chains. Apparently, I was extremely good at what I did, because week after week I brought in the top sales for Faces, and there were eleven salespeople on staff."

"And how did Roger discover your talent?"

"Oh that? He decided to buy the company. We were located just outside of Knoxville, and he wanted to take us over, move us down here to the coast, and make Faces a megabucks outfit—or so he said."

"I didn't realize Roger was into anything like that."

"Roger was into whatever would make him a profit. He bought Faces, reorganized it, brought in top talent, and made the company big—really big—and six months later he sold it to Bristol-Myers. They downgraded the products—cheapened them, if you want my opinion. But Roger didn't care what they did as long as he made a profit. In the process, he netted a few million and moved on to the next project. That's how he operated."

"And how did you fit into all of that?"

"Simple. Roger was brilliant. Anyone will tell you that. He had an intuitive instinct about him. It was almost as if he looked at a product or a line—even if he knew nothing about it—and could sense what would sell and what wouldn't. He was the same way about people. In the twenty years I was with Roger, not once did I ever see him make a bad deal. He was that good."

"I'm still not clear—" I said and remembered I was supposed to keep my mouth shut.

"Roger knew I had potential. He spotted it within minutes of our meeting the first time he came to Faces. Privately, he asked me if I would meet him for lunch—strictly business, he said. But I had classes at the university, so we settled on dinner. That night he offered to make me a vice president—one of four in Harden Enterprises."

"Just like that?" I said, and I admit skepticism rang out in my voice.

"Just like that. He said he would give me flextime to finish my degree—which he did. He even backed me so I could do an MBA. In th'··· Roger was the best."

"And in other ways?" I prompted. As I asked, Burton raised I caught the message. I'd try to keep my mouth shut.

"Roger taught me many things, and always he acted as a man conduct—"

"You mean he didn't make a pass at you?" I said and wondered if I needed to literally bite my tongue.

"Never. He was a total professional. I knew he was married—he married a few months after I started to work for him. You can believe this: No matter what a jerk he was, it was always business. Totally, strictly business. No, Roger was one of those people for whom the ultimate aphrodisiac was money, which meant success, and success meant power."

I had a comment ready, but this time I said nothing.

"I loved my work with Roger—at least I did for the first ten years. I learned more on the job and from him than I ever could have learned on my own." She paused and smiled. "Both Harvard and Princeton offered me a teaching position last year—which I turned down. But that's to make it clear how much Roger taught me, and to explain that I had become well known for my business sense."

"But you despised him?" I said softly. This time Burton didn't raise an eyebrow.

"He did teach me—I received a great education from him, but that instruction came at a price. Roger would coach me or open any doors I wanted to go through. There was just one catch."

"Total control," I said without thinking.

"Exactly that. I had to turn down Harvard and Princeton because I would be too far away from him. Everything, anything—it didn't matter what it was—Roger Harden had to be in total control." She shook her head, swiveled in her chair several seconds. "He liked my ideas—that was never a problem. But I had to bring every idea and every innovation to him. No matter what, it was as if he had to put his imprimatur on it."

"But you said he liked your ideas?"

"He never rejected one of them. Two or three times he made suggestions to improve the concepts or figured out ways for me to get more mileage, but that's all. I didn't mind that, and he never demanded credit. He didn't seem to want that kind of power. It wasn't anything like that."

"But it was the control issue, right?" I asked.

She nodded. "If I didn't consult him on every single thing, he would go berserk. One time he yelled at me for almost twenty minutes in a board meeting. Do you know why? Because I had forgotten to hand deliver to him a copy of our profit-and-loss statement—and we had netted nearly three million dollars. *Hand deliver.* Can you imagine that? I sent it by the office messenger because I was running late for an appointment."

"That must have been demeaning," Burton said.

"Demeaning? You have no idea. Another time I hired a secretary. An entry-level secretary! But I didn't tell Roger first. He was angry because I didn't tell him that I had interviewed four candidates, liked her the best, and offered the position. He made me fire her. Is that micro-micromanagement or what? I don't know how he kept all that going inside his head, because I know I wasn't the only one. Even though I realized he was that way with everyone under his powerful hand, I didn't feel any better."

"It must have worn on you," I said.

"Worn on me? Ha! That's understated. It grated on me every day—every day. I kept reminding myself that I was making a lot of money because of Roger. He also taught me how to invest wisely—which I've done."

"So where does the hate come in?" Burton asked. "He could have been a nuisance, but—"

"He lost interest in my career. It was as if I had become a finished product. He had taken me, molded me, and made me what he wanted me to be. Then he had no further interest in me. I still had to drive through his control booth, but there was a tone of disdain."

"Disdain? I'm not sure what you mean," Burton said.

"He began to make me feel insignificant and reminded me constantly that whatever I was, he had made me. Things like that. He said I would have been nothing without his guidance. And he sometimes said those things in board meetings or whenever important people were around."

"So what did you do?" I asked. "You don't seem like the kind of woman who would just take that forever." I'm sure she knew I hinted that she might have hated him enough to kill him.

"I suggested to him that I leave and move elsewhere. He went into a tirade over that. He screamed at me and called me ungrateful. That night he phoned me just before midnight and again called me an ingrate and self-centered and said I had only wanted to use him for my own means."

"And what did you say?" Burton asked.

"I said, 'If I'm so terrible, then perhaps it is better if I leave.' Then he really screamed and finally said, 'You will leave Harden Enterprises *only* when I tell you to leave. If you try to apply for another position, I'll ruin you!' "

I reached over, took Paulette's hand, and squeezed it gently. I knew enough about Roger that I could understand her feelings. I hadn't liked her before. I still didn't like her, but at least I understood her pain.

Burton and I didn't say anything more. Both of us seemed to sense if we just kept quiet, she would open up.

"Okay. I'll tell you. You're both professionals, right?"

We nodded.

"That means whatever I say to you is confidential? Burton's clergy and you're a therapist. You assure me of confidentiality, and I'll tell you."

We both assured her that we would hold everything in confidence unless she gave us permission to speak.

The words poured out. She worked most of the years for a subsidiary of Harden Enterprises, but her offices were in Roger's twelve-story office building. "I was in charge of a chemical company that wanted to develop a natural insecticide that would not harm the environment." She knew nothing about the formula, but she stood behind All-Well Chemicals as they developed their product. They spent millions of dollars, and after three years, they reached the final stages of development. They would have to test its effectiveness—especially the long-term effects, then they would be able to put it on the market within two years.

A friend had invited Paulette to a cocktail party. One of the other guests was the CEO of a rival firm. The CEO said he had asked the friend to invite Paulette because he wanted to offer her a job. She would become acting president and succeed him in five years. He was willing to write a contract. When she told them that Roger would try to block it, he promised a contract that would prevent the company from firing her. If they did release her, they would give her a five-million-dollar bonus for every year she worked there.

"It was too good an offer to pass up," she said, "but there was just one problem."

"And that was?" I asked.

"I had to steal the formula from All-Well Chemicals and pass it on. Oh, they would make small changes so that it wouldn't be exactly the same. They were working toward the same goal, and it would have saved them millions in research."

"Did you have any qualms?"

"Not really. That sort of industrial espionage goes on all the time. I also convinced myself that it was my way to get even with Roger for his years of dominance."

"So you went through with it?" Burton prompted.

"I was so filled with disgust for Roger, I said yes without even taking time to think it over." Within a week she had copied the formula and had done it so that no one could prove she had stolen it.

"The day before I was to deliver the formula, Roger called me into his office. 'Where is the formula?' he demanded. 'I want your copy of it.' I didn't try to argue with him. I have no idea how he found out I had copied it. I had simply downloaded it onto a flash drive. I took the flash drive out of my purse and handed it to him.

"He didn't fire me, and he wouldn't let me resign. He didn't yell or say anything, but the smirk on his face said, 'I know everything you do.' He finally said, 'I told you that you would stay here as long as I want you here. I choose to keep you here. For now.' "

"That was the end of it?" Burton asked.

"Almost. He sent me a memo the next morning—a memo, mind you—in a sealed envelope. His secretary brought it to me and said Roger had instructed her to wait for a response.

"He sent my confession. He stated that I was to sign it because it was industrial theft, after all—and it could send me to jail. He *instructed* me—I mean that. He spelled it all out and even numbered the paragraphs. The final item, number 6, told me to sign the confession. Then he stated that I was not to date it. That way, whether it was one year or ten—despite the statute of limitations—he had control.

"You want to know something else? He knew about the cocktail party. He knew everything. I have no idea how he got all that information, but he had it, and it was totally accurate."

"You think he set you up?" I asked.

"I don't think so, because he also had a second paper for me to sign—and that one I dated. That was to turn down the other position 'for the sake of my own conscience.' I'm sure Roger loved writing that statement."

Burton said nothing, but his eyes told both of us that he understood.

She nodded slowly, and I think she was pushing back the urge to cry. "He had it all figured out. He had me tied up for as long as he wanted me."

"Now you're searching for the confession, is that it?" I asked.

"Yes, and I have no idea where it is. I can't find it among his papers, and I know he would never leave it at the business office."

"So you figured—" I said.

"It had to be here. Where else could it be? But it's not here. I've been through everything twice. I'm now convinced it's not in this office unless he has some secret compartment." She sank back into the chair. "I hardly saw him this past year. In fact, it was quite a relief. I sent him everything by our interoffice e-mail or by messenger, because that was how he wanted it—no more face-to-face contact. Then I received the invitation—the summons—and I came." She leaned forward. "I am ambitious—ambitious enough to be a thief—but not ambitious enough to take someone's life."

I wanted to say, "I believe you," but what if she was fooling me? What if she had killed Roger? What if Mrs. Wright had seen her, and Paulette had decided to get rid of the only witness? Instead of saying anything, I gave her a quick pat on the shoulder. I had no idea how truthful she was, but she certainly had plenty of motive to kill Roger Harden.

17

We asked Paulette to put everything back where it belonged, and she started to do that as we left. I didn't think to say anything to her about fingerprints. Or maybe it's only in movies that detectives check those things.

Burton and I left, went into the hall, and headed back toward the kitchen. "I need another Oreo," I said. It was now almost midnight, and I had begun to feel tired. I confess that I liked being with Burton and felt we had already developed a camaraderie. I still thought he was good-looking, and now that I had seen him in operation with people, I liked him even more as a professional.

I also liked the fact that he didn't try to convert me to his religion. I once dated a man who did. Every time there was the slightest opportunity, he'd insert some comment about my need for God. When I resisted, he'd tell me that unless I heeded and believed, I'd go to hell. "Listen," I finally said, "I don't know anything about hell, but that's what you're making life for me right now, so cut it out. You asked for a date, and this isn't any preaching meeting. If you invited me to dinner to convert me, the price is too high."

I smile about that experience. We were sitting in a restaurant and had nearly finished the meal when I spoke up. He got up, threw his napkin on the table, and said, "I hope you enjoy your torment in hell, because it will last a long time." The jerk didn't even pick up the check. So I had to buy his dinner as well as endure his lecture most of the evening.

Burton was different—I still waited for his religion pitch—they all have it. I was sure that's why they go to seminary. Even when I opened up to him, he didn't tell me what a horrible sinner I was. But I knew he would.

They all did.

Once we were inside the kitchen, without asking, Burton plugged in the coffee machine and measured the water and the grounds. I accommodated him by putting out two cups and saucers.

"Oh, I thought I was the only one who couldn't sleep," Amanda Harden said as she walked into the kitchen. Even in her robed pajamas, she still looked attractive. I sure hoped that at her age—which must be fifty or more—I'd look that good at 12:02 in the morning.

"We couldn't sleep," Burton said. "In fact, neither of us has tried."

"Can you tell us anything?" I asked her. I pulled another cup and saucer from the cupboard. "You were Roger's wife. Surely you either know or suspect something."

She sat down on a chair. It was a large kitchen and held a table that seated twelve people—which made it larger than my dining room and kitchen combined. That was Roger. He liked everything big.

"I've thought a great deal about him this evening," she said. "I did love Roger in the beginning—and I think I made that clear—but the more I saw of who he was, the more I pulled away from him. He bought me expensive gifts—jewelry, furs, and cars—you know—things and only expensive things. He offered to set me up with any kind of business I wanted. He knew I had money and didn't need anything, but he loved to tell me how much richer he was than I was and how he had increased his wealth. He also reminded me that although I had inherited mine, he had earned his money. He used to quote that old TV commercial about getting money the old-fashioned way. 'I earn it.' I never could make him understand that I didn't want more money or homes. We own homes in six different parts of the world. Can you believe that?"

"Six? That's a lot," I said.

"I wanted a normal relationship with him. I wanted to be his companion, not his slave."

"Yes, I think we understood that," I said. "Anything else?"

"I'm not sure what to make of this—and that's why I couldn't sleep. Roger changed. I'm not sure when. Maybe two months ago. He became moody—and he was never moody before. One time—oh, maybe a week before I left him—he stood and seemed to stare at the cliff—the place where we dock. I was weeding flowers, and he didn't know I was around. He cried out, 'What's wrong with me? What's wrong with me?'

"I ducked down behind the peonies and rhododendrons until he left. He turned and faced the ocean. He screamed other words, but I couldn't hear them. He was there maybe ten minutes. Then he turned and walked back toward the house. He never glanced my way, and I never told him I had heard him. But that was such a shock. Never had I ever heard Roger entertain the thought that something was wrong with *him*."

The aroma of coffee had begun to waft through the kitchen. I also became aware that I was hungry. I opened the refrigerator, found a foil-wrapped plate of sandwiches, pulled out the plate, and unwrapped them. I took a cheese-on-rye and offered the plate to Burton and Amanda.

"Elaine made those. She was so thoughtful and always made them for late-night snacks." She stopped and wiped tears from her face. "I didn't like her very much, but I'm sorry she's dead. I didn't know about the robbery, but that certainly explains to me why she was often curt."

Burton poured coffee. He picked up an egg-salad sandwich and munched on it. "Hmm, this is good," he said. "Homemade bread. I don't get that often."

For several minutes the conversation went boring. I don't cook, and I don't like to talk about food. I try to patronize restaurants to keep the economy booming—and I certainly do my part to keep Americans gainfully employed.

"There was one other thing," Amanda said. She laid aside her half-eaten tuna-with-Swiss sandwich. "One time Roger and Simon were having a heated discussion. It may have been an argument, but it didn't sound angry—loud, strong, but not angry. Something about a book. Simon said, 'You don't have to *like* the book.' He held up a book—I could see that much. Roger yelled something back—something like, 'I don't like it, and I don't have to like it, and I refuse to like it.' "

"I'll bet Simon shrugged," I said.

"Correct. He put the book into a briefcase and started to walk away. He did stop, turn around, and say, 'But if you decide you want to read it, I have two copies.' "

"Sounds interesting," Burton said, "but I'm not sure how relevant that is."

"What is relevant is this. First, Simon spoke in full sentences. I had never heard him speak that way before—he had fooled me the way he did everyone else. Second, and this is the main thing, Simon spoke to him frankly, even strongly, and Roger didn't scream. I'd observed Roger when he screamed at Simon in the past—many times—and always over trivial things. That's what makes this so odd. Roger smiled after he said he didn't like the book. *He truly smiled.* In eighteen years of marriage, I never once saw Roger smile when someone talked strongly to him. And Simon was an employee, which made it worse. Or at least it was strange."

"Perhaps we need to talk to Simon," I said.

"That wouldn't hurt," Burton said and reached for another sandwich.

Amanda tried the phone. "Still out." She finished her coffee, threw the uneaten part of her sandwich into the garbage can, and said good night to us.

Burton quietly munched his second sandwich. I knew he wanted to go to bed. I needed the sleep, but I could always catch up on sleep, and I wanted to prolong our time together. I liked this guy. Just being around him made me feel better about myself.

I sat quietly and wondered how many people made me feel good about myself just being with them. I had a friend named Nan Snipes. She does that for me, but I couldn't think of anyone else.

"What are you thinking about?" he asked.

I know I blushed, so I said, "About you." Before he could respond, I said, "You're the first preacher I ever met who didn't start every fifth sentence with some reference to God."

"I'd love to talk to you about God—if you want and when you want."

I laughed, but I'm sure he knew I was embarrassed. "I'm not very tactful, am I?"

"No, but I like your directness. It's real."

"So I suppose almost everybody brings up God even if you don't."

"Most of the time. They either tell me some of their best friends are preachers or that they were forced to go to Sunday school and hated it. Sometimes they'll say, 'I haven't been inside a church in twenty years.' "

"How do you respond to that?"

"Come on back," I say. "God's still waiting to hear from you, and it's about time to visit again." He laughed. "No, I don't say that. I usually ask them why. Most of the time, they're open enough to tell me. I understand why a lot of people have turned away from the church. I just wish they wouldn't turn away from God, as well."

"Interesting perspective," I said. "I never thought of distinguishing the two."

"Think about it. The church means people—and all of us are flawed. God is the perfect One. That's the direction I like to point people—from imperfect people to a perfect God."

"Makes sense. Yes, one way or another, if they're around you long enough, everyone does gets around to the topic of God with you priests."

"Pastor. Not a priest. I'm a Protestant." He grinned. "But you knew that, didn't you?"

I laughed. I was doing a little harmless playing—the dumb-girl act and probably a little flirting. I didn't think a pastor-type would be interested in me, but then, I loved his curls and nice smile. He was the most attractive man and the nicest I'd met in at least two years. Okay, he was maybe half an inch shorter than I am, but no one is perfect.

"You don't act like a preacher—at least not the kind I was exposed to as a kid."

"Maybe it's time to be exposed to a new type."

He looked directly into my eyes when he said those words. *That's not fair,* I wanted to say. *I'm trying to flirt and you're getting serious.* "Uh, well, maybe. Right now I'm trying to get a few things straight in my life—my boring life."

"I'm sure it's not boring," he said, but he continued to focus his total attention on me. "Have you tried God?" he asked quietly. The words were spoken so softly I wondered if I had imagined them.

"Not yet, but I'm running out of options."

"God may be your best option and not just your last one."

"If a belief in God helps you, by all means, you need to believe it or practice it or whatever you tell people to do."

"Belief is a good place to start."

This conversation wasn't going the way I wanted. I needed to switch topics. "You make it easy to talk. And you're pretty funny."

"You're pretty. Period."

"I didn't know preachers had a sense of humor."

"It comes from arguing with nonbelieving redheads." He smiled before he said, "We preacher-types work on it. I took a course in seminary called Laugh 101. I was the only student."

That was a silly remark, but he said it with such a serious voice, in spite of myself, I laughed.

Just then I thought of something.

"I have no idea why I thought of this now, but Roger phoned me twice. Oh, it's been a month or more since he called. We talked about general things, mostly about my workload. It was something he said just before I was ready to hang up. At the time I thought it was odd, but now it seems even odder."

"What did he say?"

"He asked me if I ever thought about religion. Did I think God had forgiven me for the accident?"

"And you said?"

"You know me. I'm the smart mouth. So I said, 'I have no idea. Since God and I have never been introduced, we haven't discussed it.' "

" 'But if you did talk about it,' he persisted. 'Think about it.' I did think about it, and I told him I thought the topic was irrelevant. I tried that old line that God stays out of my business and I stay out of his."

"Did he say anything else?"

I closed my eyes and concentrated. "Let's see, that was the first time. No, he didn't. He just said good night. Maybe two weeks later he called again."

—

"Julie, do you remember our last conversation?" Roger said. "I asked you if you thought God would forgive you. I wanted you to think about it. So, what do you think?"

"I don't know. Why do you ask?"

"No big reason—"

"Sure it is, or you wouldn't have brought it up. What's going on?"

"Nothing really," he said. "I went to church last week—"

"To church? You?"

"It would take too long to explain the reason, but yes, I did. Since then, I've been wondering about a few things. That's all. So how do you feel about being forgiven?"

"How would I know? That's totally outside my experience."

"Yes, I suppose it is," he said quietly and after a pause added, "totally outside mine, as well."

"Are you turning religious?"

"I certainly hope not," he said. He laughed—more of a sneer. "The speaker at church made several provocative statements. I have never talked to anyone before who could say he or she felt forgiven by God. So it was merely a topic of passing interest."

I had kept my eyes closed—somehow it seemed to make it easier to remember. I opened them and said, "Just one thing about that conversation bothered me—which is probably why I remembered."

"What was that?" Burton asked.

"His final words before he said good-bye. He said it was merely a topic of passing interest. But the tone of his voice—something about the way he said it—made me know that it was more than something of passing interest."

"What do you think?"

"After all this? My guess is that Roger Harden may have developed a conscience."

"In what way?"

"I don't know, but I suspect he called us here to confront us and to expose us to each other. Maybe it was to tell us that he was going to turn over everything to the police."

"Could be," he said. "I do think one thing is now obvious. All the guests have something to hide—something Roger had on them—something wrong or unlawful."

"Is that true with you?" I asked.

"I came because of Jason. Remember?"

"I remember that's what Jason *thought*."

"Or perhaps he wanted to confess his wrongdoings."

"Do you think that's possible?"

Burton smiled. "As we Christian types say, 'anything is possible with God.'"

"I'm not sure God had anything to do with it."

18

My name is Dr. James Burton, but no one calls me James. I'm just Burton to everyone. Julie said she was going to write down everything that happened on Palm Island. She won't allow me to see it. She says it's her secret diary, but she wants to make sure we won't forget anything.

I'm not a writer, and I avoid writing whenever I can. But as a favor to Julie, I agreed to write this part. There is a segment of the story where she wasn't involved. So I'll tell it from my perspective.

Before I tell my part of the story, I want to point out that I like Julie. She's refreshing. We have a big gulf between us, so I don't see anything romantic happening. I was aware of her flirting—her frequent flirting. It's flattering, even though she now realizes that it won't lead anywhere. She's certainly not like that tarantula type I run into—they grab hold and keep after me.

It's nice to know she finds me attractive enough to flirt with. Like that thing about her tripping on the path. I wonder how many times females have tried that one on me. It goes all the way back to tenth grade when Jennifer Schuchmann tried it on me the first time.

As much as I like Julie, however, we don't have enough commonality. My faith is too important to compromise. I'm not sure she understands that, because faith doesn't mean anything to her. That's the big problem.

That's really too bad. I like her.

~

Julie and I talked in the kitchen for a few minutes and I began to yawn. Then she yawned. I yawned again, and she tried to make more noise with her yawn than I did.

"Enough. Let's go to our rooms," I said.

We walked upstairs, and I waited in the hallway until she opened her door.

"You're really gallant," she said. She stepped inside, and just before she closed the door, she smiled and said, "Thanks for being nice to this heathen."

I wanted to reply, but she closed the door.

103

I fell across the bed and didn't even bother to undress. I must have dozed, because something awakened me. I wasn't sure what it was, but I was instantly alert. I got out of bed, crept to the door, and opened it. I didn't see anyone in the hallway, but I had the distinct sense that someone had passed my door. It was the last room before the stairs.

I peeked into the hallway, but I didn't see anyone. I closed my door silently and left my room. On the stairway I saw nothing. I crept silently down the dark steps. Before I reached the bottom, I spotted a light from under Roger's office door.

Does everybody have a key to that office? I asked myself.

I turned the knob slowly. As I did so, I wondered if the intruder had a gun. That was a chance I'd have to take. As I pushed the door forward a fraction of an inch at a time, I peered inside.

Jason had pulled out the same files that Paulette had gone through. He did it differently. He took out the drawer itself and laid it on the desk and then pulled out the files one at a time. He was so focused on the files he didn't notice me.

"What are you doing?" I asked.

A startled Jason dropped the manila file folder. Several sheets of paper fluttered to the floor. He dropped to his knees and picked them up.

"Looking. Just looking for—for something."

I didn't want to make this difficult for Jason, so I sat down on the sofa across from the desk. "I can see that."

"You don't think I killed him, do you? I wouldn't do that—I couldn't kill anyone—not Dad, especially not now."

The best way to handle Jason was to say as little as possible. He had become active in our congregation, and I had gotten to know him fairly well.

"I know this looks so totally bad for me—like the murderer coming back to the scene of the crime, like he wanted to pick up the one piece of evidence that would, like, convict him."

"Is that what's going on?"

"Oh no. It—well, it just looks so totally that way, don't you think?"

"You certainly think that way."

"I was, uh, like, looking for something—I mean like something Dad had earlier—earlier, like when I saw him before tea."

Whenever Jason resorted to the frequent use of *like*, I could tell he was rattled. He used to say that *like* and *so totally* were part of his school style, but when he spoke with adults, he normally used an adult vocabulary.

I stuck my hands in my pockets, sat still, and smiled at him.

He laughed. "You used to do that in your office. Just like that."

"I know."

"So—is this, uh, like, some kind of counseling session?"

"Is that what you want it to be?"

"Can it be?"

"If you like."

"Okay, I'll tell you."

I knew he would. Jason is a good kid. He's amazingly mature at times, but once in a while he acts as if he's thirteen. I like the boy. Despite moments of immaturity, he's solid. His struggles with Roger Harden haven't been easy.

"It was something Dad wanted to read to us—right after dinner. That's what I'm searching for."

"What was it?"

"I don't know."

"Any idea?"

"A list of all our sins maybe? I don't know, but that's what I think. You know, Mr. Burton, every person in that room had something to hide—something bad they did and Dad found out. I don't know all of them, but I know he held something over their heads."

"So what was he going to do? Read his own emancipation proclamation? Or threaten to call the police?"

"I don't know. He was well, like acting so totally weird. I mean, yeah, weird. I can't think of another way to say it."

"In what way was he weird? I mean, you haven't told me enough to make me understand."

"You know a lot of the story," he said and sat down on the far end of the sofa from me, near enough for him to feel close but far enough that he would know this was a counseling session.

I did know a lot of his story. Jason's birth father died when he was only a baby, so he really has no memories of the man. Amanda married Roger when Jason was about two years old, which made Roger the only male parent the boy had ever known. His stepfather didn't understand children—even he admitted that to Jason. He tried to treat the boy like an employee. He never spent time with his stepson or encouraged him. Jason often complained that he wouldn't attend any of his basketball or baseball games.

"If he didn't grumble over the grades on my report card," Jason once said, "that was his way of giving me approval. If I made a lower grade than he thought I should have, then I'd get The Big Lecture on how to study."

I felt sorry for the boy. He studied hard, and I knew that. Several times he had come to see me at my office, and he brought his laptop and school books. If he arrived ten minutes early, he used those minutes to study—and it wasn't to impress me. He was just that self-disciplined about his studies. Two of Jason's teachers were members of our congregation. Both said he studied hard, was extremely bright, and never handed in late papers.

The only complaint I ever heard about him was that he tended to be moody. Later I learned that whenever he endured The Big Lecture from Roger, he would feel depressed for two or three days.

As I stared at the boy with his clean-cut American good looks, I thought what a shame it was that he had had to go through so much.

"You taught me something important, Mr. Burton," Jason said.

"Really? What's that?"

"You were—and still are—the best father figure in my life. You're the kind of dad I wished I had."

I hardly knew what to say to him. I had been aware, of course, that Jason liked me, but I had no idea I had become that important to him.

"Remember how you used to walk me to the door of your office and give me a hug?"

"Sure. I do that—" I stopped because I started to say I did it with most people I knew fairly well.

"I'd always close my eyes and think, *This is the way a dad's hug should feel.* Whenever I visited your office, you always made me feel better."

"I had no idea—"

"Yeah, I know. That's why I like you. You weren't trying to be a dad. You were just being who you are."

I felt slightly uncomfortable. I liked Jason, but I wasn't used to having the conversation focused on me. I cleared my throat and asked, "So tell me what happened after you came back to the coast." He had studied two years at Clayton University even though Roger and Amanda had moved permanently to Palm Island.

"As you know, I transferred to Georgia Southern in Statesboro this past year. Dad asked me to do that. No, he told me—he commanded it. He said that if I wasn't going to attend one of the best schools in the country, at least I could study fairly close to home. He wanted me home on weekends."

"Did you come home?"

"When I had to and when I couldn't work out an excuse to stay over."

"It must have been hard for you to come home like that."

"Yes, it was—until maybe a month ago. That's when things changed. That's when Dad changed."

I must have leaned forward, because Jason chuckled. "Now I know you're listening carefully. Whenever you do that, I know you're hanging on to every word."

I probably blushed then—and people tell me I do a good blush. This was one observant kid.

"You like me and you helped me—most of all you helped me. I went to another shrink—you didn't know that, but I had to because Dad made me. The guy was a good shrink, but he never did dig what made me the way I am. No matter how much I talked, he always kept telling me that I had to forgive myself. Like all I had to do was say, 'I forgive myself.' I just wanted to forgive Dad. That was until you helped me turn to the Lord and ask God to forgive me. And because of your help, I was able to forgive Dad—not right away—but eventually."

"Do you realize you never called him Dad before last night? At least not with me?" I had noticed that earlier. He was always Roger.

"He became my dad—he wasn't good at it—but he tried."

As I waited for Jason to continue, I became aware that the rain had softened from earlier in the evening. It was as if the clouds were running out of moisture.

"Dad did change—not a lot—but he was, well, different. At least he was different toward me. He still yelled, and I heard him really give it to ol' Holmestead one day on the phone. He used words he would have whacked me across the face for if he'd heard me say them."

"How did he change toward you?"

Jason stared into space. "Mostly, he was quieter, I think. Yeah, that's how it started. He didn't pick on me all the time. My grades were all good, but in the past, he'd still find something to diss me about."

"You're convinced that he changed and not you?"

"Oh, I changed, too. Maybe that's what started it. You helped me a lot there. You kept urging me to accept him as he was—and not wait until he became a good father to me. That was hard, but I did. You told me to pray for him every day."

I remembered that time very well. I had suggested to Jason that instead of trying to change his father, he might pray for himself—pray that he would be able to accept and love his stepfather. If he could love his stepfather, he could accept Roger's imperfections. Jason told me that he would pray for Roger at least once a day. I also know that a year later, he said he still prayed.

"I told you the others had a secret—something wrong they did," Jason said.

"Yes, you did."

"I did, too. I'm not here just because I'm his stepson. I—I did something wrong—really wrong."

"Want to tell me about it?" I hated using those words because that's a standard phrase in counseling, but I meant them.

"It started with a phone call on a Thursday evening. Dad said, 'I want you home by four o'clock tomorrow.' When I asked him why, he said, 'You'll find out when I tell you. Just be here.' "

"Did you know why he wanted you home?"

He nodded. "I would have had to be stupid not to know. Do you remember one time you read from someplace in the Bible where it said, 'Be sure your sin will find you out'?"

I didn't remember quoting the verse, but that wasn't the point.

"My sin sure found me out. About five months ago, I forged his name on personal checks. I stole a book of his checks from his desk." He shook his head slowly. "I didn't need the money. I was just mad. I wanted to do something to hurt him. I ordered dumb stuff to be delivered to his office—you know, stuff from Victoria's Secret—really dumb things—and I paid for them with his forged checks."

"Didn't you know he'd catch you?"

"If I had stopped to reason it out, sure. I was so filled with anger I wanted to do something to—to get even—to make him really as angry as I was."

"Was there something in particular?"

"I turned twenty. He hadn't remembered my birthday—but then, he hadn't remembered my nineteenth, either. I was trying hard to forgive him and—" Jason's tears stopped him from saying anything more.

I moved over and put my arm around Jason and let him cry. I wasn't sure why he needed to cry, but I sensed he needed me to understand and to care.

"I always thought he hated me," Jason finally said.

"Do you still think so?"

"I—I need to find that paper—that paper he planned to read. Then I'll know for sure how he felt."

19

Jason's body convulsed with tears. "I was wrong. Really wrong. And stupid."

I held him until the tears subsided. The rain had definitely passed. Now the aftermath of the storm threw all its energy into wind. The house creaked. Trees banged against the side of the house, but I heard no rain.

"See, when I came home, I was ready to get The Big Lecture—and I assumed he'd give me another on ethical and moral behavior."

Jason lapsed into silence again. When he spoke, he told me what had happened Friday afternoon, before the rest of us arrived.

—

"Come into my office, young man," Roger ordered. "Sit down." Jason started to say something, and Roger said, "Shut up and listen."

Jason had prepared himself for the worst possible consequences. The worst would be if his stepfather told him to leave the house and never come back. He didn't care if the old man cut off his allowance. He had saved money, and his mother had her own money. He couldn't think of a really bad thing Roger could do that would hurt him.

Jason sat stiffly in front of the desk, his head bowed. He listened without response and stared at his watch as the seconds ticked by. He always surreptitiously checked the time whenever Roger lectured. So far, the old man's record had been twenty-three minutes and eight seconds. He expected to hit thirty minutes today.

"I'm ashamed of you," Roger said. "Very ashamed."

Jason looked up briefly, made his face look extremely contrite, and bowed his head again. He considered whether to fake a few tears.

"I'm more ashamed of myself than I am of you," Roger said. "You are a good boy—an extremely good boy. I have failed you."

Jason waited. He knew Roger wouldn't say, "I'm sorry," because those words weren't part of his vocabulary; however, he figured this was as close as it would ever get.

"I assume this was some kind of payback. I deserved this kind of treatment."

Jason's head jerked up and he stared at his stepfather.

He wanted to hate the man, wanted to tell him how rotten he had been through the years, how cold and indifferent he had always been. Instead, he said, "I'm sorry."

Roger held up his hand. "Let's say no more about this, but I'd appreciate it if you would return the checks you haven't used." He smiled at Jason. "I'm going to try to be a real father to you. It's not exactly my strong suit, but I intend to try."

"That is a great start," Jason said, not knowing what else to say. Then he did something he had never done before: He grabbed his stepfather and hugged him. It felt as if he had hugged a marble statue, but Jason didn't let go.

Roger finally relaxed—slightly. He didn't pull away, so Jason held him for a long time. When he finally let go, he whispered to his stepfather, "Thank you."

Roger shook his hand, and Jason grinned. "It's a beginning."

"There are things we need to talk about," Roger said. He held up a folder with a number of sheets of paper tucked inside. "I was going to save this until tonight when everyone is here, but maybe you need to see it first."

"What is it?"

Just then, Wayne Holmestead knocked on the door and pushed it open. Without being invited inside—something Jason had never seen anyone else do—Holmestead said, "We need to talk."

"I'll be free in a few minutes," Roger said.

"This can't wait. We need to talk. *Now.*"

Roger patted Jason's shoulder. "We'll talk tonight."

Dismissed and confused, Jason left the room, bounded up the stairs, and went to his own room. This was one turn of events he had never expected.

As he lay on his bed, he replayed the scene inside his head a dozen times. His stepfather had never acted that way before. *He's never been human. What's wrong with him? Is he afraid of dying or something? What would make a mean old man like him change like that?* he wondered. *Maybe it's an answer to prayer. Maybe God has changed him.*

"I hope so," he said aloud. "Oh God, I hope so."

About twenty minutes later, he went down to Roger's office. He didn't hear anything until he was just outside the door.

"...won't get away with this. You're a tyrant!" That was Mr. Holmestead's voice.

The response was muffled, but he heard the words *police* and *jail.*

Mr. Holmestead swore—and those words were clear. Then his tone softened and he said, "Can't we talk—?"

Jason turned around and went back to his room. He waited until teatime, but his stepfather walked into the dining room, sat down, and said nothing. Jason could detect no difference in his looks or attitude. He leaned close and whispered, "Uh, Dad, I wonder if we could talk." It was the first time he had called him *Dad*.

Roger shook his head. "Later. We'll talk later."

A disappointed Jason said, "Okay."

"Promise," Roger said.

Jason smiled. Roger had never used that word with him before. Something was definitely different about the old man. He even smiled when he said that single word.

As Jason sat next to his stepfather, he stared at him. Roger had a strict rule about teatime. He allowed no important conversation. Jason always thought that was stupid, but that's what the old man said. "This is the time not to think of serious issues," he said more than once.

Roger kept his conversation focused on the weather. Holmestead commented on the impending rain. Paulette said they needed more rain. Beth Wilson commented that the state of Georgia showed a five-inch rain deficit for the year. Jason tired of listening to the small talk and found himself thinking again about the strange experience with his stepfather. He watched Roger and listened whenever he spoke, but he didn't seem any different than he had been at other times. Maybe the old man was going crazy. Maybe he had started to take drugs. He stared at the man's eyes—the first giveaway sign—but he couldn't see any unusual dilation.

Roger's gaze met his. The two stared momentarily, and Roger gave him the barest nod and a hint of a smile.

———

"I know it sounds weird to you, Mr. Burton, but I felt something happen inside me. Like I said, I've been praying and praying for him. When I looked at him, I loved him. *Just like that.* All my anger evaporated. That's the only way I know to say it. It was—well, like a miracle or something. He didn't look any different and he didn't say anything. But I felt as if I had changed. I wanted to get out of my chair and go over and hug him or something."

"What did you do?" Burton asked.

"Nothing. I just sat there trying to figure out what had happened to me. Maybe it was something that happened to him. I don't know."

"You felt your prayer had finally been answered, huh?"

"Yes. And you know, I did care. I still do. I wish—I wish we could have talked—even for just a few minutes. I wish I could have told him."

"Maybe he knows."

"Yeah, maybe. . ."

20

"What are you doing in here?" Julie stood in the doorway of the office.

I sat in the dark. Jason had left minutes earlier, and I sat ruminating over all the things that had transpired since I first reached Palm Island.

Julie was dressed. Different slacks, different blouse, but the same casual style. I don't know much about clothes, but she looked good in those muted colors.

"I might ask you the same question," I said.

"You might, but I asked first."

"I thought I heard someone in the hallway—or maybe I didn't. I awakened and came downstairs." I told her what happened with Jason. "Now it's your turn. What made you open the office door?"

"I don't know. I didn't have any sense of anyone being in here. Maybe I just wanted to assure myself that it was locked."

"Okay, so why did you come downstairs?" My watch showed 4:03.

"I couldn't sleep. And I got hungry again. I dressed to come downstairs and eat the rest of the Oreo cookies." Instead of going to the kitchen, she came into the office and sat down. She kept her eyes averted from Roger's body.

I moved the office sofa just enough to hide most of it. She could see only the end of the blanket. Although Simon had covered him, it was still a body. I hoped that by not seeing him, we could push him out of our consciousness.

"After Jason went back to bed," I said, "I decided to stay here in case anyone else came to pay a visit."

"Good idea," she said. She locked the door from the inside, turned off the light, and felt her way over to the sofa.

I got up and opened the blinds. A half-moon had sneaked across the horizon. Only a few scattered clouds drifted above, and the night sky was ablaze with stars.

"I keep thinking about Paulette and Jason both coming here to the office." I kept my voice low in case someone else tried to come to the office. I didn't want my voice to carry.

"I didn't even know about Jason, naturally, but I kept thinking about Paulette," Julie said. "Just suppose Roger had a file that contained the truth about everyone here on the island. Suppose he planned to confront us tonight—"

"Confront may be the wrong word. He said *announce*, didn't he?" I asked.

"Regardless of the word, wouldn't that scare some of them?"

"Did it scare you?"

Julie thought for a minute. "Not really. You know why? Roger had kept the incident a secret for years. Why would he bring it up now? I had always done whatever he asked."

"But what if some of them felt the burden had become intolerable?" I asked. "What if that led them to think he might plan to expose them?"

"That's exactly what occurred to me," Julie said. "We've already heard several confessions. Maybe the police can figure out who had the strongest motive. So far, I can't."

"Nothing quite fits into place," I said. "And what about the attempt to kill Wayne Holmestead? That just doesn't fit. We can figure out the reason for Roger's death, and we can assume that Elaine Wright saw someone or heard something."

"But where does Wayne fit in?" Julie asked.

"I don't know. That's what doesn't make sense."

We sat in silence, but I knew both our minds were working. Two people had come into the office. Both had searched for some papers. Paulette wanted her confession, and Jason wanted whatever it was his stepfather had held up. Were the searches connected with the murder? That seemed logical.

Julie said she would curl up on the large chair on the other side of the office. I wanted to act like a gentleman, so I told her to take the sofa. She lay down on the sofa, and I got on the floor and used one of the sofa cushions. She did try to dissuade me, but I assured her I could sleep on the carpeted floor.

I stretched out, loosened my shoe laces, and tried to relax. I closed my eyes, but I couldn't think of anything except the stories the people had told me. I assumed they were true—at least largely true—but even if they were, things still weren't making sense.

I wasn't aware of falling asleep, but a gentle tap at the office door startled me. I jumped up and stumbled toward the door and opened it.

"I went to your room and you weren't there," Amanda said. "I looked everywhere else downstairs and finally figured you must have come in here."

Julie sat up, rubbed her eyes, and smiled.

I looked at my watch. It was 4:38. I felt the stubble on my chin and thought about whether to opt for more sleep or a shower and shave.

"I'm so glad you're here, because I need to talk to you," she said.

"Come on in," Julie said and snapped on the light.

"I killed Roger. It was an accident, but I did it."

"Tell me what happened."

"We had an argument—"

"About what?"

"That's not important—"

"I think it is. Tell me."

"It was about Jason."

"What about him? Please, don't make me pull every word out of you."

"Jason did something bad—really bad."

"What did he do?" Julie asked.

"He forged Roger's signature on eight checks. There may have been more, but that's all I know about. He had Victoria's Secret deliver several packages of skimpy clothing. Two parcels came from some horrible place called the Super Sex Shop. Roger was appalled. Roger found out after I left him."

"When was that?" I asked.

"About three weeks ago."

"Three?" Julie said. "Are you sure?"

"It may have been only nineteen days—but yes, it was close to three weeks. Roger called me in Savannah and told me."

"I know about the forgery and the delivery," I said, "but are you sure it was approximately three weeks ago?"

"Yes. Why? What difference does it make?"

"It means Roger knew and didn't do anything—not until yesterday," Julie said. "Doesn't that seem odd?"

"Nothing Roger did would seem odd," she said. "How did you know about the forgery?"

"Jason came down here earlier. He told me."

"Did he—did he tell you anything else?"

"Was he supposed to tell me something? Come on, Amanda. I'm tired and I've hardly slept."

"Roger was furious over what Jason had done. He's been furious a lot of other times, but this was—it was the worst. He swore at me and called me names—well, terrible names—and accused me of being a bad mother."

"Anything else?"

"I offered to give Roger the money, and he laughed at me. He didn't need the money, but I was afraid—"

"Afraid of what?"

"That he would send Jason to jail. That was typical of him. Punish the guilty or punish the innocent. It didn't matter which. He was good at punishing."

"So you were angry?"

"Of course. Jason didn't need the money. He has money. I have money."

"Wait a minute," I said. "Let's get back to Roger's death. Tell us what happened."

"I was furious—the angriest I've ever been with him."

"Why?"

"He said he had—had decided to have Jason prosecuted. He would send my son to jail, and he would forbid me to have any contact with him."

"That would make anyone angry," I said. I didn't believe her, but I had to play this out.

"And the gun? He kept the gun in his desk," I said. "How did you get it?"

She hesitated only a second before she said, "I lunged for the desk, pulled the drawer open, and grabbed the gun. I didn't plan to kill him. I'm not sure what I meant to do—maybe to frighten him. Yes, I only wanted to frighten him—to make him say he wouldn't send Jason to prison. When you're a mother, you—"

"When you're a mother," Julie said, "you'll do anything to protect your child, right?"

"He wanted Jason to go to prison. I couldn't allow that. Jason is a good son. He's never been in trouble before. He was—well, he had been angry and had acted stupidly. Roger didn't remember his birthday for two years in a row, and I think he just acted out of immaturity and anger and forged the checks."

"Hmm, I see."

"So tell us—what happened?" Julie asked. Something about her voice told me she didn't believe the story, either.

"We struggled. The gun went off, and Roger fell to the floor. I—I panicked and ran from the room."

"With the gun in your hand?"

"Oh yes, yes."

"What did you do with the gun?"

"I threw it over the cliff. I went out the east door—and no one saw me. I tossed it over the cliff and then raced back inside."

"When you threw away the gun, was that after you shot at Wayne Holmestead?"

"Wayne? I—I didn't shoot at him," she said. It was obvious she had forgotten to take that into account.

"I see," I said.

"And you killed Elaine, as well?" Julie asked.

"Oh no. I would never hurt Elaine. Neither would Jason. I didn't like her very much, but I felt she was badly treated by Roger."

"So there is another murderer here," Julie said to Amanda, but she looked at me. She and I were operating on the same wavelength. "You killed Roger, and then someone else killed Elaine. Why would anyone kill her?"

"I have no idea."

"Did Elaine see you leave Roger's office?" I asked.

"I'm sure she didn't. I mean, even if she had, I wouldn't have hurt her."

"I believe you," I said. "In fact, I don't think you killed anyone."

"You think Jason killed Roger," Julie said, "and you're trying to protect him. After all, isn't that what mothers do?"

"No, that's not true. I killed Roger. I've confessed. Let's leave it at that, please."

"You have watched too many TV programs," Julie said and smiled at Amanda. "Jason didn't kill him, either. Why did you think he did?"

"Jason didn't?" She dropped into a chair. "You're positive?"

"As positive as I can be until we find out who did," I said.

"Why did you think Jason killed Roger?" Julie persisted.

"It was what he said just before he went downstairs to see Roger—in the afternoon, maybe a couple of hours before tea. He said, 'I hate that man. I've tried to love him. I've tried to forgive him for making you miserable and for being such a lousy father. I'll do anything to make him suffer. Anything!' "

"So you naturally thought he killed Roger?"

She nodded.

"If Jason is the boy I think he is—and if he had killed Roger—do you think he would have allowed you to take the blame?"

"He would have stepped in and confessed," Julie said. "Isn't that the kind of kid he is?"

"I hadn't thought of that," she said. "I feel like a fool. I love my son, and he hasn't had an easy life with Roger. I only wanted to protect him. I felt I owed him that much for all he's had to go through."

"You haven't talked with Jason about this, have you?" I asked.

"No. He came upstairs before tea and said he and Roger hadn't finished their conversation. I tried to get information from him, but he said, 'Not now, Mom. I'm too confused to talk.' "

"Just that?"

"No. He turned around and said in a flat voice. 'This isn't over. Not yet. We haven't settled it yet.' "

"You're a good woman," I said. "You have a good heart."

"There is one other thing that you probably need to know. Jason did threaten to kill Roger once. I'm not sure, but I think it was maybe six months ago. We had guests here, and Wayne was one of them." Amanda said she didn't know what the argument had been about—something about school or grades. She had been weeding on the far side of the house. Just as she came in through the front door, Jason screamed at Roger, "I'll kill you! I'll do the world a big, big favor! I will kill you someday."

"So you thought he had kept that promise?"

She started to cry and barely nodded. I hugged her and said, "It must be a big relief to know that Jason didn't kill Roger."

"But if he didn't do it, and I didn't—"

"That leaves seven suspects," Julie said. "Wayne Holmestead, Jeffery Mark Dunn, Paulette White, Tonya Borders, Beth Wilson, Lenny Goss, and Reginald Ford."

"I can't believe any of them would—"

"Roger didn't kill himself," Julie said. "And we don't think Elaine's death was an accidental fall."

The three of us spoke together in hushed tones, but none of us came up with a solution.

The clock struck five. "It will be sunrise soon," I said. I debated whether to go upstairs to bed or just to have a long, hot shower. Julie and Amanda left the room. I turned the light off. As I debated what to do, I settled down into the sofa and went to sleep. I don't even remember putting my head on the cushion.

21

I don't know how long I slept, but I awakened, unsure of what startled me. The dawn had just begun. Gray light seeped in around the drapes. It was too dim to reveal the details of the furniture, but it was bright enough to deepen the shadows and distort the shape of everything, so that the room seemed like an alien place.

Julie unlocked the door and opened it only an inch or so and saw me sit up startled before she threw it fully open and snapped on the light. Simon stood next to her.

"What's going on?" I asked.

"Make coffee," he said. "We talk."

"Are you trying to sound like the old Simon?"

"I spotted Simon sneaking in the front door," she said. "I tried to talk to him, and he's reverted to his bad English again."

"Sneaking in the front door? Why?"

She shrugged, and this time I laughed. "You do that just like Simon."

"Glad you noticed. I've practiced a lot," she said. "I think Simon was out all night. I didn't think of it then, but he was the only person not present when we found the bullet in the doorpost."

"Make the coffee. I'll be right there," I said.

My head felt rotten. I'm always grouchy until I've shaved. I'm not sure why, but my face always feels heavy, and this time it was also achy from lack of sleep. I tried to argue myself into getting off the sofa, going upstairs, and cleaning up before I confronted Simon. Instead, I closed my eyes.

The aroma of coffee filled my nostrils, and I opened my eyes. Julie smiled. "You don't snore when you sleep on your back."

Not sure where that conversation could lead, I looked at Simon, who held out a cup of coffee. I waved away the sugar and cream.

"Caught," he said. "Out all night."

"Oh, cut it out, Simon. We don't want to listen to the pidgin English anymore," I said. "I already have a headache."

"Sorry, habit." Then he laughed.

"So tell us."

"I was out all night, that's true."

"What were you doing?" Julie asked.

"That's not important for you to know," he said.

"That answer isn't good enough," I said. "As soon as the telephone is working, we'll call the police."

"The telephone is now working. I called the police. They will be here as soon as they can."

"How soon?"

"Does it matter? This is a small island, and I have the only key to the Boston Whaler." He pulled the key from his pocket. "So no one can leave before they arrive. The police know that. They will probably wait until the new shift goes on at 8:00, and then someone will come."

I looked at my watch. It was five minutes before six. "Seems like a long time."

"Does it matter?" Julie said. She held up a notebook. "I've written down everything we've learned so far, and I can tell the police. It also means that none of the other suspects can change his or her story."

"Back to you, Simon. You admit being out all night. What were you doing?"

"Praying."

"What?" Julie asked.

"I was on the beach. I prayed all night."

"All night? That must have been five or six hours. How long does it take to say a few prayers?"

"Sometimes it takes hours."

Simon and I looked at each other, and he smiled as if to say, "Okay, I'll try to explain." He turned to her. "You see, it is more than repeating words. Prayer—the kind of prayer of which I speak—means to open my heart to God. It's not so much words I speak, as that I feel such—such a heaviness—a burden that is so heavy it makes me—"

"Oh," she said. "I see."

She obviously didn't, so I said, "He was deeply troubled. He needed to get alone and talk to God. He wanted to find inner peace. For some of us, that's how we do it: We pray. So, yes, I understand."

"Okay, I really don't understand," Julie said, "but let that go. Why aren't you soaked if you were out all night?"

"I keep a small tent in my room, and it takes ninety seconds to set up. I often put it up at night and sleep near the edge of the island. It's peaceful. But it's more than that. It's a place where I can be alone with my thoughts and with my prayers."

"Oh," Julie said. "Now I have something else I want to ask you— something I think is important."

"Of course, just ask."

"What did Roger hold over you? What is your secret?"

Shock registered in his eyes. "Why do you ask such a question?"

"Everyone else has a secret of some kind. Why should you be different?"

He smiled, and his face had a boyish look. "You're correct. In my own way, I was a prisoner here like the others." He paused to drink deeply from his coffee and poured himself a fresh cup.

"I was a lawyer—a good lawyer as a matter of fact. By age twenty-four, I had earned more than six million dollars a year by representing pharmaceutical companies in court."

"And you killed somebody or stole money or—"

He shook his head. "No. I sampled their products. That's where I got into trouble. At first, it was only an occasional upper. It's an old story, and thousands of other people have the same sad tale. A few pills on bad days. Before long, every day became a bad day. But, I reminded myself, it was only temporary until I got past this big case or until I could get my schedule down to normal. Eventually, I had to pop a couple of uppers to get going in the morning, another couple to handle the work of the day—I'm sure you know how the story goes."

"So the company found out that—"

"Not exactly. I switched to meth."

"Methamphetamine?"

"Right. It's a form of speed, you know."

"I also know it's cheap to make," I said.

"That's the point. Cheap. Easy to get. I didn't have to pilfer the company's products."

"So what happened?"

"At first I thought I was free. I never had to peep over my shoulder. I forgot one thing, however—"

"Which is?"

"Drugs are drugs. And most drugs, even the most benign ones, if taken regularly and over a long period of time, become addictive. Of course I was strong and I could always kick the habit.

"Although we addicts lie to ourselves for a long time, and I did, eventually I faced a reality: I couldn't function without meth. I couldn't go to a business meeting without my own brand of insurance."

For several minutes, Simon told us his sad account of how he had wrecked his life. His wife divorced him and moved away. He had no idea where she was or where she had taken their two children. The police nabbed him one day after a high-speed chase up I-95. "I was lucky I didn't kill somebody."

He received a seven-year prison sentence.

"And you learned your lesson?" I asked.

"No, I was still the tough guy. There were ways to get drugs and there were ways to make meth. The truth was that I didn't want to kick the habit. I hated it when I was down, but when I had a hit—a good hit—there was nothing in my life that felt so good."

"You're not on drugs now," I said. "That seems obvious."

"You want to know why?" He pointed to a barely visible scar on the left side of his face. It ran from his temple to the top of his lip. "See this? This scar saved my life."

I must have looked startled, because Simon laughed. "You did that to shock me, right?" Julie asked.

"Yes, I did, but it's also true. I was a mess in prison. My entire first seven months were like a buzz of forgetfulness. As I said, there are ways to get the drugs we need." Simon told us that his cell mate was a man named Michael Kamen. "If ever there was an innocent man in prison, it was Michael." His cell mate had been accused of armed robbery. He did resemble the criminal (and the police caught the real one after Michael had served almost four years).

The two men shared common interests and both were college grads—the only ones in the prison population. They were both bright and articulate and had been successful in the corporate world. Michael had been a contract lawyer.

"Michael took no drugs, nor did he have any bad habits. He called himself a 'born-again Christian.' He cared about me and often talked to me about God. I didn't want to listen, but he talked anyway. Some nights he'd read portions of the Bible aloud or tell me what he had read in religious books. He was my friend, so I couldn't tell him to shut up." Simon laughed. "Okay, I did tell him to shut up a few times, but he never gave up.

"He was concerned about my drug habit and gently tried to talk to me about it. I tuned him out. He became stronger and more adamant. He was on my back constantly about quitting."

Michael started a Bible study group in the prison library. He successfully recruited two of Simon's drug-addicted friends. Then others came. Soon there were about fifty regular attendees, and the gangs that had run the cell block were losing their power. One hardened criminal determined to put a stop to the religious fervor. He came after Michael with a shiv.

Simon jumped into the melee, and the man with the knife attacked him. It ended when Simon broke the man's wrist. That man was moved to another prison.

"I had this cut on my cheek, but that wasn't the worst. He also struck me in the kidneys. I was rushed to a civilian hospital. For two days no one knew if I would live. Somehow Michael received permission to be there with me. He sat at my bed. Most of that time he prayed."

Simon told us that he saw the reality of love and compassion in Michael. It was Michael who made him realize how he had wasted his life.

"I was a slow learner, but Michael was patient with me. I joined his Bible study. You see, something powerful happened to me while I was in prison. I also became a born-again Christian."

"Oh yeah, like Jimmy Carter," Julie said. "Or that healing evangelist on TV."

"Okay, if you want to say it that way," Simon said with no defensiveness in his voice. "My life changed. Truly changed. It wasn't that I didn't have yearnings for meth. I did, but I also had God in my life, and I knew I would never go back."

"And did it last—that—that change?" Julie asked.

He smiled at Julie and nodded slowly before he said, "On my thirtieth birthday I was baptized. That was five years ago. I still believe. And you know, you could—"

"And Michael? What happened to him?" Julie asked, and I was sure it was more out of her discomfort than truly wanting to know the answer.

"Three months after I was baptized, Michael's sentence was overthrown, and they released him from prison."

"Ever see him again?" Julie said. "I've heard that former convicts don't like to visit."

"Michael never forgot me. He wrote regularly. Every week he visited me. He brought me books. He spoke with the chaplains about me and asked them to encourage me. Eventually I took over Michael's Bible studies."

"Oh," she said. She still wasn't comfortable, but for once Julie West didn't know what to say next.

"You've stared at my scar several times," Simon said to her.

"I didn't intend to stare—"

"It's all right." He pointed to his scar. "I could have had it removed. Roger was willing to pay for it, but I refused. It's a constant reminder that my life is different. That scar is there to tell me who I used to be and who I am now."

"Are you still in contact with Michael?" I asked.

Tears welled up in his eyes. "He died in an automobile accident just before I was released from prison."

"I am sorry—"

"I miss him every day, but I'm grateful he stayed alive long enough to share his faith and friendship with me. Sometimes I think of him as an angel from God—like Michael the archangel, you know. I know people aren't angels, but he seemed like an angel from on high to me. After I surrendered myself to God, I had a long time to think and to get my life in order. I got out of prison after four years because I didn't cause any more trouble and the parole board agreed that I had been rehabilitated. I kicked the habit in prison and began to get my life in some kind of order."

"So Roger held your past over you?" Julie asked.

"No, no, not that. I served my sentence, and I could hold up my head. No, Roger got involved because I violated my parole."

"That was stupid," she said.

"Yes."

"But you did violate it, huh?" Julie asked. "And in the process, you went back to drugs?"

"Oh no. Never." Simon stared at Julie in surprise. "I told you, I would never do that."

"Okay, how did you violate your parole?"

"That's where I was stupid."

"There are a lot of ways to be stupid," Julie said.

"I visited some of my old friends. They refer to them as 'known criminals.' They were guys I had done business with—felons—and some of them had been in prison two or three times."

"Why in the world would you go to see them if you weren't back into drugs?"

Simon turned and looked at me. "You're a preacher, you can understand this part. Something powerful had happened to me while I was incarcerated. My life had changed, and I discovered something I had never known before."

"What was that?" Julie asked.

"Peace," he said simply. "I've always been a hustler. I was one of those people who rushed, pushed, and never stopped. I graduated at the top of my college class at age twenty and had my master's degree and passed the bar before I was twenty-two." He paused and played with his hands before he continued. "I guess deep inside I knew something was missing in my life, but I had no idea what it was. It took prison to slow me down enough to face myself."

"Can we skip forward to the parole violation?" Julie asked.

"Are you afraid to hear about God at work in my life?"

"Afraid? Of course not. It's only—"

"It's only that you are probably running, too, aren't you?"

"Okay, Simon, don't push it," I said. "Julie doesn't want that part of the story. I'd love to hear it, and perhaps you'll tell me more later."

"Yes, sir, I'd like that. Well, one of the things that Michael kept saying, and I think he was correct, was that it wasn't enough for me to find inner peace. My responsibility—and my privilege—was to pass it on. That's how he constantly said it. Responsibility and privilege. So two weeks after my parole, I learned where several of my old friends lived."

"So you went to their home?"

He shook his head. "I learned the name of the bar where they went regularly. Part of my parole was that I was not to go inside any drinking establishment and not to socialize with any known felons. I went to see my friends anyway. That's when the police caught me. You know, one of those random checks when they were looking for something else—I never did learn what—and they found me with four known felons. To make it worse, one of them had two kilos of hash with him. Get the picture?"

Both of us nodded.

"I pleaded with the arresting officer. I asked him for a chance. The others also told him I had come to talk to them and that I was clean."

"He wouldn't listen but took me to jail to book me. On the way I talked to him some more." Simon laughed self-consciously. "The officer stopped the car and told me to sit tight—as if I could get out of the car. With five of us handcuffed together in the backseat and the two smallest sitting on our laps, I wasn't going anyplace. Besides, the lock was on the outside of the door. The officer got out of the vehicle, walked several feet away, and used his cell phone. A couple of minutes later he got back inside. He turned around in the front seat and said, 'Presswood, this must be your lucky day.' He took me to Mr. Harden's office first, let me out, and booked the others."

"He just took you there and left you?" Julie asked.

"That's it. I met Roger Harden standing in front of his office building. I spent twenty minutes with him, and we made a deal."

"What kind of deal?"

"The kind Mr. Harden made with every one of us. Essentially, it was extortion. I didn't want to go back to jail, and he knew that. He wasn't interested in the reason I went to the bar, but he said the police officer believed in my innocence. After I gave him my word that I wouldn't run away, he put me up in a hotel and told me to come back in three days."

"Why would he do that?" Julie asked.

Simon laughed at that question. "Because he was Roger Harden. He had to show me his control. One time I started to leave the hotel to eat, and a bellman stopped me. He said I was to order from room service and not to leave my room. He was to bring me anything I needed, but I wasn't to leave."

"For three days?"

"Like being in prison again—of sorts," Simon said. "It also gave Roger time to find out everything about me. I had a phone call that said, 'Mr. Harden's car is on the way. Be in front of the hotel in fifteen minutes.' When he summoned me back—and summoned is the right word—he held up a thick file. 'This is all about you,' he said.

"The deal he offered me wasn't as bad as I had expected. He told me that if I would work for him for two full years, he would pay me well and I would never have to go back to jail. Of course, there was the downside—"

"Which was?"

"I was his private snoop. I had to constantly report on his wife, his son, and all visitors on the island. That's why I acted as if I didn't know English. That was Roger's idea. He thought it was a great trick. He was right—you'd be amazed at how freely people spoke in my presence."

"And you reported their words to Roger?"

"Every word. I didn't like it, but I had promised."

"Didn't it trouble you?" I asked.

"Very much," he said. "In all honesty, sometimes I walked away so that I didn't have to hear some things."

"How long have you worked for him?"

"Two years and two months."

"I thought you said exactly two years?" Julie said. "Why didn't you leave at the end of that time? Wouldn't he let you go?"

"I stayed for several reasons—but none of them have anything to do with his death."

"Convince us," Julie said. She had a determined look in her eyes, and she wasn't going to let him stop now.

"He never planned to let me go. He made me sign a confession—an undated one. He had also dug up evidence of other crimes I had done—drug things. So he could easily have sent me back to prison."

"That sounds like a good reason to kill him," Julie said. "All you had to do was kill Roger Harden, get the confession back, and you were free."

"I have the confession. He gave it to me two nights ago—okay, I guess it's now three nights."

"And you're still here?"

"Yes, I was the only one to whom he gave back the implicating evidence. He told me so."

"Why you?"

"I don't know. That's the truth: I don't know."

"Let me backtrack." He turned to Julie. "This involves God again, so it may bore you. Maybe you want to make fresh coffee while I tell Mr. Burton."

"I can handle it," she said.

"A month before my two years ended, I asked him about when I could leave. He laughed at me. He said he liked me and liked the way I did things.

He said I was the best servant he'd ever had and wanted to keep me a little longer."

"A little longer?" I asked. "What did that mean?"

"It meant he wasn't going to let me go. He had enough evidence on me to keep me here. Even with the statute of limitations running out, it wouldn't matter. He had enough power to keep me here the rest of my life."

"So you shot him?" Julie asked.

"I won't even answer that," Simon said. "I was angry. Hatred raged inside me, and you know what? I think he liked seeing me so angry."

"What did you do?" I asked.

"I ran out of the house—down to the water's edge—down near where we found Elaine's body. At first I just wanted to jump into the Atlantic and drown. But I had met Jesus Christ in prison. I stopped and I prayed." He looked at Julie and said, "You'll have to take my word for this, but I fell on the ground and cried out to God for help. I pleaded with God to forgive my anger and to take away my hatred."

"Did it go away?"

"Not then—not instantly. It took two days because I couldn't forgive him, and my soul was tortured. I didn't hate him, but I wanted to be free from him. Two nights before everyone came here, I was able to forgive him."

"I can just about believe that story," Tonya Borders said. "*Just about* believe it, but not quite."

We looked up and saw her standing at the door. We had no idea how long she had been there.

She walked into the office. "Roger was not the kindest man in the world, but if he knew you had violated your parole, he would have told me. And I would have gone to the authorities."

"You seem to be an authority on Roger Harden," Julie said. "Maybe you have something to tell us."

"I loved Roger Harden. I truly loved him. If it hadn't been for Amanda—oh, well, you know how those things go."

"She's lying," Simon said.

"How dare you say I'm lying," Tonya said. "I loved him."

"Perhaps you did," Simon said, "but you also stole from him."

22

S tole from Roger? How can you dare to say such—such a vile thing!" Tonya Borders screamed, her accent fully in place.

I didn't realize Tonya had that much of a voice range. She had always spoken in low, unemotional tones, but her voice now reached a semihysterical pitch.

She turned from Simon and faced me. "This—this convicted criminal stands before you and dares to accuse *me* of a crime. How dare he!" She pulled off her glasses and wiped the perspiration from her face. "I told you: I loved Roger."

"Love I don't know about," Simon said. "But I know you stole from him."

"This is preposterous," she said. "Burton. Julie. Are you going to listen to this—this convicted felon?"

"I know what Roger told me."

"Oh, now that he is dead, you become familiar and call him by his first name? What kind of person are you?"

"He asked me to call him Roger, and I have done that for the past three days. Something else—I became his friend." He looked at me and added, "That's why I didn't leave. He told me I could go. He offered to do what he could to help me get my license restored or do whatever I wanted so I could obtain a good job. He also promised to help me find my wife—my former wife—and see if there was a chance for reconciliation."

"Why didn't you go?" Tonya asked.

"He needed me," Simon said simply. "He needed me."

"How preposterous," Tonya said. "That was his problem: Roger never needed anybody."

"Let's get this back on topic," Simon said. "I accused Tonya of stealing from Roger."

"And I said—"

"Yes, I know what you *said*," Simon interrupted, "but—"

"Are you going to listen to that—that convict? I would not do such a thing as—"

"Roger said that you had falsified records and that he could prove you had cheated him out of slightly over six million dollars."

"I did not steal from Roger."

"I believe she is telling the truth." Wayne Holmestead stood in the doorway. I have no idea how long he had been listening to the discussion. He came inside and took Tonya's hand. "You don't have to listen to such—such ridiculous charges."

"I know what I know," Simon said. "And besides—"

"Besides nothing! I was Roger's partner and best friend for more than twenty years. I was his business adviser. If Tonya had cheated or stolen anything, I would have been the first to know."

"Unless you were part of it," Simon said.

"How dare you!" Wayne raised his fist—something that seemed totally out of character.

"I know what Roger told me! Even better, I can prove it!" Simon said.

"Oh sure, the convict now becomes the police sleuth," Wayne said. "Who would listen to you?"

"You don't have to *listen* to me," Simon said softly. "All you have to do is read." He stepped so close to Wayne that he was less than six inches from his face. "You can read, can't you?"

Wayne stepped back and turned to me. "Will you get this—this person—out of here?"

"Why don't we all calm down and let Simon talk?" I said. "You'll have an opportunity to refute whatever he says."

"I'll even bring in chairs for everyone." Before anyone could protest, Simon rushed out of the room and came back with two chairs from the dining room.

"Now if Wayne and Tonya will be quiet, I'll tell you what I know."

Tonya started to object, but Wayne held up a hand. "Let him talk."

"Roger wrote something—I don't know what it said—I mean specifically. He planned to read it to us last night. I do know this much. It concerned all of us. Roger had held all of us captive to his capricious will for years. He had everything documented. He put the documentation inside a folder along with the paper he planned to read."

"Oh sure," Wayne said. "And I suppose now you're going to whip out the document and point out who killed Roger and poor Elaine and also tried to kill me."

"Why don't you give your mouth a rest?" Simon said.

Julie laughed, but the rest of us stared in shock. Such a statement from Simon seemed out of character. But then, Simon had portrayed a character whom Roger had created, and none of us had known who he truly was.

"I have the document. I haven't read it, but it's in my possession." Simon paused and let the words sink in.

"You have the documents?" Tonya repeated numbly. "All of them?"

"Everything," Simon said.

Tonya and Wayne stared at each other. I tried to read their faces, but I couldn't understand what was going on.

"Yesterday morning Roger called me into his office, and we talked for perhaps forty minutes, maybe a little longer. What we talked about isn't significant except for what he said just before I left the room."

"I suppose he told you someone would try to kill him," Tonya said, and the snicker was on her face as well as in her voice.

Simon shook his head. "He certainly had no idea that anyone would murder him. In fact, he told me about his plans."

"Plans? What plans? He certainly never discussed anything with me," Wayne said. He started in on his being Roger's friend and confidant.

Simon waited until Wayne stopped speaking and continued as if he had not been interrupted.

"Roger called me into his office. And just to make the relationship clear, he didn't order me. He saw me walking from the kitchen toward the front door. 'If you have a few minutes, Simon, could you come in here?' Those were his words. Not a command as you said—"

"Summons," Julie said. "That was the word they used. A summons."

"Whatever the word," Simon said, "Roger asked me to sit down. He told me about the dinner party and that everyone would stay overnight. He said, 'I have something here.' He held up a manila folder filled with papers. It was about two inches thick, and a rubber band held the folder tight. He slipped the folder into a large envelope and laid it on his desk."

"So where is this—this alleged envelope?" asked Tonya. "I don't see it."

"I stole it," Simon said.

"You did what?" Wayne asked.

"Whoever killed Roger wanted the envelope. I figured that out immediately, so I took it and hid it." He turned to me and said, "You see, the murderer didn't know—at least not then—that the important material was in an envelope."

"This is most confusing—and perhaps a little too melodramatic for my tastes," said Tonya.

Simon sank into a chair and turned his attention to Wayne. "You claimed to be his friend. You were the worst among us here. Roger trusted you. He thought of you as a brother—a brother he never had. He felt more betrayed by you—and by Tonya—than he did the others."

"What others?" Paulette White stood in the doorway with Jeffery Dunn and Beth Wilson next to her.

"It looks as if everyone is here except Amanda, Jason, Lenny, and

Reginald," Julie said. "Why don't we all go into the drawing room and get comfortable? Simon has some interesting things to tell all of us."

"This is totally prepos—"

"Just stuff it," Simon said to Wayne. "Let me have my say, and then you can object or squirm." He laughed. "I think you'll tend to squirm."

"Let's all calm down and go into the drawing room," I said.

No one objected. Amanda and Jason were in the kitchen, and they must have heard us, because they came through with coffee and tea. Julie ran upstairs to get Reginald and Lenny.

Simon called me aside and hurriedly gave me information that shocked me. He also told me what he planned to do when we were all gathered. "Are you sure you can pull this off?" I asked. He gave me the old Simon shrug, put his arm around my shoulder, and led me into the drawing room.

"I'm going to cook omelets," Amanda said. "Is that all right? It's about the only thing I can cook besides scrambled eggs."

"We don't need any food now," I said. "We'll stay here in the drawing room. The coffee and tea are fine. Simon wants to talk to all of us."

"Why don't we wait for the other two?" Tonya said with a smirk. "We don't want anyone to miss out on this—this fabulous tale we're about to hear."

In less than five minutes all of us were gathered in the drawing room. Several more minutes lapsed before everyone had poured themselves something to drink. I opted for water and sipped from my glass.

"Simon started to tell me several things," I said, "and most of your names came up in the middle of it. I'd like Simon to start from the beginning and tell us everything."

Tonya sighed. "Must we go through—?"

"I would like to hear," Amanda said and stared at Tonya. "This is my house, and you're my guest."

"Wow, Mom!" Jason clapped his hands. "I wish you'd done more of that in the past."

"Be quiet, Jason," she said softly. "Let's listen."

"You're cool! Mom, you rock!"

Simon waited until everyone had given him his or her attention. I smiled at that. It was as if he were in a courtroom and we were the jury.

"Roger and I became friends quite recently," he said. "He opened up to me and talked to me."

"I can hardly believe he would discuss anything with you," Jeffery said.

Simon held up a hand. "Then indulge me. After you've heard everything, you can decide whether I'm telling the truth." He smiled and added, "Please."

As if he were making his closing arguments in a criminal trial, Simon paced the room and stared at us one at a time. "Each of us is guilty of a crime. Each of us has something to hide—something illegal we have done—and something we want to keep hidden. It is also something that Roger knew and held over us."

Without giving anyone a chance to interrupt him, he told us that Roger had discovered all of our crimes, even though he had no idea how Roger had learned everything. "He loved having you under his control. He didn't want anything except control." He walked up to each person and pointed a finger at each one.

As he walked, I found it interesting that as soon as he approached a person, stopped, and stared into that person's face, none of them could return the stare.

Not even me.

Simon's talk forced me to think about things I didn't want to contemplate. Yes, Roger had control over me, as well. I had not mentioned that to anyone, not even Julie when she confessed so openly.

Julie stared at me. Her lips formed the words, "You, too?"

I nodded and looked away. I was too ashamed to look at her again. From then on, I avoided meeting her glaring eyes.

"Everyone here is guilty—and I am guilty, as well."

"I can't stand any more of this grandstanding," Wayne said and pulled down his vest. "This is like one of those cheap crime dramas on TV where you gather everyone together and call out the murderer—"

"Of course you can't stand anymore," Simon said quietly and pointed his finger at Wayne. "I know about you. You stole from Roger. You had a scheme going, and you systematically pilfered over the years. Notice I used the word *pilfer*. He knew you had accumulated nearly a million."

"That is a lie—a terrible—"

Simon leaned forward and placed his arms on Wayne's shoulders. "He had less respect for you than anyone in this room. You know why? He said you were a cowardly crook. It took you twenty years—twenty years—to steal a million. He said you took such small amounts and you could have taken more. He said you were a total coward."

"That's not true. Not true." His voice lacked conviction, and he dropped his head.

"You were here in the afternoon. I saw Jason leave. I heard you with him. I know he showed you the letter and maybe the folder—whatever he wrote. He did, didn't he?"

"No, he showed me nothing. We talked—we talked about a riverfront project at Brunswick. He wanted to dump the project after I had invested months of time and effort and—"

"Stop lying!" Simon said. "Stop talking. Listen!" When he had control of the group again, Simon said, "I have the documents—although I have not read anything."

"So now you're going to tell us that Roger entrusted you with them? You, a convicted criminal," Tonya said.

"He didn't give them to me, remember. I stole them." Simon explained that when we rushed into the office, he saw the envelope on the desk. While everyone stared at Roger's body, he pulled the envelope off the desk and stuck it in the back of his pants. "It's like this. Wayne knew about the letter, and he knew about the documentation, but he didn't know where it was. Possibly some of the others knew. I thought the police would get here last night, so I was going to hold it and give it to them."

"What does it contain?" I asked.

"I can only surmise," Simon said. "Roger had shown me the letter and the documentation. I don't think Wayne saw it. If so, he would have grabbed it, right? No one would have had to search the office again."

"If I had killed Roger," Wayne said, "which I didn't."

Simon walked around the room and finally said, "Whoever killed Roger Harden wanted the evidence. And I still have it."

"If you have the envelope," I said, "why don't you show it?"

"It's in my room," he said. "I can go and get it, but I'm not sure it's something to show everyone. If it's what Mr. Harden said it was, it contains information about everyone in this room."

As Simon and I had planned, I said, "Go and get it. I'll see that no one leaves the room while you're gone."

I expected Wayne or one of the women to grumble about the procedure, but no one did. I had no idea about the contents, but I knew I didn't want everyone in the room to know about my past. There was no ethical way I could display the contents and not show my secrets if Roger had included mine.

As soon as Simon came back into the drawing room, Wayne tried to rip it from his hands. "As his best friend and adviser, I should look at it first."

Simon pushed him away. "No." He thrust a thumb into Wayne's chest. "I think you killed him. I'll continue to believe that until I find evidence to the contrary. So you won't be the person to open the envelope."

"How dare you—"

"You killed Roger to prevent his reading his announcement to all of you, didn't you?" I said, hardly aware of the words until they tumbled out of my mouth.

N o no—" Wayne said. "It's true I wanted to get rid of the letter. It wasn't just about me. Remember, Simon said that. I didn't kill Roger." He dropped his head. "I wanted to destroy the letter."

"You knew about this material," Simon said. "I have the documentation you wanted."

"Wait a minute," I said. I turned to Paulette. "You knew about the documentation, didn't you?"

"How would I know?" she asked.

"What were you searching for in Roger's desk?" Julie asked. "That had to be it. You knew about the letter or whatever it was Roger wanted to announce. You wanted to find the letter and the proof so you could destroy it all."

"That is a pathetic lie," she said. "But quite imaginative."

"We'll get back to Paulette in a moment," Simon said. "But first, I want to accuse Wayne Holmestead—and I don't have to read the contents of this envelope."

"How dare you!"

"The reason I have said nothing until now is that he had to have had an accomplice. She searched for this." Simon held the envelope so that everyone could see it. "The only way she could have known about the documentation was by being in cahoots with the killer."

"Maybe she killed him herself," I suggested.

Simon shook his head. "No, I know who killed Roger."

"You think I did it?" Wayne Holmestead said.

"I know you did," Simon said. He turned to the rest of us. "Remember the little incident with the gun last night. Wayne said someone had shot at him and missed."

"Everyone knows that," Beth said.

"So someone else had to have had the gun, right?"

"If we assume it was the same gun."

"Oh it was." Simon reached inside his pocket and pulled up a plastic bag. Inside was a gun. "It's a .32 caliber Beretta, and it holds seven shots. I'm sure the police will discover that it has been fired twice. It's not a bad weapon if the person knows how to use it. This Beretta has a three-and-five-eighths-inch barrel that—"

"We don't need a lecture about guns," Amanda said. "Especially—especially *that* one—if it's—if it's the—the weapon."

"Oh, it is the weapon all right," Simon said. "Would you like to know how I found it?"

"Sure—right inside Roger's desk," Paulette said. "That ought to be proof enough—"

"Then it would have to have my fingerprints on it, right?" Simon smiled. "The police will be here soon. You'll notice it's inside a plastic bag. There will be fingerprints on the gun, and they won't be mine."

"What are you trying to say?" Amanda asked.

"They will have Wayne's prints on it. I'm sure they'll also have Paulette's on it."

A visibly shaken Wayne said. "I—I don't—I don't—"

"Save your breath," Simon said. "Wayne, you killed Roger Harden, and Paulette was your accomplice—or the other way around."

Wayne shook his head violently. "No! I wouldn't—I wouldn't—"

"Oh yes, you did."

"By what brilliant process of logical deduction did you arrive at such a conclusion?" Paulette asked. She folded her arms across her chest. Her look defied Simon to prove his allegations.

"Two things," I said before Simon could reply. "First, you had to know about the document or you wouldn't have searched the office—"

"You can't prove that's what I wanted."

"No, that's true, and that's only circumstantial," I said. "Simon and I have discussed this. After I told him about the gunshot, both of us figured out something obvious—there had to be an accomplice."

"So why me?"

"We made an assumption. Because you were the person we discovered going through Roger's desk. We assumed—"

"And fingerprints," Simon said. "Unless you wiped your prints off the gun, I'm sure they'll find at least one or two."

"That's right," I said. "And how else would your fingerprints get on the gun? Someone other than Wayne had to have fired the gun in the hallway, which was obviously a ruse to throw suspicion off Wayne. The accomplice fired from somewhere down the hallway. Wayne couldn't have fired the single shot and run down to his room. He's too large a man to run silently. Besides, even if he could have, he had no way to know that others wouldn't run from their rooms in time to see him. So, like Simon says, unless you wiped the gun clean, your fingerprints will also be on the Beretta."

"I agree with all that," Julie said, "but, Simon, how did you get the gun?"

"Yes, how did you?" Paulette said. "Maybe you're the one who fired. None of us saw you upstairs after the shot."

Simon stared at me, and I said, "Tell them."

"Last night I was broken up. I had just begun to know Roger. I can't say I knew him well, but we had an excellent beginning of—"

"We don't have to hear the entire commentary," Jeffery said. "Just tell us what happened."

"I went out to the beach to pray."

"In the rain?" asked Paulette. "I hardly believe that."

Simon explained again about the small tent. "I like to go there so I can be alone with my thoughts and with my prayers."

"Prayers?" asked Paulette. "Now you're going to tell us that you're some kind of saint who—"

"I was a lawyer and a drug addict," Simon said quite simply, "and then I became a convicted criminal. After my release from prison, I went to work for Roger. Like many of you did when he learned of your crimes."

"Are you trying to call us criminals?" Paulette asked.

"I am not *trying*," he smiled at her. "The difference between me and the rest of you is that I have paid for my crimes."

"How dare you!" Wayne said. He grabbed for the plastic bag.

I took the bag from Simon. "He dares, Wayne, because it's the truth," I said. "Now let him finish."

"You see, I became a serious Christian during my time in prison. My life and my values changed and—"

"Oh dear, here comes the awful story of his rehabilitation in prison and a lengthy sermon," Paulette said. "Can we skip that, please?"

"Just listen to him," Julie said. "He might make sense."

"This is so totally okay," Jason said.

Paulette dropped her gaze.

Simon told us that he went down to the beach. He referred to the oak tree that Mrs. Wright often climbed. "I made space on the ground next to the tree. It gave me a wonderful view of the mainland—when the weather permitted." He told us the rain ended shortly after midnight. He did not hear any shots, although he did see the lights go on at one point. He considered going up to the house but decided instead to remain and pray.

"My heart was heavy. I had lost someone—Roger—who had become important to me. I agonized in prayer for God to intervene and to help us solve this heinous crime." He told us that God had given him a deep love for his former extortioner.

"Sometime after midnight—I didn't notice the time—but the rain had stopped. I was still inside my tent, kneeling in the dark. I heard footsteps on the gravel path. I wondered if someone wanted me to do something. Roger used to call me at any hour of the day or night when I was inside the house. By my being outside, he would have to come down to look for me.

"There was just enough of a moon peeking through the clouds for me to see who it was. Wayne Holmestead walked right past me—he stopped maybe five feet away. He couldn't have seen me. Then my conscience bothered me and I wondered if he needed anything. I started to speak, but he took something from his pocket and threw it over the cliff, turned around, and walked rapidly toward the house.

"That made me curious, of course," Simon said. He had a small flashlight in his tent and walked to the cliff. "I could see nothing—my flashlight isn't very powerful." He walked down the ladder and looked around. He spotted the gun. "The nose of the gun had stuck in the sand, and the handle was straight up. It was barely on the rocks. When the tide changed again and started to come in, the gun would have been washed away." He pulled off his shirt and used it to grab the gun, which he carried up to the kitchen and put into a plastic bag.

"Why didn't you come in then?" I asked.

"I wanted to pray for Wayne."

"For me? Why would you pray for me?"

"I knew you must be deeply troubled. I knew you had reacted as you did because of something Roger held over you. I prayed for God to be merciful to you and to forgive you."

"Simon came into the house a little earlier," I said, "and he told me what happened on the beach."

"So this is all settled and we can go back to bed," Lenny said. "Good show, Simon!"

"There is something else," Julie said. "The envelope. The documents Roger had."

"Oh yeah," Lenny said. "I had forgotten."

"Or maybe you wanted to forget," Beth said.

"If this were a made-for-television movie," Lenny said, "Wayne would try to make a run for it right now."

"Don't be stupid," Wayne said.

"Well, did you murder him?" Julie said.

"No, I didn't murder him." His lips quivered, and he said, "but I did kill him."

"Shut up!" Paulette said.

"Leave him alone," I said to Paulette. "Let him tell us his story."

"I did kill him, but—but it was an accident. We fought over the gun, and it went off."

"Really?" Julie asked. "How did the gun come into the argument? I thought it was kept in a desk drawer."

"Roger pulled it out. He threatened me. He said he'd shoot me if I didn't leave."

"I think you're lying," I said. "But that will be for the police and the courts to decide."

"Why did you kill Elaine?" Julie asked.

"I didn't kill her. Yes, I did kill Roger. But I don't know anything about her death."

"What's the difference?" Julie asked. "One murder or two? And it will at least be one murder and an attempt to cover it up."

"All right, I did kill him. But it truly was an accident, even if you don't believe me. I was the one who pulled out the gun. He held the letter in his hand. He started to read it. I lunged for the paper—it was actually four pages—and he pulled back, and we fought."

"Maybe," I said, "but there doesn't seem to be any sign of a struggle. Nothing was messed up. Nothing was out of place. Everyone can testify to that. Right?"

"Did you get the paper you wanted so badly?" I asked.

"No, I panicked and ran."

"You're lying," Julie and I both said at the same time.

"Sure he is," Jason said. "Nothing was messed up in the office. I saw that. I mean, it looked as orderly as Dad's desk ever did."

"The more you lie, the more difficult it will become for you," I said. "Why don't you confess before the Brunswick police arrest you?"

He sat quietly and said nothing. "Just leave me alone for a few minutes," Wayne said. "Please. I—I want to think."

I walked into the dining room and poured myself a cup of coffee.

The morning sun slanted through the slats of the blinds, striping the table with shadows and golden light. I peeked through the blinds. The sun was a warm, bright yellow ball that seemed to chase every cloud off the horizon.

Several others followed me into the dining room. I poured a cup of coffee for Wayne. Although I had no idea how he took it, I added sugar and cream. When I walked back into the drawing room, I handed him the cup on a saucer.

He nodded his thanks but didn't look at the cup. Automatically he raised it to his lips and took a long swallow. He took two more, drained the cup, and handed it back to me. Simon stood behind me to take the dirty cup back to the dining room.

He nudged me, and I followed him out.

"I'll put Wayne's cup into a plastic bag," Simon said, "It will make it easier for them to compare fingerprints."

"You're an amazing man," I said and struck him lightly on the shoulder.
"Yes, I know."

A minute later we both walked back into the drawing room.

Wayne stared at Simon and then at me. He dropped his head. "I killed Roger, but I didn't kill Elaine. That was Paulette's doing."

"What? How dare you implicate me?" Paulette said. "You think that if you throw some of this onto me that it will make it easier for you? How dare you—"

I faced Paulette, put my hands on her shoulders, and gently pushed her back into her chair. "You'll have a chance to speak," I said softly.

Holmestead turned away from her and directed his attention to me as if we were alone in the room. "Paulette and I were both in the office. She came in two or three minutes after Jason left. Elaine saw her—saw both of us."

Paulette said, "That's a lie—"

"Shut up," Simon said. "I am strong enough to tie you up and tape your mouth if I need to do so."

As ludicrous as that sounded, Paulette shut her mouth, but the anger was apparent on her face.

"Elaine also saw us come out of the office," Wayne said.

"Why didn't she tell us?" I asked. "She could have saved herself, as well."

"Money," Wayne said.

"You mean blackmail?" Julie asked.

He nodded. "She didn't know I had shot Roger—not then—but she had seen us. We were the last ones out of the office. After the discovery of the body, while we were all standing around, Mrs. Wright pulled Paulette aside. She whispered that she had seen us coming out of the office."

"That's not—" Paulette said, but she stopped when Simon came toward her.

"She told Paulette that she had heard the shot and saw us leave the office."

"And—?" I asked.

"Paulette asked her to be quiet and said that we'd talk to her later. She told me that Mrs. Wright had also said, 'Be sure to bring your checkbook.' "

"That isn't true," Paulette said. "I have no idea why you want to implicate me, Wayne. You're guilty. You've said so. Don't try to smear me with—"

"But it was your idea to kill Mrs. Wright," he said. "That's why."

"Suppose you finish telling us, Wayne," I said.

"I don't know the details." Wayne said that Paulette told him about Mrs. Wright's comments. Wayne wanted to pay her off, but Paulette said that was never the way to work with blackmailers. Roger had never let them go and planned to expose them. She said, 'Leave Mrs. Wright to me. You took care of Roger. I'll take care of her.' That's all I know."

"So the two women met on the cliff, and she pushed Mrs. Wright off."

"Yes."

"That's a lie!" Paulette said. "The note part is right, and I did go to the cliff, but he came, too. You know there is a large magnolia tree near the oak where Mrs. Wright used to go? He stood behind it."

"But that's a dozen feet or more from the cliff," I said.

"That's right," she said. "Mrs. Wright said she would keep quiet if we paid her two hundred thousand dollars. Wayne and I had decided that I would get her to the precipice, and he'd come up behind her and hit her and push her over the cliff. He had a hammer in his hand. She never heard him coming."

"I didn't—I didn't—" his voice broke.

"Oh, shut up," Julie said. "Don't go sniveling now."

"Now I can tell you more," Simon said. "Roger knew that Wayne and Paulette had stolen from him. What they did not know is that he wasn't going to expose them."

24

"Not expose them?" I asked. "Wasn't that the point of the invited guests and dinner meeting with all of us?"

"No, that wasn't the point," Simon said. He smiled at us. "Roger was going to forgive all of you."

"Forgive us?" Julie echoed.

"And then he was going to ask you to forgive him."

"Roger was going to ask us to forgive him? Impossible." Tonya shook her head and laughed. "Roger never made mistakes. He only capitalized on other people's failures."

"Hard to believe, but it's also true."

"How do you know that?" Jeffery asked.

"He told me." He held up the envelope. "I did not see what was inside, and I haven't looked. I didn't think it was ethical to do that." He smiled. "Yes, I have ethics. I didn't before I became a Christian, but—"

"Do spare us the sermon," Paulette said. "Just speak up, and then shut up."

"I'll do that," Simon said and handed me the envelope. I took the envelope and opened it. There was a three-page letter and a manila folder held together by a rubber band. I pulled out the letter and skimmed it.

"And, of course," Beth said to Simon, "you took out the incriminating evidence about you."

"Beth. Everyone. Let's stop. I'll read the letter or announcement or whatever it is. As you'll see, this is what Roger planned to read to us last night." Burton began to read.

I've decided to put this in writing because I want to say everything correctly. I don't want to get sidetracked with questions or comments—I'll respond to them when I've finished.

First, I have been a businessman—a successful businessman—since I was in my early twenties. As a human being, I was a failure. I failed as a husband and certainly failed as a father to Jason. I have been underhanded and manipulative and interested only in myself.

"I don't think we need to sit here and listen to Roger's sad, dull, and soulful experience," Beth said. "I've heard better things at AA meetings." She smiled and said, "Yes, I am a member of AA and also Narcotics Anonymous. That's another little story that our dear, departed Roger knew."

"Read it anyway," Amanda said. "I want to hear it. I—I need to hear it."

I read the first page, and it was mostly what I'd call confessional information. He didn't mention anyone individually but said that he had gained power by finding human weaknesses and wrongdoings and exploiting them.

He also wrote that those invited here were not the only people of whom he had taken advantage.

There are others—hundreds of others. I've written to many of them, and I'm in the process of contacting others. I had a luncheon last week with nine other people and went through what I plan to do here tonight.

I wanted to see each of you in person. In many ways, you are the people who should have been closest to me for various reasons. I didn't allow any of you to get close, to know me well, or to care for me. I pushed you aside. I know that caused you to detest me. You liked what I could do for you, but you didn't like the price you had to pay.

I've already told you about the change in my life. I want to tell you what brought it about. Three months ago my life shattered. One person I had blackmailed took his own life. He sent me a letter that arrived after his death. He said he couldn't take it any longer.

In the letter, he reiterated all the demeaning things I had done to him and the demands I had made of him. He was totally correct. I had thought only of power. It had never occurred to me how deeply oppressed people felt. That was the first time in my life I saw myself as evil.

I stopped reading momentarily. Except for a few of us who knew what had happened to Roger, the rest were in shock at this unexpected turn of events. I had expected Lenny to interrupt with smart comments, but he sat there, his mouth open, and stared.

"I'm so—so happy to know Roger changed," Amanda said. "For years I tried to talk to him about God, but he refused to listen. However, I never stopped praying—not even after I left him." Tears burst from her, and she wept with a lack of self-consciousness and control. Instead of decreasing, her crying grew louder.

For several minutes, her sorrow and pain seemed to fill the room. Her wailing gave the rest of us an opportunity to realize the impact of Roger's letter.

"I wish we had known," Lenny said. "I can't tell you the number of times I've wished he'd get run down by a car or killed by a mugger."

"It hardly seems like the same Roger Harden I have known for all these years," Jeffery said. "I did not know he was capable of emotion of any kind."

I should have stopped Jeffery then, but he began a monotoned lecture about how we never know other people and how little we understand their feelings.

"Yes, that's true," Julie interrupted him. "But let's get back to Roger's letter."

I smiled my thanks to her. The others must have felt the same way, because I heard affirmations and saw nodding heads.

Until then, I had not thought I'd harmed anyone. I rationalized that I always gave them more than I took. I opened doors, gave them investment opportunities, or hired them. I thought it seemed like a good bargain from their point of view.

I say "rationalized" because that's what it was. I didn't care about what others felt. I wanted to have control over them. It was a compulsion that would not let go. It sounds easy enough for me to say it, but I never wanted to do damage to anyone—certainly not enough so that someone would feel the only way to be free of me was to take his own life.

That man's death rocked me emotionally. Nothing had ever shaken me so badly. Although he did not say it, I knew his death was on my hands. I had murdered that poor, foolish man.

I couldn't get away from the shame—the overwhelming shame and guilt. I felt as if I were the most miserable and despised person in the world. I didn't like anything about myself. How could I? I had destroyed many lives.

I realized the reason several of my trusted employees—or those I should have trusted—had stolen from me. That was their way to avenge themselves. My first inclination had been to ruin their lives, but I knew I couldn't live with myself if I caused another person's death.

I decided to get help. I met with a therapist, and he suggested I also talk with a minister. He said he felt my problems were also spiritual in nature.

Roger's letter told us that he had consulted a pastor and met with him regularly. He read several books, and every day he read portions of the Bible. At times he hated what he read in the Bible, but he kept coming back. He said that I had greatly influenced him because of what I had done for Jason. Most of all, Simon was the one who had touched him. He said that both of us had badly flawed pasts and had overcome them. We were an inspiration to him.

Yes, I became a believer. But I wanted to do more than believe. Because I believed, I wanted my life to change. I had heard of people who had great emotional experiences. That was not mine. I had discovered peace—a deep, deep inner peace. I knew God had forgiven me. The minister urged me to contact everyone I had wronged and ask their forgiveness.

That is why I called you here. I have saved every paper or document I have used against you. I wanted you to be here tonight so that I can give them to you and you may destroy them yourselves.

I have chosen to forgive you.

Two of you are here because you have been systematically stealing from me. I will erase that. I can no longer allow you to work for me, but I will do nothing to prosecute you or prevent your getting a new position. For the others, I will do whatever I can to help you in any way I can.

I have only one thing to ask of you: I ask you to forgive me. I have been a tyrant and I have been evil. I know God has erased my sins, and I plead with you to forgive me.

"You knew?" Amanda asked Simon. "You knew he had become a believer and you didn't tell me?"

Simon nodded. "Blame me that he said nothing. I may have been wrong—and if so, I apologize. I suggested that he tell no one, and he agreed with me."

"Why? Why wouldn't you want everyone to know?"

"In time he needed to tell everyone, but first I wanted to see Roger change. I have known many who had what we called jailhouse conversions. They had powerful experiences, but once they received parole or their parole was refused, they lost their Christianity."

"That makes sense," Jason said. "I *saw* the difference the day he died. It wasn't just the things he said to me, but I knew—I knew something had changed." He hugged his mother. "I hope that will give you peace to know that he is in God's presence right now."

"You see, Amanda, Roger wanted to reconcile with you," Simon said. "He wanted to tell you—in the presence of these people." His hand swept to indicate everyone in the room. "He wanted you to know that you were the most important person in his life. He felt he had hurt you the most by his demanding ways. He wanted you to forgive him."

"To forgive him?" Amanda broke out in fresh tears. "I prayed, but I never believed—not really—that he would change."

"He changed. He also wanted you to help him grow. Once he became a believer, he was able to look back at the way you lived. He told me that you were far, far kinder to him than he deserved."

"She was," Jason said. "That's part of the reason I hated him. Mom let him yell at her. Sometimes he acted as if she was an idiot or a first grader."

Simon smiled, and his eyes moistened. "In some ways, he was like a boy himself—after his change. He had found something wonderful, better than anything he had experienced before, and he wanted to be the one to share the news. I respected that right."

"He was going to tell us at dinner," Jason said. "I knew—sort of—that something had happened. I'm a believer, too. That's part of what helped me forgive Dad."

"This is quite extraordinary, isn't it?" Reginald said. "Our two murderers committed unnecessary acts of violence. Of course, murder is always unnecessary, but Roger was going to forgive them. If they had only waited." He shook his head in wonderment.

"Why didn't he tell me?" Wayne wailed. "If he'd just hinted—"

"Did you give him a chance?" I asked.

"No, perhaps not." He hung his head. "Roger said, 'I know what you've done. I know the money you've stolen from me. That's why I've called you here to the island.' He smiled at me and said, 'I have a major announcement to make.' It didn't occur to me that he would forgive me. Certainly not Roger Harden. I expected him to step on me as if I were a mere bug. So I screamed at him that he couldn't do that. I knew where he kept the gun. I grabbed it, and I shot him." He stared at the floor. "You know all the rest."

The ringing of the telephone interrupted the conversation. Jason ran to Roger's office and picked up the phone. He returned to the room. "The police are on their way. They'll be here in about ten minutes."

I read the final portion of the letter, which was a beautiful prayer for all of us to follow God in our lives. I replaced the letter in the envelope.

"Aren't you going to show us the documentation?" Reginald said. "If Roger was going to forgive us, then why—?"

"Isn't that a matter for the police?" I said.

"But what if they read it? Our lives will be ruined, too," said Lenny.

I gave him my best Simon-imitation shrug.

25

This is Julie picking up again. I didn't know what Simon and Burton planned, but it worked. I do know what happened after the police came.

Everything considered, that final event was a great climax to the evening and morning. It took us about half an hour to explain everything to the two police officers. Simon would talk, and I'd interrupt with information he'd forgotten, and then Burton would remind us of something else.

The one in charge was a woman. The other, who was new to the force, stood and observed, but he never said a single word. By the time we finished, the female officer said, "I hope you can remember everything you've told me."

That's the reason both of us are writing. It's not to show each other. I'd blush if Burton knew how I felt about him—especially at our first meeting to travel to Palm Island together. No, I'm writing down everything so I can remember if it comes to trial. Wayne Holmestead is such a wimp, and he can't seem to confess enough. Paulette has denied she did anything wrong. She finally said Wayne had coerced her. She claimed Wayne killed Elaine. I'm not sure it makes much difference who did what. Eventually, she did admit that they both were guilty.

Oh yes, they found Paulette's fingerprints on the gun, and Wayne's—oh, but that came out nearly two weeks later.

We had one important moment of excitement, and I have to write it so I remember every detail. After the police officer heard the story, and after both Wayne Holmestead and Paulette White admitted to her and to the rest of us that they had killed Roger, she asked for the envelope.

"I have a question," Burton said. "We are all witnesses that Wayne and Paulette confessed to two murders. Is that correct?"

Everyone agreed.

"There was no coercion. No force used. Right?" Burton said and grinned.

Simon caught on, and he grinned. "Great idea! Yes!"

I stared at both of them, and then I caught on. I was a little slow on that one. I supposed I grinned in imitation of the two men.

"So you don't need this envelope." Burton held it up for the police officer to see.

"Not to convict, but it is evidence, you know."

"And it could be used to harm all of us, right?" I said. I winked at my two conspirators.

"If you've committed crimes, then of course it would be evidence and I would have to use any information against you."

"Even if we were all blackmailed? Even if we've all more than paid for our crimes?"

"That is not for me to decide," she said. "You hand me evidence. My job is to take it to my superiors. I bring in the evidence, and they make the decisions."

"Think about the material in the envelope," I said. I didn't look at her, but at the others in the room.

"We all know one part of the contents—our own, uh, failures—but I'm sure there was more. Is that correct?"

Everyone agreed.

"That's correct," Simon said. "If the police officer takes the envelope and the contents are revealed, who will it harm?"

"I have a wife and two teenage girls," Reginald said. "I would hate for them to know."

"It would kill my mother," Jeffery said. "She has always been proud of me." He looked around. "She's in a nursing facility, you see."

"Please—please don't give it to her," Amanda said. "There are some things in there about me, but that's not my concern. Look at all the lives this can ruin. It will be exactly the opposite of what Roger wanted."

"Exactly what I was thinking," Burton said. He turned to the police officer. "I am going to burn this. You may accuse me of destroying evidence, but I'm going to burn it anyway."

He walked across the room, and the officer made no attempt to stop him. If she had, I think she knew the rest of us would have blocked her. Burton opened the envelope, pulled off the rubber band, and extracted the manila folder. He turned the envelope upside down, and the contents fell on the grate of the clean fireplace. He took one of the matches in the container on the mantle and set the contents aflame. He lit fires in four or five places.

"You really should not do that," the police officer said. "I have to tell you that you may be committing a crime." She made no effort to move as she said those words. "I have to tell you that," she said. "I have to warn you that you may face criminal charges."

"It would be a greater crime if anyone read the papers," I said. "Please, let it go."

"I can't stand here and give you permission. That would make me an accessory. If you prevent me from doing my duty—well, there is nothing I could do to stop you, is there?"

"And there is no one to report it, either, is there?" I said.

All of us watched the fire consume the pages. I got a little impatient and didn't want anyone to filch partial pages from the ashes, so I reached down with a poker and spread the flame so that everything burned to ashes.

"My law-officer conscience sometimes argues with my humanitarian conscience," the police officer said. "But you prevented me from doing anything, didn't you?"

"If you have any pangs of conscience," Simon said, "perhaps you'll think about it on the way back to the mainland. There were two murders. Both suspects have confessed. Case closed."

"I never believe in worrying about what might have been." She nodded to her assistant. "Cuff these two, and let's go."

26

Shortly after the police left, Tonya Borders and Dr. Jeffery Dunn insisted they had to leave immediately. Both of them seemed to have emergency meetings. Lenny Goss and Reginald Ford also demanded that they get out first. Tonya had four large suitcases, and Jeffery had three and a briefcase. Beth Wilson had two large suitcases. Jeffery and Reginald each had to hold suitcases on their laps—which was the only way all five of them could get into the Boston Whaler.

Burton and I said we were in no hurry. Both of us wanted to be back to Atlanta that night. As long as we left by five o'clock we could make it back.

Simon took the others ashore.

Amanda and Simon decided to stay on Palm Island. She would make funeral arrangements. "Jason and I need to be alone for a couple of days," she said. "He and I need to talk and to take all of this in. It's still—well, a shock."

Simon planned to leave as soon as he was sure everything was in order, and he would do what he could. Amanda found a manila file folder in Roger's bedroom. It contained information about Simon's wife, her whereabouts (she was still single), and his two children. As soon as Simon had taken all of us off the island, he planned to phone her.

While we waited for Simon to return, we walked around the small island. It was the first time I had ever seen the entire island in the daytime. The flora amazed me. Peach trees showed their unripened fruit. Black-trunked elms crowded against the sides of the path on the windward side and swayed gently in the wind from the ocean. The aroma of oregano and lemon balm filled our nostrils until we picked up a whiff of honeysuckle and then reached a small bed of roses. Roger must have had at least thirty varieties, and all of them actually smelled as beautiful as they looked. I lost track of the variety of flowers. It was obvious that someone had taken great pains to make it restful. I understood why Simon enjoyed being out there alone.

In the distance we could see the ocean liners that appeared no larger than toys. I turned away and then looked back every few seconds. It was almost as if they got slightly bigger each time.

Amanda brought us a pitcher of iced tea—true Southern style: The tea was weak and very sweet.

"I wish I had known about Roger's change of heart," I said to Burton as we sipped our tea. "When he called me a couple of weeks ago, he did act different. But I didn't think too much about it."

"You're a psychologist," Burton said; "I'm surprised you didn't wonder. I mean, wonder enough to ask or do something."

"He played games with people. I thought it was just another game."

"Yes, I suppose that is the way he was."

"And you know from experience?"

"I know from experience," he said.

I thought Burton was going to open up to me, but just then we heard the Boston Whaler approaching. Roger had a yacht, but he preferred this for guests on the island.

"It takes, what, three minutes to reach shore in the calm waters?"

He shrugged. "Maybe four."

We got into the boat, and just for fun I timed the trip. It was exactly three minutes.

"I'll miss you, Simon," I said after he helped me with my luggage and I gave him a warm hug.

Burton hugged him, as well. "What do you plan to do now?"

He shrugged.

I laughed, and then Burton laughed. It took a few seconds for Simon to catch on.

"The shrug, huh? Oh yes, I do that extremely well. For a moment, I forgot." He gave me another warm hug. "My answer is that I'm not sure. I've saved my money—what is there to spend money on around here? My former wife wants to think about a reconciliation. I believe she'll say yes. I believe that because God has kept love in her heart alive during the years of our separation. She just wants to be sure. I won't make any significant change until I hear from her."

"I'll pray for you and for her every day," Burton said. "What's her name?"

"Sheila," he said.

"Every day, you will be in my prayers."

"I don't know if God listens to me, Simon," I said, "but I'll talk to him regularly about you and Sheila. That's the best I can do."

"Is start." He burst into laughter. "That has been like performing for the tourists. I'll miss the playacting."

We thanked him again and headed for our cars.

"How about coffee?" Burton asked just before I got into my car.

"I thought you'd never ask."

We walked from the pier to the nearest restaurant—about half a mile away. Neither of us seemed to know what to say along the way. I marveled again at the sand dunes and the countless rows of sea oats. Everything smelled fresh, and the sun warmed my arms.

After we sat down and had our coffee served, I said, "You and Simon are the first Christians I've found attractive."

"What kind of Christians have you known?"

"I lived with an uncle and aunt for six months when I was in college—six months before they kicked me out. They had so many "don't rules," I finally made a huge poster listing all those rules and hung it in the hallway outside my door. I think I listed fifteen things I couldn't do."

"Is that when they kicked you out?"

"No. As a matter of fact, they liked it. My uncle was sure I was beginning to learn."

"Oh oh. That doesn't sound good."

"They got the message when I put up the next poster."

Burton smiled. "I gotta hear this."

"The first poster said, 'THESE ARE THE THINGS GOOD CHRISTIANS CAN'T DO.' On the other I wrote, 'THESE ARE THE THINGS GOOD CHRISTIANS CAN DO.' "

"And what did you write under that?"

"Nothing. I left it blank. The next day Uncle Ed asked, 'When are you going to finish the poster?' I answered, 'As soon as I can think of something to put there.' "

"And what happened? Did he fill it in for you?"

"Oh no. He yelled at me. That's all it took."

"Wait—you lost me."

"Sorry." I sipped my coffee. "You see, one of the rules was 'Christians can't get angry.' When he yelled, I pointed to the rule and said, 'You can't do that!' "

"And then—?"

"He really yelled and told me to get out at the end of the week. But I had the last word."

"Am I supposed to be surprised at that?" Burton showed those gorgeous teeth, and the light was perfect and his dimples glowed, as well.

"I said, 'Uncle Ed, I'm sorry, but I can't do that.' When he asked why, I said, 'Because I don't plan to stay that long. I'll be gone tonight.' Guess what? I never saw him again. But anytime anyone talked to me about the church or Jesus or being a Christian, I thought of him."

"I'm sorry about that—"

"I should have added, until I met you and Simon. You two guys are genuine."

"We try to be."

We both sipped our coffee and looked out the window. The day had grown extremely warm. We sat outside where the soft Atlantic wind could caress our skin. It messed up my hair. No matter how windblown Burton's hair, those curls never looked bad. Why do some guys have all the good hair?

From inside, the aroma of smoking fish filled our nostrils. I thought about food—as usual—but I didn't want to ruin the ambience.

"I want to ask you something," I said and broke the silence.

"Ask," he said. The way he answered made me realize he already knew my question.

"You had a secret, too. Most of the others told theirs, but you didn't."

"And the question is—?"

"Would you tell me—trust me—with the secret?"

"You're a therapist," he said slowly. He wrapped his hands around his cup and stared into the coffee. "You know there's a time for people to open up."

"We like to say that they'll open up when they feel safe."

"True," he said, "but it's more than safety. I still have a couple of things to work out within myself first. I hope you'll understand that—as a therapist and as a potential friend."

"As a potential convert," I said. I smiled to deflect my disappointment.

"It's not easy for me to open up," he said. "But I will—eventually."

"I am disappointed, but I'll wait."

"In the meantime," Burton said, "I'd love to talk to you about the Christian faith."

"Again, I thought you'd never ask."

"You're serious? You'd really like to talk about God?"

"I'm serious. This time. Honest," I said, and I meant it. "As I told you earlier, I never met any real Christians before—"

"Or maybe you weren't ready to meet real Christians. Maybe you let a few of the odd ones scare you away from opening up."

I laughed. He had me, and he knew it.

"There is a Sufi saying, and maybe you know it: 'When the pupil is ready, the teacher appears.' "

"That's not fair," I said. "I quote that to clients all the time. In fact, I even have a lovely poster of that on my office wall that one of my appreciative clients made for me."

"Maybe it's time for someone to quote those words to you—and for you to listen."

"Okay, teacher, I want to be a ready pupil. Truly. I mean that."

He leaned forward. "I know you do."

"Isn't this the time where you grab me and kiss me and—"

"Not yet. One day, maybe. Not yet."

"I can wait. I can be patient, too."

"It will also give me a chance to know you better."

"I'm counting on that, as well."

"After we get back to Atlanta," Burton said, "may I take you to dinner one night?"

"Do you take all inquirers to dinner?"

"No, not all," he said and smiled. "Only two kinds."

"Oh? Who are they?"

"Serious males and women with red hair."

"Titian."

"What are you saying?"

"My hair. It's not red. It's titian."

"Okay, I'll amend that to say serious males and titian-haired women."

"In that case, I'm always free on Tuesday evenings."

EVERYBODY
WANTED
ROOM 623

1

When the desk clerk first mentioned Stefan Lauber's death, I didn't react. The truth is, I was only half listening. Although I came to see Stefan, I had agreed to meet him at the Cartledge Inn for my own reason. It was a good excuse to get away from the Clayton County Special Services, where I headed up the mental health unit.

Today I was in an especially low mood. The reason was James Burton. Burton, as he likes everyone to call him, is pastor of a church in this area, and we met at the Georgia coast a few months ago. He's the first genuine Christian with whom I ever talked. That's the trouble. I like him. Okay, more than that, I might even be in love with him, but I don't love his God. That is, I *think* I love Burton—and about four days a week I'm positive that I do. It's been a long time since any man has aroused my emotions like that curly-haired preacher.

Even if I do love him, the friendship can never lead to anything—not even a single kiss. Burton is so stubborn, he wouldn't let anything develop in our relationship—I mean a male-female connection. I can be his parishioner or a professional to whom he refers people in need. (And he's done that twice since we met.)

He also angers me. He's so likable. And kind. Okay, and he's cute—really cute. He's no hunk, but I'd settle for those dark blue eyes, and I'd love to run my fingers through those soft, dark brown curls.

Many times I've wished he'd make some kind of move on me, but he's so hung up on his religious commitment, and I'm too honest to fake the faith.

So that's how all of this started. As I approached the desk of the Cartledge Inn and asked for Mr. Lauber, my thoughts were centered on Burton.

It was the first time I had been to the inn, which was built out of red brick that had weathered and lightened over the decades into a pale, rose-colored patina. The double front door was made of thick, dark cherrywood. The place had originally been an inn, built around 1920, just after World War I. A few years ago, the present owners turned it into a retreat center and motel. It's located about three miles outside of Atlanta's Stone Mountain Park.

Because his words hadn't sunk in, I said to the clerk again, "Lauber. Stefan Lauber."

He stared at me.

"I think he's registered here."

"Didn't you hear what I said? He's dead." He leaned forward and whispered, "Murdered."

"Murdered?" I mouthed the word. "But how? I mean. . .I talked to him on the phone only yesterday." My response didn't make sense, but I was so shocked I wasn't thinking logically.

"Someone put him away last night." The clerk tugged at his magenta blazer. "I'll probably get in trouble for telling you this, but he was murdered right inside his room. Room 623."

The clerk adjusted the pin above his pocket, which read CRAIG BUBECK. "He was a nice man, too, and had been with us for several months. He didn't deserve to get murdered."

I wanted to ask whom he thought deserved to be murdered, but I didn't. Temporarily I had forgotten Burton. Right now I needed to process this information.

"He asked me to come see him this morning," I said, although I was talking to myself more than to the clerk. "He said it was important and. . ." I stopped myself before I began to babble.

"The police were here last night for more than two hours. At least that's what Doris said. She's the other clerk, and sometimes she exaggerates. They came back again this morning. They don't seem to want to stay away. Ghoulish, if you ask me. But after all, how much time do they need to search one room? A hotel room is a hotel room, and I have no idea why they searched the room again and again. I mean, how long does it take to search *one* room?" The fiftyish, wimpish clerk must have tipped the scales at 115 pounds. He rambled on, but I had stopped listening, to his obvious disgust.

"How was he murdered?" I asked to break his monologue.

"Shot. With a gun, you know. Right in the heart. At least that's what I heard." He pulled back slightly and looked around to make sure no one could hear. "I didn't see the body, you understand, but that's what Doris told me this morning. You see, this month, because of vacations, we're doing twelve-hour shifts and—"

"Do they know who did it? Do they know why someone killed Stefan—uh, Mr. Lauber?"

He shook his head. "The police don't know anything, or at least nothing that I've heard. Since you're asking, I'll tell you what I do know. Mr. Lauber called for room service at 4:22 and asked for a meal to be brought to him at 7:00. Wasn't that considerate of him? None of our other guests would think to order in advance. Anyway, when the waiter arrived, he knocked, and no one answered. The door was slightly ajar, so he assumed Mr. Lauber had left it open for him because maybe he was in the shower or something. Just as he pushed the door fully open, he called out, 'Room service.' "

"Yes?" I asked. "And what happened?"

"That's it."

"What do you mean by 'That's it'?"

"The body. Once he had stepped into the room, he spotted Mr. Lauber's body sprawled on the floor, facedown. Blood. Lots of blood."

"That must have been horrible."

"It certainly is. They'll have to replace the carpet. The owners hate it when the inn incurs unexpected expenses like that. He was shot. Didn't I mention that? Shot right in the heart with a .38. I don't know anything about guns, but Doris—"

"The other clerk—"

"Right, Doris told me. I didn't see anything myself, you understand, but this morning one of the detectives stopped at the desk and we talked. He told me a few other facts."

"Really?" I didn't mean anything by the question. I was processing information.

Craig must have assumed I doubted him, so he leaned forward again and whispered, "All right, he didn't actually tell me, but I overheard him on his cell phone when he told someone else. I was clever at it. I kept my back to him so he wouldn't think I was listening, but I heard every word. *Every single word.*"

Stunned, I couldn't say anything, and I must have looked like an utter fool with my mouth hanging open.

"Mr. Lauber didn't suffer, so that's a blessing. I'm sure of that fact, because on his cell, the detective said he died instantly."

I wondered why people thought that the news of instant death was supposed to comfort anyone. Whether they suffered three seconds or ten minutes or died instantly, they were still dead.

"Dead," I said. I finally had enough presence of mind to move away from the front desk. I walked toward two sofas upholstered in apricot-colored fabric. The antique tables matched the walls. The lobby definitely had an elegant look about it. I sat on the end of the sofa and pondered the situation. How odd that Stefan had been insistent—almost demanding—that I come to the inn to see him. He had apologized for asking but said it was extremely important. Now I wondered what "extremely important" meant.

I didn't know Stefan that well. I'm a therapist, and he had started to come to our mental health center. Because I'm the director, I don't see many clients. His coming in itself was odd because he could afford a private therapist. Most of our clients come because they have no insurance and they pay on a sliding scale, which goes all the way down to five dollars a session. Stefan said a friend had recommended me—a psychologist named David Morgan, whom I respected. Stefan freely admitted he could pay, and we billed him at the rate of sixty dollars an hour, which is our highest payment level. The fee hadn't seemed to faze him. Later I realized that money was certainly no problem for him.

At first he came once a week, and then he asked for twice-weekly appointments. "I have a number of things to think through," he said. "Business issues mostly, but being with you pushes me to return to my room and think seriously."

I studied him to be sure he wasn't flirting with me. Not that I would have minded, but I'm a therapist and nothing else, and now and then a man thinks he has to hit on me. I wouldn't have been able to date him if he had asked—which he didn't—but he was still quite a hunk. A little old for me by maybe ten or fifteen years. The wrinkles of wear around his eyes and mouth made him appear to be in his late forties—about ten years older than his actual age—but he could still get any woman's attention when he entered a room.

A week ago he asked if he could see me privately and if I would come to the Cartledge Inn. I don't usually do that, but I sensed he had serious problems—the kind that he was determined to resolve—and I was willing to provide individual attention to such clients. At our center we're moving toward a behavior-model therapy for everything, and we'll eventually do only group counseling to save money. Consequently, we've been mandated to accept fewer individual patients. Even though I granted Stefan personal sessions, he paid the center. I don't do private counseling as a sideline; that had never seemed ethical to me. Because of our policy change, the board of directors encouraged us to take a limited number of private patients if we felt they needed special help.

For the next few months, we're still able to accept patients who can pay the minimum scale or more if we believe they'll benefit. I felt Stefan Lauber was one of those individuals who had made amazing progress and wouldn't need a therapist long.

"Stefan is dead," I said to myself.

I was so caught up in the shock of the news that I didn't notice when someone walked past me to the counter, which was perhaps fifteen feet away. Only when I heard his voice did I look up.

"I'd like a room, please."

"I suppose you want room 623," Craig, the clerk, said.

"Sure, that's fine." His back was to me, but I would have recognized his voice anywhere. Sometimes I hear it in my sleep.

"Everybody wants 623," the clerk said. "And I can't let you have that one."

He chuckled. "Okay, give me something else."

Impulsively I got up and walked toward him. "Burton!"

He turned around and smiled. I hate that smile—it melts me every time. And those dark curls ought to be illegal on a man.

"Julie West!" he called out. "What are you doing here?"

"I came to see someone, but he's not in," I said.

"He's not in because he's dead," the clerk said. "Murdered."

"What's going on?" Burton looked from me to the clerk.

"That's why you can't have room 623," Craig said. "The police won't let me give it to anyone. With blood stains all over the carpet and the room all torn up,

I have no idea why anyone would want it anyway."

Burton moved forward and hugged me. It was a nice, friendly, brotherly kind of embrace. "Nice to see you again, Julie."

I hated that I had worn my lime green four-inch heels today. I'm five ten in bare feet and about half an inch taller than Burton anyway. Now I towered above him. But my colors were right. My hair is a shade of red someone called titian, after the painter, and it sounded exotic to me, so I tell everyone that's my color. *Red* is so, well, mundane. I wore a lime green suit with short sleeves. It wasn't formfitting, but I felt it made the best of my assets. Any shade of green seems to flatter me the most. For jewelry I wore only a copper-and-green malachite bracelet that complemented my complexion and my light brown eyes. I may not have looked chic, but it was my best outfit.

"She wanted to see Mr. Lauber," Craig said. "But then, everyone either wants to see him or wants his room. If you ask me, this is a strange place today."

I stared at the unprofessional clerk. He held a pen in his right hand, but it was shaking. "This has rattled you, hasn't it?" I asked.

"Rattled? That's all I can think about. My nerves are shot. Absolutely shot. I know I won't sleep tonight." He wasn't loud, but his voice had hit the higher registers, signaling that he was near hysteria. "It's bad enough to be a clerk in an inn where someone was murdered, but everyone keeps asking for that room—his room—for room 623. What kind of ghoulish people come here?"

Burton touched the man's hand gently and said, "You have had a bad time of this. I'm sorry." That was Burton in action. I've told him twenty times he ought to be a therapist instead of a pastor, but he has never listened to my advice. Burton's soothing voice worked its magic. "Can you take a few days' vacation or—"

The clerk snorted. "And miss all this action? Nothing like this has ever happened before." He spoke in a normal range again.

"But you are upset," I said. "Don't you think it would help if you took at least a day off?"

"My nerves are shot," he said, "but I'll. . .well, I'll carry on."

Burton continued to speak softly to the clerk, and I nodded at everything he said. That Burton is a natural at getting people to open up to him. Within two minutes the poor man told Burton all his other problems. He said something about his mother, who was in the early stages of senility, and added that he was an only child. He had dated a woman for nine years, and she'd finally called it off. "But as long as I had to take care of Mother, I couldn't have a wife, too, could I?"

I thought it would be more discreet if I moved away, so I went back to the sofa and sat down. I couldn't hear the rest, but within several minutes the man smiled. He grabbed Burton's hand and shook it vigorously.

Burton then came over to the sofa, sat on the other end, and turned toward me. "It's such a surprise to see you."

"A good surprise? Or a shock?" I love to say things like that.

"Good. Always it's good to see you."

"I suppose you want to know why I stopped attending your church."

"Not unless you want to tell me," he said. "But I have missed you. You came five Sundays and attended three of the new believers' meetings."

"You keep score on everyone?"

He grinned, and those perfect, movie-star teeth gleamed. "Sorry. I meant only that I was aware of your not being there. That's all."

"What are you doing here?" I asked. "Okay, I changed the subject, but—"

"I'm here for a private retreat."

"A private retreat? I don't get it. It sounds like something a priest or a monk would do." As I said, I love being a smart-mouth. I knew differently, but it also kept him talking to me.

"It's something I do at least once a year. Ben and Marcia Cartledge, the couple who own this place, are wonderful Christians, and they're members of an inner-city congregation. They offer free facilities for ministers of any denomination who need to spend a few days alone."

"Oh," I said. That's always an appropriate response when I don't know what to say.

"Occasionally I need to put my life on hold while I rethink my priorities," he said simply. "It's nice—really it is—to see you again."

"You've already said that. So it means we must be near the end of things to talk about."

"Or maybe we just need to get beyond the awkward stage," he said. "I'm absolutely surprised to run into you here."

"Remember when we met?" I asked. "That involved a murder, too—Roger Harden."

He aimed that powerful smile at me before he said, "You know, I just thought of the same thing."

Burton and I had been involved in solving the murder of Roger Harden at Palm Island off the coast. It was because of our meeting that I started to attend his church. I never told him, of course, but I was more fascinated by him than any of the things he said. He was probably a fine preacher. That hadn't been the reason I attended.

Just then an attractive woman in her early thirties brushed past us and stopped at the desk. "I'd like a room," she said. "I'd like room 623, please."

Craig glanced at us, shrugged, and rolled his eyes as if to ask, *"See what I mean?"*

2

I'm sorry, ma'am," the desk clerk said to the woman in a controlled voice but loud enough for us to hear. "Room 623 is not available."

"Oh, that's too bad. I spent my honeymoon here," she said. "I love that room. Are you sure it's not available?"

"Positive, but I can give you an excellent room on another floor."

Whatever Burton had said to the poor clerk had changed him into a quiet, controlled professional.

"Perhaps the room next to it, then," she said.

"I am sorry, ma'am, but the rooms on either side, 621 and 625, are also taken."

"Are you sure?"

"Yes, ma'am, but I'll check anyway." He paused, clicked a few keys, and stared at the screen. "Yes, ma'am. They are both occupied, and—"

"Across the hall, then?"

"I was about to tell you that rooms 622, 624, and 626 are also occupied. Though two of those will be vacant later today. However, I can give you a lovely room on the floor above. Room 723 is vacant and has the same dusty salmon color with a soft turquoise base as 623. Both rooms offer a superb view of the lake, which is the reason most guests want a room on the north side. In fact, some of our guests have thought rooms 723 and 823 have an even better view because—"

"No, no, that won't do," she said. She stood there, apparently in contemplation. Her back was to me, but her burnt orange acrylic nails tapped the counter. "I so wanted to stay there. You see, my husband died three months ago. Our plan had been to come here for our tenth anniversary. That's tomorrow."

She was a tall, beautifully built woman. Because I couldn't see her face, I shifted my position. I still couldn't see, so I held up my hand for Burton to wait, and I walked within five feet of her and behind the desk as if I were going down one of the two passageways. I stopped and examined her closely for a few seconds. That's just the way I am: I'm curious about people, especially one as unusual as this woman.

My presence didn't matter; she seemed lost in her own thoughts and unaware that I had approached the desk. She wore a simple navy blue tailored suit that showed her figure to full advantage. Her cloth-covered pumps were obviously

161

made to match the suit. She had curly black hair that barely brushed her shoulders. I figured the hair was probably dyed, because the color was too perfect. She had high cheekbones and the classical line of nose and chin. Her skin texture was smooth. She would have been a beautiful woman except that only her mouth smiled. Her dark eyes remained expressionless. I thought that full, rich mouth had probably become quite accomplished at showing the full range of human emotion, but the eyes looked as if they were dead. If eyes are the windows to the soul, no one could see inside that woman.

Her thick, dark hair fell across one eye, and she pushed it away from her face. That drew my attention and I stared at those acrylic nails. Why would anyone choose such an outlandish color? Except for those nails, she could have been a model—an older version—but she definitely had that kind of beauty.

I might have remained focused on the nails except that I knew she had lied to the clerk. I could tell by her body posture. Most people have some giveaway signals, and the way she held her body was my clue. I wondered why she concocted such a story. Who cared why she wanted the room?

I walked back and sat down next to Burton. He knew me well enough that he didn't say anything. He, too, watched the action at the desk.

"I do apologize, ma'am," the clerk said to her, "but it's not—"

"Surely there is some way. If you would explain my situation to the person who currently occupies room 623—"

"I'm sorry. It truly is not available."

"But please. Maybe I could talk to him, or her, or whoever." Her right hand held up two twenty-dollar bills.

The clerk's eyes focused on the money before he said, "I'm sorry."

She added two more bills.

Even I could see the temptation in Craig's eyes, and before she could interrupt him again, he said, "You see, the police have, uh, sealed off that room. There was a crime committed there. You know, like on television—"

"That's terrible. How soon will they finish?" Her hand dropped to the counter, and I couldn't see what she did with the bills.

This time he shrugged. "I can give you 423 or 523. Would that work for you?"

"When will the room be available?" The voice was louder and slightly harsh.

"I don't know. Maybe not for days," he said. "The police wouldn't tell me."

She mumbled something and turned away. She stuffed something inside her shoulder bag, and I assumed it was the money that Craig had reluctantly turned down.

I marveled at her again. I revised my opinion: She wore a little too much makeup, but it was expertly applied. Everything about her was perfect, everything except for those garish nails.

At that moment she turned my way and our eyes met. She must have realized

I had been listening, because she smiled with only her mouth while those lifeless eyes stared at me. She cleared her throat, and I sensed she wanted me to think she was slightly embarrassed. "Just seems terrible for a murder to take place in such a quiet setting."

"How did you know it was a murder?" I asked.

"Oh, uh, I assumed. . ."

Again I knew she was lying, and I wondered why. So what if she knew it had been a murder? What was the big deal?

She turned again and faced the clerk. "All right, give me a room as close to 623 as you can, on the north side of the building."

"As you like." He attempted a professional smile. He wasn't gifted that way, and his smile appeared forced. He would have done better to have remained expressionless. He clicked on his keyboard, but I believe he already knew what rooms were available. "I can give you 629 or 631 or—"

"Fine. Anything. Give me 629."

He handed her a form to fill out and asked for her credit card. I don't know why I watched, but I did. For a second time, I got up from the sofa and edged closer so I could hear and observe everything.

"Thank you, Ms. Knight." He laid the credit card imprint on the counter for her to sign before handing her a key. "We still use keys here instead of the magnetically keyed cards. Our owners think it retains more of the ambiance of a quaint and quiet—"

"Whatever," she said, grabbing the key and walking toward where I assumed the elevators were. Because she didn't hesitate, it was obvious she really had been here before. Maybe she had come on her honeymoon. But after ten years, would she still remember which way to the elevators? Maybe she wouldn't.

As soon as she was out of view, Burton turned to me. "Doesn't that strike you as odd? Several people wanting room 623?" He got up and walked to the desk. "How many people have asked for 623?"

"Three. Maybe four. Five. I don't remember, but this is strange," the clerk said. "I mean really strange, as in insane. The police haven't released the information that he was murdered in room 623, only that a man was found dead in the Stone Mountain area. They certainly didn't say it happened here at the Cartledge Inn, and I've watched the news on CNN and Channel 2. So why would all these people want the same room?"

"Yes, that is strange," Burton said.

"Bizarre," Craig said.

Again Burton asked for a room and told Craig he had a reservation. He added, "You can put me anywhere you want." He pulled a card from his wallet. "This is to show I'm an ordained minister and—"

The clerk nodded. "Thank you." He found the reservation and said, "Yes, there is no charge for the room." He asked Burton how long he planned to stay (three nights) and gave him room 430. "Unless you don't want to be part of this ongoing stream of traffic; in that case I can put you in 315 or 316—that's in the south wing."

"That's fine. I don't need traffic." He smiled and added, "I came here to be alone."

After Burton filled out the information card and received his key, he turned to me. "It's been good to see you again," he said. "My luggage is in the car, so I suppose I'd better get it." He started to walk toward the entrance.

I didn't want him to walk away, but I couldn't think of anything to hold him. As I turned around, I bumped into a tall, broad-shouldered man.

"Sorry, miss," he said.

"Ollie! What are you doing here?" Burton called out. He turned around and walked back over to the man. They did the male, A-frame-hug thing with about five pats on each other's back, which doesn't make any sense to me.

"Hey, Julie," Burton said, "I want you to meet an old friend of mine." He introduced him as Oliver Viktor. They had been classmates in college. "Ollie was a member of our church for a couple of years until he moved over here to the east side of town. What was that? Five years ago?"

"Yeah, five or six."

I smiled at Ollie, but I immediately didn't like him, and I wasn't sure why. I usually like most people, so I figured my reaction spoke more about me than it did about Ollie.

"This is the man who tried to lead me astray many times!" Burton said and laid his arm on his friend's shoulder. "We did a lot of crazy things in college—"

"No, *you* did the crazy things," Ollie said. "I was merely the mastermind behind the brilliant ploys and fabulous activities."

Burton laughed. "He's right, you know. He was the trickster—"

"The brilliant thinker and mastermind genius is what this low-level pastor means—"

"Uh, as I said, Ollie was the trickster and planner behind a lot of pranks and—"

"But always in good taste," Ollie said.

"Oh, really?" Burton looked at me. "Good taste? How does this sound? We had a boring speaker at our commencement—"

"Boring sounds mild," Ollie said, but he grinned and obviously enjoyed this trip down memory lane. "I felt I was doing something uncommonly good for the entire graduating class."

"We'd heard that speaker a couple of times before—"

"And he always ran over the allotted time when he spoke." Ollie shook his head and frowned. "That's what got me the most. If they allotted him thirty minutes, he took forty or forty-five—"

"Right, so Ollie got the idea of how he could shut him up." Burton blushed and looked away to hide it. "What we did. . .well, it—it wasn't kind."

Ollie shrugged. He looked like a man who shrugged a lot. "We weren't trying to be kind. Only effective. And it was fun."

"Okay, yes, to a couple of twenty-two-year olds, it *seemed* like fun when we planned it, but—"

"It was fun," Ollie said, "and it worked."

I had already entered Zone Total Boredom by then and I honestly didn't care, but it was obvious that such pranks were an important part of their relationship. So I asked the right question: "What outrageous things did you two guys do at your commencement?"

Burton rewarded me with one of his heart-melting smiles. "Uh, well—"

"The president of the college knew I was into all kinds of—uh, well, youthful pranks," Ollie interrupted in a voice he intended to come across as modest. "So I had to divert him."

"Yeah, divert is right." Burton shook his head, and his eyes made me realize he thought it was a terrible thing to do. "You see, Julie, it did seem like fun at the time. We thought only of ourselves, not about the feelings of anyone else or—"

"Hey, don't start that," Ollie said. "He was a stuffy jerk, and he deserved what happened. So tell her."

"Ollie convinced me to give up my alarm clock and set the alarm for 4:00— the time the speaker, Dr. Garrar Terashita, was scheduled to end."

"What a hoot! What pandemonium!" Ollie laughed and whacked Burton on the shoulder. "The old buzzard was in the middle of a sentence, and the alarm rocked the building. Everyone just stared for a minute or so. They couldn't figure out what caused the noise or where it came from. Seven of us knew what was going on, and we laughed the loudest—"

"I didn't laugh," Burton said. "I saw that poor man's face and realized what a mean—"

"Oh yeah, I forgot," Ollie said. "And after the ceremony, my good friend lectured me over the evils of our ways. That's what he said, but I really think he was most upset because he had lost his alarm clock." Ollie winked at me as if I were supposed to laugh with him.

I didn't laugh.

"Yes, it was insane with noise. Our little group laughed," Burton said, "but I felt sorry for the faculty, especially the president and the others sitting behind Dr. Terashita."

"What happened?" I asked. "I assume they figured out the source of the noise." I didn't like playing the straight role for Burton's comic friend, but I felt I had to do it.

"Finally the dean of students and a couple of the profs ran toward the podium." Ollie's voice had become louder, and he roared as if it were the first time he had ever told of his great escapade. "It took the dean a few more seconds to find the alarm clock. You know why? Because I had taken Burton's clock and buried it inside the flower stand that was in front of that podium."

That still didn't seem funny to me, but I hadn't been there, so maybe it had been funny. Regardless, in my newly volunteered role, I knew the next question to ask. "Did you get into trouble?"

"Nah," Ollie said. "They questioned me, and I said, 'I did not put that alarm clock inside the flower stand'—deep inside so they had to remove the flowers to get to it." He winked at me. "See, I told the truth."

"That was because they didn't ask if you had planned it."

Ollie shrugged. "But Burton here was such a good boy, no one ever would have suspected he would do such a devious thing."

"So you got away with it?"

"We got away with it, but—"

"But what?" I asked. There. I had done my duty. That would be my last question.

"Preacher boy confessed."

"You did *what*?" I hadn't planned to ask that one, but it made me respect Burton a lot more. Not that I needed to respect him more. "That must have taken a lot of guts."

"I don't know about guts," Burton said. "What we did wasn't right, and it disrupted everything. Dr. Terashita was so embarrassed and hurt that he didn't try to finish his speech. As he threw his papers together, I saw the pain in his eyes, and I knew I had done a rotten thing." He turned his gaze toward Ollie. "And it was a very, very mean thing to do."

"Aw, c'mon, it was fun—"

"Not that one." Burton shook his head. "But the other things this evil genius did weren't so bad. At least that's the only time I was aware of someone being hurt."

"What about the effigy?" Ollie prompted. As he said those words, I began to realize why I didn't like him.

"I didn't have anything to do with that, and if I had known, I would have refused to participate," Burton said. "It was one of your few plans I refused to join in with. Remember?"

"Yeah, I forgot. You had gotten so lame by then, but that was all right, because I got some other guys—guys who appreciated a good joke."

I hoped we were ready to move on, but Ollie explained that he detested one professor, the man who taught most of the required English classes. "Boring old guy," Ollie muttered. So he talked two other students into helping him. They stole a scarecrow from a farmer's field, hung it in the quadrant, wrote the professor's name on a placard, and pinned it to its chest. "You know, I can't remember the old buzzard's name."

"Hawkins. Dr. Robert Hawkins IV," Burton said softly. "I liked him and learned from him—"

"Oh yeah, maybe you did, but he bored me."

"Are you easily bored?" I asked and hoped that would change the subject.

Ollie shrugged for the third time. I had been correct—he was one of those frequent shruggers. But then, he had the shoulders for it. "Oh, before you ask, I'll bet you can't guess why I'm here."

"It certainly can't be to ask for room 623, can it?" That was a smart-mouthed remark said in my most sarcastic tone. I felt I was back in my own territory—at last.

"How did you know about that room?" Ollie stared at me and seemed genuinely surprised.

This time I shrugged—exaggerating the movement for his benefit. I don't think he caught my mockery.

"Hey, I don't know how you figured that out," Ollie said, "but yeah, that's why I'm here. It's room 623. But how—"

"The clerk told us," Burton said quickly. He knows me, and he could see I was getting ready to make another smart remark.

"Okay, okay, dumb clerk," Ollie said. He turned to me and grinned. I think he thought his conversation charmed me. Okay, for some women that would have been charming, especially when those green eyes lit up. I admitted to myself that he was as handsome as any man I'd ever met. He probably pumped iron five hours every day. His ash blond hair had barely begun to recede on top, so it was nice to see that he was flawed, even if only a little.

"You see, Julie, I work for the DeKalb County Police Department. I'm here to investigate a murder."

"A murder?" I said and batted my eyes a couple of times. I figured out that the Cartledge Inn was in DeKalb County and not inside Stone Mountain, which made it a county matter.

"Yeah, scary stuff, huh?"

"The murder? Who was murdered?" Burton asked.

"Stefan Lauber," I said. "In room 623. Right, Detective?"

"Yeah, that's right."

"Who was he?" Burton asked.

Ollie held up his hand. "Wait a minute, missy. How do you know about this murder and his name? Don't tell me the clerk blabbed that much. We haven't released his name to the public."

"Not exactly the clerk's fault," I said because I didn't want to cause any trouble for Craig. "I'm a therapist. Stefan is a client. . .was a client, and—"

"And you make house calls?" There was that grin again, but it soon disappeared as the upper lip curled into a sneer.

I wanted to slap the expression off his face, but I restrained myself. "Not ordinarily, but this was special," I said. "Mr. Lauber asked me to come here. He said it was extremely important.".

Ollie's eyes traveled from my head to my feet and back to my face. "Yeah, I can guess that it was special."

His attitude shocked me so badly I was momentarily speechless. If I had been fifteen years old, I would have punched him in the nose, regardless of his size.

"She really is a therapist," Burton said.

"Okay, so you're a real shrink," he said. "Sorry if I misunderstood, but with looks like yours and—"

"Let's leave it at that," I said.

He gave another shrug. "Lauber told you it was extremely important, or so you said?"

"That's correct. *He* said it was extremely important."

"In what way?" Ollie asked. "What made it important? Was it also urgent?"

I smiled softly to deflect my response. "As I've already said, I'm his therapist. That's privileged and confidential information." I knew I could tell him what he wanted to know, but I've heard that line in so many movies, I wanted to use it. It felt good to say those words.

"But he's dead now. So you can tell me, right?"

"It was confidential. He bared his soul to me because he trusted me."

"What do I care about his bared soul? You want to help us catch the murderer," Ollie said, "so come on, open up."

I didn't want to tell him anything except to say firmly, "Get out of here and leave us so I can talk to Burton." But there was something else. I couldn't understand why I hesitated. Ollie was a detective, and I couldn't think of a single reason not to tell him everything, but that intuitive nudge held me back.

Something about that detective bothered me, and I no longer blamed it on myself. This man's hat wasn't worn right, as my dad used to say. I stared at his ash blond hair, his green eyes. I estimated him at about six three or perhaps even an inch taller. Broad-shouldered, he had probably played football in college. I suppose it was his attitude that put me off. Maybe he was used to pushing people around. When he talked, it was almost as if he expected people to give him whatever he wanted—as if it were his right. Maybe that's why Burton had yielded to him in college. Ollie must have always been heavy-handed and demanding like that.

"I thought you detectives always came in pairs," I said in what I hoped was my innocent voice. "You know, so that one keeps the other honest."

"Yeah, usually. Two police officers investigated last night—"

"And you can handle everything by yourself?" (I knew he wouldn't catch the sarcasm.)

"Yeah, sure, but that's not the reason. In follow-up work like this, they usually send only one detective."

"I'm sure you'll do a thorough job," Burton said.

"Could we get out of here?" I asked as a ploy so I could do some quick thinking. "This is rather public, and you're asking about a man's inner life." Instead of waiting for him to take charge, I started to walk toward the front door and smiled to myself. It felt good to take control of the situation, even if it would last only another twenty seconds.

I turned and he followed. I motioned for Burton to join us, and to my delight he raised his right eyebrow as if to ask, "Me?" I nodded and said, "Sure. Come and join us." I turned forward and moved on. I heard Burton's footsteps behind me. From the front door, I spotted a sign with arrows that read NATURE WALK. Apparently I could have turned either way. I read once that most people automatically turn right, so I turned left.

Although I had never been to the Cartledge Inn before, people who live in metro Atlanta know the grounds are lovely, featuring large sections of native Georgia plants. According to a small sign at the far end, we could walk among forty buddleia bushes of five different colors. Buddleia was one of the few names I knew, although most people just call them butterfly bushes. I love the fragrance the plant sends out and the constant attraction of butterflies and bumblebees.

Because I wore my heels, I used that as an excuse to walk slower. I didn't know how much to tell Burton's buddy, and the walk gave me almost a full minute to think. A slight breeze caused the rosemary plants' evergreen needle–like leaves to hang heavily in the air.

About thirty feet ahead, I saw two comfortable-looking benches that faced each other. They had been placed between Southern magnolia trees. It was early June, and several of their creamy white flowers already filled the branches. I think the magnolia is not only the most fragrantly beautiful tree, but the flower itself has such a fragile look. I have rarely seen anything nicer than the white blossoms, although I hate the long, hard leaves that take four or five years to become mulch. Still, the flowers are worth the nuisance of the leaves.

I sat on one bench. Ollie and Burton took the other. I knew Burton well enough to know that he wanted to be alone for his private retreat, but he was also curious enough that he didn't want to leave and miss out on the conversation. I smiled to myself, because I was quite sure I was reading his struggle accurately.

Somewhere behind me the overpowering fragrance of honeysuckle wafted through the air. I don't mind honeysuckle, but it causes some people to sneeze or develop sinus headaches. I didn't like it today because the cloying fragrance overwhelmed the magnolia.

"So what can you tell me?" Ollie asked, leaning toward me.

"Aren't you supposed to take out a pen and a little notebook?" I asked. "They always do that on *Law and Order*."

"This is just plain law. Georgia law and my order," Ollie said, impatience apparent in his voice.

"That's a good line," I said. "Do you use it often?"

"Nah. Just popped out." He smiled, oblivious to my sarcasm.

Most women would have called him a hunk, and I suppose he was. Underneath the gray shell blazer, I sensed he had taut, well-toned muscles.

"What do you want to know?" I decided not to make it easy for him.

Burton leaned forward. "Julie, please don't. Be nice to the man. Okay?"

"You know me too well," I said to Burton. "Okay, here it goes. First, did you know Stefan Lauber had been in prison?"

"Tell me about that," Ollie said. He took out the obligatory notebook and pen. This time he played the role of a cool cop. He wanted information, but he wasn't going to tell me anything he knew.

"Suppose you tell me about his prison term, and then I'll tell you why he came to see me." I stared into his eyes, daring him to intimidate me.

"How well do you know this dame?" he asked Burton.

"Dame?" I said and laughed. "That sounds like something Humphrey Bogart would have said in a 1941 movie. In fact, he did say that in the *Maltese Falcon*, didn't he?"

"We just bumped into each other a few minutes ago," Burton said, "but Julie and I were involved in solving the murder of Roger Harden, the multimillionaire. Do you know about that case?"

"Yeah, that's right. I saw it reported on TV, but I had forgotten. Great amateur work, but this is a professional investigation and—"

"Very good," I said. "And since we're all professionals, let's share." This time I not only told him I was a therapist but added that I held a PhD (and that did impress him). "And Burton—"

"Yeah, he's got a doctorate as well. I'm lucky to have finished college and received an undergrad degree. So we're all professionals, but different kinds of professionals." He stared back as if daring me to argue.

"You share. I share," I said. "If you don't want to share, you'll have to get a legal order for me to talk to you." I didn't know if that was true, but the police shows use that kind of insipid dialogue, and it felt good to repeat the words.

"Hey, Burton. It's easy to see why you like this broad. She's a real hottie and she's—"

"A broad? A hottie?" I stood up. "Obviously, this is not a meeting of *professionals*." I wasn't really offended. I liked the crude flattery, but I wouldn't let him know that.

"Ma'am, I apologize," he said with exaggerated emphasis. He spoke the words, but his eyes told me his apology was insincere.

"So you start." I gave him what I call my alluring smile, the kind that's supposed to make others think I'm enchanted with everything that pours from their lips. "You already knew he was in prison, right?" I decided to throw that in so he could see that I used my professional intuition. Actually it was only a guess, but his face told me I was correct.

"Very good. I'm impressed." Ollie rewarded me with a full grin. "Yes, I knew he was in prison. He received a three-year sentence for receiving stolen goods. Which was all they could convict him of. That is, they found the stolen money but not the diamonds—"

"I think I remember that case," Burton said. "It was a jewel robbery of a courier from Antwerp."

"Amsterdam," Ollie corrected. "The courier carried about one hundred million dollars worth of polished diamonds and half a mil in cash."

Ollie told us the background. A known criminal, Willie Petersen, and a woman later identified as Cynthia Salzmann ambushed the man in the long-term parking lot of Hartsfield-Jackson Airport. Apparently the man struggled, and in the altercation, Petersen shot him. The couple fled with the pouch of diamonds and money. Forensics was able to lift Petersen's fingerprints from the door of the courier's car, and the police tracked him down. When accused, he implicated Lauber.

"I wasn't involved in that case," Ollie said, "but I've read the report. They found the cash, which Lauber said Petersen had brought to him and asked him to invest. According to Lauber, who was a legitimate investment broker, Petersen said he had never trusted banks and had been saving the money in his home, or some incredibly dumb story like that."

"But Petersen said Lauber had planned the heist. Wasn't that the story?" Burton asked.

"Exactly. Lauber was a stockbroker. In the previous few months, the SEC and the police suspected—" He held up his hand and said, "Only *suspected*, but were unable to prove, that he was involved in several shady dealings. When it finally came to trial, it was his word against Petersen's."

"That hardly seems like enough to convict anyone," I said.

"Petersen had brought the money into Lauber's office in cash. All in hundred-dollar bills, all still banded with the name of an Amsterdam bank. The information was in the media. Now how many people would have blithely accepted that much cash without some questions?"

"Good point," I said.

"So the jury convicted him. If Lauber had reported the money, nothing would have happened. But the dumb jerk stuck the money in an office closet, and get this—" Ollie raised his voice as he added, "Not only was the money there intact, but it was still in the attaché case that Petersen had stolen. The name of the diamond-polishing firm was on the case—Coster—one of the best-known firms in Europe. The name was right on the case. Petersen insisted Lauber was the brains behind the robbery."

"Didn't they connect Lauber with the diamonds?" I asked.

"They tried, but they had no case," the detective said. "They didn't find the diamonds in his office or anyplace else they searched."

"A jury did convict Lauber, but only of receiving stolen property, is what I remember," Burton said.

"And what about the diamonds?" I asked. "What happened to them?"

"They never turned up. Dead end no matter where the investigation went. I've always believed Lauber hid them and had them ready for a nice retirement plan when he was paroled about five months ago."

"So you think Lauber was murdered for the diamonds?" I asked.

"Reasonable guess, wouldn't you say?" Ollie said. "But we have absolutely nothing to link him to the diamonds. The missing diamonds aren't within my purview—"

"Purview? Nice word," I said.

Burton frowned at me.

"Makes good sense," I said.

"I wish I knew a little more about Stefan Lauber," Ollie said and leaned back. "Now why don't you talk to me? So far I'm the only one giving information. Now it's your turn, so you can help me learn something more about Lauber."

"I also can speak to the answer of that question," a man's voice said. "Did I not know him? Was I not his friend?"

All of us looked up and stared at a man with the smoothest ebony complexion I'd ever seen.

3

Yes, for a long time I have known Mr. Stefan Lauber," the man said as he walked from behind one of the magnolia trees. I hadn't seen him approach, and his presence took us by surprise. I wondered if he had been hiding behind one of the trees.

Not only his syntax but his accent made it clear that he was an African. All the black men I had ever seen were one shade of brown or another, but this man was truly black. His head was shaved, although he had roots for a full head of hair. I assumed he was in his early thirties or maybe late twenties. He was about my height, when I don't wear my heels. He looked healthy enough, but he also was like a man whose skin was stretched over a live skeleton. I didn't know how he could be so thin and yet not look emaciated. Maybe it was his grin and the beautiful white teeth that made me know he was strong, wiry, and healthy.

"And who are you?" Ollie asked.

"Was I not listening to what you say here?"

"I suppose you were," I said. "And you knew Stefan Lauber. How? What was your connection?"

"May I sit with you?" he asked. Without waiting for a reply, he came around and sat on the bench next to me. He wore a plain white T-shirt and sharply pressed shorts, bright red and made of coarse cotton, like muslin.

"My name is Jason Omore," he said, "and I am from Kenya, and I am the grandson and the son of a chief of the Luo tribe from Suna Location." He held out both hands to me and asked my name. After I told him, he turned to Burton and then to Ollie.

"What do you have to tell us?" Ollie asked instead of giving his name.

"Please indulge my cultural background," Jason said. "In my country it is not polite to discuss anything if we are not introduced."

Ollie must have realized the sensible thing to do was to introduce himself, so as to not antagonize the man. He gave his name and said he was a DeKalb County homicide detective. "And now, tell us something besides your name."

"I am here to study as a foreign student, and I am enrolled at Emory University where I am writing my dissertation."

"A dissertation? That means a doctoral degree." I looked at Jason, but I said that for Ollie's benefit. I'm sure he knew, but I wanted to antagonize him a little more.

"In what field?" Burton said a little too quickly. He must have sensed my attitude and tried to intervene.

"In the field of behavioral psychology. Has not my government sent me here to earn my doctoral degree so that I may return and teach behavioral psychology?" He smiled, and his face seemed to glow. "I did my intern work at the Floyd County Prison in Rome." He meant Rome, Georgia, which is about an hour north of us under good driving conditions. "Mr. Lauber was an inmate, was he not? I was able to have many interviews with him. As a matter of great fact, I did a case study of six different inmates. He was the most fascinating, was he not?"

"Do you always give information by asking a question?" Ollie asked.

"Do I?" He laughed. "It is a habit. You Americans seem to like that style, so I have cultivated it. And now I use it often, do I not?"

Burton burst out laughing, and so did I.

"I don't like it," Ollie said.

"Should I then choose not to use it?"

"That's enough," Ollie said. He had obviously figured out that he had become the butt of the joke. "Tell me what you know about Lauber."

Jason Omore was sharp. He was my kind of man.

"He was a criminal and convicted of a lesser crime for which he had committed a greater crime," the African said. "He is—he was—a most complex man and one that many thought had no conscience. Even I did not think so during the first two interviews I had with him."

"But you changed your mind about him?" I asked before Ollie could stop me.

"Yes, that is so. I changed my mind because he changed his way."

"He changed? He reformed? Is that what you mean?" Burton asked. "Or did he just hold back at first?"

"Is that not a good question you have asked about Lauber?" Jason gazed into space as if to measure his words. "I shall have to consider that."

Jason's gaze shifted among our faces. In the distance someone started a lawn mower. The constant rustle of leaves and the gentle breeze against my bare arms felt good. I love Atlanta weather, although the humidity is sometimes a little much for tourists. A male and female cardinal flew into the closer magnolia tree and flitted around for several seconds. I assumed it was some kind of mating dance.

As we waited for Jason to continue, Ollie tapped his foot. His eyes hardened. His chin jutted out. He had all the signs of a man of intense anger. I wondered if he'd explode at me. Maybe I could help him a little and see how long it took.

"I shall tell you, but sometimes you Americans do not seem to understand." He took a deep breath. "Mr. Lauber underwent a conversion experience less than two weeks before his release."

"A conversion? You mean like being born again?" Burton asked.

"Yes, is that not so? Is that not exactly what I mean?" Jason smiled at him. "So you do know the meaning of such language?"

"I'm a pastor. I've also undergone a conversion experience, have I not?"

I couldn't help myself. I roared at Burton's response because I knew he felt as I did about Jason.

Ollie only tapped his foot faster.

"Ah, then you do understand. That is most good."

"Just get on with it," Ollie said. "We're all Christians, okay? We understand the lingo."

I didn't know whether to object to the label that included me, but it didn't seem appropriate to correct Ollie, so I kept still. Besides, I wanted to hear the story.

Jason told us that Lauber made drastic changes in his behavior. "Because you understand the language, I can say it to you in the language of Christians, may I not?" Before Ollie could interrupt, he said, "My friend—that is, Mr. Lauber, who became my friend—truly repented of his sinful ways and chose to follow the Lord Jesus Christ and was baptized while he was an inmate in prison. Is that not the way it is done here in America, as well?"

"Yes, that's the way," Burton said. He laid a hand on Ollie's shoulder. It was obvious Burton had realized Jason wasn't going to go any faster or give any more information than he chose. It was also obvious that Ollie's irritation was nearing the explosion point.

"That is also why I am here at the Cartledge Inn to work. Mr. Lauber became not only my friend, but my mentor, as well. He has paid for me to stay here in this place for six months. I could have stayed near Emory and worked part-time, but he chose to help me. I think it will not take me much longer to finish my dissertation and then to defend it. Is that not so?"

"Probably," I said and intentionally veered from the subject of Stefan Lauber. "It took me about five months, and I did nothing else. I was exhausted when I finished mine."

"Can we get back on topic?" Ollie asked. It was obvious that he was working hard to control his voice.

"Yes, and there is one thing more I can tell you," Jason said. "Because you are an *askari*—pardon, I mean a policeman, I think this is what you must want to know. Mr. Lauber had in his possession a certain number of stolen diamonds." He paused and stared at the detective. "You knew that much, did you not?"

4

"You *knew* Stefan had the diamonds?" I asked Jason. "So he was involved in the theft."

He nodded. "And does not this policeman also know that fact?"

As we sat outside the Cartledge Inn, Jason Omore's words shocked us. Or maybe they shocked only me. Ollie jumped from the bench and took a step forward, almost as if he were intent on grabbing Jason's T-shirt, but Burton's arm on his shoulder pulled him back.

"Easy, my friend," Burton said softly.

"But you know—you know for certain that he was in possession of the diamonds?" Ollie's voice grew louder.

"If your question is to ask if I saw the diamonds, the answer, of course, is that I did not see them."

"So you don't know—"

"But if you want to know what he told me—told me but did not show me—then, yes, I can tell you most assuredly that Mr. Lauber had the diamonds."

I liked Jason better all the time. He had that delightful sense of humor I love in people. He might be a foreigner, but he knew how to get to people like Ollie.

"Of course that's what I want to know." Ollie sighed loudly. "Are you trying to play some kind of game with me?"

"Would I do such a thing?" Jason asked.

Ollie glared at him.

"But, yes, to respond to your question, Stefan had possession of the diamonds. He also told me that he planned to return them. Did you not know that as well?"

"How would I know?" Ollie said.

"Is that not why you have come?"

"I came to investigate his *death*," Ollie said, and it was obvious from the tight-lipped way he spoke that he was nearing the explosion point. "A few people in law enforcement assumed Lauber had the stones, but we could never prove it. If we could have proven it, he would still be in prison."

"Did you believe he had them?" I asked.

"I came to finish up the report on the death of a man in this hotel. Just that."

"Did you know he had the stolen diamonds?" Burton asked me. "I mean,

176

when he met with you, did he admit that to you?"

"He never said anything directly to me about them." I thought about my last conversation with Stefan. "I wonder if that's why he wanted me to meet him here. . .to talk about them."

"Yes, is that not so?" Jason said. "He told me that he was going to speak with you today because you are a person of good conscience."

"Good conscience?" I laughed. "What does that mean?"

"Those were his true words. He also told me that he would compensate you well for your efforts. More than that, I cannot say. My *rafiki*—my friend—told me he trusted you. That is how much I know."

"That's news to me," I said, but I felt quite flattered.

"Yes, it may be news to you," Jason said, "but I know he trusted you and wanted you to be the one to return the diamonds."

"Me? Why would he ask me to—"

"So where are the diamonds?" Ollie interrupted. "You said you haven't seen them, but do you know where they are?"

Jason shook his head. "No, it is true that I have not seen them, *bwana*—uh, sir. He said he had placed them in a safe place. 'A very safe place' were his exact words. He said he placed them there before he went into *gaol*—uh, prison. He told me that he also had funds—large sums of money—secreted in a total of twelve places, but I do not know where, so do not, please, to ask that question."

"I'm trying to get all the information I can," Ollie said. He scribbled a few notes in his notebook. "And I think you have more to tell me, so how about if—" Ollie's cell phone buzzed, and he excused himself and walked about ten feet away. He turned his back to us. We could hear nothing—and it wasn't that I didn't try to listen.

As he stood there, I detected a slight tremor in his right hand. *Nerves?* I wondered.

He closed his phone, turned toward us, and said, "I have to leave now." His gaze shifted to the African. "I know where to reach you, Jason, so don't leave here." Before Jason could respond, he said to me, "And I have more questions for you to answer, so tell me where—"

"Are you going to arrest me?" Even nonsuspects said that on the TV cop shows.

"Don't act stupid," he said. He handed me his business card. Burton stuck out his hand and took one as well.

"In that case, take this." I handed him my card. "If you want to call, try my cell first. That's the easier way to get me."

He snatched my card and hurried away from us. I thought the action was abrupt, but the phone call may have been the reason. Or maybe that's who Ollie Viktor was and the way he always behaved.

"I must also leave you," Jason said. "I am here in room 300. I take only two breaks during the day. This is my first one, such as I am doing at this moment. I go outside on these grounds so that I may stretch the legs, as you call it." He grinned before he added, "Do I not?"

Burton patted him on the back. "I love your humor."

"And so do I," I said.

"Yes, is it not wonderful to be able to laugh?" Jason shook our hands and hurried away from us past the magnolia tree.

As he left us, I looked at my watch. It was only 11:20. "I know you came here for some kind of spiritual retreat," I said, "but you probably eat lunch. Unless you're here on some kind of fast. Even though it's a little early, would you—"

"Good idea, and you'll be my guest."

"And, Mr. Burton," I said, "I was taught that the person who invites, pays. Or are you going to be one of those old-fashioned macho types who insist—"

"But you didn't ask."

"Was that not implied in my question?" I tried to do my best to imitate Jason Omore's accent and cadence.

He held up both hands. "Surrender. You win. Why don't you buy me lunch?"

He and I turned and started back toward the hotel. His eyes focused on the building, and he obviously counted to the sixth floor. He had been there before, so I assumed he knew where 623 would be.

"Look! Someone's in that room! In 623!"

I followed the direction of his pointing fingers. A woman moved quickly past the window. I recognized her. "It's the widow," I said.

"The who?"

"You met her. The woman with those hideous orange-colored nails?"

He stared at me, frowning.

"Never mind." I grabbed his arm. "Let's go. I don't know how fast I can travel in these heels, so I'm hanging on." Of course, I had another reason to hang on, but that excuse worked.

Burton led me to the elevators, and one of them was open. In less than three minutes, we were outside room 623. The police had not put up one of those yellow ribbons, which I thought was good. Or maybe they only put up yellow crime-scene tape on TV.

I released Burton's arm and rushed ahead. I knocked loudly on the door. "Maid service!"

There was no answer, so I yelled again and tried the knob. "Maid service!"

"Can you come back?" A woman's voice answered.

"Gotta come in now," I said. "No come later." That was my attempt at Hispanic-style English.

A few seconds passed before she opened the door. She glared at me. "You're not the maid!"

"You're not the sentimental widow either!" I said and pushed the door open. Burton and I both stepped inside. "This is the one," I said to Burton. "She claims to be a widow who wanted to visit this room because it was her anniversary. She didn't say she wanted to ransack the room."

"I know this must look bad," she said. "I can explain."

I learned early in my training that silence is a powerful tool. If I waited long enough and said nothing, she would feel obligated to explain. Burton didn't say a word.

"I lied," she said. "I'm a writer. I'm with *Atlanta* magazine. I came here to do a story on Mr. Lauber."

"Mr. Lauber is dead," I said, "so he can't give you any good quotes."

"I wanted information. . .something—something I can use for my article. I'm, uh, going to do a story about his adjustment after prison. . .and, uh, I thought that if I looked in his room. . ." Her cadence had slowed to a complete stop. She must have recognized how implausible her story sounded.

"Hmm," I said. "That story was a pretty good recovery, wasn't it?" I asked Burton.

"Not bad for someone who gets no warning. Want to tell us the truth?" Burton asked softly.

"I think I want to get out of here." She clutched her shoulder bag and turned toward the door. At the first chance, I knew she would rush out of the room. We weren't the police, so we couldn't stop her. Or maybe she thought we were the police.

For the first time, I realized how badly the room had been torn apart. "Did you do all of this?" I tried to sound like someone with authority. "Did your search reveal whatever you wanted?"

"It was already like this when I came. That's the truth." She tried to brush past us, but Burton pulled the door closed behind him.

"Let me go," she said. "Who are you anyway?"

"Who are you?" I asked.

"I told you. . .I—I—"

"You don't work for *Atlanta* magazine," I said. It was one of those intuitive statements that just came out. I have no idea how I knew, but I did.

"I write for them," she said. "I do."

"Do you really?" I asked and refused to look away.

"Okay, twice," she said. "I've sold them two articles."

"So who are you?" Burton asked.

"That's not important."

"You want the diamonds," I said, again an intuitive statement.

"Okay, I want them. Who doesn't? We all knew Stefan had them."

"Who is *we*?" Burton asked.

Instead of answering, she grabbed the door handle and pulled the door open. She raced out of the room. The quick tapping of her feet retreated down the hallway.

"What was that all about?" Burton asked.

"I don't know," I said, "but let's go to lunch and talk about it."

"How did she get into the room?" he asked. "You tried the door and it was locked."

I had wondered, as well. "That means she probably had a key and still has it with her." I looked around.

"I don't believe she would have put it down in all this mess."

"I think I know how she got it," I said. "Let's go back to the front desk."

Burton snapped his fingers. "Of course!"

That man is quick and bright. In fact, I'm surprised he didn't think of it before I did.

As soon as we got off the elevator, we walked to the front desk. I gave Craig my best smile and said softly, "How much did she pay you for the key to 623?"

He blinked several times. I could all but see the wheels scurrying around in his brain as he wondered whether he should deny or admit the bribe. "Uh."

"Never mind," Burton said. "You've answered the question. We wanted to know how she got access to the room. You've just told us."

"Please don't report me," he said. "She came back right after you walked away with the detective. She begged me."

"And I suppose fifty dollars helped," I said.

"It was only forty. I don't care what she said. That's all she gave me."

"I won't tell," I said. I took Burton's arm, and we moved away and toward the hallway leading to the dining room.

———

We walked into the elegant dining room, its walls papered with a soft gold and brown pattern. The ornate tables and chairs looked like something stolen from a *Masterpiece Theatre* set.

"I am sorry, but you are too early for lunch," the maître d' said with a slight Hispanic accent. "But if you can be accommodated with tea, I could serve you while you wait, or you might choose to return in twenty minutes."

"Tea is fine," Burton said, and we followed the maître d' to a table by the window. It faced the east, and I could see wisteria vines that had been snaking their way up the side of the building for the past three or four decades. I don't like their fragrance, but I love the soft, purplish flowers.

A matronly waitress in a black dress and white apron brought in two bone china cups and saucers and a tall delft teapot on a tray. Without being asked, Burton slipped into the role of host for the tea ceremony. He checked the pot for "nose," and with tiny silver tongs, he placed thinly sliced lemon in both cups before he poured in the pale golden liquid. He held up the milk, and I shook my head. He looked up and smiled. "I lived in England for a year," he said.

"Very nice." I wanted him to feel I didn't know anything, although I had lived with an aristocratic British family for nearly two years. I had been a nanny to their sweet-tempered boy. And he truly was easy to take care of. If he hadn't been, I probably wouldn't have lasted the two years while I did my graduate studies.

Burton reviewed what little we knew about the late Stefan Lauber, which wasn't much. Both of us seemed surprised that he wanted me to be the courier to return the diamonds.

"Why me?" I asked for at least the fifth time. "I hardly knew him."

"He trusted you. That's what Jason Omore said." Burton took a long sip of his tea. "Don't give me one of your smart responses." He smiled. "Stefan Lauber obviously grasped what a fine and trustworthy person you are."

I stared at Burton for several seconds. "That's probably one of the nicest things you've ever said to me." I wanted to hug him and let him hold me in his arms, but that wasn't appropriate considering the place and the status of our relationship. But a woman can daydream, can't she?

We finished tea, and I tried to think of what to say next to keep him around.

"This time I do need to leave you," Burton said before I could think of something clever, "but it's nice to see you again." Like the gentleman he was, Burton waited for me to move first before he got out of his chair and slipped behind to assist me. I left enough cash on the table for the tea and a generous tip.

We reached the front desk just as the phone rang. Craig cried out, "Okay, okay. Be calm." And his voice was anything but calm.

"We'll call 911. Right now!" He opened the door to the inner office and yelled to some unseen person, "Cover for me. It's room 623! Again!"

He pulled out his cell phone and was so focused on the emergency that when he rushed around the counter, he collided with Burton. "Sorry. It's that room again—that 623!" He began to run. On the cell we heard him say, "This is the Cartledge Inn. It's room 623 again." He said something else, but he was too far ahead of us for me to understand the words.

This time Burton grabbed my arm and propelled me toward the elevator. We moved faster than the clerk, passed him, and reached the elevator before he did. I pressed the button. In the seconds before the elevator arrived, the harried clerk shook his head and said, "Murder. It's another murder."

"What?" I said.

"That's what the maid just said. She's up there yelling and crying."

The elevator arrived, and Burton punched the button for the sixth floor. When we got off, we hurried down to the room. A Hispanic maid stood outside the door. Her body shook, and she cried loudly, mixing her Spanish and her English. "Dead! *Ella está muerta!* Murdered. *Matado!* On the floor!"

A second maid, an Asian, stood calmly on the other side of her cart. "There. In that way. The door was open—very wide open—and both of us saw her."

The clerk started to rush inside, but Burton held him back. "Don't take a single step into the room." He unclipped his cell and pulled Ollie's card out of his pocket. He dialed the detective. "Get back to the hotel. There's a dead woman in room 623."

While Burton talked to the detective, I moved to the door and surveyed the room. I saw the body—I couldn't miss it. It was the woman we had seen in the room before, the one with those outrageous burnt orange nails. I wasn't ready to look closely at her, so I scanned the room. It was even more torn apart than it had been when Burton and I had been there less than an hour earlier. The air vent near the ceiling had been pulled out and tossed carelessly on top of the torn-up bed. The wooden headboard for the bed had been ripped from the wall. The mattress was flipped over. I was surprised it wasn't cut open—they do that in the movies, which always seemed silly to me. The three drawers of the bedside stand had been thrown across the room. The intruder had pulled out the clothes that had once hung inside an old-fashioned armoire made of real oak. One of the doors was ripped off its hinges. Everything indicated that the search had been done in a fit of rage.

Finally, it was time to look at the body. I stared, mute. She lay on her back. Another shooting. I'm no expert, but it looked as if she had been shot in the chest and the bullet went through her. Most of the blood seeped from beneath her.

At first I wondered why someone didn't hear the noise, but perhaps there had been no one around. It was, after all, midday, and most guests were out of their rooms.

"Who is she really?" Burton asked. "She lied to us once."

"Even then she didn't tell us her name," I said. "But when she registered, she did use a credit card—"

"So who was she?" Burton asked the clerk.

"I'm still so rattled, I don't remember the name," Craig said.

"I know who she is." I turned around. A tall woman said, "Her name is Deedra Knight. At least that's the name I knew her by."

5

Before I had a chance to question the woman, she stepped into the doorway of room 623 and said, "I haven't seen Deedra for years, but she hasn't changed much. She still has those cheap-looking acrylic nails. Frankly, from the back side she looks better than she ever did from the front."

"And who are you?"

"My name is Janet *Lauber* Grand, and before you ask, I didn't like her. In fact, I detested her."

"Well, at least we know who she is," I said. "I mean, who she was."

"And you're with the police, is that correct?" She glared at me. I said nothing, and she quickly picked up on that. "You're not, are you? So why *are* you here?"

I stared at her, but I couldn't see the faintest family resemblance. Instead of answering her question, I asked, "How did you know which room was Stefan's?"

"First, because he called me on the phone yesterday and said he was now staying at this inn. Second, I have no idea who you are and why you're asking me these questions. You are not with the police, are you?"

"No," I said.

"Third, perhaps you ought to explain to me. Stefan was my brother. After I learned he had passed, I came. . .well, I came to see if there was anything, you know, anything I could do."

"Where did you come from?" Burton asked. "How did you know to come to this room?"

"I walked toward the reception desk. I came in through the side parking lot. I heard this man," she said, pointing to Craig, "shouting in a most unprofessional manner. Something about another murder in room 623." She explained that by the time she reached the elevator, it had closed, so she watched the dial above the elevator, saw that it stopped on the sixth floor, and rang for the second elevator. "When I came off the elevator, I saw you three standing in front of this door. Now, *who are you?*"

"I'm the desk clerk," Craig said.

"I don't mean *you*." The contempt was heavy in her voice. "With that blazer and your name on the jacket, that is patently obvious. I mean these two."

"I'm a therapist," I said and told her that Stefan had asked me to come to see him.

"A therapist? Stefan with a psychiatrist? You must be joking."

I'm a psychologist, but I didn't correct her.

"She isn't joking," Burton said and introduced himself.

"And now you're going to tell me that my brother decided to study for the priesthood."

"I never met your brother," Burton said. "I'm a guest at the hotel."

"Then what right do you have to ask me anything?" she said. "I'm not going to tell you anything more."

"Then tell *me*."

I jumped and turned around. None of us had heard Ollie Viktor come into the room.

He held up his badge and waved it in front of the woman.

"In that case, I'm delighted to talk to someone who obviously has the authority to ask questions." She gave me a half-second smile that wasn't worth moving her facial muscles. She turned to Ollie, eyed him, and nodded in approval of either his general appearance or his good looks. "My name is Mrs. Janet *Lauber* Grand." She accented *Lauber* again. "Stefan was my brother." She tilted her chin. "My much older brother."

I wouldn't have believed it, but she was flirting with Ollie, smiling and fawning, and she moved around so he could see her trim figure. Okay, she was beautiful—even I had to admit that much. She was also a woman who had been around—a lot. The hardness in her eyes and the tautness around her mouth were two things her expensive makeup couldn't hide. Her face, which seemed tightened regularly by a plastic surgeon to retain its youth, was expertly made up, as if she were about to walk on stage or on a runway. Her iridescent blond hair curled softly and stopped just below her ears. I suppose that was to cover any signs of the surgeon's knife. She wore off-white cashmere slacks and a silk blouse of the same color. She probably spent more on that outfit than I laid out for a full wardrobe. Around her neck and on her wrists and fingers she displayed a great many diamonds.

Ollie stared at her jewelry.

"You like this? It's my daytime wear," she said and rewarded him with a generous smile. "You are so very observant."

"How could he miss it?" I wanted to say but held my mouth shut.

"And you came to this room because? . . ." Ollie asked.

"Because—because I heard my brother's name shouted—quite loudly, as a matter of fact—by the desk clerk."

"I did not mention his name!" Craig said.

She waved him to silence and sighed deeply. From her purse she took a silk handkerchief that matched her blouse. It reeked of gardenias. She sniffed a few times and wiped her eyes as if tears had fallen. She wasn't a great actress, but she was pretty good. Most men probably fell for her performance. I wondered if that was why she had so many jewels.

"I'm sorry you have to go through this emotional ordeal," Ollie said. That was the softest I had heard him speak. Maybe a real heart beat inside his chest after all. Or maybe he had just been overwhelmed by her obvious attention.

"I didn't know—I didn't know he—what to do—Stefan was my brother— and I wanted to do something—anything during our time of deep grief." She handled that line extremely well. She not only used the Southern expressions, but her drawl was so good I expected honeysuckle to drip from her fingers. "I didn't know until I heard the desk clerk—"

"I'm sorry," Craig said with contriteness written across his face. "I was excited and—"

Ollie waved him to silence. "Go on back to your desk," he said and moved out of the way so Craig could get past him.

Ollie turned to Burton. "I got your call just as I pulled into the parking lot. The team will be here in a few minutes." He pushed past me as if I didn't exist, walked the few feet into the room, and knelt beside the woman's body. "So who is she?"

"Deedra Knight," I said. "Or so she says." I nodded toward Janet.

"Any of you know what she was doing in this room?"

"Obviously searching for. . ." Janet paused and added, "For—for something. It must be something of immense value. Why, just look at this terrible chaos." She put her hand to her face, and I thought she did that better than Vivien Leigh in the old film *Streetcar Named Desire*. Next I'd expect her to dim the lights in the room because they were too harsh on her face.

"The room was in disorder from before," Ollie said. He paused and looked around. "Maybe not quite this much of a mess when we arrived last night." He turned to face me. "I was here last night just before the uniformed officers left."

I gave him my best dumb-little-me smile.

"So you think people—someone—is looking for the diamonds?" Burton asked.

"Maybe. My supervisor doesn't think so—"

"But you felt he had them—even before Jason said anything."

"Yeah."

"Because—"

"Professional intuition," he said.

"So did you look?" Burton asked. "I mean, last night, did you—"

Ollie nodded. "They weren't on his person, and the two officers who searched last night didn't find anything of value inside this room. It was already a mess when they came, so they tried to be careful not to disturb any evidence."

"So the point is," Janet said, leaning against the doorjamb as if posing for a photo shoot, "you did not find anything that belonged to my dear, dearly departed brother."

"What they searched for didn't belong to your dear, dearly departed brother." I think my accent was almost as good as hers. Burton's slight shaking of his head begged me to stop poking fun at her. "They were stolen diamonds."

"And at least we're fairly sure the first searchers didn't find them or there would have been no second murder," Ollie said. I'm not sure what a man looks like when he preens, but that's how I'd describe the way he straightened his shoulders. "Yeah, this second murder and more destruction probably says the second search didn't yield anything either."

"Or the person found it and stopped the search," I added.

"You may be correct," Ollie said. "But for now we'll go on the assumption they have not found the diamonds."

"And the diamonds the other gentleman mentioned?" Janet's eyes widened as if she were portraying shock in a silent flick. "Surely you don't mean the diamonds from that utterly terrible, terrible robbery that—"

"That's the one," Ollie said.

"You never found them?"

"No, ma'am, we never did," Ollie said. "They're worth a lot of money, and we'd sure like to recover them. That's not the reason for the investigation. This started purely as a murder—"

"And you just happened to tie him in with the diamonds?" I asked.

"Not until we ran his name through our computer." He shrugged. "I returned to look over the scene, but there seemed no hard evidence to connect him to any diamonds—"

"Until Jason Omore said something. Right?" I asked.

"Yes, that's correct," Ollie said. "I thought I'd look this over one more time before I reported—"

"I had no idea, absolutely no idea the diamonds were still missing." Janet Grand really laid it on thick. As I watched her, I sensed she was lying about being Stefan's sister. I kept trying to remember what Stefan had said about his family of origin. He had an ex-wife and admitted to having affairs with several women. Was she one of those women? The more I observed Janet Grand—if that was her name—the more she seemed to fit into that category.

"Can you prove that you're his sister?" I asked.

She turned her back on me and faced Ollie. "I shall be delighted to answer any questions you have for me." She sighed deeply again. "But please, only questions from you."

"This is a police matter," Ollie said. "You don't belong here—"

"But we're here," Burton said. "I hope we can be of help. We'll stay out of the way." He looked at me. "Won't we?"

Instead of making a rude remark and getting another shake of the head from Burton, I interrupted, "Did you notice the connecting door?" I motioned toward the door that led to 625. "It's all but closed." I tiptoed past Miss Mint Julep and pointed to the bottom of the door. "See?" It was a fraction away from being closed.

Ollie walked over to the door. He didn't exactly push me out of the way. Or maybe he did, but I assumed he was focused on the door. He reached forward to pull it when he must have realized that it pushed inward toward 625. So he nudged it and the door swung open. Because I stood near him, I could see inside. It hadn't been torn up like 623. It looked like any other upscale hotel room to me. I knew it was occupied, because I spotted a small stack of books on the desk in the corner.

Ollie turned back to all of us and held up his right hand. I was sure he'd seen that done on TV, because he was just too perfect at it. "Just stay where you are." He walked around inside 625. I couldn't see everything, but I heard him pick up the phone and punch a number. "This is Detective Viktor upstairs. Who is registered in room 625?"

After a lengthy pause, he asked, "Do you have a phone number for his office? A cell number?" He muttered something, and I heard the rumble of his voice for a full minute or so before he replaced the phone.

After he returned to the room, he spread his arms out to usher us into the hallway. "What do you say we all go downstairs and find a quiet place so we can talk?"

"Who's in room 625?" I asked.

He smiled. "Let's go downstairs. All four of us."

Obviously he wasn't going to tell us, so we let him direct us away from the room and down the hallway. No one said a word until we got back to the main floor. Ollie told us to wait while he left us and spoke to Craig. I had remained focused on Janet.

"How long has it been since you last saw your brother?"

"Awhile."

"How long is that?"

"I prefer not to discuss this, especially with you. The pain is already so—so intense." She pulled ahead of me and stood next to Ollie.

"Follow me," Ollie said and waved toward us. He led us to the end of the reception area, and we made a left turn and entered a small room. It had already been set up for a business meeting with a whiteboard and memo pads and pens in front of every chair. Every table had two pitchers of ice water and a stack of glasses. PowerPoint equipment was ready for whoever had booked the room. "Desk clerk says this room is free for about an hour." He tried to smile, and maybe he actually did, but it looked forced. "Sit down."

"Let's start with you," he said and focused on Janet. He took out his little notebook, thumbed through several pages, and wrote on a new page. "Tell us about Deedra Knight."

She shrugged as if she felt confused. Again she touched her cheek with her right hand, and the large diamond on her ring finger sparkled. "She was. . .I think the word is. . .Stefan's *coliguillas*."

"No, a coliguillas is a man," I said gleefully, using the proper Spanish pronunciation. "You probably mean something old-fashioned such as *courtesan*. *Doxy*, maybe? Or perhaps—"

"Enough of that, Doc," Ollie said to me. "Just let the lady speak."

If I had thought about it, I would have given him an Ollie-type shrug, but instead I nodded. I really wanted to hear her myself.

"She was, uh, I suppose what I mean is that she was intimate with both my brother and Willie Petersen. She played them both. This is conjecture, of course, but from what I know of her and of Stefan's past, it fits. She also had something to do with the robbery. In fact, Stefan once hinted that she was the one who set it up." For a second her mask fell as she realized she'd told us more than she was supposed to have known. "By that I mean Stefan never said anything about a robbery, but he did mention a big business situation in which he was closely involved. And then, of course, he was arrested and sent to prison."

"And why do you think Deedra had anything to do with that?" I asked.

Her contemptuous glare should have made me back down, but it only pushed me to pursue the question.

"You seem to know a great deal for a person who supposedly knows nothing," I said. I didn't know what I meant, but it sounded good to my own ears.

"I know little," she said and faced Ollie. "In fact, I know almost nothing." She paused as if embarrassed, but I figured she did that for dramatic effect. "You do understand that I am telling you only what I assume is true. Everything I have said or could add would be purely conjecture."

"I had understood your brother was the one who planned this," I said. I wanted to push on about that matter.

"I doubt that." She still refused to look at me. "It was not the sort of ugly, evil thing he would have done."

"As his therapist, I can say with authority that he planned the robbery." Again, I have no idea where that statement came from and hoped no one would push me. That woman was lying—probably about everything.

"If you choose to think so, but I can assure you that—that horrible woman— that Deedra Knight originated it. Stefan was so easily influenced by. . .uh, by women of sordid reputations."

"Oh, really?" I had to throw that one in.

"Neither man—Stefan nor Willie—would have done such a thing without being goaded by her." She leaned toward the detective. "You believe me, don't you?"

Ollie nodded before he flipped a page in his notebook and jotted down a number of items. He kept his left hand over the page so I couldn't see the script.

"So why do you think Deedra came here?" he asked.

"Wasn't it obvious?"

6

"Obvious? In what way?" Ollie Viktor asked.

"To search for the diamonds. Didn't you say as much?"

He shrugged. So we were back to that gesture. "What else can you tell me?"

"Nothing. I'm sure. I don't know anything. I came to see my brother. That was the sole purpose for the visit." She pulled out the off-white handkerchief again and held it to her dry eyes. She must have practiced that before a mirror, because she did it exactly the same way again.

"I have some interesting news for you," Ollie said. "Your other brother is also a guest in this place. What's his name?"

"Lucas? Lucas is here? In this hotel?"

"He's checked into room 625. He may have been one of the people who wanted 623 but couldn't get it."

"Lucas and I haven't spoken in years, and it has nothing to do with this matter. We stopped speaking more than twenty years ago." She smiled and added, "I was willing to forgive him, but he refused to apologize for his—his bad behavior."

"Do you have any idea why he's here?"

She shook her head. "None." She stood up. "I must go. I have an important appointment. If my brother is not alive, there is nothing here for me, is there?"

"Don't you want to see Lucas?"

"Absolutely not," she said.

"Perhaps the mutual grief would unite you," I said.

"Perhaps you ought to stay out of things that do not concern you."

Before I could conjure up a rejoinder, Burton shook his head, and she had reached the door.

Ollie stopped her and asked for her address and phone number. He said he'd let her know if he learned anything else.

"Now I need to get back to you," Ollie said and glared at me. "This morning you were ready to tell me about your sessions with the victim."

"You mean my sessions with Stefan Lauber?" Okay, that was evasive and out of line, but I didn't like him, and I wasn't going to make it any easier.

"When we spoke this morning, there was only one victim." Although his voice hadn't changed, his fist had knotted and his eyes showed agitation. I decided to push him to see how upset he would become with me. At the same time, I

190

wondered how he ever solved crimes if he was so impatient.

"Yes, of course," I said. Just that one question and his impatience was already showing.

"What do you want to know about our sessions?" I leaned slightly forward. "Do you want his personal history? His romantic secrets? His—"

He slammed his fist on the table. "Don't be cute or coy. I don't give a dead man's noose about his personal life. Stop being evasive. I want to know why he came to see you."

"Just that?"

"Yes. That's a simple question, isn't it?"

I hesitated, not sure how much to say. Burton leaned close and said softly, "Tell him. This isn't you and me at Palm Island trying to solve a murder. He's the professional here."

Although I like Burton, a brusque retort formed in my mind. But he was right. I didn't like the detective, but he was the professional. "Okay, I'll tell you," I said. "First, of course, Janet isn't his sister. I don't know who she is, but Stefan had no sister." I hoped he wouldn't ask me to prove that, but the feeling was so strong, I trusted my intuition.

"You're sure about that?" Burton said. "Maybe we need to stop her."

Ollie leaned back in his chair. "Very good, Julie, but I already knew that. Stefan was an only child until his parents adopted Lucas, who was five or six years older."

"You knew that?" I was surprised.

"Yes. I also know the reason for the adoption. The parents felt Stefan had gotten unruly and that an older brother was what he needed." He met my gaze. "Is that correct?"

"For a man who has no direct interest in this case," I said, "you certainly know a great deal."

"Computers. Everything's on computers these days," he said.

"I didn't know about the adoption, although I knew the brothers didn't get along. That was one of the issues Stefan talked about. After they were both grown, he cheated Lucas out of a large sum of money—"

"About a hundred grand," the detective said.

"If you know all this—"

"So far you haven't told me anything new, but you will." He poured himself a glass of water and gulped it down in one long swallow. "I'm still listening. A little impatiently, but I am listening."

"Did you get all that information from computers?" I asked. "Wow, what's the URL?"

"Julie." Burton spoke my name softly, but I knew he wanted me to back off.

"I'm not giving information now. I'm receiving it."

"Okay, then what about that woman—Janet Grand?" I asked.

"I know who she is. She was one of those—how did she say it?—intimate people with Stefan. Somehow she found out about the murder and knew about the diamonds."

"Really?" Burton asked.

"She tried to book the room by phone this morning—about an hour before she showed up." He smiled as if to say, *"See, I'm ahead of you on his case."*

Even though Stefan was dead, I didn't feel comfortable telling the detective anything. My intuition said he wasn't a man I could trust. Or maybe that was only my prejudice. Maybe I just didn't like him as a person—which I didn't—and that may have distorted my reasoning. Besides, he was so different from his college classmate, and I had as low an opinion of him as I had a high one of Burton.

"I didn't know about any religious experience he may have had," I said. "Or his *conversion,* as Jason Omore called it. That's not an area we talked about. However, I knew something had happened—something that changed him. When he first came to me, he told me, quite up front, that he had a number of unresolved issues in his life and said he wanted to change." I paused, shrugged to imitate Ollie, and plunged on. "Actually, he said it even stronger. He said he was determined to change."

Ollie threw more questions at me. Each time, he wrote something in his little book and must have flipped six or seven pages. I wondered if they had to buy those things themselves. They must use a lot of them.

I asked Ollie to give me a couple of minutes to review my professional relationship with Stefan. I didn't need that reflection time, but I wanted to see if he'd push me to hurry.

He said nothing, but it was obvious he didn't like the silence. While I reflected, his fingers drummed on the table.

"I saw him a total of six times," I said.

"Yeah, okay," Ollie said.

I got up, walked to the far side of the room, stalling for time, unsure of how much I wanted to tell him.

"Any day now," Ollie said.

"Yes, there were six sessions. The first time, a Monday afternoon, not much went on, mostly his giving me information about himself. He did speak of significant issues in his life and said he was trying to figure out the right thing to do.

"He refused to say more except that he wanted to be sure he could trust me before he went into details. We set a second appointment for Thursday of the same week. Ordinarily I don't do two appointments in the same week, but he had insisted, and I felt he was nearing a crisis stage about something. I agreed."

I lapsed into silence again, wanting to think about how much to say. By the middle of the second session, he had begun to trust me. I can always tell when that happens. It's not just the way the clients talk, but their bodies relax and their voices grow softer. At the first session, Stefan had sat tall, straight, and stiff. During the second session, he relaxed, and for the second half of his appointment time, he sat in my office with legs wide apart and arms stretched across the back of the couch.

I decided to omit whatever I didn't want to tell Ollie. I walked back to my chair and said, "Okay, I have it sorted out."

"At last," Ollie muttered.

I ignored that. "Okay, what you need to know is that Stefan cheated several people," I said. "His brother was only the first. That was some kind of obscure business deal. Stefan didn't go into detail, other than to say he did it and his brother found out—and he wasn't supposed to know. When Lucas heard, he vowed to kill Stefan."

"Hmm. Really?" Ollie said and scribbled hurriedly on the pad.

"That happened long ago, you see, and I don't know if—"

"Some family feuds can last a long time," he said. "Go on."

"Stefan never mentioned the diamond robbery, but he hinted. I mean, in retrospect, it seems to fit. Several times he referred to himself as the big kahuna—"

"The big guy, the top dog," Ollie said. "It's a Hawaiian term—"

"So you also saw all those dumb beach movies," I said.

Ollie blushed. He actually blushed when I said that. I liked him a little for that unconscious act—not a lot better, but somewhat.

"Yes, any number of times he said that he had become the big kahuna with a brilliant idea that had gone wrong. Now I can see that's what he meant. He said he had been involved in something illegal and dangerous and people got hurt—something for which he had never planned."

"That was as specific as he got?"

"Pretty much," I said.

"And?" Ollie prompted.

"During our third or fourth session, he asked pointedly because he wanted to be certain: 'Please assure me that, no matter what I tell you in these sessions, you cannot be compelled to testify against me in court.' I told him not only that it was true, but that he already knew that."

"How did he answer?" Burton asked.

"He said he needed to know for his own peace of mind."

"So I guess he didn't trust you," Ollie said. "Is that it?"

I stared at him for a moment and then closed my eyes and rethought that session. "No, I don't think so. In fact, I think it was an odd, perhaps subtle way of affirming that he felt he could trust me."

"Doesn't sound like it to me."

"That's why I'm the professional." I said the words quietly, but from the corner of my eye I saw Burton's head shake slightly. Who appointed Burton to be my conscience? Okay, maybe I did, and he was right.

"Okay, sorry for that," I said. "He admitted that it was for his own peace of mind. This may not make sense to you, Detective, but in my professional assessment, Stefan wanted me to say *out loud* that anything and everything he said in our sessions was privileged communication. It was almost as if he did that for the benefit of anyone who might be listening. And, of course, I never tape such sessions. But then, perhaps, his having been in prison—"

"Perhaps he taped *you*," Burton said.

"If he did, I never saw a recorder anywhere," I said. "But that thought went through my mind at the time. However, it didn't matter. If he had asked, I would have allowed him to tape any sessions—"

"Okay, let's move on, please," Ollie said. "Tomorrow will be here before you tell me anything significant."

I gave what I assumed was a warm and apologetic smile before I said, "Stefan told me he wanted to make full restitution for his crimes. Those were his exact words: full restitution for his crimes."

"Did he say what his crimes were?" Ollie leaned forward as he asked.

I ignored his question. I had decided to tell him, but it would be in my own way. "Stefan didn't look like the kind of person I would consider a criminal." I laughed at myself. "Okay, he was, but he didn't act like one. He had none of the signs." I turned to Burton for help.

He nodded slowly before he said, "I understand, and I think Ollie does, too."

"Okay, he didn't give off any bad vibes. He was a genteel, reformed criminal," Ollie said.

"And if he had changed," Burton said, "if he had become born again, surely that would have made him behave differently."

"Yes, I suppose it would," I said and knew my words didn't sound very convincing, because I wasn't sure his conversion—or whatever he had experienced— was relevant. I had met a number of the born-again types and—okay, I don't want to digress and go on that diatribe. "I can say that he seemed to be genuinely honest and a man who was determined to grow." I leaned forward to match Ollie's posture. I also wanted him to know the sincerity of my client—my former client. "He listened to everything I said. He probed within his own heart. At times it was painful, but he faced things about himself—his personal values and attitudes. He was definitely committed to change."

"Change in what way?" Ollie said. "To make restitution sounds good, but you still haven't told me anything new."

"He mentioned the names of several people he had hurt. They're names I know now. He referred to Deedra—by first name only—and someone named

Willie and his brother, Lucas. There was also another woman, but he never mentioned her name. His struggle, so far as I could figure out, was how he could right the wrongs he had done with his business associates—again, that was his terminology—through his illegal actions and yet make things right so that he could live with himself."

"And you believed him?" Burton asked. "You believed he spoke the truth?"

"Absolutely," I said. "I've been at this profession too long to have been taken in."

Ollie snorted, and I gave him my most intense glare.

"Okay, okay, you believed him," Ollie said. "And?"

"Stefan felt that if he made things right with the people he had hurt and gave them what they insisted they deserved, it would be an immoral act. If he didn't make things right with them, he felt it would not be ethical for him." I paused and thought back to his words. "He may have used the word *God* once or twice. People often do, but they don't usually mean divine power or anything like that."

"Do you think he meant *God*?" Burton asked.

"Not at the time I didn't," I said. "But after our conversation today with Jason, I think he probably did."

"Okay, okay," Ollie said. "I don't care. You're holding back on me, aren't you?"

"Okay, it's like this. Stefan wanted to make everybody happy, and he knew he couldn't do that," I said.

"How could he make everyone happy?" The detective looked at me. "What was he trying to do? Become some kind of saint?"

"I don't know. I can only tell you what he told me—"

"As well as a few of your insights," Burton said.

"That, too. Stefan continually asked himself one question—"

"What question?" Ollie asked.

Ollie was impatient. I paused, stared at him, and finally said, "Please. You asked me to tell you what I know, so don't constantly interrupt."

"Yeah, okay, but just get on with it."

"Stefan had several things to resolve, but what troubled him the most was the one question he would ask aloud. By asking, he didn't mean he wanted me to give him the answer—"

"Then why did he ask?" Ollie interjected. Aware of what he had done, he looked away.

"Some people need to talk aloud. They need to say the words to another person before they know what they think. Make sense?" I got a slight nod from Burton and a blank stare from Ollie. "Here's the way I say it: I only know of myself what I say of myself. That means I don't really know how I feel about something until I say it to someone else."

"Yeah? What good does that do?" the questioner interrupted yet again.

"Two things take place," I said. I decided to act gracious and ignore his impatience. "First, and in this case, Stefan was able to put his emotions into words. In our field we say that when a person like Stefan feels safe—feels understood and trusts the therapist—he'll speak from his heart. Things come up that he might not otherwise say."

"Okay, I get that. So what's the second?"

This detective would provide a great venture for a team of therapists. Besides his impatience, I sensed his high level of anxiety. "Are you always so intense and so. . .anxiety-ridden as you are now?" I asked him.

He opened his mouth, and I think he was going to swear at me, but he glared at Burton and said, "Look. This isn't about me, and I didn't hire you to be my personal shrink, okay? Just tell me about Lauber. You may be a good therapist, but it sure takes you a long time to get to the point!" His voice had raised in pitch, and he stood up. He mumbled something about being sorry but he was eager to solve the case.

"Eager or anxious?" I asked.

Ollie stared blankly.

"Okay, I'll let that go," I said. I actually enjoyed watching his responses. He might be a hunk, but his wires were so tight they were ready to snap. "Stefan sat in front of me, often leaning forward, his head down, and he would say, 'What is the right thing to do?' He didn't ask that just once, but repeatedly: 'What is the right thing to do?'"

"The right thing about what?" Ollie asked.

"He didn't say. As a therapist, I didn't feel I needed to probe for that. He knew. That's what counted." I scooted forward until our heads were only about three feet apart. "You question people all the time, don't you?"

He nodded.

"But you do it to elicit information. Correct?"

"What else?"

I held up my hand. "That's not how a therapist works." I turned to Burton for help, not because I couldn't express myself, but because I sensed Ollie would listen to his old friend.

"I think she's trying to say that she wasn't probing. There is a time to probe—a time when a therapist asks the questions that open people up and enable them to get in touch with their deeper selves—their inner child or their—"

"Okay, okay, I think I get it."

"I'm not sure you do," I said. "He had already begun to open up. I sensed the trust level was high. Once that happened, my role was to allow him to work out the problems by himself. Instead of trying to hand him answers—"

"More psychobabble!"

"Not really," Burton said. He gently laid his hand on Ollie's shoulder. "She's trying to explain how this works. She's saying that Stefan had to resolve the problem himself. Her role was to remain objective, to be open to listening, and to encourage him so that he kept moving forward."

"Very good," I said. I wanted to hug Burton for that. But then, I wanted to hug him for a variety of reasons.

"Okay, I get it," Ollie said. "I ask to get information. You ask to get a person to look inward. I understand, and now I've passed Psych 101. Now, Dr. West, what else can you tell me?" He spoke softly, but the words were uttered as if he were ready to sock my jaw.

"He said nothing directly about the robbery or the diamonds; however, from what I've heard since I've been here, I think he wanted to return the diamonds to their rightful owners."

"That's a consortium based here in Atlanta," Ollie said. "I'm sure that long ago, however, the insurance paid for the loss, so I don't know how that works. That's not the issue anyway."

"The issue was his dilemma of trying to figure out the right action," I said, "and how to do that so he hurt the fewest number of people."

"But he had the diamonds. Right?"

"How should I know?" I asked, but I added, "Yeah, probably."

Ollie's cell phone buzzed again. He held up his hand for me to wait, which was quite unnecessary. I didn't want to say anything more, and I did want to hear what he had to say on the phone.

"You're kidding me!" Ollie said, followed by a series of one-word responses. "Was he obsessed with that number?" Those were the two longest statements he made before he hung up.

I raised my eyebrows as my silent way to ask Ollie to share information with us.

"You're both in the head-and-heart business," he said. He still held his cell and turned it over and over in his hand. "So maybe you can help us with this one. It's the number 623. That Lauber was obsessed with 623. Weird, huh?"

"Obsessed?" I asked.

"Yes," he said and raised his right index finger. "First, he lives here in room 623. He's been here for months. Second," and he held up another finger, "he rented post office box 623 in Stone Mountain and also box 623 at Decatur's main post office." He now held up three fingers.

"That's certainly odd," Burton said.

"Fourth, he bought a house on Royal Path Court in Decatur. He hadn't moved in because construction isn't finished. It's a tract of land that will eventually have eight houses. His is the only one that's almost finished. They plan to finish the others before the end of the year. His house won't be finished for another month or so. But guess what the number of Lauber's house will be?"

"Another 623?" I asked.

Ollie genuinely smiled. "And even crazier, he bought the first of eight large homes, and all the others—all eight—had already been assigned addresses, and all of them were four digits, but he insisted on his being 623 and said he didn't care what any of the others were."

"How could he do that?" Burton asked. "The builder doesn't assign—"

"He paid cash. Then he turned around and bought the other seven houses as well. He spent 5.3 mil for the entire tract of completed houses. For California that might be nothing, but here in Georgia, that's a big, big hunk of cash."

"For money like that," Burton said, "I guess he could get what he wanted."

"What's the compulsion about 623?" I asked. "Those three digits don't mean anything to me. What about his birthday? Is it possibly 6/23—June twenty-third?"

Ollie shook his head. "His birthday is November something."

"Was he born in 1962 perhaps? That would account for the 62." But I knew the answer. "Too old. He was in his late thirties, wasn't he?"

"Thirty-seven," Ollie said.

We batted around various possibilities for the number for a while, but nothing seemed to make sense.

"One more thing I'll tell you," Ollie said, "but it goes no further than this room. Right?" He stared first at Burton and waited for him to say yes before he turned to me. I nodded my agreement.

Ollie got up and paced the circumference of the small room three or four times. "There is one more thing that might have some value." Ollie told us he had been the first detective to arrive at the inn. The two uniformed officers touched nothing but waited at the door until he arrived. "When I turned over Lauber's body last night, his right hand clutched a piece of paper—more a fragment of a piece—ragged, but only about the bottom two inches. I don't know what happened to the rest of it, but it fits in with this."

"You mean the number 623?" I asked. "It was on the fragment?"

"Yes, and just above it a capital *R* and a small *o*—as in the word *room*. That was printed from a computer, and his handwritten signature was below those two letters."

"What does that tell you?" Burton asked.

"Room 623," he said. "What else?"

For a few seconds I tried to figure out what else would fit. Nothing came to mind. Burton seemed as puzzled as I did.

"I thought maybe you two could add some insight to that." He rubbed the back of his head. "This obsession with 623 is nuts. Just plain nuts."

"Prison cell?" I asked.

He shook his head. "Good thinking, but I checked on that this morning. No connection. In fact, another detective went to the prison and asked around, trying to find some meaning to 623. He came up blank."

For perhaps two minutes more, the three of us sat in silence. Ollie poured himself a second glass of water. The ice had melted, and I wondered if the water would be cold enough for the group that was supposed to use the room a little later.

I decided to stretch as I pondered the situation. I walked to the large windows and looked outside. I admired the cerulean hue of the cloudless sky as it contrasted with the hydrangeas along the small path that wound from the sidewalk to the lake. The hydrangea bushes were a bright purple or a soft pink—my dad said the color had something to do with the amount of aluminum in the soil.

I stood in silence; Ollie paced; Burton stared at the ceiling. Just then, the soft noise of the air-conditioning kicked in.

"Is it a code?" Burton asked. "You know, where each number is a letter?"

"Okay, suppose it is," Ollie said. "If 1 is A and B is 2, that means 6 is G, and that gives us GBC. Does GBC mean anything?"

"Or he may have used a different base," I said. Instead of 1 equals A." Then I laughed. "It's just as confusing to try to figure that out as it is to stay with 623. After all, if we want to make sense of what went on inside Stefan's head, we need to understand those three numbers and keep them in that order."

We all agreed.

Aside from the low, indistinct sound of air moving into the room, there was no noise. Ollie reached for a fresh pitcher of water. He poured and gulped down a third glass.

"Something has been bothering me," I said. "It's something Craig, the desk clerk, said."

"What was that?" Burton asked.

"When that woman—Deedra Knight or whoever she was—came to the desk and asked for 623, Craig told her it was taken—"

"Yeah, we know that," Ollie said.

"He also said 621 and 625 were occupied. We know 625 is Lucas Lauber's room. Who's in 621? It also has a connecting door, you know. I checked and it was closed. Even so—"

"Wait here!" Ollie hurried from the room. Less than a minute later he returned. "Scott Bell-James from Muscatine, Iowa, is what the registration says." He walked around the room and then said, "Sounds like a dead end to me."

"Are you sure?" I asked. "The name doesn't mean anything to me, but from the way Craig talked, I felt it meant more than just somebody taking the room by chance."

"I think you're right," Burton said. "Almost the clerk's first words to me were, 'Everybody wants room 623.' "

"Right!" I said. "When Deedra Knight asked for room 623, Craig insisted that everyone wanted that room and went on to say that 621 and 625 were taken—"

"As if they chose those rooms because they couldn't get 623," Burton said.

"Maybe we need to locate Scott Bell-James," Ollie said.

I wondered what took him so long to figure that out.

Ollie Viktor asked us to leave the tracking down of Scott Bell-James to him. He reminded me—not too sweetly—that he was the professional detective and we were in this only because he allowed us to participate. "And as long as you have something of value to add, you can stay."

He didn't add a threat, but the tone of his voice made his meaning clear. He left us and said he'd be back within half an hour.

That left Burton and me alone.

"I suppose you can start your retreat now," I said without enthusiasm.

He laughed and shook his head. "Now? And not stay involved in this? Don't you know me better than that? Besides, this might be a good diversion for me."

"Diversion? I thought you wanted rest."

"Change. Time away is what I want—what I need."

"I don't know much about how you preacher types work, but I assume you holy Joes have immense theological problems to grapple with so you can make thunderous pronouncements from the pulpit."

"You really love to play the ding-a-ling, don't you?"

"Do I? Do I really?" It was my best Southern accent and my most innocent look.

"Enough of that." He took my arm and said, "Let's go back into the garden area. Ollie will figure out where we are. You don't object, do you?"

Why would I object to walking with Burton?

As we walked out of the room, Ollie stood near the desk. He talked on his cell, but Craig hovered and didn't miss a word. Burton signaled that we were going out to the benches again and that we would turn right instead of left as before. Ollie waved us on.

We walked slowly down the path. By then, of course, he had released my arm, and I couldn't think of any way to get him to take it or to hold my hand. We found a small alcove with two benches that faced each other. On three sides of us grew an assortment of daylilies—some bright yellow, a few tiger lilies, and a variety of tall pristine white. Around the flowers the gardeners had planted sage and mint. I closed my eyes. Instead of being overpowering, the fragrance was just enough to enjoy.

This time we both sat on the same bench, and Burton leaned forward. "I want to tell you something."

I started to make a crack about liking to have him tell me anything, but the seriousness in those deep blue eyes told me to keep my mouth shut.

"You're the reason I'm here," he said.

"Me? You found out I was coming here?" I knew that wasn't what he meant, but I wanted to hear him say what he really meant. I liked the way this conversation had started.

"No, that's not what I meant." He turned away from me and played with his watchband for several seconds. "It's more than that. I'm in a dilemma. . .a real dilemma. I felt I had to get away for a few days to think." His voice became softer and lower so that I had to strain to hear the last few words. "It's you I need to think about."

"Me?" I asked. I loved hearing that but decided to play naive. "Why would you need to think about me?"

"You know I like you," he said.

"And I like you."

"A lot. I like you a lot."

"And I like you a lot, too."

"There you go with that ding-a-ling thing again," he said. But the hint of a smile made me know he liked it when I did that. He turned his face toward me. "I have feelings. . .strong feelings toward you, but—"

"But I'm a fallen woman, and you're the pure gentleman—"

"Don't, Julie."

"Don't what?"

"No game playing, at least not for a few minutes. Please," he said. "You know what I mean."

"Yes, I do." And of course I did. "I had no idea—really—that you felt, you know, that you liked—"

"It's this way. God is truly the most important thing in my life. He comes first. I—I, well, you're not a Christian, and—"

"Okay, I'll help you with this one," I said. When we met at the coast, I had told him about living with my religious-but-legalistic uncle. More than anyone else, my uncle Rich had turned me against the church, preachers, and Christianity. Burton had started to rebuild some of that destructive mind-set. I visited his church several times, and to my immense surprise, I liked the people. They were friendly, and I enjoyed the warm atmosphere. I had never felt that before inside a church building. Best of all, no one cornered me or tried to get me to rush down to the front and cry out for salvation.

"You mean you understand what I'm trying to say?" Burton asked.

I held up my hand. "My uncle had a saying. Okay, he had a lot of sayings, and most of them were aimed at me and my waywardness. One time a certain young preacher visited him and I liked him. Tall, blond. You know, a real hunk.

And best of all, he wasn't married. He and I hit it off rather well, and I flirted with him."

Burton cocked his right eyebrow as if to ask, "Where is this story going?"

"After the man left, my uncle told me how shameless I had acted. He was correct, of course. I wouldn't have used the word *shameless*, but I knew what he meant. He raised his right hand. He always did that when he was getting ready to preach for my benefit."

Yes, it was one of those memories that sticks inside the brain and never seems to diminish.

———

Uncle Rich stood in the middle of the room. Usually his voice started low, and as he warmed up, it rose in pitch and volume. This time he started on a high octave, and anyone in the house could have heard him. "You're shameless. You're a hussy. You're a tempter sent from the devil himself."

I had heard Uncle Rich so many times that his preaching had begun to wear thin, and I had become immune to his insinuations. He had the amazing ability to read the vilest intention into everything I did. I wasn't quite ready to leave his house—that came about six weeks later—but I was tired of all his accusations.

"And what did I do this time?" I sighed loudly, but I knew that gesture was lost on my uncle.

"You have to ask? You flaunted yourself! You think I didn't see you lean toward him? You touched his hand! When you came back with the iced tea, you sat so close to him that I couldn't have put a piece of paper between you!" He raved on for at least a full minute.

"Really? You were watching me and all the sinful things I was doing? I thought you were listening to his talk about sanctification and the need for people to turn from idols of iniquity." I smiled at my uncle. "You see? I listened."

"How dare you mock me! You—you Jezebel! You temptress! You seductress! You wanton woman!"

"My, my, Uncle Rich, you must think about sex and sin a lot." I had overstepped that time. His face filled with anger, and I wondered if he was going to hit me.

"Let me warn you, young lady. You may end up corrupting that innocent man, but—"

"Corrupt? We had iced tea together in your presence. What kind of mind do you have?"

"He invited you to church, didn't he?"

"Yes, he did. And he said they had three hundred members."

"It's a beginning. I know how women like you work. You'll go to church and you'll play up to him and then trap him like a spider traps a fly."

"Can you really see all of that in my future?" I laughed. "I like him. Yeah, I like him a lot."

Uncle Rich came up to me and stopped only inches from my face. He stared into my eyes and said, "If a man marries the devil's daughter, he'll certainly have trouble with his father-in-law."

"That's a good one! Probably the best one-liner you've ever come up with!"

I actually laughed. He must have heard that line somewhere, because Uncle Rich wasn't clever enough to think of anything original.

He slapped me.

I stared at him in surprise. It was the first time he had struck me. Several times in the past I had expected it, but he'd restrained himself.

"I hate you," I said calmly. "I hate you, and I detest your religion and despise your god and everything else you talk about."

"That's because you are of your father the devil."

"Okay, that's fine. So it's a family issue. I'm the devil's child and you're my uncle."

He slapped me again.

I ran from the room. That's when I determined I had to get away from there. I was still a college student and had no place to go. But I knew I had to find a place—any place. If he struck me and I put up with that, where would the abuse lead?

Two weeks later I met Dana Macie, had a quickie romance, married him, and a few weeks after our wedding, I learned he was into drugs. Later Dana died in a car accident.

As my mind came back to the present, I knew exactly what Burton struggled over. "If you marry the devil's daughter, you'll have problems with your father-in-law," I said. "Isn't that what you mean?"

Burton winced. "That's a bit strong."

"But the principle is right, isn't it?"

"Yes," he said softly. "Yes, I suppose—"

"So you came here to the inn because—"

"Because I had to figure out what to do. I care about you—I care a lot—a lot more than I ever thought I would—"

"So that's bad, is it?"

I'm not sure he heard my smart reply. "Julie, Julie, I've tried to hold back, but my feelings for you. . .well, I've never felt this strongly about a woman. Any woman. Ever."

"And the problem is?"

"Don't do that," he said. "You know the issue."

"You're right," I said. "I'll also tell you that I like you a lot, more than I ever thought possible. I don't know if I love you. I'm afraid to think about loving anyone." I was lying when I said those words, because I knew I did. "You know, one time down the chute with Dana Macie—"

"I remember your telling me."

"But it's more than your feelings, isn't it?" I asked. "Okay, I'll make it easier for you. According to your religion, we have no common foundation. You're committed to—to your God, and I'm a—"

"Yes, but you make it sound petty—"

"It is petty—and cruel—to me," I said, "but I also know it's absolutely serious to you."

"I could never marry a non-Christian."

"My uncle Rich was right about one thing. You're a son of God, and I'm a daughter of the devil."

"Now you've gone from sounding petty to harsh."

"Maybe that's my protective barrier you've just crashed into. I don't want to be hurt. Not again."

"I wouldn't want to hurt you, Julie. Not ever," he said softly. "I hope you believe me."

"I know that."

"It doesn't have to be like this—"

"You mean if I turn to Jesus and—"

He stared at me, and I knew he wanted to take my hands, but I couldn't let him. I stood up. I wasn't ready to hear a long lecture on what I needed to do to get my life right with God. "I don't believe—at least not like you do, Burton. I'd like to believe. I'm open, or at least I try to be."

"What's the problem?"

"I suppose it's mostly my uncle Rich. His and other voices like his still lurk inside my head. Until I met you, I thought Christianity was for old people and idiots."

"And now?"

"It's not just for the old," I said. "No, I'm sorry. There I go. I'm at my worst when I'm tense or have to talk about my feelings."

"I know," he said. "You're good at picking up others' feelings, but not so clear about your own."

I sat on the bench across from him because I didn't trust myself. As I looked at James Burton, I knew—for the first time with absolute certainty—that I truly loved him. I also knew I didn't want to mess up his life. I'm too honest a person to say I believe in God unless I mean it.

"That's why I came here," he said. "I've missed you. I've wanted to call you half a dozen times every day, but I couldn't, and I won't. I had to get away and pray and ask God to help me."

"How did you ask? How did you pray?"

He hung his head, and light reflected on those gorgeous curls. "I prayed for God to—to give me a sign. If I was to hang on or if I was to totally avoid you. I had become desperate. I couldn't hear anything from God. I felt if I got away—"

"Away from any contact with me?"

He lifted his head and smiled. "Something like that."

"So we're both here at the Cartledge Inn and neither of us knew the other would be here. Do you think God arranged that, or was it a trick of the devil? Uncle Rich would say the latter."

"I prefer to think more about God than I do the devil."

Our eyes met. I didn't know what to say or do. Obviously he didn't either. So we stared.

I love this man, I said to myself. *I do. But I can't—I can't go his way.*

8

A lovers' quarrel?" Ollie asked.

I hadn't heard him approach and wasn't aware of his presence until he spoke. Despite his being a large man, he walked quietly. I wondered if that had been part of his police training.

"Hardly," I said. I was glad he had come, because Burton and I didn't know what to say to each other. I wanted to kiss him and he wanted to run away, but neither of us had moved.

"Did you learn anything about room 621?" Burton asked.

"I still don't know anything about Scott Bell-James, but he did write down his cell number when he checked in. I left him a voice message and asked him to call me."

"Thanks, Ollie, for letting us be part of this," I said. "I know we're amateurs—"

"And you are," he said without rancor in his voice. "But I'm open to any kind of help."

"I wanted to ask you something," I said. "It's about Deedra Knight. Why would someone kill her? I assume she wanted the diamonds. At least it makes sense that she was looking for them. But why murder her? If she found the diamonds, wouldn't it be easier to take them from her?"

"Probably," he said.

"But why kill her?" I persisted. "Unless, of course, she found them and the murderer could only take them from her by shooting her. Seems drastic."

"Or maybe the killer didn't want anyone alive to identify him," Burton said. "Or her."

"A strong possibility," Ollie said.

Burton looked at Ollie. "But until you know that's the reason, what do you plan to do? What's your next step?"

Ollie sat next to his former classmate. "I plan to talk to anyone who can shed any light on this situation." His voice was calm and pleasant. As a professional, I wondered how his moods could shift so easily. I wondered if this erratic behavior was typical or if this case was causing a big emotional strain.

Ollie talked for a while, but I didn't hear him. I was absorbed in watching him. His hand had shaken slightly before, but now it was steady. He smiled the way he had when we first met. Something was different about him, and in the back of my head, something clicked. I had worked with clients like him before, but I couldn't pull the information into my conscious mind.

"Good idea," Burton said, and I snapped back to attention.

"Jason Omore will be here in a minute," Ollie said. "I called his room and asked him to join us. I told him we'd be out here." He smiled at me. "After we learn everything he knows, perhaps you'll open up and tell me the rest of what you know about Lauber." He leaned forward, about a foot from my face. His green eyes narrowed as if he were trying to see inside my head. "And I know you're still holding back."

Before I could reply, Jason Omore came into view. He had picked a yellow rose and held it out to me. "I don't have permission to do this from the owners," he said, "but I do not think they will mind if I pluck one rose to give to such a beautiful woman. Does not beauty attract beauty?"

"I like you better all the time," I said. I took the flower and held it to my nose and inhaled the scent. So many of the roses these days have little fragrance, but this was different. The pungent aroma filled my nostrils.

Jason sat next to me and faced the detective. "You wish to ask more questions, is that so?" Before he looked at Ollie, he glanced at me, and I think he winked, but it was so quick I wasn't positive.

"Tell us more about you and Lauber at the prison."

"Is there much to tell? I do not know, but I shall try." Jason held his hand to his face. "Even the odor of the rose remains. Do you say *odor*? Is that not a negative word?"

"Try *fragrance*," Burton said. I could tell from his expression that he knew Jason was creating a diversion on purpose.

"As you know, I am a Christian," Jason Omore said. "I am also a student sent here by my government so that I may return and develop—"

"Yeah, yeah," Ollie said. "You can skip that part. Get to Lauber."

"Yes, but of course, I shall do that. At the prison in Rome, I spoke with many of the inmates. As you may know, in prisons and jails, many volunteer groups come regularly to present worship services and Bible studies. I chose to talk to them individually. Because I was a doctoral student from Emory University, I had no problems in moving freely around the prison."

"And how did you meet Stefan?" I asked.

"First, as you may know, he was at two different prisons before they transferred him to Rome—"

"Yeah, I know how the system works," Ollie said. "With good conduct come better conditions." He cleared his throat and added, "So answer the question."

"I had posted the information at various places in the prison that I wished to study individual inmates and their behavior. All things were confidential. More than sixty of them showed up."

"That's a lot," I said.

He laughed, and his whole face participated in the exercise. I had rarely seen a person so happy. I wondered what made him so joyful. It was more than his face; something about the way he behaved exuded a kind of aura of peace and quiet joy. The more I was around Jason Omore, the more I liked him.

"That is easy to explain, is it not? Some thought it would help them make early parole. I had to assure them that their participation would not make a difference. For others, they came to the meeting out of boredom. Some left the facilities during the day for work details, but the others had nothing much to claim their attention."

"And Stefan was among which group?" Ollie asked.

"He worked on detail, is the way I think it is said. He often worked for ten hours each day. It was volunteer work, but he seemed always the first to volunteer for any task."

"Did you wonder why?" Ollie asked.

"But of course, and I asked."

"And what did he say?"

"I had seen Mr. Lauber before, of course. He was different from most of the others."

"You didn't answer my question," Ollie said, "but maybe you'll answer this. In what way was he different?"

"Many of the inmates had marked themselves—tattoos, many tattoos. Others carried scars from fights. Too often I saw old faces, hard faces on young men. He was in age maybe, I don't know—"

"Thirty-seven," Ollie said. "According to our records, he would have been thirty-eight in November."

"Yes, but it was more. He shaved and dressed as if he had a purpose each day. How can I say it? Most of them seemed to have nothing. Something else also. He read. He read many, many books, did he not?"

"What kind of books?" Ollie asked.

"Everything. The prison had no real library, even though I tried to get them to start one. A few books were in the recreation room, and there is a room where they may enter and read, but little of intellectual stimulation. People cannot send books to individuals, but only publishing houses can do so. So he received many such books that way by ordering them from the publishers. Once he read them, he left them in the reading room for others."

"How did he pay for them?"

"I did not ask, but one day he said his brother gave him money."

The three of us looked away from Jason and at each other. Our silent faces asked how that could be. They supposedly hated each other.

"Do you know anything about his brother?" Burton asked.

"Of that I know little. I met him but one time in the prison. He came to visit.

By then, Stefan was truly my friend, and he introduced him to me. We did not exchange words. He seemed to be in great haste to leave."

"That was the only time you saw him?"

"Yes, of course, except for yesterday."

"What?" Ollie jumped up and grabbed Jason's T-shirt as if he wanted to strangle the African. "What are you holding back?"

Jason said nothing, but his eyes met Ollie's and he did not flinch. Ollie finally released him and moved back.

"You did not ask if I had seen him here. It was a surprise to me to see him, of course."

"When did you see him? Where? Here in the hotel?"

"I saw him but yesterday. I did not look at the time, but I know it was before 6:30. Perhaps ten minutes, but I do not know."

"How do you know the time?"

"Because my doctoral adviser promised to call me at 6:30." He held up his cell phone. "I wanted to get out of my room, and I was moving toward the front entrance of the building. I wanted to walk away from the inn and toward the expressway. I do not have a motor vehicle, and I wanted to see a different landscape. That is when we met."

"And exactly where did you meet Lucas?" Ollie asked.

"When he exited from the elevator, is that not so?"

"Did he acknowledge you?" Burton asked.

"At first not. I think he recognized me, but he would have walked past as if he must be in a large hurry. He walked quite rapidly. Perhaps he did not remember my name, but—"

"Did you speak to him?" I asked.

"Would it not have been rude for me not to do so?"

Ollie took a long, deep sigh and said, "Please, Jason, just tell us. Don't make me pull out every tiny fragment of information."

"Yes, that I can do." Jason momentarily closed his eyes. "He wore a blazer that was of the color gray, a light gray. His trousers were of a darker shade of the color gray. And as I said, he walked very fast, as if in a large hurry." He turned to me. "Large hurry? Is that correct English? I think it is not correct?"

"We understand what you mean," Ollie said. "Just move on."

"I greeted him and extended my hand," Jason said. "I introduced myself, and he said he did remember me. We both were going in the same direction, so I walked out of the inn with him and to his car. He drove away. That is all."

"That's all?" Ollie asked. His anger was almost at the exploding point. "What did you talk about as you walked to his car? What kind of car was it? Did he say where he was going? Did he explain why he had been at the hotel?"

"Oh, is that what you wish to know?" Jason said. "He told me that he had been to see his brother, but he was not in his room. I had seen Stefan perhaps an hour earlier when he stopped at my room."

"Why your room?" I asked.

"To give me a Bible and—"

"Okay, and then Stefan left you? Is that correct?" Ollie asked.

I wondered how Ollie solved any crimes if he was always so uptight and explosive.

"Lucas said he had come because Stefan needed to sign a paper, and he was late for a place he had to be for a meeting, and he regretted that he could no longer wait for his brother."

"Just that?" the detective asked.

"I said I would drop by his room later and ask him to call, but Lucas said I should not bother. That was all."

"Nothing else."

"My cell phone rang then. It was exactly 6:30. My adviser is punctually absolute." He laughed. "Sorry, absolutely punctual. English is so difficult, is it not, especially with where to place the adjectives, is that not so?"

"And he drove away?"

"Yes, and it was a green vehicle. A Mercedes, but the year of the vehicle I do not know," Jason said. "But it was not a vintage model—not—not old, I mean."

Ollie waved at him to stop explaining.

"Was there anything unusual about him? Anything that struck you as strange or unusual?" I asked.

"But one thing only. It was a paper he held in his hand. I could not read it, but it was, how do you say it? Crumpled? No, it was also that, but—"

"Torn?" I asked.

"Yes!" His eyes lit up. "Sometimes I forget English words. It was torn—no, ripped. Fragmented. Yes, that is the word. It was but almost all of one page, and does that not make it a fragment?" Without waiting for an answer, he said, "I noticed it because the fragment was not straight at the bottom. You know, if I take a sheet of paper from a tablet, both top and bottom are even—"

"Okay, okay, I got it," Ollie said. "Torn. Ripped. Shredded. Fragmented. Whatever. Could you read it?"

He shook his head. "And would it not have been rude to try to do so?"

"Did your people find the remaining portion of the paper?" I asked.

Ollie shook his head. "Not that I know. It certainly wasn't among the evidence collected."

"It would have been such a small portion," Jason added. "But a pinch—I think is how you say it."

Ollie waved him away.

"I have a couple of questions I want to ask," Burton said. "Would you tell us about your time together in prison? What happened?"

"Yes, that I can do. I did not like Stefan at first because he said rude things—perhaps rude is not the word. Vulgar? Yes, he spoke with vulgar—with vulgarity—about my faith and about God."

"Tell us, will you?" I asked.

"Let's go back to the room," Ollie said. "This is a little too public."

We followed him back to the meeting room.

9

This is the story Jason Omore told us:

I had noticed Stefan because he was different, and that I have already said. He told me the first time in the meeting that he didn't want to hear me talk about God.

"Then you must close your ears or walk away," I said to him. "God is not something I can push aside because you are afraid to hear of Him."

"Afraid? What makes you think I'm afraid?" His voice was very low, what you call a bass.

"Are you not afraid?" I asked.

"I just don't want to hear anything about religion," he said. "I had a couple of injections when I was a boy, and now I'm inoculated. I don't need another dose."

"That I can understand for your sake," I said, "but for my sake, if I cannot speak about God, it is as if I would be forced to walk with only one leg." I turned from him and spoke to the others in the room. I did that to enable him to get up and leave if he chose to do so. I did not wish to embarrass anyone. By then we had only fourteen men left in the room. "Each of you has volunteered to come here. If you choose to remain with my program, I will record the information, but your names will never appear. I must do this to defend my work at the university." I looked around. "There are liars and crooked people in this place, you know."

Most of them laughed, and several hooted and clapped.

"No one will hear your voice—unless it is because my supervisor wishes to up-check."

"Check up, you mean!" one of them called out, and many laughed. I made that error on purpose, of course. From their responses I knew they wanted to trust me.

They had a few questions, but most of all, they simply wished to talk, and I waited patiently for them to speak. I explained that I studied quite diligently to understand behavior in humans. "It may surprise you, of course, but we truly have criminal activity in Kenya. We wish to understand behavior of every kind."

They truly loved it when I spoke like that. They thought I was extremely naive, and I did not mind that they thought so.

After that I looked around, and Stefan Lauber had not left. I was surprised, but I made no mention of his presence still with us.

In the middle of my first session with the group, one of the men stood up.

"Why would you come here? You're not like some of those who want notches on their guns to record each of the converts they've shot out of hell and landed in heaven."

This time Stefan clapped loud and long. It was the first time he had responded as a member of the group.

Did I not laugh at that? Yes, indeed, I did laugh. Then I explained that I had once been a very bad person in my native Kenya. I had used *pombe*—native beer—every night without fail. I beat my wife if she argued with me, and I stole cattle from other farmers. But one day God changed my life.

I told them about a man named Erasto Otieno who had come to our village and told me that God loved me and God's Spirit would never give me peace until I surrendered. He also said he would not leave our village until I believed in Jesus.

"Is this not strange?" I asked the men.

I must explain our African custom to you. That man, Erasto, stayed in our village for five days. In our culture, a guest stays until the host tells him to go. That is the way it is, although Western culture is changing our ways, those of us who live far from the cities still honor the ways of our ancient parents.

I explained to the inmates that I could not ask Erasto to leave because my wife wanted to hear him speak and so did my parents. My two sons begged me to let him say his many words. Unlike your culture, I could have not walked away from him. He was my guest. For me to do so would have been a serious insult.

So Erasto spoke to me, to each of us, and he seemed never to be without an excuse to preach about Jesus. I would offer him a drink of water, and he would tell me that Jesus was living water. We had just gotten electricity in our area, and when I turned on the lights, he would say that Jesus was the light of the world.

Yes, he irritated me, but he also did it with love in his voice, and something made me listen to his words. I could not have walked away—that would have been a rude thing. I seemed to have no choice but to listen. He was not there to get me to join some *dini*—some religious group—and I believe he came as a man of love for other human beings.

Before the end of the fifth day, I believed. I believed because of the words he spoke, but I also believed because of the way he spoke the words. In his face I saw that he would die for Jesus if asked to do so.

I confessed my sins and promised to follow Jesus. I was weak, and I stumbled many times, but I kept on. One day, perhaps a year later, I learned that Erasto had died. A witch doctor in the primitive area of Kadem Location had poisoned his food. When I heard that, I knew—deep inside my heart—I knew that I must carry on Erasto's work. I would not be a preacher as he was, but I could become useful to God in whatever field I chose.

After I answered that call, did I not witness openness in many hearts?

But about the men: After I answered their questions, they had nothing more to ask. I waited and I knew they trusted me, so I gave them forms to fill out. They were simple questions and asked only for basic information about themselves, their crimes, and how they felt about what they had done in breaking laws. I was careful not to ask if they were guilty.

When everyone had completed the papers, I said, "If any of you wish to stay and talk about Jesus, I shall be most pleased to do that."

After I dismissed them, eleven men stayed. They sat at heavy wooden tables and on hard chairs. One of those who did not leave was Stefan Lauber.

I spoke to them. The others had all been to church, had all thought they were members of the kingdom of God at one time, but they also committed crimes. None of them were murderers. Not those in that prison. Most of them were there on drug charges, theft of vehicles, and other nonviolent crimes. Two of them had been in prison before, but the rest were there for the first time—and I hope the only time.

As I have said, Stefan Lauber was different from the others. He was the only one with a college education, and there was another factor about him. Dare I use the English word *mystical*? It was as if God had chosen me and sent me to the prison to give him the information for which he had been waiting many years. He did not know he was waiting, but had not God put a deep longing into his heart? Later he would tell me these words: "I felt as if I have waited all my life to meet you."

I provided him with books to read—as many as three a week. One of my professors was kind enough to pay for them and have a publisher send them. Stefan read the books—every one of them. One day I saw him reading the Bible, but he did not understand much of what he read, so I helped him, did I not? From then on, he spent at least one hour each day in reading the Bible, mostly the New Testament. He would stay with a chapter or a portion until he could say to me, "Yes, I understand."

Four days before his early release, Stefan asked to see me. The guard normally escorted inmates from place to place, but they did not do that with Stefan. Yes, a guard was present, but he walked beside him, as if they were two friends. Like Paul the apostle of old, he had won the respect of those who were his captors.

He came into the room, and the guard stepped outside. As soon as the door closed, Stefan fell on his knees in front of my desk. "Please, please help me."

The agony written across his face showed such severe pain, I went around to him, pulled him up, and embraced him. I said nothing and waited for him to speak.

"I have been a terrible sinner," Stefan said. "And I know I must change."

"Yes, that is good," I said. "We must all change."

"But it's more than that. I have stolen from people."

"Can you not return what you have taken?"

"That's the problem. I want to follow Jesus, but I want to keep what I've stolen because I'll end up back in prison if I attempt to return the stolen items." He laughed at himself. "That sounds terrible, but it's true."

I embraced him tightly—I had been doing that for some weeks. He embraced me just as tightly. Before I released him, I prayed that the Holy Spirit would make him want to return what he had stolen. Just that much.

As I started to walk away, he said, "You are the happiest man I have ever known. Why is that?"

"Is that not what my name says?" I answered.

Most strangely he stared at me and said, "I don't understand."

"My name. My African name. It is Omore. In my language, which is called Luo, the word means a happy person or one who reflects happiness."

"Yes, you are a credit to your name," he said.

The words came with such softness, tears leaped from my eyes. I am a happy person, that is true, but I am far from the kind of person I wish to be. Instead of answering, I could speak only a word of thanks.

He opened the door and started out, stopped, and turned. "Omore, my happy friend, you are the kind of Christian I would like to become."

Those words touched me deeply, and once again the tears leaped from my eyes.

The next day I had to return to Emory University for research and to meet with two of my professors. When I returned, I learned that Stefan had been released. I thought that was the end of our relationship.

To my surprise, three days later I received an e-mail from him; he invited me to come here to the Cartledge Inn and to study. He informed me that he had sufficient funds to pay all my expenses and that they were not stolen funds. Was I not most pleased to accept such an offer?

When I came to Cartledge Inn, he met me and greeted me before he introduced me to the members of the staff. We were together every morning for at least an hour at a time. Some days it was for longer.

—

Jason wiped tears from his eyes. "He was my friend. My good friend. Never have I had a friend I have loved so much as Stefan Lauber. He planned to return to Kenya with me to meet my wife and my children. But now that cannot be."

I thought he was through, but he said, "It is now my intention that my next son will be named Stefano in his honor. Among my people it is the highest honor we can give another—the greatest honor I can offer in his memory—to name my child after him."

"Very touching," Ollie said. "Very."

"And you have no idea how Stefan resolved the problem?" Burton asked.

Jason shook his head. "No, I do not *know*. I cannot say such a word; however, I believe that he did the right thing, whatever that was. That is how my *rafiki*— my friend—behaved. He had many, many struggles inside his heart, but in the end he always did the right thing."

I glanced at Ollie and asked, "Do you suppose that's why he was killed? To prevent his returning the diamonds?"

"I can think of another reason," he said.

"Which is?" I asked.

"Someone else wanted the diamonds, and Lauber refused to give them up. He wanted to hold on to them himself."

"Makes sense as another possibility," I said, but I didn't believe my own words. I sensed Jason had been right about Lauber.

"But what did he do with the diamonds?" Burton asked.

10

"Excuse me." Craig opened the door without knocking. "Your new room is ready for you, Mr. Viktor." He was quiet and quite professional. He smiled at me—and he almost pulled off that friendly-but-plastic smile many professionals develop. Maybe if he worked at it, he would learn to fake it well. I liked him better in flustered mode.

What Jason told us of his experiences with Stefan presented me with a different picture of the man than what I'd heard from anyone else. He must have been a good man—or maybe he had *become* a good man.

As if he had read my mind, Burton said, "God can change people. That's the divine specialty, you know."

"So they tell me." That smart answer came out before I realized what I had said. I opened my mouth to apologize, but Burton smiled as if to say, "Apology not needed."

He knows me well—maybe too well.

Ollie thanked Craig and turned to Jason. "You can leave. I'll call you if I need anything else."

I thought Ollie's tone was a bit dismissive, but I said nothing. Burton shook Jason's hand as if to make up for Ollie's harsh treatment.

"You are also a good man," Jason said, "for I can see it in your eyes. Yes, you are truly a very good man."

Burton turned his head away, but I think he blushed.

Ollie had already dismissed Jason and said to Burton and me, "I've arranged for a suite where we can talk and meet with anyone who has anything to tell us." Without waiting for a reply, he led the way.

I patted Jason Omore's shoulder and said, "Thanks. That helps me understand a few things." I wanted to talk to him, perhaps alone, and I hoped I'd have the opportunity. Like Burton, this man exuded a vital connection to God. This was so unusual. Other than Burton, I had met only one man who had exuded any kind of vital, warm relationship to God. A man named Simon Presswood whom I'd met at Palm Island. So here I was again with two men, both of whom lived a vital relationship with God.

Has God decided to gang up on me? I didn't want to answer my own question; it might be true.

Instead of going to the elevators, Ollie led us past them. We made a left turn and went directly to room 127, a suite with a large sitting room and a bedroom, although the bedroom door was closed. For my tastes, the room was far too austere with an overabundance of pale colors, pale fabrics, pale woods, and delicate paintings. The room needed vibrant colors, rich fabrics, and exciting new paintings. But then I don't suppose guests rented the suite to admire the room. Aside from the usual desk and several floor lamps, the room held two large sofas, both of a boring ocher color, and a wing chair of equally drab yellow.

"Sit down," Ollie said in a commanding voice. "In order to make us comfortable, the owners of the Cartledge Inn promised to send in refreshments this afternoon."

I attempted a smile as I watched Ollie's hand tremble slightly. Earlier the harsh tone was there along with the tremor. Was it Parkinson's? Surely he wasn't on some kind of drugs, was he? Although I didn't like him much, I could hardly think he'd be into something like that. So why did his hand tremble at times?

I checked my watch. It was nearly 2:30. I could hardly believe the time had passed so quickly. Burton and I had not eaten lunch, but I didn't mind. That might give me a good excuse to snag Burton for a long, quiet dinner.

Not that we had gotten far in solving the murder, but I had spent a few minutes alone with Burton. I knew how he felt about me, and his confession had surprised me. Until then I thought the attraction was only a one-sided romantic infatuation. When we met at Palm Island, he had playfully said he liked me a lot, but he'd also told me then about his unwillingness to get involved with someone who was of a different faith. I laughed to myself after I thought about those words. No, it wasn't a different faith. Mine was simply no faith, but he had tried to be gentle and sweet and wouldn't have said anything to hurt my feelings.

For several minutes I seriously considered an attempt to fake the faith, but I knew I couldn't do that. If anything ever worked out between us—and that meant I'd have to become a Christian first—it would definitely have to be real. I had given serious thought at one time to becoming a true vamp as my uncle Rich said I was, and had a few nice daydreams about saving Burton from all the bondage of religion. But I knew he was too determined, and even if I had succeeded, he wouldn't have been happy.

So if there was to be a change, I had to be the one to make it. But I didn't want to change. I didn't want to become one of those holy-holy types. Why did I need to have some kind of religious experience or change? I was a good person—not perfect, but I was an ethical person. But why did Burton have to be such a kind, sweet person? Why did he have to be so accepting of others?

A uniformed waiter came into the room with cold water, juice, and Cokes. He had hardly gone when someone knocked.

"Come in!" Ollie yelled.

A muscular African American man, about five feet five, walked into the room. More accurately, he swaggered into the room. Stocky, with a big chest and bigger arms, he had a neck as thick as a wharf post. He looked as if he snapped railroad ties in half for exercise or fun.

His dark brown eyes were far lighter than his skin, and his bushy black beard was lightly salted with curly white hairs. That touch of frosting was the only thing about him, other than the whites of his eyes, that was not very, very dark. I guessed his age to be early forties. Probably to emphasize his dark features, he wore black slacks and a black shirt. I might have been afraid of him if I had met him on the street, except for one thing: The brightness of those dark brown eyes twinkled in a way that would have pushed aside any trepidation.

To me he seemed such a strange contrast—except for those eyes, he looked like a man ready to confront anyone who stood in his way. Or as my administrative assistant would say, "That dude shows plenty of 'tude."

"You left a message on my business phone. Said you wanted to see me." He looked directly at Oliver Viktor. "I'm here. What do you want?" As he stared at Ollie, his eyes lost that softness.

"Well, well, so we meet again after such a long time," Ollie said. "Hey, Burton and Glamour Girl, this is Nicky Harrison. On the street they call him Chips."

"They call me Chops. C-h-o-p-s," he said, "but you knew that."

"Yeah, that's right," Ollie said. "I'd forgotten." But it was obvious he hadn't forgotten. I wondered why he wanted to antagonize the man.

The stranger stared at me, looked me over carefully, and said, "Mr. Smart Mouth here think he so funny, but don't know nothin' about crackin' jokes. Yeah, they still call me Chops."

"That's an unusual name," I said because I didn't know how else to respond.

"That's 'cause I usta be a tough guy. If anyone messed with me or my boys from the hood, I chopped him good with my fists."

"Do you still chop?" Burton asked.

"Not since the Lord Jesus chopped me down to size. No, sir."

"Yeah, that's right," Ollie said, "I heard you got religion in prison."

"Not *religion*, Mr. Policeman; you done heard wrong," Chops said. "I was sentenced to ninety-five years in the federal prison for murder and four cases of rape."

"Yeah, I remember."

"You should!" Those eyes, so soft minutes ago, blazed in anger.

"I'm surprised you're out and able to breathe real air like the rest of us."

"No, you ain't. You knew."

"Guess I did," Ollie said.

"And it prob'bly ruined your already miserable day." Before Ollie could make another wisecrack, Chops said, "The man with the big, scary badge is right. I was in prison, but I was innocent. And to be honest about everything, I did a lot of bad things—never murder or rape—but plenty of bad things, and I got away with them all. But in prison I prayed and—"

"Oh, here it comes," Ollie said. "Sorry I brought it up—"

"Listen, Mr. Policeman, you let me set the record straight. I started to pray in prison—right in the federal pen here in Atlanta. I promised God that if He'd set me free, I'd serve Him forever." He stopped and smiled. His face changed when he smiled, as if all the 'tude had vanished. "And that's what happened. The government began to introduce all that DNA stuff, don't you know? And they proved I couldn't have done any of those crimes. Not any of them! And now I've gotten an official apology, have a pending case against the police department—your police department and your former partner. I've been out in the big world. I'm free from prison and free from sin. Best of all, I've been born again for five years."

"Yeah, so I heard." Ollie made no attempt to hide the sneer in his voice.

"And so you still hate me, don't you?" Chops said. "But I'd like to tell you something." He stepped up close to Ollie, who was several inches taller, but Chops didn't look intimidated. "You did your thing, and that was okay, 'cause while I was inside, God did His thing. After I got it figured out, just like with ol' Peter, the doors swung open for me, and I ain't never looked back no more. Been out a year."

"Yeah, well, that's, uh, very nice," Ollie said, and he didn't back away, "but that's not the reason I asked you to come."

Chops Harrison laid his beefy arm on Ollie's shoulder and then straightened his tie. "Yeah, you remember good. Real good. I don't like you, and God don't say I gotta do that, but I forgive you."

"Like I care a great deal," Ollie said. But the harshness of his voice seemed to have diminished. As I watched the exchange, I felt as if Chops had finally intimidated him.

The black man patted Ollie on the cheek. "Notice, I didn't give you no kiss of peace, but I ain't gonna put a hurtin' on you."

"Uh, so, uh, you and Ollie know—"

Chops interrupted me. "Know each other? How about that, Mr. Policeman?" He smiled at me, and the twinkle was back in his eyes. "Yeah, this dude don't only knowed me. He knowed me 'cause his partner it was that turned over all the so-called evidence. He knowed I was innocent."

Ollie shrugged. "What's the difference? It got you off the streets—"

"You are sure right about that, Mr. Policeman. Even if you allowed your partner to pump up the evidence." He stressed the last word so that all three syllables received the same inflection.

Ollie shrugged again dismissively. "You know how it is—"

"Oh, I know," Chops said, "and I ain't never expected an apology from you. And 'course, you ain't big enough to give me none neither."

"I was just trying to do my duty," Ollie said, "just trying to do my duty like I'm trying to do right now."

"And may I assist you to do your duty?" Chops asked. He gently pushed Ollie into the wing chair and sat on the sofa across from him. "As a public-minded citizen in good standing in this community, how may I render assistance to the police department?"

The change in his voice amazed me. He had come in sounding like some tough guy who bounded out of the Wide World of Wrestling or Atlanta's inner city. But this time his tough, uneducated street talk was gone.

"Okay, let's cut through all the garbage and get this straight," Ollie said. "I didn't like you before, and I don't like you now, despite the DNA—"

"You know, that's funny," Chops said. "I didn't like you before. Now I just feel sorry for you. You're such a small man on the inside. An extremely small man."

Ollie flushed, but to his credit, he didn't say anything.

Chops spotted the refreshments, hopped off the sofa, and went over to the ice-filled box. He took out a bottle of water. I half expected him to bite off the end. He slowly turned the cap, peeled it off, and took several sips of water. Even in taking the water, there was both a gentleness and a grace in his movement that seemed so different from the man who had walked into the room only ten minutes earlier.

"So you wanted me here to answer questions," Chops said. "As a law-abiding citizen in good standing with a clean police record, I have come at your request." He bowed from the waist. "How may I assist you?"

"You called room 623 eight times in the last five days," Ollie said.

"I don't know about eight times, but if you say so. After all, why would you lie to me? You represent the —"

"You deny you've called room 623?"

"No, I don't *deny* anything. I called Stefan Lauber. I didn't know what room he was in. When the receptionist answered, I asked her to connect me."

"Yeah, right," Ollie said. "Okay, let that go for now. Why did you call?"

"Why do you want to know?"

"Maybe I'm just a curious kind of guy." Ollie leaned forward, and anger filled his face.

"Stefan Lauber was murdered last night," Burton said. "Ollie Viktor is investigating the crime."

Chops paled when he heard the word *murdered*. He staggered backward and sat on the sofa next to me. "Stefan? Murdered?"

"You didn't know?"

He shook his head. Tears filled his eyes, but he said only, "Stefan? Stefan? But why?"

"Tell us about the phone calls," Ollie said. The anger had disappeared from his face and voice. I think he believed Chops.

"I can't believe. . . I just can't—"

"Sorry if I can't give you time to mourn," Ollie said, "but this is a murder investigation, and—"

"Stop it," I said to Ollie. "Can't you see the shock on his face? Even you can give him a minute to absorb this."

"Whatever," Ollie said, but I felt he heard me and was ashamed at his behavior.

For perhaps a full minute no one said anything. We just stared at Chops. If we hadn't been watching, I think he would have broken down and cried. I didn't know anything about the relationship between Stefan and Chops, but it was obvious the man cared for the late Stefan Lauber.

"He had planned to help me—help us—with a project in Decatur." Chops said the words so softly I strained to hear him.

"What kind of project?" Ollie asked.

"Does it matter to you? It was legitimate. That's all you need to know."

"Make it easy on yourself, Chops. Just tell me what I want to know."

Chops Harrison stared out the large window for several seconds as if debating whether to speak. He sighed and mumbled, "Okay."

"Okay, what?" Ollie said.

"I have nothing to hide. It's just so—so—" With his large right hand, Chops wiped both of his eyes before he turned his face toward the detective and said, "You see, I met Stefan when he was in prison up in Floyd County." He turned to me and smiled. "I was only a visitor. I came to see Too Tall Tom Tomlinson, one of my boys who had messed up. I thought he was clean, but police caught him. Two *honest* policemen. Too Tall was slamming ice."

"He was injecting ice—the purest form of meth," I whispered to Burton. In the past year, I heard that term a lot at our center.

Burton nodded his thanks, because he obviously hadn't understood.

"Yeah, and it was a tough one and his second knockdown, but Too Tall Tomlinson is going to make it this time. He's now in rehab, voluntarily."

"Okay, so you were at Floyd County," Ollie said, "and that's where I lost the trail."

"So while I was there, I met a neat dude from Africa named Jason Omore. I can give you his cell number if—"

"Jason is here at the inn," I said.

"Really? I'll look him up. Great man of God. You know him, huh?"

"We do," Burton said. "And we like him."

"How could you diss him? Mr. Policeman, Omore and I, man, we started rappin' about things, you know, and we got pretty tight, and he introduced me to Stefan. We chilled for maybe ten minutes."

Chops had reverted to his street talk, and I wondered if he had done it to antagonize Ollie.

"How long ago was that?" Ollie asked.

"Don't know. Don't matter none now, do it?"

"Just answer," Ollie said. His voice sounded angry again.

As I listened to the two men, it seemed as if they both shifted from one style to another. Ollie's hand shook just a little more than it had before Chops entered the room.

Chops closed his eyes as if in thought and said quietly, "Maybe a year ago. Yeah, just a year. After that I wrote Too Tall a letter every week."

"Yeah, right, of course," said Ollie. "You wrote—actually wrote—letters?"

"Excuse me," Chops said, "but I have earned a master's degree in journalism from the University of Georgia. That's what I do now. I'm a journalist. In case you don't know what that means, I'm the assistant bureau chief for the AP. Uh, sir, that's the Associated Press."

"Well, miracles happen, don't they?" Ollie said.

"Indeed, they do," Chops said. "And by the grace of God, I'm one of them."

"Okay, point well taken," Ollie said. "Tell me more about the project in Decatur to which Lauber was *purportedly* going to offer help."

"Oh, it was more than an offer," Chops said and genuinely smiled. The glint in his eyes had returned, and his voice softened. "We finalized plans to set up a series of homes there. It's a new concept in children's homes—what we used to call orphanages. Instead of one large, institutional setting, we have decided to set up group homes. They're clustered together, but we will have such group clusters in other parts of the country. He had already put up a grant for a similar cluster near Auburn, Alabama."

"Yeah, yeah, I got it," Ollie said. "Just tell us about the place in Decatur."

"Stefan bought eight houses. One is built and ready to move into. That was to be his house. The second is—"

"What's the address?" I asked.

"It's off Columbia Drive, and the street is called Royal Path Court."

"And is the house—the one already built—numbered 623?" I asked.

"Exactly. Yes, that's the one. Have you been there?"

"Okay, okay, I understand. I know everything I need to know, okay?" an extremely irritated Ollie said. "Can we just stay with basics?"

"First I don't tell you enough; now I tell you too much," Chops said. I saw the faintest hint of a smile. This man was bright and about ten yards ahead of the detective.

"And the phone calls?" I watched Ollie's face; he concealed all trace of emotion while Chops spoke. "Why did you call him?"

"All the calls had to do with minor problems and details about the program.

We wanted to name the cluster after him, but he said no. I pushed him, but he refused. We finally decided to name it after Jason Omore." He turned to Burton and said, "His name—Omore—means a happy person. So we're calling the venture Happy Face Homes."

"And you can prove all this?" Ollie asked.

"You'll have to ask Jason. He told me that was the meaning of his name."

Ollie slammed his fist on the arm of the chair. "You know what I meant."

"Oh, that? Yes, I can prove it about as well as you can disprove it," Chops said. "I have all the paperwork, but I don't record telephone calls."

"Too bad the government will have to take it all away," Ollie said. "Lauber used stolen money, you know."

"No, he didn't," Chops said. "That's what part of the phone calls were about, especially the last one."

"Okay, so tell me," Ollie said, and his voice was about as sneering as I had ever heard it. "And try talking loud, will you? If you shout, the argument becomes even more convincing."

I'm not normally an angry person, but I wanted to get up and slap Ollie's face about ten times. And if he still kept that smug look, I would volunteer for another ten times.

To my surprise, Chops didn't react. "You may or may not know that Stefan had been an investment broker. He started out totally legit and made a lot of big bucks doing that. Good money. In fact, extremely good money."

"Oh, but of course," Ollie said. "Another innocent in the world."

"I refer to the period prior to the diamond robbery. We can prove his honesty. I investigated him thoroughly before I became involved. For example, Stefan invested fifty-five thousand dollars in a start-up company close to thirty years ago—I think it was around 1977 or 1978, but I'd have to check my research. You see, another factor is that I wanted to write his biography. He refused but said maybe one day. So I collected information and—"

"Yeah, I got that," Ollie said. "About 1977 or 1978, what happened? I can hardly wait to hear this."

"Good, because it's a great story. Stefan invested in a start-up company owned by two guys named Bernie Marcus and Arthur Blank. They called it MB Associates—"

"Okay, so—"

"So they later changed the name to Home Depot. Maybe you've heard of them. That fifty-five grand has made so much money that maybe a year before the diamond robbery, he sold his share of the company, reinvested in Google. com, and—"

"Oh, I am so impressed."

"Ollie, cut it out, okay?" Burton said softly. "Let's just listen."

"Yes, I have all the paper trail, and furthermore, three months ago Stefan sold his Google stock—all legitimately owned—and put every penny into a nonprofit organization. I'm on the board. Am I making sense now?"

"But again, of course you can prove—"

"Let me finish, sir, please. You see, Stefan was involved in the grand larceny deal—the theft of diamonds."

"And a murder," Ollie said. "Don't forget that. If he was guilty of the diamond theft, he's tied in with and just as guilty of the murder."

"We can discuss that later. I don't believe the diamonds and the murder are the same case, but that's not the point I wish to make. May I continue?" Without waiting for consent, Chops got up and walked in a small circle, his huge arms behind his back. "Stefan was involved in the theft of the diamonds and was ready to make a full confession."

"And we know the diamonds were never recovered," I said quietly.

"That's because Stefan had them."

"You're positive?" Burton asked.

"Absolutely. He told me. I didn't see them, but I believed him. That is, he told me in such a way that I did not have legal knowledge because—as a good, law-abiding citizen and registered voter in DeKalb County—I would have felt it was my duty to go to the police. But I knew and he knew I understood."

"And the purpose of your last call was what?" Burton asked.

"Stefan was ready to accept any further punishment for the diamonds and to return them. That wasn't even the issue. The issue was the nonprofit organization. He wanted to make sure there was no smear or connection. It's all documented. I mean legally documented to show that it's clean money."

"Okay, yeah, maybe, so tell me about the diamonds," Ollie said.

"I don't know anything except this: He planned to return them."

"Oh, right—of course he did."

"That's what Jason Omore told us," I said, but Ollie acted as if he hadn't heard me.

Ollie started to get up, but Chops still walked around the room in his tight little circles. The detective settled back into his chair. Both of his hands showed slight tremors now. "So Lauber got religion in prison and—"

"Despite your caustic and somewhat negative attitude," Chops said, "such transformations do take place."

I smiled. He was no longer talking like someone from the inner city. The more Chops talked, the more I liked him; the more he talked, the less I liked Ollie. He talked the way I would have in his place. I not only enjoy being a smartmouth; I like other smartmouths.

"Okay, let's move on to the return of the diamonds. How do you know?"

"Simple. I was to be the go-between."

11

It took a few seconds for Burton, Ollie, and me to react to Chops's statement. "Yes, I was the go-between to return the diamonds. Not to deliver them personally, you understand. I was the go-between to work this out with the police and the insurance company. He had someone else in mind to actually deliver the diamonds."

"And Lauber planned to return the diamonds? Just because he had a change of heart?" Ollie asked, his tone reflecting his disbelief.

"Yes, because he had a change of heart," Chops said. "Stefan asked me to come here today." He looked at his watch. "Actually, it was to have been at 4:00 today—in less than an hour." He turned his back to us. But I saw the tears spilling out. He pulled out a handkerchief and blew his nose. He walked over to the window as if to stare down at the lake.

"Okay, let's say I believe you—"

Chops turned around. "You believe me, do you? I tell you what I would like you to do, Mr. Viktor. When you go to your home tonight, I want you to get down on your knees, look deeply into your heart, and ponder how little your opinion means to me."

I roared with laugher.

Chops winked at me. "In short, I don't care if you believe me. You didn't believe me when I was innocent of a serious crime; I expect nothing has changed."

"Let's say I believe you," Ollie said. "Where are the diamonds?"

"I have no idea. Stefan didn't tell me. I assumed they were in his room here at the hotel."

"The room has been searched," I said.

"At least twice and also by the police," Burton said.

"Searched and ransacked," I added.

"Really? What happens now?" Chops asked. "If you don't have the diamonds to return, there's nothing I need to negotiate. Is that correct?"

"Don't leave town—"

"I love it when you say things like that," I said, cutting off Ollie. "It sounds so TVish. Aren't you also supposed to tell him that you expect to be in touch with him?"

"Get out of here," he said to Chops. He turned his back on him and glared at me. "I don't think you like me very much, do you?"

227

"You're extremely perceptive." I gave him my best smile.

"I'm only trying to do my job," Ollie said. "Give me a break."

Immediately I felt bad for being smart-mouthed. "You're right. I apologize for my rudeness."

"Now what?" Burton asked. "Anyone have any idea what we do now?"

"I think we need to wait," Ollie said. "I expect at least two more visitors before the day is over."

"Who might they be?" I asked.

"Lucas and somebody named Scott Bell-James—"

"Is that the man in 621?" I asked.

Instead of answering me, Ollie said, "I've left messages for both of them."

I didn't want to sit in the room with Ollie and just wait. I decided to take a walk beside the lake. When I announced my intentions, Burton asked if he could accompany me. I readily agreed. Ollie said he had phone calls to make anyway.

Frankly, I also wanted to get away from Ollie for a few minutes. He was quixotic—one minute he acted like a normal person, and then he'd shift and act like a man on drugs who was waiting for the next fix. I didn't think he was an addict, but his habits were peculiar.

—

The sun was a white ball, and even though it was midafternoon and I put on my sunglasses, I still had to squint. Part of the reason was the glare from the lake itself. In the warm afternoon sun, the impatiens were clumps of red, white, pink, and orange. They seemed to peek out from the immense variety of monkey grass and hostas. A small sign boasted of sixty-four varieties of hostas, and I didn't doubt it. I had never seen such a variety in stripes and solids, variegated and in colors ranging from blue-green to chartreuse.

When we reached the SOUTHERN HERB HAVEN (or so the sign declared), I wanted to pause and inhale the fragrances that teased my nose: rosemary, sage, mint, the peppery scent of savory, and the fragrance of sweet marjoram. "Oh, this is wonderful, isn't it?"

"It's nice," Burton said, which made it obvious that flowers and spices weren't high on his list of favorite things.

We moved on down the path and saw a glass-enclosed area of Jerusalem cherry plants. They smell terrible, but they were made untouchable because their bright orange fruit is poison and a part of the foxglove family. I could have stayed all day as we walked among the blue, violet, and white lobelia.

"You didn't come out here just to wander among nature," Burton said. "Something is troubling you. Right?"

"Either you're highly intuitive or you read me well—maybe both."

"Maybe," he said and rewarded me with that gorgeous smile.

"I feel as if there's some kind of conspiracy going on around me."

"Conspiracy?" he asked. "Maybe. The diamonds are worth a lot of—"

"I didn't mean the diamonds."

He stopped and stared at me. "You've lost me."

"You talk to me about God—"

"Yes, but specifically about Jesus Christ the Savior."

"Okay, specifically about Jesus Christ. Then Jason Omore is a Christian, and I learn that Stefan is a believer. Chops Harrison becomes the newest surprise," I said. "Oh yes, and Ollie is one—or at least he's supposed to be one, too."

"You don't think he's genuine?"

"I don't know," I said. "You're the preacher. You ought to know."

Burton laughed. "Long ago I stopped judging people. At best I'm a fruit inspector."

Now it was my turn to look confused.

"Jesus said, 'By their fruits you will know them.' So I test fruit from time to time, but it's still not my job to decide who believes and who doesn't. My role is to encourage and help those who are open. If they are good fruit, I do whatever I can to help them grow."

"I like that," I said. "Great attitude." Immediately I thought of Uncle Rich, who always knew with pinpoint accuracy—or so he implied—precisely which people would enter the portals of heaven and those who rushed toward the pit of utter destruction.

"So about this conspiracy," Burton said. "Want to tell me more?"

"I feel as if I'm getting crowded, that's all."

"Am I pushing too hard?"

"No, of course not." I bent down and pinched the top two leaves off a chocolate mint plant and handed him one. I chewed on my leaf. He watched me and did the same. "But, Burton, it's as if you had programmed each of the others to come in and recite their stories—their experiences of faith—just for me."

Burton stopped walking and grinned at me.

"So now you're going to tell me that it's some kind of divine conspiracy."

"Is it?" he asked.

"Is it?"

"I don't know," he said softly. "I know that I pray for you every day. I want you to experience deep inner peace—the kind of peace I've found."

"You pray for me?"

"Every day."

As I stared into his dark blue eyes, I knew he meant every word. "I don't know, Burton. I think—I think maybe I want to believe all this. Maybe I will."

"Maybe you will," he said, and we continued walking. We had made a complete circle, which I estimated to be about three-quarters of a mile.

After he said those words, I didn't respond at first. Frankly, I didn't know what I wanted. "Maybe," I finally said.

12

As soon as Burton and I completed the circle around the small lake, we decided to join Ollie. We had gotten within ten feet of the room when a man came from the direction of the desk. He stopped at the door of the suite the inn had given us and knocked.

Burton stepped up and introduced himself and me. Before he had a chance to tell us who he was, Ollie opened the door. "Come in, come in," he said.

We entered the room, and all three of us turned to the stranger.

"I had a message on my cell that Detective Oliver Viktor wanted to see me. My name is Scott Bell-James."

Although he was probably about five seven, I estimated his weight to be in excess of three hundred pounds. His tan suit pants strained to encompass his enormous thighs. The buttons on his shirt met, but there was no possibility he could button his chocolate brown blazer. He wore a tie of yellow polka dots on a field of rich russet, which clashed with his blazer and emphasized the extraordinary circumference of his neck. His face was extremely round, and his almost-auburn eyes glinted with intelligence. In spite of his great size—or perhaps because of it—he was compulsively neat. His clothes were immaculate. His hands were pink and his nails manicured and neatly trimmed. He looked as if he had just come from the barber, with not a single strand of his graying-brown hair out of place. He carried a briefcase that he clutched tightly.

Ollie approached him silently and appraised him for several seconds in a way that probably would have intimidated most people. "Yes, Mr. Bell-James. I'm Oliver Viktor." He pointed to a chair and asked the man to sit. "It's really quite a small thing, sir." Ollie sounded as if he were trying to imitate Peter Falk as Columbo.

"Certainly, Mr. Viktor. Just how may I help?"

"You are booked in room 621?"

"That is correct."

"You asked for 623 first?"

"Yes, I did."

"Why did you want 623?"

"Is there a crime against requesting a particular room?"

"Oh no, sir, of course not," Ollie said quietly. He scratched the back of his head. "It is a bit unusual, but not illegal." Ollie's hands were no longer shaking, and he seemed calmer than he had been since we first met.

"But why did you want 623? Why didn't you ask for, say, 519?"

The man stared at Ollie for what seemed like a long time. He blinked a couple of times. "That information is not quite correct. I did not ask for 623."

"Well then, the information I have contradicts that, and this whole thing seems confusing to me," Ollie said.

"No, I might as well tell you. I asked *about* 623—but that was only to verify that Stefan Lauber had that room." He took several deep sighs as if he felt relieved to explain. "If the room had been vacant, then I would have known he wasn't there. I knew he had been there the week before. You see, I, uh, hired a private investigator to locate him for me. Very simple, right?"

"Go on."

"Once the clerk informed me that Mr. Lauber was in room 623—I pointedly asked him, and it cost me a small bribe to get the information—I requested the room next to 623." He held up his hand and said, "I did not explain my reason, and I'm not sure what I would have said if the clerk had asked. He didn't."

"And he gave you room 621."

"That is correct."

"When did you check into room 621?"

"Three days ago."

Ollie sat in silence as if waiting for Scott Bell-James to add more. Outside a mower started up at the end of the building.

"Why did you want room 621?"

"I didn't care if it was 621 or 625. Either one would have been satisfactory." As he spoke, not only was his pronunciation precise, but I detected the slightest British accent.

This time Ollie sighed. "Okay, Mr. Bell-James—"

"Please call me Scott."

"Okay, Scott, why did you want the room next to Stefan Lauber?"

"It is quite simple. In fact, the reason is very, very simple. I came to the Cartledge Inn to kill him."

All of us were so shocked by Scott Bell-James's confession that he came to murder Stefan Lauber that for several seconds we simply stared at him.

Ollie recovered first and said, "You admit you killed Lauber?"

"I did not say that, and I made no such confession." Scott straightened up as if to make his short stature taller. "I came to the Cartledge Inn for the precise purpose of putting an end to his miserable existence. However, I did not commit the deed." He smiled. "I was quite fortunate, because someone took care of that untidy task for me." He walked over to the wingback chair. Without being asked, he sat and carefully pulled the creases on his slacks to avoid wrinkles.

"Okay, I want to be sure this is correct," Ollie said. He pointed to Burton and me, introduced us, and explained who we were. He emphasized that we were not police but we were professionals. He didn't say what kind of professionals, and Bell-James didn't ask. We sat on the couch and turned so that we could face Scott.

Ollie sat on the opposite couch and pulled out the ubiquitous notebook. "If needed, they will act as witnesses to this conversation. Do you have any objections?"

"Of course not. Ask whatever you wish. I have absolutely nothing to hide."

"Okay, let's review this." Ollie went through all the information Scott had given us and ended with, "You admit you came here to kill him. You were here two nights before the murder, and you claim you did not kill him."

"That is correct. I did not murder Mr. Lauber."

"If you came to kill him," Burton said, "why didn't you do it the first or second night?"

"The first night, Monday, I wasn't ready. Although I am a man of great determination, I am not a person of great courage, you see, and I had to work up the courage—the ability—to commit the deed."

"And the second night?"

"Tuesday night, I was almost ready. I knocked at his door, but he did not answer. I went to the lobby and used a hotel phone to call his room. He did not answer and I left no message."

"Why didn't you call from your room?"

He smiled. "Perhaps I've watched too many episodes of *Law and Order* or reruns of the old *NYPD* series, which was my favorite, but I assumed there was the bare possibility that the Cartledge Inn might maintain a record of calls from room to room. I knew they would not have a record from the lobby."

"Wait a minute," I said. "You've been so open about all this, why were you devious about that?"

"Oh, that is extremely simple," he said. He tugged at his tie to loosen it slightly. "I had not settled on whether to make my crime public. I had planned to shoot him, but I had yet to decide if I wished to go to the police and confess or attempt to hide what I did. That does take considerable thinking, would you not agree?" He stood and took off his blazer. He folded it neatly and carefully laid it on the arm of the chair. "Would you mind if I had a bottle of that water? I am quite parched."

Burton was closest to the cooler, so he grabbed one and handed it to Scott. The man drank greedily. The three of us sat and watched while he finished all eight ounces.

"Would you like another?" I asked.

He shook his head. He laid his briefcase carefully on the floor, walked over to the cooler, picked up a paper napkin, wiped the bottom of the water bottle, and set it on the table. He came back to the chair and sat. For a man of his girth, he moved gracefully. "So what is your next question?" Scott asked.

"Well, perhaps it's too obvious," Ollie said, "but why did you want to kill Lauber?"

"Oh, I apologize, I truly do. You see, I've never been interrogated before. This is quite an adventure. I assumed you knew all of that and that was the reason you had asked me to come in for an interrogation."

"All of that? What do you mean?" Ollie leaned forward as if this were the most fascinating witness he had ever questioned. I wondered what kind of role he now played.

"Permit me first to explain my background," Scott said. "Please indulge me and try to be patient with me. My late wife said that it sometimes takes me a grand loop around Piccadilly Circus before I make my point."

He told us that he was British by birth and an American citizen by choice. He went into lengthy detail to explain why he had a hyphenated surname, and it had something to do with a family named James that was disreputable and it was his father's way to distinguish between them.

I was already bored, but I wanted to watch and see how Ollie handled this. To his credit he said nothing, although he crossed and recrossed his legs three times.

Scott Bell-James told us, eventually, that his wife of twenty-three years had died of cancer a year earlier, and she had been his total life. "Without Edna, I really have little else to live for." He said that during her lingering illness of more than two years, he diverted himself by thinking about the terrible crimes committed by

Stefan Lauber and that he ought to be punished "for his dastardly deed."

"But why that crime?" I asked. "It seems, well, so offbeat. I'd think you'd focus on something more—more like rapists or—"

"Again, I need to make myself clear. You see, Edna's brother was Jeremiah Macgregor."

The three of us stared at each other. Ollie raised his hands and shrugged.

"Who?" I asked.

"Jeremiah Macgregor," he said. "May I have another bottle of water?"

We went through the same ritual again, including drying off the bottom of the plastic bottle. After he was seated again, Scott said, "Oh, perhaps you did not know or you did not make the connection. Forgive me. I live with such inner pain and become quite obsessive, and I quite forget that others do not know. You see, Jeremiah Macgregor was my late wife's brother. That may not sound like a strong bond, but I wish to assure you that he was far, far more than my brother-in-law. He was more like my own brother. No, he was more than that. In my entire life, I have never had such a friend, someone who understood me so well, accepted my faults, and truly, truly loved me. I often said he was the brother I never had. For almost twenty years, the four of us spent our holidays—sorry, our vacations—together and were the closest friends."

I was the impatient one this time. I was ready to say, "Stop circling Piccadilly Circus."

He must have read my face. "Please forgive me," he said and nodded my way. "I shall attempt to condense this. Edna and I were never able to have children. Jeremiah and Roberta. . ." He paused and smiled before he added, "Roberta is my younger sister. I have two sisters but no brothers—"

"Yes, we understand," Ollie said.

"Well, this is important, I think. You see, I married Jeremiah's sister, and he married my sister. Is that not rather amazing? Actually, I have two sisters—"

"So you've already told us," Ollie said.

"Oh yes, so I did."

"Just get to the point before I die of old age." Ollie had stopped being Columbo and now segued into a bad-cop routine.

"Yes, yes, of course. But you see, Jeremiah and Roberta have sons—three wonderful boys—and I have had to assume some degree of responsibility—"

Ollie got up, walked over to Scott Bell-James, grabbed his tie, and jerked him forward. "I don't care about Roberta or Jeremiah or their five sons—"

"Three sons."

"Two. Five. So what?"

"Oh yes, but of course that would not matter to you," Scott said. He didn't seem the least bit uncomfortable that Ollie had yanked him forward, although that quick jerk must have hurt his neck.

I got up and walked over. I removed Ollie's hand from the man's tie and straightened it. "Scott, please forgive us for our impatience, but your late wife was correct. You're taking a long time to get to whatever it is you want to tell us. Can you be just a little more direct?"

"Yes, yes, I can do that." He reached for a third bottle of water, and Burton tossed it to him. He drank the contents and thanked us for being so accommodating. As soon as he finished, I took the bottle, and he watched me wipe away all moisture. He rewarded me with a smile.

Ollie was ready to blow up in anger, but I laid a restraining hand on his shoulder. "Why don't you sit back down, Ollie? I'll help Scott tell his story." I got down on my knees next to him.

"Okay, help us with the connection. Who was Jeremiah Macgregor, and what does he have to do with Stefan Lauber?"

"Why, he was the courier. Weren't you aware of that fact?"

"The diamond courier?" Burton asked.

"Yes, of course. That is the reason I have been so—so compulsively antagonized. Edna was his sister, and my truly beloved wife. First I lost Jeremiah, who was my best friend. My best friend in the—"

"Yeah, I know, the best in the world," Ollie said and let out an extremely loud sigh. "Finally."

I held up my hand to Ollie and said to Scott, "Go on, tell us."

"As my beloved wife declined in health, I realized I would soon be deprived of the two people I loved the most in the world. As her cancer progressed, I became obsessed over Jeremiah's death. Perhaps it was the only thing I could do at that time to cope with her illness. By allowing my mind to focus on repaying Stefan Lauber for his odious crime, I could find a reason to continue to live. Finally, Edna died. I had lost two of the dearest people in my life, my sweet, adorable Edna and my very best friend in—"

"In the world."

Scott stared at Ollie and back at me. "Is he angry about something?"

"He's a policeman and he suffers from acid reflux," I said. "He wants information quickly. Just go on."

"One evening I listened to the local news on the NBC affiliate. I don't like the Fox Channel because—" He stopped and cleared his throat. "That is, I heard that Stefan Lauber had been released from prison. He had served less than two years. Two years for accepting stolen goods—but worse—two years for a crime that included the murder of Jeremiah, my best—"

"Your best friend in the whole world." Ollie rolled his eyes.

"I could think of nothing else—I don't mean that almost literally, you understand, because although most people use that word, they only mean it as a figure of speech that—"

"Yes, it's a figure of speech," Burton said.

"Anyway, I decided I had to have justice. I searched online for a private investigator." He smiled as if pleased with himself. "I remembered how they did such things in the TV shows. I actually interviewed three, but I finally settled on Terrance Waylin. He is local, you see, and his office is located on—"

"Let me see if I can help here," Burton said. "You hired the investigator, and he located Lauber for you. You learned he was staying here at the Cartledge Inn, and you decided to come here, meet up with him, and kill him."

"Exactly. And I must say you are excellent for putting it so concisely. Thank you so much."

I glanced at my watch. Scott Bell-James had been in the room nearly twenty minutes and had given us perhaps three minutes of information. I stayed on my knees and said, "Scott, help us. How did you plan to kill him?"

"Oh, I was going to shoot him. You see, I went to a pawnshop in Avondale Estates. It's at an intersection with a strange name—Sam's Crossing. It intersects with College Street."

"Yes, I know where that is," I lied, but I wanted him to move on.

"You can surely understand that I did not want to go to a regular gun store because—"

"Yes, I understand," I said. "What kind of gun did you buy?"

"The weapon I purchased was manufactured in Switzerland. It is called, I believe, a SIG-Sauer 9mm semiautomatic pistol. It is a compact, short-barreled handgun and holds an unusually large number of rounds in the magazine. Sixteen the man at the pawnshop told me. And unlike most other pistols, it has a double action, which means that it did not need to be cocked to be fired. All I needed to do was pull the trigger. That was why I purchased the SIG-Sauer. Oh, I do not mean because of the bullets, but because I didn't have to do anything but fire."

"Thank you," I said. "Where is the pistol now?"

"Oh, I discarded it. I threw it as far into the lake as I could. I mean the lake here at the Cartledge Inn. I understand that it is more than twenty feet deep, but I assumed there was, is, virtually no likelihood of draining—"

"Okay, enough," Ollie said softly as he paced the room. To his credit, he didn't add anything more.

"Did you ever see Lauber?" Burton asked.

"Certainly. I went to his room Wednesday night—the night he was murdered. I had the gun concealed in my left pocket. I'm left-handed, you see, and I could still knock with my right hand. I thought that was a rather good ruse to—"

"So you knocked!" Ollie said.

"Well, yes, I did. I mean, I tapped on the door, but it wasn't locked. So I pushed it open—"

"And?" I asked.

"Why, he was dead, of course. But you certainly know that, don't you? For a few moments, I was quite upset. Actually, I was disappointed because someone else had brought justice in the world. I didn't know whether to cry or to leap with joy."

"Did you search the room?"

"You must be joking. The room was a complete mess—all torn up. On TV don't they say the room was tossed? And why would I want to search the room? I went there to kill him, not to steal from him."

"What about the diamonds? Didn't you want them?"

"Diamonds? What are diamonds to me? Diamonds cannot purchase happiness or give peace of mind or provide solace in my grief. No, I wanted only revenge." He stared at me, and his eyes pleaded for me to understand. "Oh yes, and you see, I did resolve the situation. I had decided to go to the police station—I even knew where it was located. Right off I-285 and Memorial Drive. I even made a practice run earlier during the day. I was afraid I'd be so unstrung that—"

"And give yourself up?"

"Not exactly. I planned to write a confession, hand it to the policeman at the desk—I did not go inside, but on TV they always have a desk. Then I planned to stand there and shoot myself in the head. I read that those who shoot themselves in the stomach or the heart do not always succeed, and that would be a great tragedy."

Burton came over and knelt on the other side of Scott. "How do you feel now?"

"Now? I'm grateful I did not have to take his life or my own. But, yes, I would have done it. Yes, I certainly would have. So I believe justice has been served."

"*If* he was involved in the murder of Jeremiah," I said.

Scott stared at me. "Are you trying to say he was not?"

"No, because I don't know," I said, "but I have a feeling—call it only intuition or a gut feeling—but I don't think he was connected with the murder."

"How can you say that?" Scott asked.

"I was Stefan's therapist."

"And he told you he did not kill—"

"No, we did not go into that, but I don't think he did. He did many wrong things, but I do not believe murder was anything he'd be involved in."

"Yes, but if that—that horrible Willie Petersen did the killing—Lauber would not have literally pulled the trigger, but he would have been guilty."

"I'm stepping out—way out," I said, "but I don't think the murder of the courier and the robbery were the same crime."

"How can you say that?"

"Stefan once said that he had done many wrong things, but he'd never been involved in any form of violence, and he made a point to say that he would never have tolerated it."

"Yeah, right," Ollie said.

I ignored him. "Stefan also said that one time there was a crime of violence in which he was implicated, but he wasn't connected with it."

"And you believed that slime bag?" Ollie said.

"I believed *my client*," I said.

"Oh dear, dear, if he was not in any way involved," Scott Bell-James said, "I might have—I might have committed a crime instead of exacting revenge."

"Yeah, well, I hope that was true—but you have only Lauber's word, for whatever that's worth," Ollie said.

"It's worth a great deal to me," I said. "I believed him."

"How sweet," he said, his voice heavy with sarcasm. "However, as far as I'm concerned, he was a felon. Any man who would be involved in that kind of theft could just as easily be involved in murder. Right now I'm not sure anyone cares whether he was involved. Lauber is dead. The diamonds are still missing—at least we have not found them."

Ollie turned to Bell-James. "Okay, Scott, you may go," he said in a calm voice. "Did you throw away the gun?"

"I said—"

"I know what you said. Did you throw away the gun?"

"No." He looked away. "I was afraid that it might—might implicate me in some way."

"Of course," Ollie said.

Scott picked up his blazer with one hand and his briefcase with the other. He opened the briefcase and held it out with his left hand. "Here it is. You will notice that it has never been fired. That is, I have never fired it, but the previous owner might have. As I explained, I bought it at a pawnshop and—"

"Yeah, whatever," Ollie said and pulled out his handkerchief and took the gun. He laid it on the table.

I smiled as I watched Ollie wrap the gun and lay it aside. It was exactly how they do it on TV. Maybe those shows do have some reality to them. Or maybe Ollie watches them and imitates the detectives.

"Just one more thing," Scott said. "How will I know—about whether Lauber had anything to do with—?"

"It will be on the news," I said. "You said you didn't like to watch the Fox Channel, so you can see it on CBS."

Scott started to give each of us a good-bye, but Ollie stopped him again. "We're glad to have met you and appreciate your forthrightness. If there's anything else, I'll be in touch."

"What about my gun? I certainly don't plan to use it, but I surely would not wish it to fall into the wrong hands. I heard of one case where a policeman took an innocent man's gun and—"

"You'll get it back," Ollie said sharply. "Just leave us alone now." He spoke those last words through clenched teeth.

Scott stared at each of us for a few seconds and hurried from the room.

"Now what?" Burton asked. "So far everything comes up empty."

"Not quite. We still have a few things left to explore," Ollie said.

"Such as?" I asked.

Just then someone knocked at the door.

14

"I'd like all of you to meet someone," Ollie said and stood aside while a couple entered the room.

The woman came in first. She was small and thickset, and at first I thought she was elderly. As she stepped into the room, I figured she was probably not more than fifty, but with a face full of premature wrinkles and furrows—a face that had seen a hard life. Her long black hair, streaked with gray, was drawn back into a knot at the nape of her neck. Her lips and cheeks were colorless. A plain, no-nonsense woman, even to her ankle-length black skirt and long-sleeved, high-collared blouse.

The man wore a crumpled white suit. Thick glasses had the effect of magnifying his pale blue eyes into great round hypnotic orbs. He was tall, angular, and hard-faced.

"We are the Boltinghauses, Dennis and Fillis. We were told that we could speak to Mr. Stefan Lauber," the man said. "The clerk at the desk sent us here." He looked around at the two men.

"Oh, this is the man you want," Ollie said. Before Burton could react, Ollie added, "They said they wouldn't talk to anyone else."

"Mr. Lauber? I hate to break in on a meeting, but this gentleman"—he nodded toward Ollie—"said it would be all right."

"What brought you here?" Burton asked.

"Uh, well, we are not used to talking in, uh, well, a crowd—"

"These are my consultants," Burton said smoothly. "I wouldn't discuss any business without them or keep any secrets from them."

"If you're sure." The man looked from Ollie to me and then to Burton.

"Positive."

"Well, sir, this is an unexpected pleasure," the woman said. "We have heard many excellent things about you—"

"Such as?" Burton tried to hide his confused expression, but I knew him well enough that I could see he hadn't fully succeeded.

"Well, sir, you see," the man said and peered through his thick lenses, "the word we have heard is that you have jewelry to sell. Uh, rather expensive, upscale jewelry. That's all I'm prepared to say in the presence of these others."

"We are totally discreet," Ollie said. "You can say we're in this business together."

241

"Please continue," Burton said.

"It is like this," the woman said. "We hear you have diamonds for sale and you need someone to dispose of them for you."

"Dispose?" Burton asked, and he was now in his role. "And by that you mean—what?"

"You know quite well what we mean," the man said. "We're prepared to, uh, take them off your hands and, uh, sell them—for a price, you understand—and you'll get as good a deal from us as you will anyone else."

"And what price do you have in mind?"

"We're prepared to offer you thirty million dollars."

"Do you have that much? In cash? In what form?"

"Bearer bonds," the man said and smiled.

"Bearer bonds have been illegal in the United States since the early 1980s," Ollie said quickly.

"But not in other parts of the world," the woman said. "And they are like cash."

"I don't know," Burton said, and it was obvious he wasn't sure how to go with this.

"How did you learn about the availability of the diamonds?" I asked. "We haven't sent a message through CNN."

"I prefer not to say," Boltinghaus said.

"I prefer to hear," Burton said.

The couple stared at each other for a minute, and she nodded for him to speak. "Uh, well, you see, there was a certain woman who was supposed to, uh, entice you to sell or give them to her and to meet us by 2:00 today. She did not show up, and, uh, she said she had no other means of disposing of the diamonds—"

"So we decided to see you ourselves," the woman said. "In fact, we can offer you a better price—"

"What is her name?" Burton said. "I've spoken to a number of people."

The couple looked at each other before he said, "We are, uh, prepared to match or better any other offer—"

"Tell me her name," Burton said more firmly.

"Knight. Deedra Knight. She assured us—"

"Deedra Knight is dead," Ollie said.

"A likely story," the woman said. "You only want to hold us up for more money." As she spoke, her words faltered as if she wasn't sure whether to believe Knight was dead.

Ollie held out his badge and identified himself. "What else do you have to tell us?"

"I don't know anything more," the woman said. "That's the truth."

"I can tell you only that Ms. Knight approached us and said there was a profitable deal for us. I have been in the diamond business for more than thirty years, sir, and I assure you that—"

"These are stolen diamonds," Ollie said.

"Oh, well, in that case," the man said, "I'm not interested."

Ollie laughed. "Actually, I know who you are. You own that shabby little jewelry store one block off Main Street in Tucker—"

"Shabby?" the woman said. "I would certainly not call it shabby."

"And you've been implicated in several jewelry-fencing operations," Ollie said. "Go on, get out of here."

They rushed from the room.

As soon as the door slammed behind them, Ollie said, "We've learned one thing from that episode—"

"Yes, the diamonds are still missing," I said.

Ollie smiled—a genuine, honest smile—before he said, "Exactly right. Either the person who killed Deedra has them, or no one has located them."

Maybe he wasn't as much of a jerk as I had thought.

———

Ollie's cell rang, and he turned his back on us and listened for several minutes. "Hmm. Yes, interesting. Thank you so much!"

After he hung up, he smiled again. With practice, that smile could be as enchanting as Burton's—well, almost. I might even learn to like the man.

"We may have had a very, very interesting break." Ollie picked up the phone on the table and called the desk. "Craig, would you come down to the room? If you could get someone to cover for you for the next ten minutes, I'd appreciate it very much."

Although I wanted to know what he had learned from the cell call, I knew it would do no good to ask. Ollie liked to be in control—and I understood that. If I asked questions, that would make him enjoy his power role even more. If the circumstances had been reversed, I probably would have acted the same way.

While we waited, I decided to open a bottle of water. I took a few sips I didn't actually want. It was really a nervous gesture to do something while we waited.

A knock was followed immediately by Craig opening the door and coming inside. "Here I am."

"Please come in and sit down," Ollie said. He indicated the wingback chair.

"Did I do something wrong?" Craig asked. He was small and almost elfish. When he sat in the large chair, he seemed even smaller and thinner.

"Did you do something wrong?" Ollie asked.

Craig's gaze went from face to face, and none of us said anything.

"Okay, I took that—that woman's money so she could get into 623. Honest, that's all."

"Really? Is that all?" Ollie asked.

I didn't understand the role he was playing, but he had shifted into a soft, quiet voice.

"Yeah, sure."

"Your name is Craig Bubeck, age fifty-four. Is that correct?"

"Yes," he said. The wariness in his eyes said he sensed what was coming next.

"And how long have you been employed at the Cartledge Inn, Craig Bubeck?"

"Uh," he said and cleared his throat. "Almost a year."

"And, Mr. Craig Bubeck, what did you do before you were employed by the Cartledge Inn?"

He dropped his head and said nothing.

"Tell us, please," Ollie said. "We're all extremely eager and anxious to know."

"I didn't have anything to do with—with the murders and that stuff." His voice sounded as if it might have come from a child. "Honest."

"Suppose you answer my question," Ollie said, and his voice had become even softer.

He cleared his throat again and picked invisible lint from his uniform blazer. "You know, don't you?" It was a voice about ready to break.

"Yes, Craig Bubeck, I do know. Indeed, I know," Ollie said. He turned from Craig and faced us. "He was in prison for six years."

"Uh, no, only four. The sentence was six, but I was paroled early."

"Oh, forgive me for making such a serious mistake," Ollie said. "I would certainly not want to hold a convicted felon's past before everyone, but suppose you tell my two friends here why you were in prison."

"Armed robbery."

I almost laughed. I couldn't believe that short, thin, frightened little man would have the courage to rob anyone.

"I was only the driver," he said. "I didn't do anything—but, yes, because I was involved, I was equally guilty." He looked up at Ollie and said softly, "I paid for my crime."

"Oh, of course you did, Craig Bubeck, and I won't dispute that," he said. "But tell my nice friends what kind of robbery you and your three misguided friends were involved in."

"Jewelry mostly. It was a jewelry store they held up."

"And there's more, isn't there?"

"I was supposed to—to fence the merchandise." He took a deep breath and said, "Okay, here's the whole story. It started with my brother-in-law. He—he owned a jewelry store near Lenox Mall. He has sometimes done things that—

okay, he was a fence. He had connections with an organization in Atlantic City."

"And where is your brother-in-law now, Craig?" Ollie stayed in that sticky-sweet tone.

"Back in the jewelry business. He copped a plea and—"

"Yes, I know that," Ollie said. "When I heard that from my department only minutes ago, can you possibly guess what I thought? Surely you must have known we would learn about your past."

"No, I didn't think you would. I mean, what is there to implicate me? I mean, I only operate the front desk—"

"And have access to the room keys."

"Yes, I do, but I have never, ever used—"

Ollie shrugged indifferently.

"Honest, sir. Never. Not once."

"And there's one more thing, Craig Bubeck. Were you ever away from the desk last night? I mean, even once during your shift?"

"Oh no, I wouldn't—" He stopped. "Okay, I was gone for maybe five minutes." His eyes pleaded with us. "I smoke. It's against the rules. I told the Cartledges that I had quit, but—"

"So you went out for a smoke. Where did you go, Craig Bubeck? To room 623 perhaps?"

"Why would I go there? No, I went out the side door of the inn and got into my car. The windows are tinted, so no one could see—"

"But you had to walk past the elevators to get to the side door. Am I correct?"

"Well, uh, yes, but I didn't—I didn't go to room 623 or to any other room. Honest, I—I—I just went to sneak a smoke. That's all."

"And you want us to believe you, don't you, Craig Bubeck?"

"Yes, of course I do."

Ollie squatted in front of him and said, "I would like to believe you. So here's how I can believe you. You return the diamonds and I'll believe you."

"But I don't have them! I don't know anything about them."

The poor man perspired, and I saw fear in his eyes. I also believed him.

"I'm reasonably sure we can assist you and get you some slack on your new prison sentence because you came voluntarily and gave us information." Ollie stared into the man's brown eyes.

"What are—are you crazy or something? I don't have any diamonds. I don't even know anything about any diamonds. What diamonds are you talking about?"

"You didn't know about the stolen diamonds from room 623?" Ollie asked.

"Diamonds? Is that the reason for the murder?" He shook his head. "I saw on the TV and in the papers about the murder. They said robbery was the motive, but I didn't know it involved jewelry—"

"Not just jewelry," Ollie said softly. "It involved diamonds. Millions of dollars worth of cut diamonds."

"Search me. Search my car." He pulled his keys from his pocket. "Search my apartment. You won't find anything."

Ollie walked around the chair several times and glared at the poor man. Finally, he said, "You know what, Craig Bubeck? I believe you—"

"Thank you—"

"I believe you because I don't think you're smart enough to pull off a job like this. It's too big for a little man like you. You're just too small, too simple, and lack the courage to do anything big."

The words obviously hurt Craig. I saw it in his eyes, and I started to object, but Burton held up his hand to silence me.

This time I ignored Burton. I walked over and touched Craig lightly on the shoulder. "The detective sometimes acts like a bully," I said. "Don't take it personally."

"How do I not take it personally?" he asked. I thought the poor man was going to cry. "He's not a very nice person, is he?"

"I'm sorry you have to go through this," I said.

"Can I go now?" he asked Ollie.

"Do you have anything else to tell us?"

"Nothing. Absolutely nothing," he said.

As I watched his face, I knew he was lying. He held back something. But I understood. If I had been in that chair, I wouldn't even have told the big man my name.

Craig got up and started toward the door. I touched his shoulder. "I am sorry." I lowered my voice and said sotto voce, "We'll talk later. Okay?"

Craig blinked twice. He smiled.

15

You acted like a cold, insensitive beast to that man," I said to Ollie. "That poor man."

"I thought it was a pretty good imitation of Rod Steiger in that old flick where he played a Southern sheriff. Did you notice how I continued to use his full name and talked softly and condescendingly and yet with authority?"

"Oh, I noticed," I said. "You were convincing, all right."

"It *was* a little heavy-handed," Burton said.

"Yeah, well, that's how it works sometimes." He nodded slightly and said, "You're right. Sometimes I rush things too much."

I tried to decide if I ought to give him the benefit of a few more words about how much I hated what he did. "You hurt that man. You didn't need to act that way."

"Okay, you're right," Ollie said.

Just then his cell rang, and he opened it and said, "Yes." His hand wasn't shaking, and I realized something rather obvious. When his hands shook the worst, he was harsh and vile tempered. When they weren't shaking, he acted as if he played some kind of role in a film. He was truly a strange man.

After a brief silence, he said, "Send him in. We'd love to talk to him."

Ollie motioned for Burton and me to sit, and he went to the door. As soon as someone knocked, he opened it halfway and kept the other person in the hallway. We could hear only muffled voices. In less than a minute, Ollie returned and a man followed him. He introduced Lucas Lauber, Stefan's older adopted brother.

I was amazed because there was a strong family resemblance. Like Stefan, he was lean and sinewy. Although Stefan's hair was dark, Lucas's hair was a medium brown, neatly trimmed and salt-and-pepper. His features were sharp and economical, as if God hadn't been in the mood to waste anything the day He had edited Lucas's genetic file. He had hazel eyes and a long nose. Although he wore no tie, his expensive dress shirt indicated that he felt more comfortable in that than he did in anything sporty. His suit trousers were charcoal gray with a thin blue pinstripe. My guess is that the suit must have set him back at least a couple of thousand dollars.

"You look a great deal like Stefan," I said.

"Our parents tried fourteen organizations before they picked me. They wanted a skinny kid that would look like his brother. They wanted people to think we were truly birth brothers." He smiled in what came across as deprecating. "I

was the right age—six years older—and had the right body style and hair color."
He laughed. "But Stefan's hair darkened to deep brunet. Mine stayed a lighter shade of brown."

"Did you like your adopted brother?" Ollie asked.

"Do you mind if I sit down?" Lucas asked and sat without waiting for a reply. "Did I like him? That would depend on which period of time you're asking about."

"Oh, not another long-winded—"

Burton put out his hand. "Mr. Viktor is tired, so please forgive him." He gave Lucas his heart-melting smile and said, "Tell us about your feelings for the past three or four years and move on to the present." He looked at Ollie. "Okay?"

"Yes, of course," Ollie said. He actually sounded courteous this time.

"It started maybe four and a half years ago, perhaps even five, when I learned that Stefan had cheated me. I'm not positive about the time element, but it was long before the diamond robbery. Months at least. Perhaps a year or even two." He closed his eyes as if he could visualize the past. "I still had my office in what used to be called the Bank of America Tower at Peachtree and North Avenue. Pat Fields hadn't yet become—"

"It doesn't matter," Burton said. "We have an approximate time."

"Your relationship with Stefan. Do you want to tell us about it?" I asked. That's always a good, neutral question for therapists to ask when they can't think of anything else.

"Of course," Lucas said. "The first thing you should know is that Stefan was one of the most insightful, most savvy investors I've ever known. It was as if he could smell good deals." He paused and shook his head. "You've heard of Google, I assume. That was one of the last big-profit deals he ever made. He initially invested a small amount—small for Stefan—of $40,000 and then another $600,000. It made a fortune for us."

"For us?" I asked.

"We were business partners. He was the risk taker, and I was the numbers counter—as Stefan called me. I played safe. I didn't make the huge profits on investments the way my brother did, but I never lost anything either."

"Did Stefan lose a lot of money?" I asked.

"Do you mean on investments or on people?"

"Tell us about his investments in people." Ollie leaned forward. His voice was exactly the right tone to elicit information.

Maybe he's not really so bad, I thought.

Lucas cleared his throat and waved away a bottle of water that Burton held up. "Pam Harty—she was the worst, but there had been a few unwise decisions before. He liked women—perhaps he liked too much variety in women and ran from affair to affair. Several of them cost him a few hundred thousand, but nothing big until she came along. I assume you know about Pam Harty. You do, don't you?"

We shook our heads.

"Really? I assumed you knew everything about her, the affair—sorry, my brother liked to call it the romance—but whatever anyone calls it, the whole thing was an awful situation. So far as I have been able to understand, she was the cause of the problem. He never blamed her; in fact, he refused to say much about her, even though she took him—us—for close to four million dollars."

"And he never blamed her?" I asked. "That seems strange to me."

"No, never. 'It was a weakness in me,' he told me when I confronted him. 'Pam was a thief, but she only exploited that weakness. She didn't cause it.' That's as close to his exact words as I can remember."

"Sounds noble of him," I said.

"That wasn't his reaction when I first learned of the theft. He said that later—much later."

"Tell us a little more, please," Ollie said. "Help us. Explain it to us."

"It starts easy and simple enough. Pam Harty went to work as a personal assistant to Stefan perhaps seven years ago. For the first couple of years, she was the total sponge—the kind of employee everyone wants. She wanted to know everything and was available to take on any job, no matter how trifling. She often said, 'Please teach me, Mr. Lauber.' Stefan loved that, by the way. If anyone wanted to get on his good side, just ask him to teach you. And to his credit, he was an excellent teacher."

"And? But?" Ollie asked softly. "What happened?"

"Pam bewitched him or something. I have no idea how this all came about, but somehow she twisted his thinking. She guided him into making several shrewd deals, very shrewd; I must say that much." He paused and turned to Ollie. "Is that important? If not, I'll go on."

"Oh, please go on," Ollie said. "This is new information."

"We can always come back to any of that if it's important," I said.

"Yes, of course," Lucas said. "I don't know all the details, but Pam totally and absolutely bewitched him."

"In what way?" I asked.

"Without permission—without my express permission—he invested one hundred million dollars in some oil scheme in East Africa. *There is no oil in East Africa.* Because it's part of the rift that begins in the Middle East and continues through the heart of Africa, some entrepreneurs claimed they had strong indications of oil. There has never been any oil found there—not a drop. It was some kind of con game that Pam either started, played, or cooperated in. She bilked him. That much is clear. She had an array of falsified documents and geological surveys. She brought in experts with thick accents and impressive-looking credentials. They were all part of the scheme. She bilked him totally. Then, of course, she disappeared. She left with the firm's money, which was mine, as well."

"Did you go out of business?" Burton asked.

"For six months I assumed we would, but we did recover—barely." He shook his head. "I lost almost everything, but by giving heavily from my own portfolio, I was able to save the company. Stefan had taken money that belonged to other investors. And I mean *taken*. He had forged their names to documents. I could have made life bad, really bad for him, but I knew it was the allure of that woman."

"Did you prosecute?"

"No. Stefan did turn over one of his personal accounts, which helped save the firm from bankruptcy. Just one, and he could have done more, but that plus the money I pitched in was enough to keep us solvent."

"You're saying Pam Harty left no trace behind?" I asked. "You didn't think you could find her or—"

"We did investigate. We hired a firm of discreet investigators. Apparently she had taken on the identity of a woman who died in a car accident years ago."

"So you let it drop? You did nothing?" Ollie raised an eyebrow. "That's a lot of money to lose—"

"I saw no way to recover the money. If word leaked out that our firm had been taken by such deception, we never would have recovered. In the end I chose to do nothing."

"Okay, so tell us about Stefan," Ollie said.

"Did you ever reconcile?" I asked. "You and Stefan?"

"Well, that's a long, long story."

"I don't mind listening to long stories," I said before Ollie could interrupt.

"Yes, we've already heard a few today," Ollie said. This time he laughed.

"When Stefan was in prison—you know that jailhouse-religion thing? He wrote me a long letter. It was ten handwritten pages, and he asked me to forgive him."

"Did you forgive him?" Ollie asked.

"Absolutely not. I believed he was sorry for the wrong things."

"What do you mean by 'the wrong things'?" I asked.

"I'm sure this sounds strange to you, but he seemed most upset about himself. He had been hoodwinked. He had been taken advantage of by Pam Harty or whoever she was. He had violated the trust placed in him. It was all about him. It was as if nothing else mattered but that he was able to be forgiven so he could clean up his dirty little conscience."

"I suppose that would have been hard to accept," Burton said.

"He had no regard for what he had done to me—the pain he had caused or the months of strain and worry—"

"That was when you received the letter, right?" I asked.

He nodded slowly. On his right hand, he wore a large ring with diamond chips. He twisted the ring several times as he spoke.

"You never reconciled?" Burton asked.

"Later," he said. "Yes, later we did."

"What happened later?" I asked. "Did you forgive him?"

"You mean after he repaid the money he had stolen?"

"He repaid it?" Ollie said. "One hundred million dollars and he repaid it? Hey, come on—"

"No, it's true. That's when I was willing to consider forgiving him."

" 'Consider' means you didn't?" I asked.

He smiled sadly. "He gave me the access code to a numbered bank account in the Cayman Islands. I took out enough to repay everything."

"Those things really exist?" I asked but felt embarrassed. "Sorry, I've read that kind of thing so often in books or seen it in films that I wondered."

"But he paid you back the whole amount?" Ollie questioned. "I find that incredulous."

"Incredulous or not, there was enough in the account."

"Enough? How much was enough?" Ollie asked. "How much was left?"

"I'm not sure that's relevant, but I took out enough to pay me back for all he had, uh, borrowed of mine, after I covered our investors. He had nearly eighteen million dollars left, so he wasn't going to suffer when he got out of prison."

Ollie whistled and repeated the amount.

"He had at least one other account. That was in Zurich. That's all I know, but it would not have been a small amount."

"He must have been a sharp investor," I said. "I mean, really sharp."

"Brilliant. Except, of course, for the incident with Pam."

"Yeah, yeah," Ollie said. "And it's a good thing she didn't get it all."

"He was in love with her," Lucas said. "He was beguiled by her, but he wasn't totally stupid."

"Okay, let's move on," Ollie said, "but I can't believe that crook would have made everything good."

I shook my head at Ollie and turned back to Lucas. "And when did you meet again—in person? I know it was at least once while he was in jail at the state prison in Hall County."

"How did you know we had connected again?"

"Just tell us when." Ollie sounded more like a therapist than a detective. "Please."

Lucas stared at his hands and played with his ring. His head bobbed slightly as if he were arguing with himself. "He wrote maybe three or four times and asked me to come see him, but I refused to meet with him."

"And why was that?" the detective persisted.

"I didn't like my brother. As I've already said, I resented him, and I knew he had never liked me, even from the first days together in our childhood. I was good to him, but I detested the spoiled brat. He got whatever he wanted, and quite often he did so at my expense."

"And as children, what did you get?" Burton asked.

"Leftovers. Always what was left after he got what he wanted." He looked up briefly and went back into the staring mode before he finally said, "Okay, I really have nothing to hide. I detested him. I didn't shoot him, although at one point I probably would have said that whoever did it might have done me a big favor."

"Because?" I asked.

"Because he got the big inheritance and I received half of what he did. Our parents insisted there was no difference between us, despite his preferential treatment. But when they died—both died in a head-on collision when I was twenty-five—it showed how they truly felt. I was worth half as much to them as he was."

"So shouldn't you blame them and not Stefan?" I asked.

"Blame? I'm long past blame. Try anger. Try—try feeling rejected and unloved and unwanted. That will give you a hint—a bare hint of the pain I felt. Nothing ever hurt me worse than my having to listen to our lawyer read the contents of the will. The amount of money meant nothing, because I was already successful and so was he. By the time he was eighteen, Stefan was already worth three or four million that he had built from a thousand-dollar birthday present from an uncle. So it had nothing to do with the amount. It was the percentage. Dear little brother Stefan never allowed me to forget that he was the favored one."

I felt sorry for Lucas and wanted to say something comforting, but nothing came to me. The expression on Burton's face told me how sad he also felt. Neither of us seemed to know what to say.

"Yeah, right, sad and painful," Ollie said. The words would have sounded harsh except that his voice remained so quiet, I had to strain to hear him. "So wouldn't that be reason enough for you to kill him?"

"Possibly. I thought of it several times. At one point I seriously considered trying to hire someone to kill him for me. Too impractical. I don't know anyone in the criminal element. But the hatred was that deep."

"So let's fast-forward to the day of Stefan's death," Ollie said. "You saw him that day, didn't you? We know for a fact that you did."

"If you know, why do you ask that question?" It was the most belligerent his voice had sounded. He dropped his head for a moment before he said, "I apologize for that rude remark. Right now I feel as if I'm walking around blindfolded in a maze of emotions." He paused and took several deep breaths. "I have no idea how you found out, but, yes, I did see him."

"Do you want to tell us about it?" Ollie asked.

I smiled. Ollie had learned something about how to proceed.

"I don't *want* to do so, but I will. Stefan called me twice on Monday and again on Tuesday. He begged me to talk with him face-to-face. He *begged*." Lucas actually laughed then. "I never thought he'd ever beg me for anything. It was the first time in our lives together that he had ever done anything except demand."

"So you gave in?"

"Yes, yes, but with great reluctance. We met for lunch at Anthony's on Peachtree. He paid, too." Lucas smiled. "That sounds like a small thing, but it was the one action that convinced me my brother had changed. He had never paid for my lunch—not ever. He used to laugh at me and say the older brother was always supposed to take care of the younger. That had been his joke since I had my allowance as a child."

"What did you talk about?" Ollie stood in front of him and gazed down on the man.

"Oh, mostly about God. That is, he talked about God. Mostly I listened."

"Did you believe him?" Burton asked.

"Hmm, that's an interesting question," Lucas said. "As I sat and listened, I focused my attention on his face. I knew my brother rather well. He had been an excellent manipulator, but as he continued to talk—"

"How did you react?" I asked. "Did you believe he had changed?"

"That's difficult to answer. The best I can say is that I believe *he believed* something powerful had happened to him."

"Was it powerful enough that you believed it was a genuine change?" Burton asked.

For several seconds Lucas stared at Burton as if trying to frame an answer. His emotions betrayed him, and his lower lip trembled. He tried to cover it up with his hand, but that didn't work. He started to cry. "Okay, I did believe him."

"And your feelings toward him?" I asked. "Did they change?"

"Yes. Or maybe—maybe I admitted what I had always felt. This must sound unintelligible, but I truly loved him. I had always loved him. I also hated him—hated him enough to want him dead—back then."

"I think I understand," I said. "I've had clients before with similar feelings."

Lucas made an attempt to smile at me. "I realized why I had refused to see him. I knew—I knew I would forgive him—the way I always did. Stefan had been unethical and—and done criminal things, but—"

"But you loved him, didn't you?" I asked.

Although he made no sound, Lucas cried for another minute or so. He nodded, and when he could trust his voice, he said, "Love isn't logical, is it?"

"Not in the least," Burton said. "Not in the least."

I turned my head, and my gaze met Burton's. I don't think he said those words for my benefit, but in that instant, something strange happened to me—something I wasn't ready to admit. In fact, I wasn't even sure what happened, but I knew one of life's supercharged moments had taken place. I couldn't have explained it if anyone had asked, but I knew it had happened. Later I would understand what *it* was.

"I'm the skeptic here," Ollie said. "Let me see if I understand what you're saying. This younger brother had always been mean and manipulative—"

"That's true."

"And you hated him? At one point you hated him enough to kill him."

"I thought—at the time I thought I did."

"And he buys lunch and you get emotional with all that brotherly love business. I want to believe you," Ollie said, "but—"

"You may believe as you choose. My brother is dead, and I really don't care what you think." A tautness came into his voice, and his body stiffened.

Ollie leaned down in front of Lucas until their noses were perhaps three inches apart. "If you loved your brother, why wouldn't you see him in prison when he begged? I'm just not able to believe you held back because you were afraid that you'd forgive him."

"You don't think he could have such conflicting emotions?" Burton asked.

"Maybe I live too much in a good versus evil world, and that usually means it's white or it's black. I'm open, Lucas, but you have to make it clear."

"I don't think I could make you understand."

"Try me."

"For many years I railed against him and against the way he treated me. He was so—so condescending. In small, understated ways he reminded me that I didn't belong to the family. . .that they had found me in an orphanage and no one else wanted me."

"So you had a motive to get rid of him?" Ollie spoke so quietly it took several seconds for his words to penetrate Lucas's thinking.

"Oh no!" The shock on Lucas's face made me wonder if Ollie was right.

"Sounds like it to me," Ollie said. He stared into Lauber's eyes. "It sounds like the perfect reason to kill him."

"I didn't know how I felt. Intense anger filled my heart. And pain. Rejection, I suppose." He leaned forward, and Ollie pulled back. "Do you have any idea how it feels to love someone who constantly rejects you? To hate someone with deep intensity and yet feel loving and protective at the same time?"

Ollie had the good sense to say nothing. Burton nodded.

"That's the best way I can explain it. You see, I never knew I loved my brother. Or maybe I didn't want to admit I loved him. I think. . .I think that if I had seen him before—before we met across the table at the restaurant—I would have broken down. I had visited him once in prison, but we had a glass wall between us. I stayed as emotionally cold and removed as I could."

"Okay, maybe I understand," Ollie said. "I'm not sure I do, but please go on."

"I didn't want to love my brother. I wanted to erase any positive feelings toward him. I wanted to hate him."

Ollie straightened up and walked in a small circle around Lucas's chair twice before he said, "So if you loved him so much, why did you shoot him?"

H ow dare you?" Lucas said. "I didn't kill Stefan. Whether you choose to
believe it or not is of little consequence to me. I know I am innocent."
He buried his hands in his face.

I wanted to kick both of Ollie's shins the way I'd kicked bullies when I
was a kid in elementary school. That was a mean thing for him to say. I felt
confused. Minutes ago he had been calm and perhaps even compassionate. I
didn't understand how he could change so abruptly. Was he playing both roles of
the good cop/bad cop the way they do on TV?

Ollie pointed to him and said, "But you were registered in the next room—
in room 625."

"What does that have to do with it?"

"You registered in room 625 so you could be next door and kill your brother."

"That's insane and irresponsible," he said.

"But we know you used that door to go into his room and back out. Right?"

"Yes, but—"

"What else can we believe except that you went into his room? You shot him
and—"

"That's totally untrue," Lucas said. "I'll try this again and hope you can follow
me. Or maybe I haven't said it well. After we met for lunch, he talked and—well,
I knew he was different. I still held back, but I knew Stefan had changed. I didn't
understand what was different, but I knew he wasn't the same. He was warmer.
Softer." Perhaps he sensed that Ollie was ready to interrupt him, because he held
up his hand and said, "Please. Just listen. Let me try to explain."

"Oh, far be it from me to stop anyone from implicating himself in a crime."

"Stop it!" I yelled at Ollie. "Let him talk."

"I'm a detective," Ollie said. "I'm willing for you to convince me."

"I was—I am registered in room 625. And if you check at the desk, you'll see
that the payment for the room is on Stefan's credit card." He smiled at me. "That's
what I meant about his change. The old Stefan never ever would have done that.
This may sound quite strange, but it was the second thing that convinced me he
was not the same Stefan."

"Just because he paid for the room?" Ollie asked.

"Yes, just because of that. You see—"

"Hold it," Ollie said. He picked up the phone in the corner and called the front desk. He asked about the room payment. Then he said, "Thanks, Craig."

"Your brother paid for the room, all right."

I knew Ollie was disappointed to learn that Lucas had told the truth. I wanted to smile and dance around the detective, but I sat motionless.

"Now do you believe me?" Lucas asked.

Ollie did his characteristic shrug again. "I believe *that* part. I'd like to believe it all."

"As I said, my brother wanted me to have that room, and he paid for it. Before that, he begged me to come here to the Cartledge Inn. He wanted me in a connecting room so that we could talk all night if we wanted to and we wouldn't disturb anyone. That's something else. My brother never would have been concerned what anyone else thought. If we made noise, he wouldn't have cared. You see what I mean? Not just his story about his changed life, but he—he had developed a lifestyle that was different from the old Stefan." Lucas stopped, and his eyes pleaded with me to believe him.

I moved over to the edge of the couch, reached over, and touched his hand. "I believe you."

"So do I," Burton said.

"Stefan said he wanted to get everything straightened out. And that he wanted my help."

"And did he straighten things out?" Ollie asked.

"Somewhat. If you check the hotel's records, you'll see that I was in room 625 Tuesday evening, the night before he was killed. We spoke from eight o'clock that night until six in the morning."

"How can you be sure about the time?" Ollie fired back.

"Check room service. We both ate our evening meal in his room. We ordered as soon as I got there. We had breakfast a few minutes before six Wednesday morning. Both of us were too exhausted to talk anymore. Besides, I needed to process what I had heard. So I left him and went into my room."

"Through the connecting door?" I asked.

"Yes, of course," he said in a peevish voice, as if he couldn't understand the reason for the question. "That's why he chose connecting rooms. I shut my door when I slept, because my brother snored."

"And after that?" Ollie asked.

"I slept until maybe 11:00—I'm a bit vague on the time. I got up, knocked on his door, and peered inside. He was gone. So I shaved, showered, dressed, and drove to the office."

"And you never came back?" Ollie asked.

"No, I did come back," he said to the detective. "And you probably have all this recorded someplace." Lucas explained that he had planned to stay at his office only a couple of hours and have lunch with Stefan, but an emergency came up and he canceled. "The nature of the emergency isn't important to you, but you may call my personal assistant and my associate. Both of them were with me until I left."

"What time did you leave your office?" Ollie asked. I realized he had been writing notes. He held his pen poised as he stood directly in front of Lucas.

"I don't remember exactly, but I think it was about 5:30. I thought I'd get back here in about half an hour, but there was a bad accident at the junction between I-285 and the Stone Mountain Freeway. It tied up traffic and blocked two lanes."

"I can check that, you know," Ollie said.

"I don't care if you do." Lucas got up, walked into the bathroom, pulled a box of tissues out of its container, and closed the door behind him. He must have stayed inside a full five minutes. When he came back, his face was flushed, and it seemed obvious to me that he had been crying. Lucas returned to the chair and dropped the tissue box beside his feet.

"And you arrived here at what time?"

"I think it was about 6:20, maybe 6:25."

"Please be as exact as possible," Ollie said.

"That's as exact as I can remember, but that's not what you want to know, is it?"

"What do I want to know?" Ollie said.

"I'll tell you. I went into my room. At noon I had sent out an assistant to buy a large box of peppermints—it's something called Nevada Parade. It's made only in Las Vegas, and only a few shops in Atlanta carry it—"

"Forget the candy," Ollie said. "Just tell us."

"But I think the candy shows we had reconciled. It was the first time I had bought it for him since—since he was maybe twelve or thirteen. It was my way of expressing—"

His voice cracked, and I said, "Ollie, leave him alone. I know you're in charge, but just back off, okay?"

"Okay, so tell us at your own pace," Ollie said. He actually smiled at me as if to thank me for the interruption.

"I went into my room, took off my jacket, and with the box of peppermints in my hand, I knocked on his door."

"And? What did Stefan say?" Ollie asked.

He shook his head. "There was no answer. I thought that was odd, because he had called me on his cell earlier and told me that he ordered dinner for 7:00."

"And so what did you do?" Ollie asked.

"I pushed open the door, and then I saw—" He burst into tears, grabbed a tissue, and wiped his eyes. "He was lying there on the floor. Blood all over the place. The room had been torn apart."

"You're sure the room was torn up?"

Lucas waved away Ollie's question and said, "He clasped something in his hand—a paper. I bent down to pick it up, and then I heard a noise in the corridor. It was the food cart, and it stopped in front of his door. I didn't know what to do. I think I must have dropped the box of peppermints—I really don't know what I did with them—"

"We found them in the room, not far from his body," Ollie said.

"Then you believe me?"

"I believe you dropped the candy on the floor. Go on."

"So I—I reached for the paper in his hands. Purely instinctive, I suppose. I'm not sure why, but I did."

"And what kind of paper was it?"

"Just plain white. When I pulled, it tore. I got most of it—"

"Why didn't you get the rest of it?"

"The waiter. I didn't know if he'd try to come into the room. So I panicked and ran into my room."

"And?"

"I grabbed my jacket, put it on, and hurried out of the inn."

"Did you see anyone? Talk to anyone?"

Lucas shook his head. "No, I don't think so." Then he snapped his fingers. "Oh yes, yes, there was one person. I've forgotten his name, but we had met once while Stefan was in prison. I had gone there to get his signature. We never talked then except in the most formal tones."

"Jason Omore," I said.

"Yes, yes, that's the man."

"What about the paper?" Ollie asked. "That paper you grabbed from his hand?"

"I stuffed it into my jacket pocket."

"When? When did you do that?" Burton asked.

"I don't know. Maybe in the room." Lucas closed his eyes as if he could relive the scene. "No, perhaps not. I remember. In the hallway—near the reception desk when I met the African. He stared at the paper in my hand, and I was hardly aware that I still held it. That's when I stuffed it inside my jacket pocket."

"May I have the paper?" Ollie asked in a remarkably calm voice.

"I don't have it. I tore it into tiny pieces and threw it out the window of my car as I drove away."

"Why did you do that?" I asked.

"Because I didn't want anyone else to know what—what he had written."

Burton and I exchanged glances.

Both of us knew he had lied. It was the first time I had felt that way.

"Why do you want to lie to us now?" Burton asked. "I believe everything you've said. So does Julie. But you lied just now."

"Why?" I asked.

17

Lucas stared at us as if unsure what he should say.

"Yeah, don't start getting evasive with us now," Ollie said. "You've been very helpful—"

"What would you have done with the paper?" Lucas asked. "I mean, if I had kept it, what could you have done with it?"

"Does it still exist?" I asked.

"Please—indulge me." He looked directly at Ollie. This time I sensed defiance in his hazel eyes as he stared unflinchingly into Ollie's face. "If that sheet of paper still existed and I could find it and show it to you, what would you do with it?"

"How would I know until I'd seen it?"

"Give me the possibilities."

"If it was a confession or something incriminating, it would have to go into evidence."

"But if it was merely something personal? What would you do? I mean, what would you do after you'd read it?"

"I don't know. I suppose I'd give it back."

"One more question." All the time his gaze never left Ollie's face. He peered at the detective as if he were trying to read his thoughts. "If nothing on the page contained anything of importance to you or to my brother's murder, would you return it?"

"Probably," Ollie said.

"That's not good enough."

"If it contains nothing that pertains to your brother's murder, you can have it," Ollie said. "That's a promise."

"Thank you." Lucas sat quietly as if he were replaying the words inside his head. He got up and walked around the room and stopped at the large window. He seemed to stare at the lake, but his back was to me, so I wasn't sure.

Lucas turned around. "I lied to you. I mean about the sheet of paper. But only about that." He hung his head. "I still have it. I will read it to you, but I won't give it to you. I won't let you touch it."

"Now wait a minute," Ollie said.

"If you want my memory to improve, you'll have to agree."

Ollie looked at Burton and then at me.

Ollie nodded.

"Let's do this." I turned to Lucas. "Bring the paper into the room. You stand right where you are and read it. I'll stand next to you to make sure you're reading exactly what's written on the paper. If it has no direct bearing on your brother's death, you keep the paper. How does that sound?"

He nodded. "You agree, Mr. Viktor?"

"If there's nothing incriminating—"

"I want your word," he said.

"Okay, I agree," Ollie answered.

He looked at us a little longer as if weighing whether he could trust us. He smiled before he pulled out his wallet, took out a single sheet of paper, and unfolded it. The page was raggedly torn off at the bottom, but he had folded it carefully.

"This is, well, almost sacred to me," he said.

Before Lucas began to read, I told the others, "The words are printed, single spaced, in 10-point serif and continue for five paragraphs. I didn't see a printer in the room, but the place was pretty messed up."

"No printer. No laptop," Ollie said. "I saw a list of contents from the room. My men were very careful not to disturb anything, but they checked every area of the room."

"So he must have done this before 4:30 Wednesday," Burton said. "That's when we knew he was back in the room and called room service."

"Makes good sense." Ollie, notebook and pen in hand, turned to Lucas. "Okay, read it."

"Thank you." Lucas began to read. Stefan apologized to his brother and to the world for his "sinful behavior" (he used those two words) and said he had hurt more people through the years than he could remember. The second and third paragraphs gave a summary of his "born-again experience" and his "entrance into forgiveness and life eternal."

Paragraph four said he was in the process of making restitution for his crimes. He admitted having been involved in stealing the diamonds and that he was going to return them.

The last paragraph read: "A few days after I turned to Jesus Christ, my special friend, Jason Omore, told me to choose a life verse from the Bible, memorize it, and repeat it every day. I have done that."

The tear came just below that, and I saw a partial word: *mans.*

"Now I get it! I get it!" Burton yelled. "Now I understand the 623. The *R-o* and 623 didn't mean room 623."

I stared at him. "What did I miss?"

"He meant *Romans* 6:23. It's a verse in the Bible. In fact, it's such a well-known verse I can quote it for you."

"Then please do it," Ollie said. It was obvious he was disappointed by the contents of the letter. He put down his pad and pen.

"For the wages of sin is death, but the gift of God is eternal life in Christ Jesus our Lord."

"That's it? Just that?" As Ollie said those words, Lucas carefully refolded the page and returned it to his wallet.

"You're saying that's why he was obsessed with 623?" Ollie asked.

"Just because of some obscure statement he read in the Bible?" I said. "I find that difficult to accept. That's not the kind of thing that obsessive-compulsives focus on."

"Who said he was obsessive-compulsive?" Burton said. "It's not obscure, by the way. It's well known, but more than that, Stefan Lauber chose a Bible verse. But not just *any* verse—it was a *life* verse. Life, get it? A verse that he would use and quote often."

"Okay, okay," Ollie said.

I was ready to say, "Whatever," but I decided to keep my mouth shut.

"No, I don't think either of you get this," Burton said. "This is powerful." He looked directly at me and said, "It tells us that Stefan was serious about his conversion. He had truly changed."

Was that a message aimed at me? I wasn't sure, but I wasn't going to ask. Instead, I said, "Do you suppose that's why he was murdered? Not just because he had the diamonds, but because he was going to return them? That way no one would profit from them except the rightful owners."

"That's probably right," Ollie said. "So we have a repentant thief, and that means someone whacked him to get the jewels, right?"

"Do you suppose they got them?" Burton asked.

"Obviously not on the night of the murder," I said. "If they had, why would they have also killed Deedra Knight and—"

"And done more searching after killing Deedra," Ollie said. "That assumes, of course, that it was the same person. The room was worse after her murder."

"And do you think the killer found them?" I asked.

That question hung in the room a few seconds before Ollie said, "Let's assume not. If the murderer found them, we're probably out of luck unless some new evidence turns up."

"But if the gems weren't recovered or haven't been so far," Burton said, "we have two murders and millions of dollars in missing diamonds."

The three of us threw out ideas and theories—a lot of talking aloud that amounted to nothing. I finally turned to Lucas. He still stood by the window with his back to us. He was sobbing softly.

I came behind him and laid my arm on his shoulder. He turned and stared at me. Abruptly he grabbed me and held me tightly. With his head on my shoulder and his chest racked with pain, he cried with great sobs. After a few minutes, he pulled back. "Forgive me. I'm sorry for—"

"Thank you for trusting me enough to use my shoulder," I said.

The gratitude showed in his hazel eyes.

Ollie came toward us, and Burton held up his hand. I couldn't hear what he said to Ollie, but I assumed he told him not to interfere. A few minutes later, Burton brought over the box of tissues and thrust them into Lucas's right hand.

When Lucas finally pulled away, he started to apologize to all of us for being emotional. He tried to wipe the tears off my shoulder. "Don't bother," I said.

He thanked me for not pushing him away. "I loved him. I loved him. No matter how much I tried to hate him, deep inside I loved him." Through tearstained eyes, he said, "When I left his room Tuesday night—Wednesday morning—you know his last words to me? His very last words?"

"We can't know unless you tell us," Ollie said.

I resisted the urge to stuff a gag into Ollie's mouth. "I'd like to know," I said.

"Please tell us," Burton said.

"We had a lot of talk between us, as I've already told you. Most of the time he talked to me about Jesus Christ. I listened, but religion wasn't something our family ever had much interest in. This was all new talk to me."

"And?" Ollie prompted.

"Just as I turned to go to my room, he hugged me. Then he prayed for me. *He prayed for me.* Can you believe that?"

"Yes," Burton said softly. "Yes, I can believe that."

Ollie shrugged.

That seemed just as odd to me as it probably did to Ollie.

"He asked me to make him a promise. The promise was that I would give God a chance in my life. When I hesitated, he added *please*—a word my brother had never used with me before—before our reconciliation."

"So you told us," Ollie said.

"How did you answer him?" Burton asked.

Lucas wiped his eyes, and I thought he was going to cry again, but instead he sniffed back his tears. "I said I would consider it carefully."

"That was all?" Ollie asked. "Did he say anything else?"

"One more thing. He said, 'Lucas, I have been praying for you for several months and for two things. The first is that you would find it in your heart to forgive me. You've done that. The second part of my prayer is that one day we'll be together in heaven.' "

Ollie said nothing, and I couldn't think of anything to say.

Burton impulsively hugged Lucas. "I'd like to continue to pray the second part of that prayer on your brother's behalf—that you'll meet in heaven."

This time Burton got the wet shoulder, and the sobs were even louder than before.

As I watched, something else happened to me. I had felt it earlier, but now it was even stronger.

I was hooked.

I believed, and I had no idea how that had taken place.

Just then Lucas pulled away. Burton turned his head slightly, and our gazes met. It was a strange, perhaps mystical moment.

Burton knew.

He knew I had changed.

18

Lucas asked if he could leave. "I need—I need to be alone," he said.

Ollie nodded and said nothing until after Lucas left.

Burton and I looked at each other. I wanted to say something, but I couldn't put into words what had transpired inside me. So I stared.

He smiled, and that face lit up as it always did.

"Okay, boys and girls, any ideas where we go now?" Ollie asked. He perused his notes, flipping pages.

"Maybe we all need a break," I said. I wanted to talk to Craig, and just as much I wanted to get away from Burton for a few minutes. I wasn't ready to talk to him. What would I say?

"Good idea," Ollie said. "I need to check in with my office and do a couple of things." He glanced at his watch. "I have a minimum of an hour's worth of stuff I have to do, so take your time."

As I turned to leave the room, Burton said, "Mind if I walk with you?" He followed me into the hallway. "Let's talk with Craig."

I didn't trust my voice, so I said nothing. We walked down the corridor, and I couldn't tolerate the silence, but I didn't want to talk about me—about him—about us, so I asked, "You caught that look in Lucas's eyes?"

"I'm not sure what I caught," he said, "but right at the end, just before Ollie let him go, I sensed he either lied or held something back."

I turned and smiled at him. "That's exactly what I meant."

"You know, you're pretty sharp," he said.

"And you know, you're wasted as a minister."

"That's part of what makes a good minister," he said. "We ministers listen and try not to condemn others."

"Sounds like a therapist."

"And we learn to sense when people hold back or when they need to say something."

"Again, like a—"

"And especially, we notice when someone we like needs to talk to us but tries to hide it."

Inadvertently I stopped right then and stared. I still wore those four-inch heels that elevated me above him, so I had to look down at his eyes. "You don't miss a thing, do you?"

He shrugged, and I burst out laughing. It was a perfect imitation of his old college friend.

"Whatever," he said.

"And whenever," I said.

He smiled and arched his right brow. "And that means?"

"It means you're right that I do want to talk to you, but not quite yet. I have a few things to sort out inside my head."

"Maybe talking will help sort them out."

"Maybe," I said. "But not yet."

Burton gave me a quick hug. It wasn't quite the churchy hug, and it wasn't what I'd call a romantic hug. It was what I would call nice.

"I'll take more of them—and longer."

"Whenever," he said and smiled.

———

When we reached the front desk, three people leaned against the counter and five people stood in line behind them. I looked at my watch. It was a few minutes after four. Check-in time.

"We're a little shorthanded today," Craig announced. "My colleague is ill, so I hope you'll be patient."

He said that to the customers, but when I turned to Burton, the uplifted eyebrow confirmed what I thought. The message was for us. I got in line, and Burton stood next to me.

"Excuse me," Craig said a few minutes later and waved at me. "I'm sorry your room won't be ready for another hour, but here's the number." He held up a small yellow Post-it.

I took the Post-it from his hand and read the number. "Thank you," I said. "I'll be back."

As I walked away, I held it up for Burton.

He snapped his fingers. "Of course! I had totally forgotten about them."

Craig had written ROOM 624.

We didn't speak until after we both got out of the elevator. I wondered why we hadn't checked on that room before.

"Why didn't Ollie remember?" Burton said. "It's not like him to miss a detail like that."

"And Craig made it obvious this morning that the rooms on either side were taken and so was the room across the hall. He emphasized that room as much as either of the others. He wanted to tell us something even then."

We reached 624 and Burton knocked. The rooms were fairly well insulated, so we couldn't hear any movement inside—it wasn't that I didn't try. I leaned my ear against the door. I pulled back when I heard the interior lock being turned.

A man gazed back at me. I guessed him to be in his late sixties. His bristly white hair curled thinly across the top of his head and thrust out around his large ears, but his neck was scrawny and wrinkled; his shoulders were slight, and he was about as thin as anyone I'd ever met. He wore a simple sport shirt with vertical lines that made him look even thinner. He might have been five six but no taller.

"I would like to ask you a few questions about room 623," Burton said. "You probably know a man was killed there—"

The man stared at him for a long time, his gaze moving from head to foot. After he scrutinized Burton, he did the same with me.

"Who is it?" called a voice from inside.

"The good-cop-bad-cop team has arrived," he said.

Before Burton could tell him we weren't the police, I impulsively threw myself into the part. "Look, just move back inside, answer a few questions, and we'll be on our way."

"Do you have some kind of warrant?"

"What TV shows have you been watching?"

The woman, obviously his wife, came behind him. With nearly white hair, a thin, pretty face, and alert blue eyes, she looked almost as thin as he did and even more wrinkled. She nodded to Burton. "You come inside. We won't talk to the bad cop." She stared defiantly at me. "One is enough, but at least we assume you'll be polite."

"Oh, I'll be very polite," Burton said.

"I'll be at the front desk," I said.

Strange people, I thought as I walked down the hallway. Did I look like someone from the police? Were they just freaked out? It didn't matter anyway. Burton would find out.

I went back to the front desk. Two people were in line. Craig looked up, our gazes met, and he shifted away quickly. I didn't move out of line, and he said nothing. It may have been my imagination, but it seemed that Craig slowed down a little. A man came up behind me to stand in line. I motioned for him to get in front of me. "I'm in line, but I'm waiting for someone, so go ahead."

He smiled and thanked me. I had said the words loudly enough that Craig got the message.

While I waited, one more person came to the line, and I let her in front of me. She wanted only a duplicate key to her room.

I finally leaned against the desk. Before Craig said anything, I blurted, "I don't want you to get into any trouble—please believe me."

"I believe you," he said.

"Tell me what you know. And you were holding back, weren't you?"

"I'd rather see someone get away with a crime than tell that—that—"

"You don't like Mr. Viktor," I said. "Sometimes he rubs people the wrong way." I focused my attention on Craig and determined not to look away. I wasn't trying to intimidate him, but I wasn't going to let him hold back this time.

"Okay, listen, I get a break in a couple of minutes," he said. "Wait for me in the parking lot." He pointed to the one that he had used for his cigarette break.

"Burton might be coming down before we get back."

"I'll leave a message with my relief," he said and pointed the way.

Just then a man and woman with two children came up to the desk with several suitcases.

I walked outside and waited. I stood among the roses. The day was warm. The late-afternoon light was golden—and utterly mysterious. The sky was partially overcast, so the landscape was dappled with sunshine and shadows. I couldn't focus on the weather. I kept replaying the events of the day inside my head—especially *that* moment. I had to sort that out before I could talk to Burton.

I didn't pace—not in those shoes on that concrete, but I did shift weight back and forth a number of times. Just then I remembered that I had a pair of sandals in the trunk of my car. They didn't match my lime green outfit, but they were soft and easy on my feet. My car, however, was on the other side of the hotel. I didn't want to go over and possibly miss Craig, so I waited.

He breezed though the doorway and said, "Follow me," and walked on. We ambled to the edge of the car park, and he led me to a lovely gazebo. He sat down and pulled out a pack of cigarettes, but he must have read the expression on my face. "Okay," he said and put them away. "I need to quit anyway."

"So please tell me about room 624. Who is that couple? What's the connection?"

"They didn't know Lauber, if that's what you mean," he said. "It wasn't anything like that. I mean, they had no involvement with the theft."

"Okay, so?"

"It's what they saw."

"You mean they witnessed the murder?"

He shook his head. "I doubt that. Look, I'll tell you what I know and then you'll leave me alone and let me puff away on my little cancer stick, okay?"

"So tell me."

"It was about 8:30—just barely dark. The police had stopped harassing everybody. Two policemen were still inside room 623, but that was all." Craig said he had gone out to his car for a smoke. No one was around, so he stood outside the car and puffed. He had barely finished his cigarette when he heard a man and a woman talking. "They walked within five feet of me. I had my back to them, and I don't think they paid any attention to me, but I'm sure they smelled the smoke."

He said they sat inside the gazebo, and he would have had to walk right in their line of vision to get back to the inn. "If the Cartledges learned I still smoked, they'd fire me," he said, "and I want to keep this job. It's the first real job I've had since—you know—since—"

"Yes," I said simply.

According to Craig, the conversation between the couple went like this:

"But what do we do? Just—just keep our mouths closed?" the woman asked. "I'm frightened."

"What else can we do? You know from those television shows what happens when witnesses speak up."

"But those are made-up stories," she said.

"Made up, all right, but they're made up from real events," the husband insisted. "Haven't we heard enough times that the story is based on real events?"

"So if we say nothing, then what?" the woman asked. "Does he get away with it? I mean, if he truly did it?"

"Aw, c'mon, they always leave clues and make mistakes. Haven't we seen that a thousand times, as well?"

"So you mean we say nothing."

"Yes, that's exactly what I mean."

"Maybe that's the best," she said.

"Look, I'm scared, too. How was I to know that just because we stepped out of the room when we did—"

"I suppose," she said. "And if we speak up, who knows how long they'll make us stay in Georgia. I want to get home—"

"He said to stay two more days as we had planned and then we could go and we would be safe."

"Yes, yes," she said. "But if police officers come to our door—"

"Then we'll deal with it," he said.

~

"That's all I heard," Craig said. "They got up and started to walk away from the gazebo. They were probably going to go inside through the other entrance to the grounds over by the lake. It's well lighted at night."

"So you went back to your desk?" I asked. "And you never said anything to anyone?"

"Are you crazy? Why would I do that?" Craig said. "If that Mr. Viktor had been a little nicer to me, maybe I would have told him, but he's like some of those tough criminals I met in prison. It's safer and better to stay away from them."

I didn't say anything. His fear seemed a bit irrational to me. But if I were a skinny little guy like him and had been in prison among brutish, tough men, I might have been a little more fearful, as well.

He got up from the gazebo. "That's all I know—honest, it is. Please—"

"Please what?"

"Can you tell that detective the truth without implicating me? Maybe—maybe you could mention asking the people in 624 if they heard or saw anything."

"Burton is with them now." I didn't want to go through what had happened, so I said, "Whatever he finds out, we can tell Oliver Viktor."

"Okay, that's all right, I guess," he said. "I just want this to end."

"Me, too," I said.

19

We got back to the desk, and Burton still hadn't come down. I told Craig I would walk along by the lake and he was to tell Burton he should join me. I went immediately to my car and exchanged my heels for the sandals. The relief was immediate. Okay, so they didn't match my outfit, but I didn't care. The comfort was worth it.

Besides, after that hug, I didn't think he'd focus his attention on my feet.

Now I was ready to walk. I don't know how long I walked or how far. The day had cooled off, and the sun's rays hid behind the clouds. Other than that, I paid no attention to anything around me, because I became absorbed in my own private world. I should have focused on the crime and trying to figure out who murdered those two people, but something else troubled me.

"I've become one of them," I said to myself. "How could such a thing happen?"

I had become a believer. Just like that. That experience didn't make sense to me. How could it just happen without warning or a conscious decision? No one had used any arguments or tried to prove anything to me. I just believed. It felt strange to think that way.

"There really is a God—a God in whom I believe." Immediately I thought of Uncle Rich. I figured my experience would upset him, because I believed without going down to the front of the church and confessing my sins to everyone.

The closest parallel that made sense to me was my learning Spanish. In college I had signed up for Spanish as my required language course. I didn't get the language. I did the exercises faithfully and memorized the words. I learned to parrot everything the instructor and anyone else in the class said. About two weeks before the end of the first year, I groaned and knew I could never pass the final exam. It was like memorizing math formulas.

About a week before finals, I sat in the classroom, groaning miserably while the teacher read us a short story completely in Spanish. As I listened, I understood—just like that. It was as if the language suddenly made sense. I no longer had to translate word by word.

"Is that the way Christianity works, too?" I asked myself. "At least for me, is that it?"

Just as I decided that it was, another thought hit me: Did I truly believe, or did I think I believed so that I could be more attractive to James Burton? "Am I that self-deceived?" I whispered.

"I don't know," I answered myself, but I did know. I liked Burton—a lot—maybe even more than a lot. Yes, I did love him, but my sudden faith in Christianity was quite apart from that.

"It is, isn't it?" I asked.

I felt as if I had awakened from a daze. Peace filled my soul, and I don't recall ever having felt such tranquility at any time in my life. "This is real," I whispered to myself. "This is real."

Burton hadn't sought me out on the walk, and I finally went back to the front desk. Craig was busy with a check-in, but he shook his head. "Haven't seen him."

That meant he was still with the couple in room 624. I thanked Craig and decided to go back to the room the hotel had given Ollie to use. When I opened the door, I could see Ollie Viktor standing in the bathroom. He had injected a needle into his arm.

I must have cried out, although I wasn't aware of anything except a feeling of immense shock.

Ollie turned. He looked up and stared into the mirror. He saw my image and finished injecting himself. He cleansed his arm, rolled down his sleeve, put the medication in a small case, and walked into the room where I stood.

"Shocked?" he asked. "Don't be. It's not an illegal drug, and I'm not an addict. It's called medication."

I didn't know if I believed him, so I said nothing.

"Perhaps you noticed the tremors in my hands. They come and go. They're usually the best sign to tell me when I need a shot. Usually one in the morning and one at night are enough for the day."

"Usually?" I asked.

"Most days."

"I assume you've injected yourself several times today—"

"This is my fourth," he said matter-of-factly. "When I'm under intense pressure, the med seems to wear off quicker."

"Want to tell me the problem?"

"I wish I knew. So do my doctors. The problem is that no one knows for certain. I've been tested for Parkinson's disease, or as we call it, PD, and that seems to be the best explanation so far. In two weeks I'll have a brain scan, and that should help." He explained that PD is a motor-system disorder and is difficult to diagnose. He had only one of several telltale signs: trembling hands. He said that sleep problems were common and he had begun to experience some of them.

"So what were you taking?"

"Artificial dopamine," he said. "It's an experimental drug. So far it hasn't produced any positive results."

I nodded, not quite convinced, but open to believe him.

"Another thing is that you may have noticed my mood changes. That's not a common symptom. I get irritated easily or depressed. I can't help it. I know I've made you angry—"

"Yes, yes, you have."

"Please believe me that I can't help it. It—it just happens." Those green eyes stared at me with such intensity I no longer doubted his word. He explained that the symptoms had actually gotten slightly better during the past two weeks. "Until today. I think the tension—you know—made me need extra meds."

"Okay, then what can I do to help? You haven't been particularly nice to some of—"

"I've been a jerk. Don't you think I know that?" Before I could respond, he took my hands in his. "Please try to understand. Right now I feel fine. Why shouldn't I? As you observed, I just injected myself. I have no idea when it will wear off. When I feel the symptoms start to return, I tell myself I won't get angry or yell or—"

"I'm sorry. Honest."

"Help me, Julie; help me. When you see me act weird, just tell me to shut up. I'm not sure it will work, but when Burton did that, somehow I was able to calm down."

"You can count on me to tell you to shut up," I said. In spite of myself, I began to laugh.

Ollie laughed, too, and released my hands. "Hey, I don't know if I like giving you blanket permission—"

"Oh, I'll use it wisely," I said and laughed again. "Or at least I'll use it whenever I don't like what you say."

"Thanks," he said.

His voice was soft—in fact, so soft I don't think I'd ever heard him speak quite like that. He melted me, but then, I'm a sucker for a soft voice. His eyes moistened, and that slapped me down even further.

We looked at each other in silence before I asked, "Does Burton know?"

He shook his head. "Outside of my doctor, you're the only one. Please don't tell—"

"I'm a professional, remember? You don't have to ask me not to tell Burton or anyone."

Almost as if we had planned it that way, a soft tap came at the door. I turned toward it and it opened. Burton walked inside.

"Hey, there's our man," Ollie said. "Now we can get some things done with you back on the job!"

"Yeah, I think you're right." Burton laughed—maybe it was slightly forced, but it was a laugh.

I stared at Burton and tried to read his face. Sometimes it's easy to do that, but he can also be inscrutable when he wants. This was one of those times.

"What do you think we ought to do now?" Burton asked.

The question hung in the air.

Just then I looked up and saw Jason Omore stroll past our room. He didn't know we were in that room, and he didn't look our way.

"I'd like to talk to Jason again," I said.

"You think he knows something he hasn't told us?" Ollie asked.

"I think—I think we didn't ask the right questions." There it was again—one of those far-out statements and I had no idea how I knew it. I suppose that's part of why my colleagues say I'm a good therapist. I listen to that inner prompting, to my gut. As a therapist, I don't get it often, but I listen. In fact, this had happened to me more since coming to Cartledge Inn than it had in the past six months.

I hurried out of the room, and both men followed me. As I exited the building, I saw that Jason had gone about a hundred yards ahead of us. Wearing my sandals made it much easier to walk. If there hadn't been two attractive men behind me, I probably would have run.

"Jason!" Burton called.

He must not have heard his name the first time, but I walked even faster. About thirty feet from the African, I called his name.

Jason turned, saw me, and stopped. Even from that distance, his smile was as big and as genuine as ever. He walked toward me and greeted me with his arms raised shoulder high, as if he intended to welcome me with a hug. "Good doctor, it is my distinct pleasure to see you again." He waved to Burton and Ollie, who were both less than ten yards behind.

"How are you?" I asked.

"That is not a good question," he said. "In our country we would not say that so quickly."

"How would you say it?"

By then the two men had caught up with me and heard our conversation.

Instead of answering, Jason turned and looked heavenward. Pale clouds had drifted across the sky, and the first hint of sunset had appeared. A mild breeze brought along the fragrance of magnolia blossoms from a nearby tree. I inhaled deeply.

"In our country—in the region we call South Nyanza where I grew up—the people are still what you could call primitive. When someone dies that we love, we mourn, but we do it differently." He told us that every evening at dark, the family and friends gathered. They wept and cried all night long. So many people would be present, someone would always be crying aloud. "We do that for thirty nights."

"And after that?"

"After that we return to our lives again. We have mourned, and we have emptied ourselves of our pain. I wish to do this for my friend, but I can only carry this heaviness in my heart for now." He stared at me and said softly, "You Americans seem to think it is a serious weakness to mourn for an extended period."

Before Ollie could interrupt, Jason said that he had been in his room. "But, alas, my heavy heart is such that I have not studied. I can think only of my friend. I have already mingled many tears over his Bible."

"*His* Bible?" I asked.

"Yes, the Bible that belonged to Stefan."

"What are you doing with it?" Ollie asked. "If it's his, did you steal it from his room?"

"And why would I do that? Did he not give it to me?"

I wondered if this was the time to tell Ollie to shut up. I glanced at his hands and saw no tremor.

Burton all but pushed Ollie aside. "Tell us about the Bible, Jason. Why did he give it to you?"

"*Akiya—*" He stopped. "Sorry, that is my own language, which means, I do not know. Truly, I do not."

"What did he say when he gave you the Bible?"

"Ah, that. Yes, that was a bit strange, was it not?"

"In what way was it strange?" Ollie asked.

"He was afraid, I think. Yes, he was very much afraid."

"Of what?" Ollie yelled. "Afraid of what?"

"Of that, I do not know."

"Don't give me that kind of—"

"Ollie, Ollie, take it easy," Burton said. "Let's find a place to sit down and let Jason take whatever time he needs to explain this to us." Ollie started to protest, but Burton added, "We have four African families in our congregation. I've learned that they operate out of a different time zone. If we're patient and listen, we'll learn."

"And what's ten minutes more or less?" I asked. I looked at Ollie and hoped my eyes gave him a warning.

Ollie raised his hands in surrender. "Okay."

Jason led us away from all the buildings until we came to a small promenade that overlooked the lake. It was the highest point of the grounds, and the lake was perhaps thirty feet below. Five leather-cushioned folding chairs were grouped in a semicircle. We sat on the padded seats, which were amazingly comfortable.

"I want your help," Ollie said to Jason. "Please tell me whatever you know. I get a little impatient at times—"

"Yes, that you do," Jason said without obvious rancor, more as if he stated a fact. "Is this not a beautiful site? Is not God's creation special for us? Is it not one of your sayings that we should pause to smell the flowers?"

"Stop to smell the roses," I said.

"Ah yes, so it is." He had been looking around at the lake, and I thought how naturally he blended in with the quiet setting. He turned his chair so that he could see all our faces. "Now my soul is calm once again. I am ready to speak."

We waited several seconds. From behind me two birds called and sang to each other.

"My friend Stefan knew someone wanted to kill him," Jason said simply.

"How did he know that?" I asked. "Was he threatened?"

"To that question, I do not have an answer. He said to me, 'Someone will make an attempt on my life.' When I asked him for more explanation, he said, 'Do not be upset. I am not afraid of death.' "

"He really said that?" Ollie asked.

"Oh yes, but of course. Even if he had not said such words, of this I am sure that he was at peace. He had only one major concern. It was the one thing he felt he must do even if his life was in danger."

"And that was?" I heard a slight irritation in Ollie's voice, but I let it go.

"It was. . ." He paused and thought. "It was, as you would say, he was obsessed with his mission. He was learning our language, and he did not know many words, mostly nouns, but his favorite was *almasi*."

"Which means?" Ollie jumped ahead and asked before Jason had a chance to explain.

"Oh, it is the word for 'diamond.' You see, he sometimes spoke to me in public. He wanted no one else to understand, so he used *almasi*."

"So he was sure someone would try to stop him from returning the diamonds," I said. "Why else would he do that?"

"That is true," Jason said. "He feared that someone would kill him before he could return the diamonds to the proper owners." He dropped his head and said softly, "And he was correct, and I did nothing to help. I could have stayed in his room perhaps."

"He told you that?" Ollie asked, interrupting the African's reflective mood. "I mean, about returning the diamonds? That it was the important thing he had to do? Are you sure he didn't plan to sell them?"

"Sell them? Why would my friend choose to do such a thing?"

"For money—a lot of money," Ollie persisted.

"No, that is not true. Not ever would he do such a thing."

"Are you sure?"

"But of course. Would I lie to you? Sir, am I not a Christian?"

"Okay, okay, I got it," Ollie said without conviction. "You say you're telling us the truth, so tell us more."

"There is but one thing I must tell you, and I do not know this is so, but it is what I have come to understand." He paused and wiped his eyes with his hand. "I loved him very much. It's most difficult to speak of him. Never have I had a friend whom I have loved so much." He pulled a handkerchief from his pocket, and we waited until he was ready to speak.

The sun had begun to slip behind Stone Mountain, which was to the west. As I watched, it looked as if the sun had begun to melt into the mountain itself and cast rays of pale orange and purple across the skyline. Below us I heard the first cicadas tune up their nighttime instruments.

"What I do not know is the name of the person my friend feared. Perhaps there were many or only one; I cannot say. I do know that Stefan felt there was one special person—one man who wanted the diamonds. It was a man. Of that I am sure. He was involved in some way with the taking of the *almasi*—the diamonds. The man who carried the jewels was supposed to have given them to one man—Peters or some such name—"

"Petersen," Ollie said.

"As you say. That was a man who would be suspected because he had robbed before, you see. That act was planned carefully, and this I know from my friend. That man, the one called Petersen, gave the bag of jewels to the woman, and she was to take them to my friend. He would dispose of them. Does that not sound simple?"

"Very. So what's the problem?" Ollie asked.

"I can't think of the English, but something happened. It is like putting two crosses together."

"Double cross?" I asked.

Jason rewarded me with a huge smile. "That is the expression, yes. The double cross."

Slowly Jason told the story. He didn't know the name, but a man had instigated everything. He was someone who had influence and knew many people, but also, in Jason's words, "a man of bad character." This man set up the entire operation and used the woman named Pam Harty to work on Stefan. "You see, to have the diamonds was not enough. It had to be someone who was wealthy and influential enough to sell the stones and not to arouse suspicions."

"And that's where Pam Harty came into this, right?"

"Oh yes, she was an evil woman—I met her but once, you understand, but those are the words of Stefan. The one who planned all this—and the man's name I never heard, and I do not think Stefan knew—hired the Harty woman. She spent many weeks, perhaps months, deceiving my friend. He talked many times about being a fool for letting that woman lead him into such a wicked venture."

Now it made sense to me. I had liked Stefan, and he seemed like a man of great common sense. That's not something changed by a religious experience. But if the woman stayed after him and used her charms constantly, okay, now I could understand. His brother had mentioned that Pam Harty had influenced him, but that hadn't really sunk in until now.

"So here is the way it was to work. I mean the way the double crossing was supposed to work. The courier was to have two containers—pouches or something—and they were to be identical. One of them contained the real diamonds and the other the imitation. In the airport parking lot, he was supposed to be robbed at gunpoint and surrender to Petersen the imitation. He would later hand the real ones over to the one who planned everything."

"How was the transaction to be made? With that man?" I asked.

"Hmm, on that I shall have to think. Did he not tell me while he was still in prison? It was long ago." He turned his face upward and stared at the sky for a few seconds and then closed his eyes.

Ollie sat motionless, but his attention was fully on Jason.

"Yes, I do now remember. It was an *askari*—a policeman. Yes, that is how it was to work."

Instinctively my gaze shot to Ollie.

"Hey, we have hundreds of police in the area. I'm only one, so don't convict me because I'm of the same occupation."

I nodded. Of course he was right.

Petersen, Jason told us, used a gun to hold up the courier—Jeremiah Macgregor. A briefcase was strapped or chained to Macgregor's arm, and Petersen forced him to take out the pouch of diamonds; then he ran with it. As it turned out, Macgregor became so frightened by the robbery that he panicked and inadvertently handed Petersen the real diamonds.

As he had been instructed, the courier called the police about the holdup. The policeman who planned the event was on the scene or nearby. That wasn't clear except that he would be the first official on the scene. Jason said he thought the policeman would say that he was off duty and had been visiting friends near the airport. The robbery took place in the long-term parking lot of the airport in Atlanta. He arrived before anyone else and grabbed the second pouch. He must have looked at the contents, or maybe Macgregor blurted out what had happened. Regardless, the policeman shot the courier, jumped into his own car, and drove away. Jason could not verify that part except to say that he knew there was a woman with the policeman.

"How do you know that?" Ollie asked. "Lauber wasn't on the scene, and you surely weren't there."

"The woman came to see Stefan. Perhaps two, maybe three days before the murder. She asked for a—a cutting—a portion—"

"A cut?" Burton asked.

"Ah yes, again. At times my English fails, does it not?"

"And?" Ollie asked.

"Oh, he refused. I was there."

"You were there?" I asked.

"Yes, she visited his room and I was present. We had begun to read the Bible together and pray. Her knock at the door interrupted us."

"Please tell us everything," Burton said. "Don't leave out anything."

20

This is the story Jason Omore told us:

Each morning, did I not go into my friend's room? And to some it sounded perhaps strange, but I conducted Bible study. I did not know everything about the Bible, but I taught him what I knew. Some days we read short portions from other books, but we always read at least one chapter of the Bible together. Sometimes I would teach him the African words if he wanted to know.

I also taught him to sing some of our songs. His favorite was called "*Maler, maler ni jogo,*" which in English means "Holy, holy are the people," and it refers to those people who follow God.

One morning—it was last week, but I do not remember the exact day—we were ready to pray together when a knock came at the door. Stefan and I had been on our knees beside his bed, so we both got up, and he walked to the door and opened it.

"Well, this is quite a surprise," Stefan said. "You're probably the last woman on earth I expected to see at my door."

"May I come in?"

Before he could say anything, she pushed the door open wide and entered into the room. Truly, she was one of the most beautiful women I had ever seen in my life. Her skin was what I would call flawless—not a blemish anywhere, and she wore little makeup. She was so beautiful that makeup she did not need. She had light-colored hair—blond—and she wore it long so that it broke over her shoulders. I know nothing of expensive clothes, but Stefan did, and he stared at her.

"You must observe what my money has done for this woman," he said to me. "She has invested it well because she has invested it in herself. She was bewitching before, but she is even more so now."

He pointed to her pale blue suit. "This is by Chanel, and the handbag is Hermes, or is it Prada?" He nodded to the woman.

"Hermes," she said and smiled. "Oh, Stefan, you are magnificent and know-ledgeable and so—so gracious."

"Look at the shoes, Jason," he said and pointed. "Those pumps look quite ordinary to you, but I assure you they are not. Charles Jourdan, obviously, at a cost of at least five hundred dollars. She would never use an imitation." He stared at her hand. "Chapard? Is that truly a Chapard watch?"

"But, my dear, you taught me to value the valuable," she said and smiled. Her smile made her face even more radiant. I think that is the word. But the eyes were sad. They were light blue, almost the color of her suit. If the eyes are the way to enter into the soul, she was sad and a truly poor person on the inside.

She walked around Stefan's room, picked up the Bible from the bed. "I heard you had begun to read such literature," she said and tossed it—how do you say—carelessly?

She stopped and stared at me as if she had not seen me before, but I knew she had taken in my image when she entered the room. She stood before me and observed me carefully. She stared at my shaved head and slowly traveled down to my sandaled feet. "Is this a waiter? He isn't properly dressed for the job."

"He is my friend. He is Jason Omore."

"How nice," she said and smiled at me. "Now you may leave."

I said nothing and began to walk toward the door.

"He stays." Stefan put his arm around my shoulder. Stefan was a tall man, perhaps as tall as Mr. Viktor. I started to pull away, but his hand held me.

"I want to talk to you," she said softly and went to sit down. She did not stop the smiling all the while.

"So talk."

"I have personal things to discuss with you, Stefan. Very, very personal things."

"This man is my brother, my soul brother. I have known him for many months, and I trust him as I have never trusted another person in the world. I have no secrets from him." Stefan released me, walked over, and sat on the edge of the bed. He indicated he wanted me to sit in a chair.

As he said those words, I felt my face grow hot. I had not known he felt about me in such a good way.

"Get rid of him anyway."

"I think not." He walked over to her. "You see, he has gained my friendship. My trust. He is one person who will never betray me or deceive me. I have trusted him with my life, and he has proven faithful."

"And I haven't?" she said. "You're right. I was weak, Stefan. Weak and afraid, so I ran out on you."

"No, you ran because you thought I had the paste diamonds."

"That, too, I suppose," she said, "but I was confused and. . ."

She stood up and hugged him. Even in her stiletto-thin heels, she was perhaps four inches shorter.

Stefan was tall, lean, with very dark brown hair and hazel eyes. Momentarily he embraced her. "Hmm, you no longer use Jean Patou fragrance."

"This is a designer perfume. Supposedly designed just for me, and no other woman in the world has a fragrance quite like it."

Stefan slowly pushed her away. "As it should be. No other woman in the world. Yes, I think that's a good description."

She reached for him again. "I've missed you, Stefan. Truly I have missed you."

"How nice," he said. He turned to me. "You have never met Pam Harty, but she was my one true love, the woman who loved me just for myself and promised to stand by me no matter what." He smiled slowly and said, "After she put her hands around millions of my dollars, she moved on. And now she's back."

"You make me sound so—so awful," she said. "And I admit I have been terrible, but I want to change that. I'm different. Truly I'm—"

"Enough." The tone wasn't angry, but it was firm.

She stared at him as if not sure what to say next.

"So why did you come back?" he said. "You walked away with a fortune in cash—a very, very large fortune."

"And I was quite unwise in the men with whom I associated. Two of them in particular were thieves. Can you believe it? They conned me out of my money."

Stefan laughed. I wasn't sure why it was so humorous, but in our culture, we do not believe it is polite for one person to laugh alone, so I joined him in laughing.

"I despise you," she said to him. She no longer seemed aware that I was in the room. Or perhaps she did not care. "You are a thoroughly despicable man." Her words were harsh, but her voice remained soft—the way a woman speaks to a man whom she loves or wants him to think so.

"That, my former truelove, is honest," Stefan said. "Your tricks won't work again, so don't waste the energy. Tell me why you came to see me."

"Isn't it obvious? I came about the diamonds." She seemed suddenly aware again of my presence. She cocked her head toward me. "Please, tell him to go."

"If one of you must leave, it is not my friend Jason."

"I came to talk to you about the diamonds—the ones you still have."

"Sit down if you like," Stefan said, "but my friend stays."

"I will leave," I said. I did not feel comfortable with such conversation.

"No, stay, please."

"Your choice," the woman said. "Okay, I know you have the diamonds. The word has circulated that you are ready to dispose of them. I want a cut. It's that simple."

"And if I refuse?" Stefan said.

"I hope you won't be that foolish. You know what happened to Petersen and to Macgregor. Such sad things happened to other people, as well."

With lightning-like speed, Stefan grabbed her arm with one hand, her bag with the other, and rushed her to the door. "Don't ever come back. You will never get another cent from me."

She tried to say something, but Stefan slammed the door in her face.

After she left, Stefan said he wanted to pray alone—and I left him. That is all I know about her.

—

Jason had told us about his meeting with Pam Harty. Although it had been interesting and I had a clearer picture of the woman, he had said nothing particularly enlightening. I wondered if I had wasted my time in wanting to talk to him. I had been so sure he had something of value to tell us, but perhaps I had been wrong. I started to get up and walk away.

"Why is your face like that of the donkey?" Jason asked. "You are much sad. Did my information displease you?"

"Oh, not at all—"

"She means she expected more," Burton said. "She felt we hadn't asked you the correct questions and you had things to tell us—information that might help to solve the murder of Stefan."

"But I did not tell you everything," Jason said softly. "Is there not more for me to tell?"

Ollie had listened but said nothing. I glanced at his hands, but they were inside his pockets, although he moved his legs in a slight kicking motion. I wasn't sure, but I suspected the tremors had begun again.

"Please, Jason, will you tell us?" I asked. "I'm not even sure what questions to ask, but I feel you know things that we need to hear. Please."

"Yes, I can do that," he said. "Yesterday Stefan and I were again together in his room. We had spent more than our usual hour in reading and studying Romans—chapter 12. He was puzzled by one statement that said to consider others better than yourselves."

"Is this important?" Ollie asked. He pulled his hand out of his pocket. The tremors had returned.

I put my index finger to my lips. "Be patient, Ollie."

Ollie got up and paced the area. I didn't know if that helped or not, but as long as he was quiet, it would be all right.

Jason told us that a woman came to the door. At first I thought he meant the same woman as before, but then he explained that the two women looked nothing alike.

What he remembered most vividly was that she held a gun in her right hand, and it was pointed at Stefan.

"The woman looked at me then," Jason said.

"Get him out of here!" she shouted.

"I went through this once before," Stefan told her. "I wonder if women coming to my room will be a usual affair."

"Get rid of him."

"No. He stays."

"My gun says he goes."

"You won't shoot me—at least not yet," Stefan said casually. "You must want something, and it would be utterly stupid to kill me and my friend Jason and have nothing to show for it."

She stood in silence and weighed her options. She did not put away the gun, but she did lower it. "Okay, at least make him sit in the corner. This is just between you and me."

"Jason, sit across from me. You don't belong in a corner," Stefan said. "You know all my secrets, so you might as well know this one. In fact, this is such a secret that I don't know what's going on inside her brain." He turned to her. "I don't know you, do I? To my knowledge I have never seen you before. But you come into my room with a gun and you start to make demands."

"I've come to talk to you about the diamonds."

"Is that a big surprise? Is it, Jason? I could have guessed that one myself." He looked at me and grinned, and then he turned toward her again. "Have you come to rob me? You think I have them in my suitcase or my closet perhaps?"

She stared at him. "I don't want the diamonds. I wouldn't know how to get rid of them. I only want money."

"How much money would you like me to give you?"

"Five million dollars. That really isn't much money for you. Give it to me and you'll never see me again. And you'll never see my partner again either. I'll make sure of that."

"Who is your partner?"

A confused look passed over her face. "I thought you knew. Never mind who he is; I'll take care of him."

"You'll shoot him?"

"If necessary. Five million dollars can encourage me to do a lot of things."

"Who are you?"

"I suppose it's all right to tell you," she said. "Especially if we're going to be partners. My name is Janet Grand."

"And what do you know that would make it worth my giving you five million dollars?"

She said she had been in the car with the policeman when the courier was shot. "I know there was a mix-up and you ended up with diamonds and my friend ended up with paste."

"Hmm, is that how it is?"

She said she knew that Stefan had the jewelry or at least the proceeds from the sale of them. "Just give me five million dollars and you'll never see me or hear from me again."

"No."

"Think it through seriously. I can give you a day or two to get the money. That's not a large amount. I mean, it's not when you think how much you'll make off the deal, even if you have to discount them to someone."

"That's quite true. It's not a large amount, but I plan to return the stones."

"What? Are you insane? The insurance has already paid off—"

"I have had a change of heart."

"You haven't asked what I can give you for five million dollars."

"No, I haven't, but I assume this is more than a robbery."

"That's correct, and you know, of course, when you try to return the diamonds, they'll pin the courier's murder on you."

"Yes, I've thought about that. I had nothing to do with his death—"

"I know that fact and you know it, but you can't prove it. I can prove it."

"Really? How is that possible?"

"I was there when he was murdered." She told Stefan and me that she sat in the car. Until then she had not known anything about the theft. "But I was sort of dating that man. I don't even know his real name, but he liked me to call him Mastermind."

"Maybe he was trying to impress you."

"And he did. He wasn't a very nice man to be around most of the time, but he spent money on me and promised there would be a lot more in the future—a lot more." She shook her head. "But it never happened, and I have expensive tastes."

"So what do you know? What did you see?" Stefan asked.

"He shot the courier, and he grabbed what he thought were the real diamonds."

"Thank you for clearing this up, Janet."

"He'll kill you if you don't give me the money."

"Really? Is that something you know or something you hope?"

"He sent me today as his courier." She laughed. "Sounds like an important job, doesn't it?" She leaned closer to Stefan. "Let's keep it simple. You give me five million and—"

"I will give you nothing. Not a cent. Not a diamond."

"The Mastermind won't like this. He'll kill you and get everything."

Stefan stared. Never had I seen his eyes so hard and so determined. Finally, he spoke quietly. "I am in God's hands."

She swore many angry words, but he said nothing more.

"You think God will protect you?"

"I am in His hands."

As if she had not heard, she asked, "Will God protect you if I shoot you?" She raised the gun.

"You won't kill me, because if you do, you won't find the diamonds. Neither will he."

"You think you're rather smart, don't you?"

Stefan stared at her and said slowly, "No, not really. If I had been smart, I wouldn't have gotten involved in such a nefarious deed. But as it is, I'm in God's hands."

"Will God protect you if he comes after you?"

"God will be with me because the Lord is with me now and won't forsake me or—"

"Whatever that means," she said. Vile words streamed from her mouth once again. "I suggest you rethink this visit. I can call you later tonight if—"

"No, don't bother. I won't change my mind."

"Maybe you'll think about it and decide to be sensible."

"No."

"I have one more proposition to offer you."

"I might as well hear it before I escort you from the room."

"I can give you a sworn statement about my partner, including the gun that fired the bullet that killed the courier. The gun still carries his fingerprints on it." She laughed. "But of course I'll have disappeared by the time you are ready to use the evidence."

"No."

"You don't want me to clear you of murder charges and keep you out of prison again?"

"My friend here, Jason Omore, once said something to me—something I've never forgotten."

"And I suppose I must listen to a sermon."

"Just this. At one point I wanted to do something morally questionable to achieve a moral objective—"

"What does that mean?"

"Forget the background. Jason's words were simple. He said we must never use the devil's tools to achieve God's work. He was right."

"Rather stupid reasoning—"

"No. This is the end of the discussion." Stefan stood up, took her arm, and led her toward the door. "I am not afraid. If you have a conscience, you'll turn over the evidence. If not, I won't buy my freedom from you. You or your Mastermind friend may kill me, but I will do the right thing."

"Don't be too sure—"

"You will never get the diamonds or the money. Never. I assure you of that."

———

Jason said, "That's how I remember it." He again wiped tears from his face.

"I'm sorry you had to relive that," I said. "Is there anything I can do?"

"No," he said and then added, "Wait. Come back in the morning. I do have something I should very much like you to do."

"What is that?" Ollie asked. "Did he give you the diamonds?"

"To me? Why should he have done that? Oh no."

"Okay, then tell us," Ollie said.

"Is not tomorrow satisfactory?"

"Tonight. Now. Right now is more satisfactory," Ollie said.

As he turned away from Ollie, Jason winked at me.

22

"Before I say more, I wish to have each of you wait for the morning light," Jason said. "My heart is very, very heavy over the loss of my friend, and it is most painful for me to speak."

"Why don't you take a short walk?" Burton suggested. "What you have to say may be important information." He nodded toward the detective and said, "He wants to clear this up as soon as possible."

"Yes, to be alone with my sorrow is a good idea, even for a brief time," Jason said. "I should like perhaps an hour."

Burton took Ollie's arm and mine, and we returned to the room. Once inside, Ollie picked up the phone and called the desk. He asked if we could have four sandwiches brought up. "Anything," he said and hung up. "So we wait."

I looked at Burton and tried to read his expression, but his face was inscrutable. He had learned something from that older couple, but he wasn't ready to tell me. And obviously he wasn't ready to tell the detective, who was his friend. I felt thoroughly confused.

Within fifteen minutes a waiter brought us sandwiches. Ollie started to dismiss him, but Burton handed the man a generous tip. All the sandwiches were chicken salad with fries on the side. The three of us ate while we waited for Jason.

Both men seemed to relax while they ate. Ollie lamented over a time when he and Burton had ordered hamburgers and fries at the Varsity—the original fast-food place—located near the Georgia Tech campus. It's supposed to have the longest counter in the world. I tried not to listen, but it was something about Ollie putting sugar in the saltshaker. He did it while Burton went to the restroom, and the other two students at the table eagerly waited for Burton to become the butt of the joke.

"But you got the best of us," Ollie said and turned to me. "Can you believe this part? That guy ate every single fry with all that sugar on them. At one point he sprinkled on even more sugar. The rest of us watched and were ready to laugh at him."

"I believe I also asked for a second serving—and ended up eating half of yours," Burton said.

"I've never figured out how anyone could put sugar on fries, not know the difference, and enjoy them."

"Oh, I didn't sprinkle sugar on the fries," Burton said.

"But I saw you. All three of us watched you!"

Burton shook his head. "I figured out what you did, Ollie. Sugar and salt are white, but they don't look exactly the same. Before I got to the table, I spotted the goofy expression on your faces. Just as I started to sit down, I watched Damon's eyes—he sat next to you—and he kept looking at the saltshaker. I caught on quickly. You didn't notice, but I grabbed a saltshaker from the table behind us and put the other in my pocket."

"Hey, he's smart." Ollie roared. "That's good! That's very good. All these years and I never knew."

"You always said I was smarter than you are," Burton said.

"But I didn't mean it," Ollie said. "Yet maybe you are. Maybe you are." He smiled, but something about his expression wasn't quite true.

Before I could figure out what was going on between them, Ollie launched into another story, but I stopped listening. I wanted to talk to Burton. Surely he had learned something from that couple in 624, and I felt increasingly anxious about it. I walked over to the window and looked out into the darkening evening as I tried to figure out how to get Burton alone.

Nothing came to mind. When I finally turned around, Ollie's back was to me, so I signaled Burton with my thumb, pointing to the door. He gave me the barest shake to indicate he didn't want to talk just then. I cocked my head and gave him my most quizzical expression.

Ollie must have noticed something and turned toward me.

Burton smiled at me and said to Ollie, "She grows on you, doesn't she?"

"Whatever," Ollie said. But what was supposed to sound indifferent carried a warm tone. He could be a nice man if he tried. And I wish he tried more often.

Exactly one hour later, Jason returned. To his credit, Ollie offered him the remaining sandwich. Jason took it and said, "To refuse a gift is to refuse a person. I shall eat it later, if I may. My heart does not desire food now."

Characteristically, Ollie said, "Okay, whatever works for you."

"You wish to know the rest of what I have to say," Jason said. The words came slowly at first, as if he had to force each one to the surface. "I shall tell you everything that I know."

The morning of the day that Stefan Lauber died, he and Jason met again for their regular study time together. Stefan asked questions about heaven—questions he had never asked before.

"I have not been there," Jason said and laughed, "so I can tell you only what appears in the Bible." For perhaps twenty minutes, he answered the things that troubled his friend. To most of the questions, he responded by turning to places in the Bible that provided answers.

"Of this you can be sure," Jason told him. "God will reward us by our deeds—by the things we have done after we have believed."

"And God does not hold our sins and failures against us—those we did before we believed?"

"God has promised us that it is like a marred sheet of paper that has been totally erased."

Jason said he felt those words brought comfort to Stefan.

"I believe that," Stefan said, "but I needed your assurance. I did many terrible things earlier in my life."

"But has not God forgotten them?" Jason said.

"But I still remember—"

"If you remember them, are you not doing a wrong thing? Why would you wish to remind God of things he has chosen to forget about your life?"

Instead of speaking, Stefan laughed before he hugged his friend.

After that they had prayer. When Jason got off his knees, Stefan said, "Wait. There is one thing." He handed Jason a large envelope. "My Bible is inside, and a letter."

"Why are you giving me your Bible?"

"I want you to have it," Stefan said. "I have another Bible here in my room, so I can read that one."

"This I do not understand."

Stefan put his hands on the young man's shoulders. "You have become the best friend I've ever had in my life. Ever. If something should happen to me—"

"Oh no, surely the woman did not mean—"

"She meant every word. Will her friend kill me? I don't know, but I will not change my mind. I must do what God wants me to do. I must return the diamonds."

"Where are they?"

As if he had not heard the question, Stefan said, "If something happens to me, inside this envelope is a letter. It tells my conversion story. At my funeral—"

"Oh, do not say such—"

"At my funeral, you must read the letter."

Jason began to protest, but Stefan hugged him. "Shh. This is not the time for protests from you. If I am still alive on Friday morning, you may return this envelope."

"Yes, I shall be most pleased to return this to you, but do not think of such thoughts—"

"If I am alive, you will return it."

Despite the continued protests, Stefan persisted and Jason agreed. "But I shall pray for our holy God to keep you alive."

"I would like to live, but I have made arrangements for myself and for all my funds to be used for the kingdom of God if I am not here."

———

Jason's voice cracked, and he couldn't talk anymore. I walked over to him and squeezed his hand. I had known Stefan only well enough that I had some sense of the African's loss.

"Where is the envelope?" Ollie asked. "Do you still have it?"

"Why would I not have it?"

"Would you get the envelope and bring it to us?" Ollie asked in a tightly controlled voice.

"It is for the funeral, is it not?"

"Bring it to me. Now. Here. To this room."

Jason looked at me and then at Burton as if to ask, "Should I?"

Both of us nodded.

"I shall do so," he said. "But one request: May I please hand it to you beside the lake? Outside I feel more—more at peace than I do in such a place as this."

"Whatever! Whatever! Just bring it."

As soon as he was gone from the room, Ollie said, "This is an interesting development, don't you think?"

"Yes," Burton said. "It's just as Julie said. We needed to ask the right questions."

The evening sky changed from crimson to ultramarine and finally to a dusky rose, and soon it would become a flat gray. In the metro area, the sky never becomes dark enough to see the fullness of the stars that look down at us. The three of us walked down toward the lake. The cicadas and the frogs seemed to compete in a cacophony of off-key notes. Despite that, the noise was soft enough not to distract.

We stopped by a small corner with chairs. A lamppost provided enough light to read.

Within minutes Jason found us. Without saying a word, he handed Ollie a large sealed envelope.

Ollie tore it open. He moved a few feet away to the lamppost where he could read and scanned the one-page letter. He could have read it where he stood, but I think he wanted to make certain none of us saw the contents.

I got up, walked over, and stood next to Ollie—more than anything just to show him we were in this together. Immediately I saw what the single sheet of paper was. "It's the same thing Lucas read," I said. "May we give it to him after the funeral? I'd like him to have a clean copy."

Ollie handed the single sheet to me and pulled out the Bible. It was large, mahogany colored with a cover made of skin.

"That is the skin of the zebra that covers the pages of the Holy Bible," Jason said. "Did I not give the Bible to him myself after his baptism?"

"A Bible," Ollie said. "This doesn't lead us anywhere." He almost tossed it aside, but he paused to flip idly through it as if he might find paper inserted between the pages. The Bible opened near the end, and at about the same time, both of us spotted a small key taped in the center between two columns.

"Ah, what is this?" Ollie untaped the key.

Jason walked over and watched Ollie carefully remove the key. "Do you not see where my friend placed it?" Jason said. He pointed to the underlined text: Romans 6:23.

"Guess that fits," Ollie said. He held the key to the light. He squinted to read the words. "It's the key to a safe-deposit box," he said. He turned it over and squinted again. He had to stare at it for several seconds before he said, "Bank of North Georgia."

"They have only half a dozen branches," I said. "So that shouldn't be a big task for the police."

"Where's the closest?" Ollie asked.

"Burton and I both live on the Southside, so I have no idea," I said.

"The bank? Surely it is the bank in Tucker," Jason said. "Would that not be correct? That is where I went with him on two occasions."

"Did you see what he did there?"

Jason shook his head. "But how could I? He went to a desk, held out his key, and the woman looked at it, checked his identification and signature, and took him into a room behind her."

"That's it," Ollie said. "I think we've found the missing diamonds." He thanked Jason and told him it was all right to leave. He handed the Bible to the African. "It's yours. Follow his wishes. His brother is in room 625. I assume he's already made plans for the funeral."

Jason left us, and the three of us headed back to the inn. We returned to the suite the Cartledge Inn had given us.

"One big problem has been solved," I said, "or so I assume. At least we think so. If the diamonds are there, that's one problem out of the way."

"But there have been two murders," Burton said. "That's more important than diamonds."

"Oh, we'll figure that out," Ollie said. "We won't close the door on this case."

"But some crimes never get solved, do they?" Burton said. He had a slight edge in his voice. Or did I only imagine it? I was glad he focused on the murders, because it was obvious Ollie had—at least for the moment—dismissed them from his thoughts.

"Why don't we call it a night?" Ollie said. "I'm absolutely worn out. I don't know why, but this has taken a lot out of me. You two might want to go for a proper dinner. I'm ready to turn in, and I live only ten minutes from here."

"Why don't you spend the night here?" Burton asked in a voice that was almost too casual.

"No trouble. It's a straight shoot off the Stone Mountain Expressway," Ollie said.

"I'd feel better if you stayed over," Burton said. "The desk can provide you with a toothbrush and razor."

I wasn't sure why that was significant, but I was ready to back Burton. "You know where the diamonds are, but no one else does," I said. "Jason does, too, but he was never a suspect. There has been just enough noise around here that someone—someone may still be searching."

"Two murders," Burton said. "We assume the same person killed them both. The three of us have been pretty visible all day."

"I'd like you to stay, Ollie." I turned on all the charm I could conjure and said softly, "Please."

"There are two king-sized beds," Burton said. "And one of those sofas folds into a bed. Julie could stay there."

"What? You think someone's going to shoot one of you?"

"Or shoot you maybe," I said. "Two murders. Who knows what else may happen?"

Ollie seemed to think about it for a few seconds. "Sure, why not? If you two will feel safer—"

"I'll feel much safer being with you," Burton said and laughed.

"Now I'm the hero?" Ollie laughed, too. "Yeah, okay, let's do it."

Ollie decided he did want to eat after all, so all three of us went to the dining room. On the way we stopped at the desk and asked them to make up the sofa for me.

"Immediately," Craig said.

When we stood at the entrance of the dining room, I was impressed by the soft decor with its muted tones and earth-colored table linen. The area featured two sections—the casual room and the formal room. The maître d' suggested we choose the room on our right. "Do not be concerned about your dress. This is not about clothing," he said with a slight European accent. "This is about cuisine. To your left is strictly American." He wasn't able to disguise his disdain before he smiled and said, "But in this direction is the finest European cuisine. We have three chefs, all trained in Europe and—"

"You sold me, pal," Ollie said. "Let's go continental."

A uniformed waiter came immediately and filled our water glasses and offered delicate pieces of mint, lime, or orange. At my urging, we all took mint.

Ollie didn't seem to care what he ordered, so the waiter, whose name tag identified him as Henri, suggested chicken in aspic, asparagus, coeur de crème, and wild strawberries for dessert. After Ollie nodded, the waiter said in a heavy accent, "That is an excellent choice."

I settled for a Caesar salad and yellowfin tuna on pasta and no dessert. I didn't get the enthusiasm for my choice, but the waiter did say, "Our tuna is imported, as you may assume, from Australia. It was brought in fresh this morning. You are most discerning, madam."

Burton chose the veal cutlet and the wild strawberries.

"The veal. . .ahh, my dear sir, that is my absolute favorite," the waiter said. "The veal is paper-thin and encrusted in a delicate mixture of spices, egg, and bread crumbs. It is the most delicious thing we offer this evening."

We didn't talk much during the dinner, except about the food. We all agreed that it was absolutely delicious.

"At these prices, it needs to be," Ollie said.

"The meal is on me," Burton said. "Please. I can get mine free, but I'd like to pay for all three."

I smiled at Burton and said softly, "Oh, is this like a date?"

Burton blushed.

I loved that response.

O n the way back to the room, Ollie picked up a fairly expensive "Male Pak" from the desk. The female clerk made me a "Female Pak," as well. "There is no charge for this." Her long brown hair covered up her name tag, but I assumed she must be Doris. It was the first time I hadn't seen Craig behind the desk.

When I asked about the sofa, she smiled and said, "The housekeeper has taken care of it."

We went inside the room and found that all three beds had been made and pulled back. On each bed was a small bar of Zhocolate. To my surprise, Ollie knew it. "Hey, this is supposed to be the best chocolate in the world—and probably the most expensive."

We each munched our Zhocolate and agreed it was rich and that a two-ounce bar was enough. Ollie started in on one of his stories about getting some college girl to bake chocolate pies.

"Hey, guys, how about if you go into your room and tell your stories? I'll use the bathroom while you guys relive the glory days." I didn't give them an opportunity to argue.

"I'll run out to the car and get my stuff," Burton said.

Inside the bathroom I saw two white terry bathrobes hanging up, and I claimed one of them.

"In case you're worried," Burton said, standing in the doorway of his room, "we'll lock the door. It has a lock on the inside. It makes a loud racket—in case—"

I started to make a smart remark, but instead I said, "With two strong men behind a lock in the next room, I know I'll be safe."

"Oh, and we have our own bathroom, so we won't disturb you in any way." He turned to close the door.

"Uh, about that—that visit you made to—"

"Later. Trust me." Burton closed the door. I heard the lock turn.

Despite the closed door, after I went to bed, I could still hear Ollie's voice. I didn't have to listen to his stories, but every few minutes I heard his loud guffaw.

With such discordant music in my ears, I finally drifted off to sleep. I didn't sleep well because I kept thinking of poor Stefan and Deedra Knight. I wondered if the police would ever find out who murdered them. As I lay in the dark, I tried to imagine every possible thing that could have transpired between Burton and the couple in 624. Despite his closed lips, I sensed it was important information.

By seven both men moved around inside their locked room, and they didn't do it on tiptoes. At exactly 7:45 a waiter brought us breakfast. Apparently Ollie had ordered from room service instead of our going down for it. When they came out of the room fully dressed, Ollie pointed to an ugly greenish-and-yellow omelet. I spotted cold cereal and opted for that, and so did Burton. All three of us poured from the two carafes of coffee.

"The bank opens at nine," Burton said. As he put down his third cup of coffee, he checked his watch. "That gives us forty-five minutes. I'll be glad to drive."

"Thanks, chum, but no." Ollie shook his head. "No, this is strictly police business. I'll take care of it, but I'll call you."

"I'd like to go with you," Burton said in a strong voice.

"That's not necessary." He smiled before he said, "You two are civilians. I allowed you to sit through all of this out of professional courtesy and—"

"I really want to go with you," Burton said. He smiled and added, "In fact, I insist."

Just then a conversation from the day before snapped into my head. I understood why Burton persisted. "Yes, and I'd like to be along as well," I said.

"I appreciate your help," Ollie said. He smiled at me this time. "Both of you. Because of you, I hope this is just about over."

"But it's not over," Burton said. "The diamonds won't be found."

Ollie looked dazed as if Burton had slugged him. "But I have the key—"

"No, they won't be found," I said, "because you'll have them."

"What are you—are you trying to say that I'd steal them?"

I stared at Burton. "Your old classmate catches on faster than I thought."

"Hey, where do you get off talking to me like—?"

"Okay, then prove it," I said. "Call your supervisor or whatever you call the person above you and explain about the key you found inside the Bible."

"Sounds like a good idea," Burton said.

"You're serious. You think I would rip off the diamonds," Ollie said. "You two aren't joking, are you?"

"Unless murder is a joke," Burton said. "No, we're not joking. Maybe we can't get you convicted for the murder of Jeremiah Macgregor—"

"Or Stefan Lauber or Deedra Knight," I added, interrupting Burton.

"But we can stop you from stealing the diamonds—the real ones this time."

"This is too insulting to discuss." Ollie pushed past me and started toward the door.

"Okay, Mastermind," Burton said. "Stop."

Ollie turned around and stared at both of us. "You don't seriously—"

"That's what you called yourself in college. You remember, Ollie, when you did all those pranks and underhanded tricks."

"That's what I remembered," I said. "Mastermind. You used the word yourself, Ollie."

"This is nuts," he said and walked past Burton.

Burton grabbed him from behind and held him in a headlock. "And before you tell me I'm assaulting an officer of the court or whatever you're supposed to tell me, I admit my guilt. Either give me the key or use your cell to call your supervisor."

"I will not give in to your tactics." Ollie could barely speak. "Ease up—let me breathe."

Just as Burton relaxed his grip slightly, Ollie punched him with his left arm, broke the hold, and in record time pulled out his gun with the other hand. "Now back off. You are interfering with an investigation, and you are obstructing justice."

"If we let you go, we obstruct justice," Burton said.

"You'll have to kill both of us," I said. I almost laughed at those words. I'd heard them so many times on TV.

"What are two more dead bodies?" he asked. His gaze shifted from me to Burton and back again. "I don't want to hurt either of you, but if you force me, I'll shoot you right now."

This wasn't funny, and it wasn't TV. That's when the criminal is supposed to crack or give up or do something stupid. Ollie had a gun, and we had nothing. He only needed two bullets and a second between shots.

"You will have to kill me," Burton said, "because I won't let you out of this room with that key."

Ollie raised the gun. "This is my last warning."

A knock at the door interrupted us. I was less than three feet from the door, so I lurched forward and opened it.

Ollie fired.

24

I pulled the door open at the moment of the shot.

Jason stood outside the door and stared at us. "I came because—because—"

I turned around. Burton had grabbed Ollie, and they grappled for the gun. Blood seeped from Burton's right shoulder, but he still fought. I raced over to the scuffle. I had received all kinds of training in self-defense, but none of it seemed appropriate. I did the most natural thing that came to me: I grabbed Ollie's left hand. I bit the soft spot between his thumb and index finger. And I bit down hard.

Ollie tried to shrug me away. Just that motion was all it took for Burton to use both of his hands to pound Ollie's right wrist against the floor. The crack of the bone filled the room. Ollie no longer resisted.

"Now it's over," Burton said.

I pulled out my cell and dialed 911.

Jason stepped into the room. "I came to this door because of bad feelings in my heart. I cannot explain except that I did not feel it was good for that man to have the key."

"You saved our lives," I said.

"Yes, this must be so," Jason said. "And even more so is that God helped me to do just that." He winked. "Is that not so?"

⁓

Burton's gunshot wound bled quite a bit, but it was superficial: He needed only a large bandage from the hotel's first-aid kit.

After the police arrived, Burton told them his conversation with the couple in 624. At last I was able to find out.

After I'd knocked on the door and the old man answered and his wife behind him, they had accused me of being the bad cop in the TVish good-cop-bad-cop scenario and wouldn't talk to me, so I left.

"They didn't want to talk to me either," Burton said, "but I think they were afraid not to. This is what happened," he started.

⁓

"Are you from the police?" the old man asked. "From the same place as the other one?"

Before I could answer, the woman said, "No, this one isn't cruel like that one." She walked up to me and peered into my face. "You're not going to threaten us, are you?"

"No, ma'am, I wouldn't threaten you. I don't do things like that."

"That's good. One death threat is enough."

They had already acted odd, and I wasn't sure what to make of that statement, so I decided to try humor. "Why, you're both too nice for anyone to hurt."

"What kind of cop are you anyway?" the woman said.

"I'm not a policeman. I didn't mean to mislead you—"

"Then why are you here? Why do you want to know about 623?" her husband asked.

"It's like this: I'm a pastor. The woman who came to the room with me is a psychologist. We're both guests at the hotel. Julie doesn't have a room, but she is a guest. The lead homicide detective is a close friend. He asked us to help him with this case."

"Mama, it's just like *Murder She Wrote*. Remember that? That Jessica Fletcher wasn't with the police, but she solved most of the crimes for them. And she did tricks like that—let people think she was someone she wasn't. You must be a pretty smart fella."

The woman came up close again and stared into my eyes. She nodded twice before she grabbed both my hands. Her fingers lightly traced my palms and the back of my hands, even though her gaze stayed on my face. "You have good hands. They feel honest." She turned to her husband. "Papa, I think we can trust him."

"I appreciate—"

"You have good hands," the woman said again. "I was a manicurist for forty-three years. When I see hands, I know the person. They say eyes don't lie, but I can tell you that hands don't lie. Yes, you are a good man."

"Thank you—"

"You need a little work on your nails, but your hands are good. I learn much from observing hands."

"So you'll tell me what I want to know?"

"Of course," he said. He pulled up three chairs in a kind of triangular shape. She raised her hand as if to say, "Just wait." Without asking me, she hurried into the bathroom and minutes later came out with a pot of tea. While she was gone, he told me his name was Duncan Kyle and she was his wife of forty-five years and her name was Mildred.

"Not Millie," she called out. "Just Mildred. Now you must join us," she said and poured each of us a cup. They had their cups drained before I had taken more than a few sips. I don't know much about tea, but my nose told me she had blended in several different herbs.

I took a sip and wished I hadn't. I'm not much of a tea drinker anyway, but to be polite, I took another sip while they watched.

I was afraid they were going to ask about the tea, so I said, "Look, can you help us? We think you know something about the murder across the hall."

"What are you talking about?" the man asked. "We know nothing."

"After the murder, you both went to the gazebo and discussed the matter. Someone heard you talking."

"Just like that Jessica Fletcher, isn't he?" the woman said. She shook her head, but it was obvious she was impressed. She turned to her husband. "Tell him, Papa."

"It wasn't much. We heard a noise. I'm not even sure what it was, but it was like a loud pop."

"No, Papa, more like a car backfiring. That's how Jessica's witnesses always describe it. And that is exactly how it sounded to us."

"Okay, maybe so," he said. "Yes, I did think maybe it was a gunshot. I used to do some target practice. I haven't done any for maybe twenty years, but people like me never forget the sound."

"So what did you do?"

"Nothing," the man said. "I mean, we talked about it, but that was about all—"

"And what time was that?"

"A few minutes after six. Five after at most," she said. "Remember—we had just heard the top-of-the-hour headline news on CNN."

"Right, yes," he said. "We had eaten a big lunch and didn't want dinner, but we decided to go for a walk."

As they left the room, he turned around to lock the door. Just then the door to room 623 opened.

"That man was startled, I tell you," she said. "He still had a gun in his hand."

"How long after the shot was that?"

They looked at each other and couldn't decide if it had been ten minutes or fifteen. They decided no more than fifteen, but probably a little less. That would have made it around 6:20. That still would have given Lucas time to come into the room before the food gurney.

"I don't think he was aware he still had the gun in his hand," she said. "Not until he saw my face."

"Then I was the stupid one. I turned to Mama and said, 'See, I told you it was gunfire. I knew it!' Just as I said those words, I knew I was in trouble."

"The man walked right up to us and put the gun to Mama's head. I'd seen it done on TV, but this was real and it was a gun. He said, 'I just killed one man. I can kill you two.' "

300

"'Please,' Mama whimpered," Duncan said. "I was scared, and my Mildred, she was even more scared."

She started to deny it and then said, "Yes, I was plenty scared."

"If you forget you saw me," the man said, "I'll forget I saw you. If you should remember, I'll come after you. I can get your name at the desk, and I'll come and shoot both of you and burn down your house."

"I didn't see anything," Duncan told him.

"I told the man the same thing," Mildred said.

"He told us to go back inside and count to fifty before we came back out, and that's exactly what we did. He said if we should see him again, he would be a total stranger."

"Did you see him again?" I asked.

They stared at each other. Duncan nodded.

"He was with the other police," Mildred said. "Except they were in uniforms. He wasn't. He wore a suit."

"He stared at us, and when no one else was looking our way, he drew his index finger across his throat."

By then I had it figured out, but I needed to have them tell me. "What did he look like?"

"Big, oh, he was so tall," the man said. Duncan was barely over five feet, so I assumed even I looked tall to him.

"His hair was not blond, but it was not dark," she said.

"Eyes?" I asked. "Did you notice his eyes?"

"Green with tiny specks of brown," she said. "Very tiny specks."

The eyes. I had looked into them too many times in the past not to recognize them. Sadness filled my heart. I knew Ollie was capable, but it was still a shock. I asked if there was anything else they could tell me.

"After they came—the police—we went into the parking lot and discussed this," Mildred said. "We have not been out of the room since then."

"Will you catch him?" the old man asked. "Have you collected the vital clues to solve this?"

"Not quite," I said. "There is something else I have to learn first, but I'm very close."

I don't know why but I asked, "What about this man? The man with the gun? Is there anything else you can tell me?"

"He's on drugs," Mildred said. "Perhaps not the first time with the gun, but when he returned. Definitely on drugs."

"I doubt—"

"For forty-three years I was in the business. During the last ten years, I fired many women who could not leave the drugs alone. I know what I know. He was on drugs."

301

"You're sure?" I could hardly believe that.

"Listen to Mama. She may not always be right, but when it comes to the hands, she is never wrong. Tremors. Look at the tremors. Then you know."

———

Burton shook his head and stared at me. "As she said those words, I realized that I had observed the tremors. I'd been so preoccupied with other things, that fact hadn't registered."

25

There isn't much left to tell, and this isn't an old TV script in which the hero explains everything. We had no trouble implicating Ollie. We also learned that he had come to the Cartledge Inn after he had called in sick.

It was also common knowledge at DeKalb headquarters that he and Deedra Knight had once been involved. She and Ollie hadn't been together for a couple of years. I suppose it was a case of thieves falling out with each other.

As for Pam Harty, we learned she had once been Ollie's housemate—the term used by one of his neighbors. After she was arrested, Pam didn't want to testify against Ollie. She loved him, and as she said, "I don't want to be the cause of his going to prison." At first she insisted she was afraid to speak up and that he had threatened her.

After she received a promise of immunity, was assured that Ollie wouldn't hurt her, and (even more important) was told that she was only one of his many girlfriends, she told us everything. She produced concrete evidence to convict Oliver Viktor. As they say in the old gangster films, "That canary sure could sing." She told a lot about Ollie—much more than we had expected.

When the police raided his house, they found evidence of other crimes. I also learned that he hadn't lied to me about his so-called motor-system disorder. He had a disorder, all right, but it was because he was addicted to a drug called oxycodone. It's an opiate and highly addictive. It created symptoms similar to those of Parkinson's disease, but it was caused by a lengthy use of oxycodone. That explained a lot of things about his behavior.

—

When Burton and I were finally free late that night from all the official police questions of Ollie's arrest, I was utterly worn out. And so was Burton. He went to his room, and I decided to book a room. Craig was on duty, and when I told him I wanted a room, I added, "Anything but 623."

"That's still not open anyway," he said, "so I can't let you have it."

He hadn't caught my humor, and I didn't argue with him. I was mentally wiped out. I went to the room, number 509, and fell across the bed, and I don't remember anything until the phone rang.

"Hey, this is that guy who slept in the next room last night. I liked your snoring so much, I want to take you to dinner."

"I don't snore."

"You don't know for sure, though, do you?" Burton said. "Hey, it's almost 8:00. Can you wash your face and be ready in thirty minutes?"

"How about ten minutes?"

Exactly eight minutes later he was waiting by the elevator.

He hugged me.

"That wasn't the kind of hug you give a parishioner," I said. "I know the difference."

"I'm glad you know the difference." That smile again followed his words. If we hadn't been in public, I would have kissed him.

"I don't know what happened to you," he said, "but I know it happened. You believe, don't you?"

As we walked toward the dining room, I said, "It is so weird. I do believe. I can't explain why or how or—"

"That's why we call it faith," he said. "It isn't anything we can tear apart and examine. Either we believe or we don't."

Instead of going into the dining room, Burton took my arm and propelled me right out the front door. We walked toward the car park and were perhaps a hundred feet from the main entrance.

"That's far enough," he said. He pulled me into a dark alcove and embraced me. "I love you, Julie West. You're crazy, and you drive me nuts, and there are times I'd like to put a muzzle on your smart mouth, but I can't think of any other woman in the world I'd rather fall in love with than you."

"I should hope you wouldn't." I kissed him, and then I said, "This is so special to me. When I came here yesterday, I was trying to figure out how to get you out of my heart."

"And I came to the Cartledge Inn to ask God's help to get you out of my life."

"I'll bet God is smiling at us right now."

"I don't know," he said, "but I'll bet He likes to see *us* smile."

Burton wouldn't let me answer. He kissed me again.

"I still have questions. Millions of them."

He put out his hand and touched mine.

In the alcove, we were two shadows that faced each other. The darkness blotted out our expressions and momentarily erased my questions.

EVERYBODY CALLED HER A SAINT

1

If it hadn't been for Twila Belk, I wouldn't have taken the Antarctic cruise, and I wouldn't have seen Burton again. If I hadn't gone on the cruise, I wouldn't have been there when someone murdered Twila.

Twila was a special friend—unquestionably my closest friend. Even now, tears fill my eyes whenever I think about her death. "It can't be," I tell myself. "It just can't be." If she had died of natural causes, I would have mourned, but grief and shock mingled together still overpower me at times.

"Why would anyone murder Twila Belk?" I asked shortly after we learned of her death. So did the others on the cruise.

In the year or so I had known Twila, not once had I ever heard anyone say a negative word about her. If anything, almost everybody called her a saint. And she was exactly that. Even now that it's all over, she is as revered in death as she was in life.

Burton and I had broken up. That's the reason I almost didn't go on the cruise—oh yes, Burton. You won't understand all the things that happened unless I start with him. His name is James Burton III but he likes everyone to call him just Burton. He's the pastor of a church in Riverdale, a small town about twenty miles south of Atlanta and about a ten-minute drive from the Hartsfield-Jackson Airport.

Our relationship was growing, and we began to talk about marriage. Almost a year earlier I had become a believer—largely through the influence of Burton, but God had also sent a few other surprises into my life. They were individuals who talked about God, as do a lot of people. But these folks lived the life they talked about. I had seen few others do that.

I'll say it straight. I loved Burton, even before I became a Christian. I had been married before, but my drug-user husband died in an accident. Burton knew about my past. I think I began to fall in love with him the evening we met on the Georgia coast when we solved the murder of Roger Harden. Sorry, I'm getting ahead of myself again. I'll try to make this a linear story.

I'm an inch taller and three years older than he is. He's never been married—lucky me. I have red hair that I call titian, and he has gorgeous black, curly hair; deep, deep blue eyes; and the kind of smile that melts me whenever I look at him.

Six weeks before the murder of Twila, I was sure we would get married. I wasn't sure I wanted to take on the role of a pastor's wife, but, hey, I could fake that part. I'm a professional—the head of Clayton County Special Services, so I worked past that part. Everything seemed so wonderful for about six weeks.

That's when I found out about his problem.

It was *his* problem—or at least he was the cause of the problem.

Weeks earlier we had one of those beautiful candlelight dinners. In one of those special places—you know, the kind of place where you don't read the right side of the menu or care about prices. I sat as demurely as it's possible for me to sit. He ordered the same meal for both of us: chicken in aspic and asparagus. The presentation on the plate was probably as good as the meal itself.

I knew he would propose, and I thought of at least twelve ways to sound extremely surprised. In the end, I thought a simple yes would be enough.

But I never said yes.

I knew he had bought a ring for me. I learned that from his secretary, who thought I already knew.

He didn't have some kind of wacky presentation by the server, such as sticking the ring inside my coeur de crème over wild strawberries. I hadn't expected anything like that from Burton.

After dinner we drove toward my apartment. He switched on the CD player and we listened to those old, old Tony Bennett songs like "Because of You" and "A Stranger in Paradise." He had done that for atmosphere, and I didn't want to spoil anything. He parked in front of my building, shut off the engine, but kept the music going. It was on the second playing of "Because of You." We listened in silence until that song finished.

"I have something to tell you," he said.

I held back from saying, "At last." To enhance the softness of the moment, I said nothing but clasped his hand.

"I love you, Julie. I don't know if it's your smart mouth or your quick thinking, but I love you. I love everything about you."

I kissed his cheek. I wasn't going to say yes until he asked. But I had practiced the word a thousand times.

"I want to marry you—"

Something wasn't right about the way he said that. Was there a *but* at the end of that sentence?

"I—I have a secret. It's something I've never told anyone else—"

"Funny. That's what all my clients say."

"But this is different."

"Would you believe I hear that statement about once a week in my practice?"

"This is—this is something—something important—"

I had three or four smart-mouthed answers fighting to pop out of my mouth, but once again, I shut up.

For a long time, Burton said nothing. I reached over and turned off the CD. It didn't seem right to hear that soft, romantic music right now.

I don't think it was my flip remarks; I think he was quiet because it was so difficult for him to speak about his dark past. I couldn't see his features clearly in the semidarkness, and after a few more seconds of silence, I wondered if I had said the wrong thing. He said he loved my smart mouth, didn't he? Yet I knew it was better to keep quiet and let him work through whatever conflict he had.

After two or three more minutes of silence, he said, "You remember when we met at Palm Island?"

"Do you think I have amnesia?" was what I wanted to say. Instead, I nodded. "Every person there had a secret—"

"Which was the reason we were there."

"Roger Harden knew all the secrets, and—"

Burton held up a hand. "Everybody's secret came out."

"I remember."

"Everybody's secret except mine."

"That's right!" I had forgotten. From across the room in Roger's house, I had formed the question, "You, too?" with my lips, and he'd nodded. "You never told me what it was."

"I was too ashamed."

"All of us on that island were ashamed. That's why we all had secrets." I realized that he hadn't been as self-revealing as I had assumed. That hurt, and I'm sure he caught the sadness in my voice.

"I want to tell you now."

He melted me again. And I did love him, so I took his hand and whispered, "I love you. I doubt that anything—"

"You haven't heard yet."

I decided to listen to him bare his soul. I loved him and was sure nothing would change my attitude toward him.

"I did tell one person—Roger Harden. But you must have assumed that. Roger's dead, so no one else in the world knows."

I rubbed his cheek softly. I didn't want to spoil the intimacy of the moment with any words, no matter how tender they sounded.

That night Burton told me his long-held secret. His words horrified me. I couldn't believe I loved a man who would commit such a harsh, cruel, and selfish act. He admitted that it had been sinful and self-centered, and he had never been able to tell the truth about it.

"You have to make this right," I said. "You're a Christian and a preacher. You're supposed to tell me to do things like that."

"I can't. Don't you see I can't do this to *them*?"

"I hate what you did!" My words surprised me. Part of it was the shock, but more than that, the confession came from a man I loved—the man I planned to marry. Okay, the confession came from a man I thought was only two short steps away from perfection.

"Besides—besides, it's too late!"

"It is never too late to right a wrong. I've even heard you say that. I can't believe—" I broke off, and tears filled my eyes. How could he have done such a horrible thing? Worse, how could he have lived with himself since then?

"You don't understand," he said, but without much force in his words. I think he knew he had lost not only my respect but my love.

"You're right, I don't understand. I don't want to understand." I reached for the door handle. "Don't call me again," I said.

"Please—"

"Maybe you can salve your conscience by confessing to me, but that's—that's not good enough! I can't marry you. I feel—" I was so angry and so horrified I couldn't finish my sentence. I slammed the door and ran to my apartment. I was such an emotional mess that it took me four tries before I could get my key into the lock.

I didn't stop loving him, but I tried. I decided that the only way to get past my feelings was to get away from him.

That was the last time I saw Burton until the cruise.

2

Less than a week after I broke up with Burton, I moved out of my apartment in Riverdale and rented one in Jonesboro. It was only ten minutes away from him but far enough so I wouldn't run into him at a supermarket or gas station. I didn't go back to that church—I couldn't sit in a pew and listen to him speak. I visited several other churches a few times, but I wasn't ready to join any of them. Besides, when Burton preached, his words had a way of making me examine my heart. No other minister had been able to make me feel that way.

I felt I needed to focus on one thing—getting on with my life—and that meant getting Burton out of it. But such goals aren't always that easy to reach. It certainly wasn't for me.

In time I might have been able to get away from Burton if it hadn't been for Twila Belk and the Antarctic cruise. For nearly three months, she had focused her energies on that once-in-a-lifetime trip. She had spent an immense amount of money for a fourteen-day excursion. It wasn't typical of her to be obsessed with something like that, but whenever she phoned me (at least once every day), the cruise was the top subject of conversation, and when she e-mailed me (almost every day), she expressed new anxieties about the trip.

Although the cruise seemed unlike the things she normally did, I loved her enough that I decided to put up with her strange behavior. She had reserved all forty-eight places on a ship named the *Vaschenko*, which had once been some kind of Russian deep-sea research vessel. After the end of the Cold War, it had been refitted as a tourist ship. Most of the cabins contained two bunk beds; a few handled four. She took one cabin to be totally alone—which I didn't understand at the time. But it was her money to do with as she chose.

I didn't know every person on the list, but she assured me that wasn't going to be a problem. We'd be together for fourteen days aboard a small ship. I'd get to know them all before we returned.

Two weeks before the cruise, I drove by Twila's office to tell her that I had decided not to go. She was already aware that I had broken up with Burton, and I assumed she would understand. I hadn't given her any details except the usual catch-up phrases about incompatible temperaments. I called her and said I wanted to talk to her, and it was important. She said her last client would be gone by five, so I arrived five minutes after that.

She probably anticipated why I had come to see her. At least she didn't seem

311

surprised when I said, "Twila, I love you, but I can't go on the cruise. I've thought about this quite a bit. It would be too painful for me to be on the same cruise with Burton."

"Don't waste any words working up to the topic, my dear." She laughed with that wonderfully deep, hearty laugh. "That's one quality I like about you, Julie. You say it straight."

"So now you know why I can't go on the trip."

"Oh no," she said. "I refuse to let you back out."

"You refuse?" Then I laughed. "That's one quality I dislike about you. You won't let the topic drop."

"All but a few of you on the cruise are special. I feel close to you and want to be with you," she said. "Some are former or present clients. About a dozen are close friends. You're number one on the list."

Her directness disconcerted me. To stall until I could figure out a good retort, I asked, "What about the others?"

"You know how it is when you have a party, don't you? You end up inviting a few people out of obligation or because they beg for an invitation."

"So you'll have some of them on the cruise?"

"A few," Twila said and sighed. "I'm thankful there are only a few."

Twila was a short, older woman and still trim. I don't think she had ever been beautiful, but her even features made her attractive. Time had been kind to her, and she had let it do its own work. Twila's once-blond hair had turned a silvery gray. The lines on her face weren't the etched strokes of sadness; rather, they formed patterns of contentment as if she were always happy. Her honey brown eyes made me feel that a woman of twenty hid inside a body of someone forty years older. That day she wore a cream silk blouse, black silk slacks, and low-heeled shoes. She tied her hair back with a ribbon of black moiré silk.

Excitedly she told me (probably for the fiftieth time during the past month) that she had planned the cruise around the people who were truly special in her life. "So except for those obligatory individuals, my guests are people I love or individuals who have been of deep spiritual influence in my life."

"And that list of special people includes Burton?"

"You were first on my list. Burton was second."

"I'm sorry, but you'll have to delete my name." I said those words to her in the strongest, no-nonsense voice I could muster. "I'm sure you'll have no problem getting someone to fill my half cabin."

"It's not a matter of getting someone to sleep in your bunk," she said. "I want *you.*"

"I can't."

"Yes, you can. I refuse to accept your declining the invitation," she said. I can't explain the timbre of her voice, but once in a while—and quite rarely—Twila said something with a gravity in her voice that Moses probably would have loved to emulate on Mount Sinai. "You will go."

"I can't. Please don't ask me again. I love you, but I can't." My pain over Burton was stronger than obeying an all-but-divine command. In a rush of painful words, I reminded her that Burton and I had broken up. I said I couldn't divulge the reason because that was for him to tell her. Twila, my friend, was also a professional, and I knew she would never probe once I set the boundary.

After I finished the torrent of words, Twila stared at me for several seconds. She shifted her gaze into space, and I sensed she was trying to decide what to say to me.

"I'm not going. It's that simple," I said.

"I've never asked anything of you in the months we've known each other." Before I could come up with a flippant response, she said, "This is one thing I ask of you. Please. You have become—I suppose I'd have to say like my own daughter. I've planned every detail of this trip, and it's extremely important."

"Important?" I asked. "What makes it important? Antarctica would be wonderful, but I would hardly call it important."

"It is important. *To me.*"

"This is so untypical of you."

"That's correct," she said. Her lips trembled ever so slightly before she said, "Julie, my dear one, this is the last, most important thing I shall do in my life."

That may sound like the tone of a martyr as I tell it, but it came across as a declaration—much like someone who says, "This is the last project I'll take on before I quit this job."

Although I heard the intensity, I wasn't ready to capitulate. "But don't you see? Burton will be on the ship, as well. I—I can't face him. I don't want to be around him—"

"There will be nearly fifty passengers on the *Vaschenko*. You'll see him, but you will not have to talk to him on any personal level or be anywhere near him."

"I can't. I love you, Twila, but I—I can't. Please understand."

Twila turned her head away—and that gesture hurt more than anything she said. "I beg you. Please."

I had never heard her talk like that. She was one of those cheerful, upbeat types, and nothing ever seemed to upset her. I decided to choose my words carefully. Maybe if she knew his secret, she'd understand. "You see, Twila—"

As if she hadn't heard me, she said, "I want you to know why this is so important to me and why I want you—why I need you—on the ship with me: I don't expect to live more than a few more months."

I didn't know what to say when Twila told me she would die within the year. I must have looked as if I were frozen, but I couldn't take in her words.

She grabbed my hand. "I've decided to tell you—only you—and you must not tell anyone. Promise me that?"

Still unable to speak because of the shock, I nodded.

"I have cancer. You remember shortly after we met, I told you that three years ago I underwent a mastectomy."

Again a mute response from me.

"It's back, and it has metastasized." She went into a medical explanation—she was an MD who specialized in psychiatry. Except for her personal physician, an oncologist, no one else knew how aggressively the cancer had spread. "Nothing has worked. We doctors do what we can, but sometimes God overrules."

"No, no—"

"These things are in the hands of God," she said. "I am at peace."

"You can't—you can't die—"

"Please, my dear. If you must argue, argue with God. I've made my peace with Him." She smiled and said, "I'll soon be with my Otto and Reinhard."

I knew whom she meant. She and Otto Belke (which he shortened to Belk because people couldn't pronounce the short *e* in German) married shortly after both of them had finished their residencies at Johns Hopkins in Baltimore. Otto bought a partnership with two other surgeons in Clayton County. Twila went into private practice.

Twelve years later, Otto and their only child, Reinhard, died when a truck's brakes failed at seventy miles an hour and rammed their car into a concrete abutment. Twila had been hospitalized for weeks with a broken pelvis. Her right leg never healed quite right, and she walked with a barely noticeable limp.

"Shh, no tears," Twila said. "Please don't shed tears for me. I am going to that perfect place we sing about in church."

The truthfulness of her voice made the tears slide more rapidly down my cheeks.

Twila is going to die soon.

No, it can't be.

"You're only sixty-one. You're so spry and filled with life—"

"You wish to argue with God, is that it?" Twila smiled, and it wasn't a false smile.

The deep inner peace was obvious.

"I can't accept that. There are other treatments and—" She stopped me before I could suggest she get a second opinion.

"This is my body. I know it is breaking down, and I'm ready." She took my hand again and held it. "We shall never speak of this again."

"But I can't—"

"I've told you because the trip to Antarctica is to fulfill my last dream. When we first married, Otto and I decided that one day we would go to Antarctica together. I must go. This is the last chance. Otto can't go with me, but I can take the friends who are the dearest to my heart." She seemed unaware that her nails dug into my hand, but the serenity on her face melted my last ounce of resistance. "I think Otto would have liked that. He was so good with people and had so many, many friends."

She stopped speaking and stared at me. Those light brown eyes seemed to plead with me.

She had me, and I think she knew it. "Of course I'll go," I said.

"I want this to be a big, big event."

She had no idea what a big event it would be. How could she have known that someone would take her life in the beautiful, frozen land at the bottom of the world?

4

Twila had made the travel arrangements for all of us. I didn't want to calculate what it must have cost her. She had booked forty-seven seats on a Delta flight to Buenos Aires. We all met on the E Concourse at the Hartsfield-Jackson Airport in Atlanta. Everyone arrived at least two hours before our flight. Betty Freeman later told me she was so afraid of being late that she had arrived nearly four hours early. Even two hours seemed a little extreme to me, but that's what the airlines suggested.

That meant I had two hours to avoid eye contact with Burton. I saw him, and I'm sure he saw me. It was almost like a dance routine. I moved in one direction, and he moved in the opposite. Although I was conscious of his presence and location every minute of the two hours, I successfully avoided eye contact with him.

To his credit, he made no move to come near me. I tried to observe him by looking at reflections in the glass windows or glancing at him from behind. I did have a feeling that he might be doing the same thing, but I restrained myself from trying to catch him at it. My emotions were still raw, and I didn't want any contact with him.

Heather Wilson, who knew we had dated, came over to me. "You and the pastor aren't with each other."

"You're very observant," I said in what I considered a noncommittal way.

"What's with you and Burton?"

"Nothing is what's with Burton and me."

"You know what I mean."

"We no longer date."

"Oh, that's wonderful! I mean, that's probably terrible or something for you." She smiled. "Did he cast you aside?"

"Ask him."

"So he's available, is he?"

"Ask him," I repeated and walked away.

She definitely wasn't Burton's type even though she was a lot prettier than I am. She's also six inches shorter and looks good when she stands next to him. She could wear heels and still look good beside him.

All right, she was gorgeous—one of the prettiest women I'd ever seen. Her features were flawless—alabaster skin, full red lips, patrician nose, and blue eyes. Her thick black hair was pulled back in a severe bun, which would have detracted

316

from any other woman's appearance but only enhanced hers. Heather wore a richly textured sapphire blue dress that probably cost more than I spend on clothes in a year.

Our brochure advised us to wear warm, casual clothes for the trip. At the airport the rest of us wore leisure clothes (that is, mostly jeans or warm-up suits). I wore flat shoes. I told myself it was because heels were totally out of place on such a trip—which they were—but it also brought my height down so that I was less than an inch taller than Burton—I mean, if we ever stood next to each other again.

When Heather spoke to Burton, she got close to him—a little closer than most people would. But then, Heather would never win an award for being subtle.

Until they called us to board, we moved around in small groups. Our group made up almost half of the passengers on the Delta flight.

Twila and I sat together near the rear of the plane, so we were able to board before Burton. That avoided an awkward moment for me. We left on time, which was just after midnight. It was a ten-hour flight to Buenos Aires, and we landed around ten o'clock the next morning. We were still in the same time zone, so we didn't have to worry about changing our watches.

We landed at Buenos Aires only about half an hour late. Going through Immigration was simple enough. We collected our luggage. I smirked when I saw the huge suitcase that Heather pulled. I overheard someone say that she had paid forty-nine dollars because she was above the seventy-pound weight limit.

We met together just outside Immigration. Twila had arranged for us to eat at a restaurant in the airport. I noticed with chagrin that somehow Heather had gotten Burton to pull her monstrous-sized suitcase. He traveled with one large carryall.

After our meal together, a fleet of taxis took us to the domestic airport, where we boarded a LAPA plane that flew the whole way along the spectacular Atlantic coast. Three hours later we landed at Ushuaia, Tierra del Fuego, Argentina. Ushuaia is touted as the southernmost city in the world. It's at the tip of the Andes where Chile and Argentina meet and nestles between what the tourist books call the "spectacular snowcapped mountains of the Andes and the Beagle Channel." This is one time the brochures didn't exaggerate.

From the airport, again a fleet of taxis (actually six drivers who made repeated round trips) drove us to the edge of the town, turned onto a dirt road, and wound around a bluff that overlooked the ocean. Twila had booked most of our group at the Los Niros hotel—a remote and scenic spot, high over Ushuaia. It was too small for all of us, so she reserved rooms for fifteen people at another local hotel.

We learned that the niros is a tree. I spotted *one* in front of the hotel, and the clerk proudly acknowledged, "Yes, it is our most famous tree." As far as I could tell, it was also the most infamous. With no competition, they could say anything they wanted about it. The niros stood about twelve feet tall. It was scraggly and ugly, and I suppose the only type of tree strong enough to survive the harshness of the weather. Relentless winds shook the building constantly. Despite the sun and moderate temperatures (according to the thermometer it was almost forty degrees Fahrenheit), the harsh, blustery winds brought the windchill factor to slightly above zero.

After we checked in, I felt restless. I wrapped myself in two heavy knit sweaters and two pairs of slacks. I debated about whether to unpack my heavy gloves and knit cap. I decided it was too much effort. I was still tired from disrupted sleep on the plane. Any further delay inside my room, and I probably would have been forced to lie down and rest.

I went outside. On one side of our hotel, I gazed at the Andes and the country of Chile. On the other side, I marveled at the high waves of the ocean whipped up by persistent and unyielding winds that also ripped at my face. I couldn't decide which side was more beautiful.

The wind never let up. It was cold—the kind that seems to penetrate every layer of clothing. There was no snow, only wind. Later I walked into a low-lying area, much like a small valley. To my surprise, I actually saw a copse of trees. Just for fun, I counted them. There were eight. One of them would have measured more than eight feet high if it had been able to stand erect. Even there, the wind was so severe that they were permanently bowed.

Twenty minutes later my cold feet and numb hands told me it was time to go back to the Los Niros.

I spotted Burton with someone about two hundred feet ahead of me. They were obviously walking together into Ushuaia. I didn't have to guess the identity of the other person. Heather was appropriately dressed in what looked like wool pants and a parka. She has a very distinctive walk, and I wonder if *sashay* is the proper description. She also wore distinctive, fur-lined boots with three-inch heels. As always, she looked gorgeous.

Doesn't she ever look normal like the rest of us?

"What do you care?" I answered myself.

She's a shameless flirt.

"Right, Julie. What's the saying? It takes one to know one."

He's no longer my concern.

"That's right!" I said. Okay, I shouted it. He was no longer a part of my life. But my tear-filled eyes wouldn't let me lie to myself.

I went back into the hotel. I felt lonelier than I had in years. I wasn't sure why. Twila was my friend and there were others I liked to be around, but my heart was out there, wishing I were next to Burton.

From inside, I peeked back. I'm sure he didn't see me. Heather clung, but to his credit, Burton seemed indifferent to her. His head was bowed slightly forward to brace against the torturous wind. It seemed as if she talked constantly. If he answered her, it wasn't with much animation.

You're through with Burton. Remember?

I turned and walked toward the dining room. It was closed, but when I waved a dollar bill, a nice waiter smiled at me—or maybe he smiled at the money in my hand. "Tea? Chai? Te'?"

With a full grin he led me to a small alcove where I found hot water and tea bags. After handing him the dollar, hearing his cheery thanks, and retorting, "*De nada,*" I made myself a cup of tea, went back into the fairly small lobby, sat in the corner, and began to read.

All right, I didn't read, but I had an open book. And yes, I glanced out the window occasionally—like every eight seconds. More than an hour passed before Burton and Heather came back. She pretended to trip and grabbed his arm. Such a cheap trick.

But then, I had used the same trick the first time Burton and I walked together at Palm Island.

But of course, that was different.

As I sat alone, a terrible sense of foreboding crept over me. I kept pushing it aside, trying to convince myself that it was my anxiety about Burton.

Afterward, I wondered if I had done something—anything—or just paid attention to the nagging sense of dread that came over me, would I have been able to save Twila's life?

5

I turned away when Burton and Heather walked into the hotel. I stayed in the lobby nursing my long-cold cup of tea until it was time for dinner.

I called Twila, but she didn't feel like going to the dining room. She had already arranged for her meal to be brought to her room. She assured me that her medication took care of any pain. "I'm tired, my dear, just tired." She went to bed. I was in the room next to hers with a connecting door. I wanted to leave it open in case she needed me. Twila wouldn't allow it.

When I reached the dining hall, I sat down near Betty Freeman and Shirley Brackett (who was at the table without her brother, Frank). When I asked about him, she said, "He's tired and is having his dinner in his room."

The two women chatted constantly. I smiled and made brilliant comments such as "Oh" or "Hmm." They didn't seem to notice that I didn't talk.

That inner nagging wouldn't let up.

I tried not to notice Burton come into the dining room. He hurried past me and sat with Thomas Tomlinson, Mickey Brewer, and a half dozen people I didn't know. Less than a minute later, Heather pranced into the room. Okay, *pranced* is my prejudiced word. I'll try it again. Heather entered the room as only Heather can. I didn't see where she went (my back was to Burton and the others), but I heard her say, "Oh, I should have been here earlier. I would have loved to sit with you."

No gallant man offered to give up his seat—or so I assume—because she came back and took the only empty space at our table.

The next morning after breakfast, we were told we could explore the town, but we were to meet in front of the Albatross Hotel no later than four o'clock, and we would be transported to the dock from there. They assured us the hotel was easy to find.

After breakfast, Twila and I wandered around Ushuaia for a couple of hours. For me, it was the most desolate place I had ever seen or imagined. The rugged spine of the Andes met the sea at the southern tips of Chile and Argentina. We learned Ushuaia had originally been a penal colony and about forty thousand people lived there.

Twila and I and ten others signed up for a half-day tour of Parque Nacional Park in Tierra del Fuego, which abuts the Chilean border. It was the only tour we could take, because the ship left at four thirty. We rode in a van with a guide named Nora. Although she was pretty and friendly, her English was marginal. She answered every question, but most of the time, her answers had little relevance to what we asked.

At four o'clock we were at the hotel. As I stepped out of the tour bus, Burton stood right there. There was about a three-foot space from the lower step to the ground. He held out a hand to each female passenger.

I stared into those blue eyes for a fraction of a second before I looked away. "Thank you," I mumbled. Because I looked away, I stumbled—accidentally—and he grabbed me.

"I think I've done this before," he said softly.

"Oh, really?" I hurriedly moved on. I love it when I can say something like that. Too late I remembered that was part of what Burton liked about me.

From then until the bus arrived, which was nearly half an hour later, I kept my back to him. That wasn't easy. He moved around and talked to various people—he's quite outgoing that way.

He chatted for a minute or two with Twila, but I still kept my back to him. *Take that,* I thought. *I won't look into those gorgeous blue eyes. I won't let your dazzling smile get to me.*

He walked away and spoke with the next group. The bus finally arrived. I had to laugh. We could see the dock from where we stood. We boarded a bus and rode less than half a mile to where we were to embark. Our ship, the *Vaschenko*, was scheduled to leave port at 4:30 p.m., or as they called it, 1630 hours.

The summer season was nearing its end, although there were still almost fifteen hours of sunlight. By March, no ships would leave the area of Patagonia until after the sun appeared again well above the horizon. Someone said that would be August, but I knew there would be no cruise ships until November.

I had been on Caribbean cruises twice and had enjoyed the luxury and the size of the huge ocean liners. Perhaps I expected something like that, but the *Vaschenko* seemed tiny, like something out of a 1930s black-and-white movie. No luxury here, but it looked sturdy, and I liked the warm smile of the captain.

Sunil Robert, the captain, greeted each of us as we boarded. He held a chart and personally checked off each name and told us the location of our cabins. Even if I hadn't been able to tell from Captain Robert's dark skin and straight black hair, I would have known he was from India by his delightful accent. He spoke English well, with an accent that fluctuated between British English and East Indian.

Not that I paid much attention, but he was quite handsome, about thirty-five, and just under six feet tall, with a stocky build that had just begun to turn soft around the midsection. As we got closer, I observed his wedding ring, which made him suddenly seem less attractive.

He smiled and shook my hand, and it was a warm, firm handshake. He told me that I was in cabin six, and my roommate was Betty Freeman. (I already knew that, of course.)

I went to my cabin and saw that my luggage was already in place and on the bunk nearer the door, so I decided that was mine. My bunk bed resembled something I had slept on during summer camp, except that this one was much sturdier and bolted to the floor. The room had one window, but we were right at sea level, so I saw nothing but water spraying against the heavily paned porthole. Each of us had a cupboard. One-half was shelving and the other for hanging. On the top shelf was a life vest with instructions that we were always to have it on when we left the ship. In one corner was a small desk, a chair, and a reading lamp. I have no idea why they called it a reading lamp. It had about twenty-five watts of light. The overhead light was just about bright enough so I could read. The toilet was outside our door on our left with the shower on the right. The ship had two dining rooms, each seating about twenty-five people.

The ship pulled out exactly at four thirty. Most of us scurried to the top and watched the ship navigate through the generally calm waters of the Beagle Channel. I went to my cabin, unpacked, and then explored the ship. Because of its modest size, that didn't take long. This was no Carnival ship, and we had no casino, restaurant, disco, stage, swimming pool, shops, TV, newspapers, or any outside communication. This was exactly what we had expected.

Betty Freeman and I shared the bathroom with the occupants of four other cabins—but we were the closest. We never had anywhere to go except the dining room on our floor, the lecture room down one flight, the bar up one flight, or the navigation bridge. To get alone during the days at sea, I realized there would be only one place to go: I walked up to the top deck, where the wind whipped me from all directions. Shivering with cold and occasionally facing pelting snow, I walked. I would rarely have company.

Twila chose the Amundsen Suite for herself—the one luxury cabin on the entire ship and at a cost of slightly under $8,000. That kind of luxury wasn't typical of Twila, but I understood the reason.

I had agreed to meet Twila twenty minutes later so we could watch the ship move out of the dock. It would have been uneventful except that several dusky dolphins followed us.

Twila loved the movement and the noise and the cold and the wind. I let her enjoy it. I watched her carefully. She insisted she was in no pain and told me in her firm-but-nice voice, "I did not bring you to be my nurse."

I apologized, but I didn't stop watching after her.

I wish I had watched more closely.

6

We had tea about five thirty while we listened to all the announcements and ended with a lifeboat drill. We had to report on the deck with life vests. We lined up in two rows. I paid no attention to anyone around us, but as I put on my life vest, I must have taken a step backward and somehow lost my balance. Strong arms grabbed my shoulders.

"Easy."

"Thank you," I said without turning around. I knew who stood behind me.

I heard none of the lecture, because I wondered if Burton focused on me or if he noticed that I had cut my hair shorter. Why should he notice?

Do you really care? I asked myself.

I chose not to answer my own question.

Instead, I asked myself, *Am I destined to run into Burton like this for the entire cruise?* One of my colleagues at the mental health center always insisted that we unconsciously attract what we want—good or bad. I hoped she was wrong.

The drill finally over, I stepped forward. Betty had brought along a small bag and dropped it at her feet (although we had been told to bring nothing). In my haste to get away from Burton, I tripped over the bag and started to plunge forward.

Strong arms grabbed me in midfall.

"You're good at falling," the voice said. "This is the best fall you've done since we met on Palm Island."

"That time it was deliberate," I said before I could stop myself.

"I know," he said and chuckled.

———

I made it a habit to get to the dining room early—earlier than Burton. The dining room was really two rooms, separated by a wall. The passageway led directly to the left dining room, and we had to walk a few feet to enter the room on the right. I went there where it was less crowded.

To his credit, Burton sat in the other room. I wondered why.

I must be crazy, I thought. *I don't want him around me and I don't want to talk to him, yet if he doesn't show up, I feel slighted.*

I sighed and thought about what I'd say to a client. I'd say it more diplomatically, but in essence, my message would be, "Get over him."

That's what I'll do, I thought.

I looked around the dining room. One cook was Russian and the other was Finnish. They came out before every evening meal and told us how wonderfully they had prepared for us. They stood in the doorway between the two rooms so everyone could see them.

Every midday and evening meal started with soup with exotic names and strange flavors, but I liked them all. We had a choice of meat, chicken, or vegetarian. Sometimes fish replaced meat. We selected our choices at breakfast by checking a posted list. Simple enough.

The meals on the ship were excellent. We had choices of two entrées at lunch and three at dinner, and could have seconds if we wanted. Even for the five vegetarians the chef always came through—although I wouldn't attempt to explain some of the odd combinations. We later marveled that we still had fresh lettuce and only moderately ripe bananas on the last day at sea when there were no places along the way to get provisions. The cooks had developed a system to keep fresh produce stored in such a way that it didn't ripen too quickly.

It was easier to focus on ripe bananas than to wonder what was going on inside Burton's head.

"Stop it!" I told myself.

I wished I could obey my commands as well as I could throw them out.

Around midnight on our first night, we entered the open sea. We had heard about the dreaded Drake Passage that separates South America from Antarctica and had been told it is the roughest sea in the world. After we went through the passage, I don't think any of us doubted the accuracy of that statement. I slept fairly well that night, because once the ride became bumpy, I packed clothes and luggage around my body and lay in the shape of a banana. I didn't get knocked around very much. Many passengers wore ear patches or took Phenergan for motion sickness—and I'm not sure they did much good. The next day I heard from at least two people that they had received shots for motion sickness. The ship rocked so hard that at times most of us felt as if we were being tossed from a horizontal position to a ninety-degree angle in our beds. The doctor had given me a few Phenergan tablets in case I needed them. I didn't.

I loved showering the next morning. I held on to a steel wall post with one hand while I washed with the other. It was impossible to walk across the small cabin (perhaps eight feet by twelve) without holding on. Maneuvering the short hallways tested our walking ability. As long as we held on to the railings, we were all right.

EVERYBODY CALLED HER A SAINT

Few passengers showed up at breakfast. Other than seasickness, nothing exciting happened the first three days as we went across the Drake Passage. If we wanted to go outside, we could see any number of albatross, especially the magnificent wandering albatross and the southern giant petrels. Mickey Brewer spotted two minke whales, and Donny Otis yelled when he saw a humpback. I raced to the spots, but they just looked like big globs of brown or gray in the water. It was cold, windy, and wet on the deck, so I spent most of my time on the bridge. It was an excellent lookout spot, and the captain or some excited passenger would point out the wildlife.

Our ship plowed through seas so rough that at times no one was allowed on deck. We had to hang on to tables or walls to keep from toppling over when we walked. All of us spent a lot of time in our bunks and slept a lot the first two days. I read two books during that rough travel—after I insisted on a larger bulb in the reading lamp.

One of the crew members lectured on "The Early Discovery and Exploration of the Frozen Continent." I found it fascinating, but fewer than thirty of us attended.

This is boring stuff, I know, but it's important to explain all of this—especially after we had our first two landings. That's when the cruise was no longer just an Antarctic trip.

We spotted land at the end of the third day. Almost everyone raced up to the decks. I started up and discovered Burton just ahead of me. I turned and went back to my cabin. I'd see a lot of land soon.

The next day, before we made the first landing, Captain Robert briefed us on the dos and don'ts of Antarctica. By international agreement, the continent must remain undeveloped, with no damage to ecosystems. For example, visitors must haul out their own trash. We were not to touch any animals or come close enough to make them wary or fearful.

It became quite a task for me to avoid Burton. He didn't stalk me—he isn't the type—but he seemed to be around no matter where I went on the ship and when we landed.

Or was my colleague correct that I sent invisible vibes through the atmosphere to attract him? I usually laughed when she talked that way. Now I wondered.

A few hours later, we received an announcement about twenty minutes before the first of four motorized rubber rafts (called Zodiacs) left the ship. That was our signal to put on our heavy "landing clothes" as I called them. The captain also told us of weather conditions—no matter how he stated his report, it was always cold.

We had instructions on how to get into the Zodiacs, which were large, heavy-duty inflatables with flat bottoms that allowed them to land directly onto the cobble and ice-strewn beaches.

EVERYBODY'S SUSPECT IN GEORGIA

The first time I held back until Burton had gotten into a Zodiac and it had shoved off. To be honest, it was stressful. If only I'd felt indifferent to him or hated him, I wouldn't have been so stressed over seeing him. Each time our eyes met, I looked away and wished I had not come along on the cruise.

I lined up for the next Zodiac. We had to have both hands free to get on and off. We women left our purses and personal items on the ship. Those with cameras slung them over their shoulders or, if they were small enough, tucked them inside their enormous parkas. We were told to step carefully and quickly from the launching platform and to accept the assistance offered by the crew. We were not to hold the helper's hand but instead to use the sailor's grip (grab each other by the forearm). Heather complained that she thought the forearm was "a most unattractive place to grab."

I thought of two or three rude comments, but I kept my mouth shut.

Most of the time (to my surprise), the temperatures stayed slightly below freezing, but with the winds, who would have known? I would have guessed about fifty degrees below zero, but Jon Friesen teased me and said I must have no blood flowing through my body.

"How can it flow when it's already frozen?" I asked.

"Maybe I need to warm you up."

He was smiling, but he just wasn't my type. I said, "A hot shower after our return will work better." I moved away from him.

Twila had even taken care of the biggest clothing problems. She had personally bought a blue rain suit of coated nylon for each of us (after we gave her our sizes). We put them over our clothing and they kept us dry, protected us from the wind, and also gave some amount of warmth. She also bought us heavy rubber boots—two sizes larger than our regular shoes so we could pad them with as many extra socks as we wanted—or so they said. They were slightly more than a foot high and had strong, ridged nonskid soles, which we needed for landings on rocks or ice. Each time we went ashore, I decided I would wear three pairs of heavy wool socks—that was as many as I could get inside the boots.

I brought polypropylene underwear because it keeps the body warm without adding bulk. On top of that I wore a heavy turtleneck and a hooded fleece jacket. Keeping the hands warm and dry, the brochure we received told us, was often a problem. I brought two pairs of thin polypropylene glove liners to wear under my wool gloves.

We lined up in our dorky gear on deck and laughed at how outrageous we looked. Several of the women commented on how fat it made them appear, including Heather Wilson, but I reminded her, "Honey, when they can choose between you and penguins on the white continent, they won't even notice what you're wearing."

They were all wet landings. That is, we had no piers, and our Zodiac pulled up fairly close but not close enough. Our driver jumped out and stood in water about eight inches deep. He offered us a grip to climb out. From there we waded to shore in freezing-but-shallow water.

Here's how the system worked: Four Zodiacs carried twelve passengers ashore, which was a ride of less than five minutes from the ship.

The landing at King George Island in the early afternoon was set up quite efficiently. Although Twila wasn't murdered on the first landing, it's important for me to tell you about it. The murderer—as we realized later—figured out the system and planned to kill her at a subsequent landing. Had it not been for a careful and observant captain, Twila's death might have gone undetected. No one might ever have known what had happened to her.

7

To go ashore, we lined up at the side of the ship to get into the Zodiacs. We first had to pass by what the captain called the "landing tag board." That was the most important and the first of two ways to keep track of passengers. The murderer must have taken careful note of the procedure.

Each of us had a number—assigned to us at random as far as I could see. When we left the ship, the tag faced right and we picked it up, turned it to the left, and put it back. The tag was nothing but a piece of wood with a number in bright yellow and a hole to put it on the hooks on the board. The captain checked the landing tag board before the last Zodiac left. If there were any keys on the board facing right, he either had been told the person was sick, which usually meant seasick, or someone had chosen not to go. Of course, anyone could choose not to go, but no one opted for that the first two landings.

We had to line up wearing our life jackets. The life jackets were the second way to keep track of us. After we waded through the shallow water, a few feet from the shore we were supposed to take off the life jackets and drop them on the ground (in a dry spot). A few of the people didn't bother to drop off their life jackets but wore them when they walked around.

That was the second thing that almost made Twila's death go undetected.

When we got ready to go back to the ship, we picked up a life jacket. The point of leaving and taking up life jackets was that if the number of people who left to go back to the ship was correct, when we left, there would be no life jackets on the ground.

We could switch to another Zodiac on the return. In that case, we were supposed to notify the driver and were responsible to have a life jacket on when we boarded the Zodiac. Occasionally someone came in, say, the first Zodiac and, instead of going back with that group, walked around and went back with the third or fourth Zodiac.

The fourth Zodiac would not leave unless every life jacket had been picked up off the beach. That's why the killer had to understand the second part of the counting system.

—

The azure blueness of the sky overwhelmed me. I had never seen such a vivid color before. We spotted large icebergs of many shapes and hues. Some were bluish (the darker the blue, the older the glacier they had broken off from). Others had tunnel-like holes through them, or they appeared to have turned upside down. A few resembled mushrooms. One passenger said, "This is a veritable Rorschach test in white and 3-D."

On King George Island, we had our first look—and smell—of Antarctica. The odor of penguin guano overpowered me for a minute, but I soon became accustomed to that and to the two-inch thickness of it on the ground as I walked around.

The air felt so fresh, I stopped several times and breathed deeply. The cold nipped at my toes, but I kept moving and wriggling them as I walked. Clouds lined the horizon as if to signal bad weather in the hours ahead. During the two hours or so we stayed on King George Island, the wind increased considerably.

I could only say again and again that it was the most spectacular place imaginable. This was one trip when pictures hardly did justice to reality. Hundreds of penguins, dozens of Weddell seals, two leopard seals, and two fur seals seemed totally at home in the rocky landscape of the desolate wasteland. We gazed at a huge glacier farther down the beach, and several of us hiked over to it. We didn't go far, because the captain warned us that calving action (breaking off) could happen without warning, and it would sweep us into the ocean.

As I walked along, I took out my brochure to identify the species of penguins. Five of the seventeen existing varieties lived there, and that day (for the first and only time) I was able to see all of them on the same island: gentoo, Adélie, macaroni, rockhopper, and chinstrap. The penguins, sometimes called wingless birds, fascinated most of us. We could watch them, seemingly endlessly, without getting bored.

Penguins have many humanlike mannerisms and portly body shapes. If we moved slowly, we could get within a few feet of them. They were afraid only of fast movements, because birds of prey sometimes swept down and snatched their babies or stole their eggs.

It amazed me to be able to stand so near and watch these birds climb a steep, slippery hill. Sometimes they fell backward, but they just started again. Yet when those awkward creatures swam, a transformation took place. They flipped into the air, arched their bodies, and, porpoiselike, dove hundreds of feet into the ocean to catch fish. They endured temperatures of minus seventy degrees. We learned in one of our lectures that males share the job of sitting on the unhatched eggs and also feed the chicks by regurgitating food through their beaks for the babies to suck out. Females usually have two eggs. In years when the fish supply is low, they feed one chick and push away the other, which eventually dies.

After two hours ashore, we returned to the ship to set sail for our next landing.

As soon as we returned to the ship, we partnered with one or two others to hose down our boots, which were packed thick with penguin droppings.

The captain said it delicately. "Wash your boots carefully after each landing to avoid accidentally transporting seeds or other organisms from landing site to landing site. Your cabin mate and the stewardesses will also appreciate it."

The system was simple; it was also efficient. After all the Zodiacs returned to the ship, the captain checked to make sure that all the tags had been turned back to their original position.

As far as I know, no one counted life jackets on the return to the ship. As long as none remained on the beach, there was no need to count.

That was the mistake.

—

The waters roiled again, and that night was as bad as the first one. This time the wave action was head to toe, producing roller-coaster sensations, whereas the first night it had been side to side. That's the description the other passengers gave me—I don't know; I slept extremely well.

—

Captain Robert had scheduled our second landing to be at Brown Bluff, on the northern tip of the Antarctic continent. The Zodiac trips were a bit rougher this time, and the huge waves sprayed us as we made our way to shore. Jeff Adams said his camera froze, so he bribed two of the other passengers to share pictures with him after the trip.

Before we left for our Brown Bluff landing, Captain Robert lectured us about a 1902 Norwegian expedition that rivaled Shackleton's for harrowing drama. The men endured two winters at Brown Bluff. After two years and various rescue attempts, two parties independently arrived from different directions on the same day to save them.

By then, we had already landed once, and everyone understood the routine. We felt like veterans of the Antarctic; no crew member had to remind us what to do. The killer must have counted on that fact.

I suppose that sense of rhythm and routine lulled my protective senses. I spent most of my time alone when we landed at Brown Bluff. It was more than avoiding Burton. I continually questioned myself, and I had to be alone to do that.

I loved Burton—I couldn't get away from that reality. But I couldn't marry him, knowing what I did about him.

If only he would confess—I stopped myself right there. I'd argued that one with myself only about 912 times.

In exhaustion, I would remind myself of one thing: It wasn't my choice; the decision was Burton's.

8

The Brown Bluff landing fascinated me. Besides the remains of the 1902 expedition's shack made of rock walls about three feet high, penguins were everywhere. While we walked among the birds, the winds increased considerably. *Cold* hardly describes the effect. My teeth chattered and my fingers became numb, even though I wore thick gloves and my two pairs of liners.

Two of the Zodiacs had returned by the time the weather deteriorated, but no one hurried back to the third and fourth ones. That implied that everyone left was determined to see the wildlife. The wind soon calmed, and I was glad we had stayed.

I marveled at the vast numbers of penguins and seals. Perhaps twenty minutes later, without warning, a stiff wind again battered us, followed by hard-pounding snow. And I mean hard—the snow felt like rock granules sandblasting my face. I'd take maybe five steps with my eyes closed, open them quickly for a step, and then shut them again. Other than the Zodiac staff, who wore goggles, none of us could see much of anything.

I raced for the third Zodiac. At least six people were ahead of me, and others hurried behind me. Our driver helped the twelfth and last passenger in, and we headed back toward the ship.

The waves utterly drenched us. Despite our rain-repellent clothes, the water got to all of us. The trip back to the ship seemed to take longer than the trip to land, and the weather continued to deteriorate. The wind had subtly blown us somewhat adrift from the ship, and I think our Zodiac driver was lost for a few minutes. He didn't say so, but the wariness of his normally calm face gave him away.

When he grinned, I relaxed. I knew he had spotted the ship.

We got aboard the *Vaschenko* and hurried through the boot-washing process as quickly as we could. My hands were almost numb.

Just as I started to go inside, I saw the fourth Zodiac tie up.

I didn't look at faces or count the number of people aboard.

That was a mistake.

Captain Robert canceled the scheduled landing for that afternoon. He said that if the weather permitted, we would land at Paulet Island the next day.

The storm didn't abate for the rest of the day, but I felt incredibly lucky to have enjoyed the spectacular view on Brown Bluff.

Once we were all on board, the captain carefully checked the tag board, just as he did at the end of every reboarding process throughout the trip.

"Everyone has made it back," he said and smiled. He had also done that on the previous landing.

About half an hour after each landing, we had tea in the dining room. It was much like the English tea with a variety of small sandwiches, sweets, tea, coffee, and hot chocolate.

After our return from Brown Bluff, the ship pulled anchor and started on the next leg of our trip. As we sat drinking our tea, I realized I hadn't seen Twila. We weren't on the same Zodiac going out, and I hadn't seen her on the island. Unless we were fairly close, it was next to impossible to recognize each other because we all looked alike when we wore our special "uniforms."

"Where's Twila?" I called out. "Anyone seen her?"

"Yes, she was on our Zodiac going over," Betty said. "We were the last ones to leave."

"Yeah, that's right," someone else said. "I remember now."

"What about coming back?" I asked.

"I assume she was with us," Betty said. "I didn't count—"

"There was no one left on the island," Pat Borders said. Pat was a real estate broker who attended Burton's church.

I wondered if she had gotten sick on the return trip. I asked, but no one seemed to remember. They were so busy taking pictures of icebergs, penguins, skuas, and seals that no one paid attention to other passengers.

"That's odd that she's not down here," I said. "Perhaps she's not well." I excused myself and left the dining room. *Oh no,* I thought, *the cancer. She said there would be no pain. Maybe she was wrong.*

"May I go with you?"

Without turning around, I knew Burton's voice. I didn't want to be alone with him, even to walk up two flights of steps with him. "I'd prefer to go alone." I hoped he caught the frosty tone in my voice. I'm good at frosty tones.

I knocked on Twila's cabin door, but there was no answer. None of the rooms had locks on them, so I pushed the door open. Her room was empty. She had reserved a private room, and it was truly luxury quality—with a double bed, two lamps, and a large closet.

"Maybe she's up on the navigation bridge," I said aloud to myself. We were welcome there at any time. They had three or four chairs so we could sit and get a marvelous view or simply stand at the window that stretched the full width of the room.

I walked up the final flight of steps and entered the bridge. The captain and two other officers were there.

No Twila.

I left abruptly and hurried to the lounge and the theater-lecture room where we watched films and the staff lectured on the days when we were unable to land.

I opened the door to what we called the sick bay, but it was empty. I braved the freezing wind and took a few steps on the deck to make sure she wasn't there. I knew it was useless, because no one would have been able to stand on the deck at that time. The snow had stopped, but the wind hadn't decreased.

I rushed back to the bridge and approached Captain Robert. "Excuse me," I said, "this may be nothing, but Twila Belk doesn't seem to be around."

He said nothing but gave me a skeptical look as if to ask, "How can that be possible?"

I explained that no one had seen her on the Zodiac for the return trip.

"There must be a mistake," the captain said with his thick Indian accent. "All tags have been turned back. No life jackets were left on Brown Bluff."

"I've been everywhere on the ship except for the others' cabins. They're all having tea, so I'm sure she's not in any of them."

He sent someone to the lounge and someone else to the theater.

I went back to the dining room. "Has anyone seen Twila?"

No one spoke.

"She has to be around," Pat Borders said. "On a ship this small—"

I cut him off and walked away. I went back to Twila's room, and I didn't find her. I was frantic. Even though I knew that the weather on the deck was too bad for any of us, I searched again. Was it possible that she had walked out there, felt weak, fainted, and been swept overboard? I took three steps out the door and let my gaze sweep slowly over the entire deck from the starboard side. I went to the other side of the ship and did the same thing from that door. No one. A fine skin of undisturbed snow covered the deck, so it was obvious no one had been there.

I went back to the dining room. As far as I could tell, no one had moved. No one seemed concerned. Jeff told a funny story about his trip to Alaska, and as soon as he finished, Jon had one about being lost in Bhutan.

I poured myself a cup of tea and sat alone. *Where is she? Where could she disappear to on a small ship like this?*

Twenty minutes later, most of us had finished our tea and were ready to go to our rooms to read or nap. The captain walked into the dining room. Behind him came Ivan, a tall, blond, Swedish-looking man, who claimed to be a Russian from Kiev.

"One minute, please," the captain said. "We have a problem here. We are missing one passenger."

"Twila? Where is Twila?" Betty called out. "Is she sick or—?"

"She is not aboard the ship," the captain said.

9

Everyone seemed to talk at once. The captain finally raised his voice. "Please be seated, everyone. We need to be quite clear about whatever has happened."

I had already told him that Twila had gone over to Brown Bluff with the fourth group. "Those of you who left on the fourth Zodiac," he said, "please to raise your hands." He counted eleven.

"On the Zodiac trip across to Brown Bluff, who was near Mrs. Belk?"

They talked among themselves, and Pat said, "I think she was on my right. You know, we have different groups each time, and—"

"Yes, I know, but of course," the captain said.

"Who was on the other side of her?" He grabbed a sheet of paper from the bulletin board and drew a rough sketch of a Zodiac. "The engine was here," he said. "Ivan drove the fourth Zodiac." He held it up and asked the eleven people to come forward and tell him where they stood on the way out. He said *stood,* but the sides are rounded with ropes, and most people sat on the sides and held on to the ropes.

It took several minutes of discussion, but they finally agreed that Twila had been seated between Pat Borders and Jeff Adams, an elder in Burton's church.

"Very good," the captain said. He turned the paper over, drew another crude picture, and said, "We shall now see where you stood on the return trip."

"I—I was on another Zodiac," Jon said. "My stomach was heaving a little, and I wanted to get back."

"You are all right now, are you?"

"Not wonderful, but I'm okay," he said. "That is, after I vomited twice."

"I am sorry—"

"So I decided to go on the other Zodiac. They were getting into the boat right then. I sent word to Ivan that—"

"You did not tell him yourself? You told someone else?"

"Certainly," Jon said. "I was too miserable."

I watched him for some sign to show that he was lying. I saw nothing.

"To whom did you speak, sir?"

"I don't know. I don't remember. I felt too miserable to pay attention. Someone was walking toward Ivan's boat. I grabbed his arm—or it may have been a woman—and said, 'I'm sick. I'll go back on this Zodiac. Tell Ivan.'"

"Then what happened?"

"I climbed into the Zodiac and said, 'I'm sick. I'm going back early.' I leaned over the side of the boat and barfed. That was the first time. It happened again before we reached the ship."

"Can someone verify this?"

"Oh yeah, all of us on boat three can," one of the men said.

The captain turned to Ivan. "How many people were on your Zodiac on the return?"

"Ten, sir."

"But you went out with twelve."

"Yes, sir, but someone told me that two of them had become——" He spoke with a heavy accent, and it was obvious he searched for the correct word. "Sickness—two of them had become sickness and would have make their return on the third Zodiac."

"Who told you?"

"I do not remember, sir. I was speaking to you on the VHF radio." He dropped his head, unable to look at the captain. "Someone—and who it was I do not know—said to me, 'Two of them have return the other boat.' "

"Did the person explain?"

"Yes, sickness."

"Sick. Two people sick? Is that what the person said?"

"Yes, sick. That is the word. Yes, sir."

"Two of them?"

"Yes, Captain."

"You are sure?"

"Most absolutely."

"You have no idea who spoke to you?"

"Sir, on this voyage, everyone in this group wears the same, do they not? So I could not be to know. The wind blow heavy, snow fall. They come, all of them from forward to the Zodiac with their heads."

"Bent forward? Lowered?"

"Yes, Captain, that is what I meant."

The captain was obviously displeased at the lack of precise information, but Ivan added in a defensive tone, "I had but not yet finished speaking on the VHF radio to you, sir. And, sir, I was upset because——"

"Yes, I see," the captain said. He turned to the rest of us. "It was a small matter and not significant here. I had spoken some rather harsh words to Ivan about something quite unrelated to passengers."

We accepted that statement. Ivan hung his head while the captain talked, so we were all convinced that he had received a severe reprimand for something. He must have felt bad about the call then and even worse that he had not been attentive on the return.

The captain finally asked the obvious question: "Who gave the information to Ivan that two people would go on the other Zodiac?"

After a long silence, he said, "I see that we have no answer." He stared at us for a few seconds and made his next decision. One by one, Sunil Robert questioned all ten of the passengers on the fourth Zodiac. He asked Jon Friesen twice to tell him about being sick. There seemed no question about his vomiting.

As I listened, I thought he would make a good detective. He was obviously assured of himself and in control of the situation. Everyone seemed compliant.

Even after he had questioned the ten people, no one admitted talking to Ivan. No one noticed Jon get on the other Zodiac.

"Ivan just said something like, 'All here. Others on different boat,'" was the way Heather explained it.

"That's right," Donny Otis said and imitated Ivan's voice.

"I didn't notice anyone being gone, and I didn't count," Betty Freeman said. "It was obvious that everyone else had left Brown Bluff, so we took off."

"But every tag faces the correct way, including hers," the captain said. "Her number was seven. The tag was turned to show that she went ashore. It now faces the correct way to say that she has returned."

"I've searched everywhere for her," I said.

"So have I," Burton said.

The captain stared at me and then at Burton. He said nothing, but both of us knew what he was thinking.

"Twila is still on the island," Captain Robert said.

10

The weather will not permit a Zodiac to land, so we shall stay anchored until the conditions have improved enough for someone to go back," the captain said.

He turned abruptly and left the room. About an hour later, we could feel the ship make a turn. Four hours later, the weather calmed sufficiently and a Zodiac left the ship. It was nearly 10:30 p.m., but no one had gone to bed. Because of the many hours of daylight, it wouldn't be a problem to get back to the island and look for Twila.

"Surely she wasn't left on the island," Pat said as we stood on deck and watched Ivan and two others take the Zodiac. "Why would anyone want to stay behind? There's nothing there—"

"There must be some other explanation," Thomas Tomlinson said. He was a baritone in the choir, and for a long time he had been one of Twila's most devoted admirers. He was in his late thirties. He once told me that his family was unable to send him to college. "My family was always poor," he had said. "I had five siblings, and neither of my uneducated parents ever made much money from their jobs."

When Twila learned that he was an exceptional student, she paid his total college expenses. He had returned to Clayton County and taught math in the Jonesboro High School. Only two years earlier he had become the assistant principal and next year would become the principal.

He could never say enough kind words about Twila. "She would not allow me to repay her. She told me that if I were truly thankful, I would find someone like me who needed help." His eyes watered when he said that. "My wife and I have decided to pay tuition for two students each year."

Thomas walked over and stood beside me. "I don't understand," he said. "I'm sure no one was left. I stood on the shore, and I was the last one to get into the Zodiac. I thought it was such a sad, desolate place."

He stared at me as if begging me to tell him Twila was going to be all right. I touched his arm. "Pray. If she is alive, we'll find her."

"If?" he asked, and I thought I was going to have to comfort him, but he turned around and sat down at the end of the table. He stared into space.

I walked over to the coffeepot, not because I wanted another cup but because I didn't want to hear the discussion among the other passengers. I knew they would continue to speculate, and it would end with something negative. I wasn't ready for that.

Twila is missing.

I wanted to cry, but I held back. *I knew.* That terrible sense of foreboding I had felt back at Ushuaia lodged inside my throat, and I felt as if I would have to vomit.

"Twila is missing," I said aloud to myself, because I wasn't quite ready to say the word *dead.*

That she was missing was the only fact I knew. As soon as that thought flashed into my mind, I wondered if she had taken her own life. Surely if that was her plan, she wouldn't have gone to the trouble of booking the cruise and paying our expenses. That kind of suicide would be incomprehensible.

No, not Twila. She was too strong a person and too committed a Christian to do such a thing.

But still.

Surely no one would harm her. I held a cup of tea in my hand, but my gaze shifted from person to person. I'm not sure what I expected to see, but no one had an appearance of guilt or remorse. I saw confusion on almost every face.

"I can't believe anything has happened to—," Betty said and started to sob.

"We don't know anything yet," Burton said. He wrapped an arm around her.

"Of course you're correct," she said, but her words didn't sound convincing.

As I half-listened, I thought again about Twila telling me she had cancer. On the plane she assured me that she experienced little pain and had sufficient medication to take care of it. "It will be a few months before the pain becomes acute," she said. "For now, you are not to be concerned."

She had turned her face from me and stared out the window. It was too dark to see anything, but I knew it was her way to say the discussion was closed.

No, Twila wouldn't take her own life.

But she was missing.

These people—all of us—loved her. We were her friends. I didn't know everybody, but I couldn't believe that any of them would do anything to harm Twila.

If it wasn't suicide, what other explanation could there be?

We heard the lowering of the anchor. I wasn't sure, but I thought I heard another Zodiac leaving. Along with several others, I hurried to the launching door and watched it push away from the ship. I soon lost sight of the small motorized boat. It was impossible to see the land from where we were.

It was cold standing there, but I couldn't move. My body began to shake, and I didn't know if it was from the weather or from my sense of loss. Just then, someone wrapped a blanket around my shoulders. "Thank you," I said. I didn't turn around because I didn't care who it was.

EVERYBODY CALLED HER A SAINT

I had been on the third Zodiac and remembered the desolation of the place. There was a small hillock—perhaps a rise of six or seven feet—but that was the only place that wasn't quite flat until we walked perhaps three hundred feet. After that, it was all steep, almost like mountains. It just didn't seem possible that anyone could have done Twila harm on Brown Bluff.

At that very moment, I knew what I had not been willing to say aloud: Twila was dead. I turned my back to everyone and tried to stand straight and tall, but tears slid slowly down my cheeks. I loved her. It shouldn't end like this for anyone. Especially not for Twila. I had never met anyone who exemplified the Christian life the way she did.

Just then a hand touched my left shoulder, and I knew who stood behind me. I didn't have the strength to resist him, but I didn't surrender. I stood as I was.

"I loved her, too," he whispered. "She's gone, isn't she?"

Without thinking, I twirled around and buried my face in Burton's shoulder.

This time the tears fell freely, and I couldn't hold back.

—

Several minutes passed, and I pulled away from Burton. "Please, please don't talk to me," I said.

Burton said nothing, but he didn't move.

I have no sense of how long we stood there, but I heard the Zodiac before I saw it. As soon as it got close enough, I spotted a blue-suited body lying flat on the floor. The hood was pulled so that I couldn't see the face. I didn't notice the life jacket beside her, but Burton later found out that they had discovered it next to her body.

"Someone killed her," Burton said.

His words threw me into convulsive sobs, but I didn't turn away. He tried to wrap his arms around me, but I pushed him away. "No! No! No!" I shouted.

By the time the Zodiac pulled alongside the ship, the captain was at the entrance and stepped in front of me. "Please return back to the dining room." He said *please*, but it was a command.

"She is—she was my best friend—"

"Please. Now."

Burton forced me to turn around. He wrapped his arms around me, and I didn't have the strength to resist. He kept his arms around me as he led me back to the dining room. Several others looked up as the small group of us walked into the room. I'm sure our faces told them the truth.

A hush came over the entire room.

Someone screamed.

"What happened?" Jon Friesen called out. "Did they find her?"

"How badly is she—?" Heather asked. She had enough sense to stop in midsentence. "Oh no! Oh, Lord Jesus, no!"

I couldn't answer any of them. I sat down. Burton sat next to me, his arm still around me. I knew his arm was there, and I felt a strange kind of comfort at that moment. I didn't move until the captain joined us.

11

S omething has happened to Mrs. Belk," Sunil Robert said.

I looked into his eyes, waiting for him to tell us something more. I willed for him to say that she was only sick or badly hurt.

"A heart attack? On the island?" Betty Freeman asked. "Is that what it was?"

"She looked healthy to me," Donny Otis said.

There seemed to be a long pause as if the captain tried to make up his mind how much to say.

"Mrs. Belk is dead."

"But how—?" Sue Downs cried out. "I can't—"

"She was stabbed."

He obviously didn't want to say more, but several people persisted. He finally admitted that as far as they could tell, she had been stabbed repeatedly in the neck. "She either died from the wounds or was left to die." He would say no more.

"Murdered?" Mickey Brewer said. Mickey owned the largest insurance agency in the county and was one of the church's most faithful ushers. "Not Twila! Not that wonderful, godly woman!"

"I'm not sure what procedures to follow," the captain said. "Already we have notified the American Embassy in Buenos Aires. As you will agree, the rest of the trip is canceled. We are returning to Argentina immediately."

"Aren't you going to search us?" someone behind me asked.

"I think not."

"But why not?"

"I seriously considered doing that very thing but chose not to do so. First, we do not know what we're looking for except that it was some kind of instrument—likely a knife. Second, I believe it would be impossible to search every place on board. Third, on a ship like this, it would take little effort for someone to throw the weapon of death overboard unobserved."

"So it's possible the weapon has already gone into the ocean," Burton said.

"Yes, but of course, that is a strong possibility," the captain said.

"So what happens now?" Betty Freeman asked.

"We have already turned the ship around, and, as I said, we are on our way back to Buenos Aires."

We knew it would take two full days to get through the Drake Passage and back to the continent.

Several people asked questions—most of them out of shock. He answered none of them. He waited until the noise level had lessened. "I would like to talk to each passenger, one at a time."

"All the passengers?" someone asked.

"Yes. All."

He asked Burton to send in the passengers to see him one at a time. He went into the second, smaller dining room and sat down.

No one stayed in the room with him for more than three or four minutes. From the muted conversation, apparently he asked everyone essentially the same questions, such as "Which Zodiac did you take to Brown Bluff? To whom did you speak going across and coming back? What did you do on the island? Were you alone most of the time or with someone?"

When my turn came, I told him the truth: I had talked to no one either way. "Captain, I'm going through a difficult period right now," I said. "I recently broke up with a man—he's also a passenger. I came on the trip only because Twila is—was—my best friend and she begged me to."

"Precisely what did you do on the island?"

"I walked by myself," I said. "I wanted to get away from everyone. I needed to be where I could feel alone for a little while. I walked around and avoided everyone." Again I remembered the pelting snow. A few skua birds hovered around the penguins.

He asked me two or three more questions, and I know I answered them, but at that moment, I was so heavyhearted I don't remember what they were. I think he took notes, but I'm not sure.

As he got up, he said softly, "I am sorry for the loss of your special friend. No one has said a negative word about her, which makes this so strange. People do not murder those whom they love." He shook his head slowly. "Would they lie at a time like this?"

"I doubt that you'll find anyone to say an unkind word—" I stopped. "Of course, whoever killed her must have hated her."

"Yes, that must be so. Someone stabbed her—an act of great violence. That was no accident. It might have been done in a frenzy, but that I cannot say." He said he knew nothing about stabbing, so he couldn't say whether it was a large knife or what the person had used. Medical examiners would have to make that determination. "But it is a cruel thing for someone to do such a thing to another human being, is it not?"

I lost it then. He was very kind and his voice was tender, and I could feel my shoulders heave and I couldn't stop. It was the most convulsively I had cried in my life. Just as Burton had done earlier, the captain wrapped his arms around me. I dropped my head on his shoulder and let the tears flow. He spoke in soft, quiet tones. "There, there, my little one." He patted my head gently as he might to comfort a child.

When I calmed a little, he pulled a clean handkerchief from his pocket and handed it to me. I wore no makeup and didn't worry about what my face looked like, but I completely soiled his handkerchief.

I handed it back.

"I have another one if—"

"No," I said. "I'm better now. Thank you."

When I finally turned to leave, he said quietly, "It is none of my business, of course, but I do hope you and Mr. Burton will patch up your—your differences."

"How did you know who—?"

"What is the word in English? *Lovesick*, is it? That is how he looks at you. I had noticed it earlier," he said and smiled.

I wanted to tell him that it was impossible for us to patch things up and that Burton and I would never get back together. But I couldn't say those words—in fact, I couldn't trust my voice again. I turned and left the dining room.

12

When I searched for Twila, I had hurriedly raced in and out of her room. Hours later, as I left the dining room, I realized that something about Twila's room hadn't been right. At that time I was more concerned about finding her than anything else. I decided I needed to go back to the room. To my surprise, I felt no trepidation or new wave of sadness. I made my way back to her cabin and opened the door, snapped on the light, and stared. On my previous visit, I hadn't paid attention to anything in the room itself. This time I stared at an opened suitcase. Twila never would have left a suitcase out and opened. She was too neat.

I entered the cabin and closed the door behind me. I don't think anything had changed in the few hours since I had last been there. After I stepped inside, I stood quietly, allowing my eyes to get a sense of the room. Now I saw what it was that had only barely registered in my mind.

The room wasn't torn up—I had seen that kind of situation before—but it wasn't tidy. It was even more than the open suitcase. If I hadn't been so focused on finding Twila the first time, I probably would have noticed.

Her bed wasn't made. I didn't know her habits that well, but it didn't seem consistent with Twila for her not to make the bed. Maids came every third day, so most of us made our own beds. Twila wasn't compulsive, but she was one of those people who lived with the idea of "a place for everything and everything in its place." In fact, she had quoted that to me a couple of times.

Surely Twila never would have left the room for breakfast that morning with a messed-up bed. I wasn't sure, but my immediate hunch was that someone had pulled up the mattress as if searching to see if she had hidden anything under it.

The suitcase was wide open on the desk. Why wouldn't she have laid the suitcase on the bed? It was certainly large enough and a natural spot—only a foot or so from the closet. As I stared at her suitcase, her clothes seemed to be carelessly stuffed back inside. Again, that was not Twila.

The door of the small closet was closed, but when I opened it, I saw that her clothes, no longer on hangers, had been carelessly dropped or thrown on the floor, and her second suitcase—empty—was on top of the clothes.

At that moment, the obvious truth stuck me: Someone had searched her cabin.

"Why?" I asked aloud.

On one shelf lay her jewelry—a couple of necklaces, three or four sets of earrings, and two bracelets. All of the items were expensive; Twila never bought cheap jewelry.

On the floor, next to the desk, lay her briefcase and her purse. All of us left our purses in our rooms most of the time, so that wasn't unusual. The purse was open, and I saw that the items had been hastily thrown inside—again that wasn't Twila.

The briefcase lay on its side. Some of the papers had been carelessly strewn on the floor. I scanned them quickly, but none of them seemed significant. Aside from a few letters that she probably planned to post on our return to Ushuaia, the rest of the papers were travel folders, instructions about the cruise, and maps— that sort of thing.

Inside the middle section of the briefcase was a selection of books. Automatically I counted them: She had brought six books on the cruise—that was typical of Twila. Even when we met for lunch, she always carried a book. "In case I have to wait a few minutes," she said. "It helps me not to notice when the other person is late." She seemed always to get to restaurants at least five minutes ahead of her reservation.

I stood next to the desk and stared around the cabin. It was about eight feet wide and perhaps twelve feet long. There wasn't a lot of extra space. It was obvious someone had been inside her cabin and had searched for something.

"I wonder what it was?" I asked aloud.

"I wonder if the person found it?" I answered myself.

"What would Twila have that someone wanted?" Sometimes I talk out loud to myself, especially when I feel confused. I also answer myself, which to most people must sound strange, but that's who I am.

"How could she possibly have anything that would be important enough to kill her for?"

"You're assuming, Julie, that the murder and the search were done by the same person."

"Of course. Don't be stupid!" I said. "Why else would the room look like this?"

"Robbery?"

I shook my head. "No, her wallet is in her purse with money inside. Her jewelry is still here."

"Okay, then it must have been a search for something significant and—"

"Oh, don't be dense. I know that."

"Okay, smart mouth, what is it?"

I didn't know how to answer myself on that one, so I only shook my head.

Just then the door opened. I looked up and Burton stood in the doorway. He moved inside and closed the door behind him. "Looks as if we both have the same idea. It's not as bad as room 623. Remember that room at—"

"No, it's not." I stopped him. I didn't want to go back to that time. Not only had we worked on a murder case in a hotel, but it was also the time when my life changed. That's when I knew I believed. That's also when Burton realized I loved him. I didn't want to go back to that again.

"Okay, I apologize. I know you don't want to talk about anything personal with me, but—"

"That's right. And you might as well know something else right now." I heard the harshness in my voice. He looked so sad and so much like a boy consumed with grief, I had to harden my emotions to talk to him. I turned away from him and stared at the messy desk.

"Listen, Burton, I came on this cruise only because Twila begged me to."

"I understand, and I don't blame you."

That statement almost broke me. Almost.

"We don't have to have any personal involvement," he said. "I mean between us." He sat on the edge of the bed—which was the only place to sit unless he took the chair that I leaned against.

"Suits me." I'm good at showing suppressed anger. I sat down and folded my arms.

"I have no idea who killed Twila." He leaned forward and stared at the floor. "I have no idea why. If I ever met a true, living saint. . ."

I almost could have written those words for him. When he paused after his long list of Twila's virtues, I said, "Yes, I agree." I hoped he would change his line of thinking. I didn't like playing the hard-hearted soul with the mention of Twila's name. I was trying to decide if I should walk past him or wait until he left.

"This much I know. You didn't kill her, because you were her best friend."

Despite my resolve, I could feel the tears glistening in my eyes. "She told me that," I said.

"She also told me. She gave me quite a lecture after our breakup. She didn't know the reason—and I'm grateful to you for keeping that our secret—but she lectured me for maybe twenty minutes."

"No, please," I said. He was moving back into dangerous emotional waters again. "Don't—"

"You see, I didn't want to come on the cruise because—because I knew it would be uncomfortable for me. And probably just as uncomfortable for you."

"I had the same feeling."

"She insisted," he said.

"With me, as well."

"I mentioned this because I have a point. What I've said and what you said leads to the other thing I know: I didn't kill her. There are forty-six passengers on this ship that knew Twila before we sailed. We can probably eliminate the twenty members of the crew. Agree?"

"Yes." I couldn't look at him. His words were warming my heart, and I didn't want to melt in his presence.

"Why can't we—you and I—investigate this together? It will be two days before we're back to Ushuaia."

I thought of the same thing—probably about the same time he had, but I wasn't ready to say yes.

"On this other thing—this thing about me—"

I could see he fumbled for words. That was something I'd never seen Burton do before. I wasn't going to help him by filling in helpful words.

"You're correct that I have to make things right. I—I don't know how—"

"Sure you do. It's easy. You just tell the truth. Or to put it in your language, you confess your sins."

"But I can't. I'm not thinking about myself. Please believe me. I can't hurt them—"

"I think we've been through this dialogue before. Right?" I was in control of my emotions again. I had to stay in control, or I'd rush over and hug him.

He faced me. He had no tears in his eyes, but it was what I would call the look of the damned. The pain was deeply etched on his face, as if the world was coming to an end and he had to face God without being ready. I had to look away. I fumbled through the loose papers on the desk.

"I'm working on this—this issue," he said softly. "I want to make things right. Please, please be patient with me."

"It's not a matter of my patience. It's a matter of your integrity." I love it when I can talk like that. I knew I had hit him hard, and it made me feel just a trifle smug.

"I'll try it again. Just give me a breather on this."

"You make it sound as if I'm *your* pastor." That was a good jab, and I felt a moment of triumph. I had stuck in the knife and twisted it. Sure, I was being mean, but my snide comments were the only way I knew to hold back my emotions.

"Can you—please, can you put our situation on hold until after—?"

"*Our* situation?" That was the coldest my voice had sounded.

"Julie, please let me say this one thing, and hold off your defensive tactics and smart cracks."

I closed my eyes and waited. That's why I love that man. He sees right through me.

"You're totally right. I know that. I've known all along. This is a burden I've carried for a long, long time. You understand the reason I've been quiet all these years, even though what I did was wrong. It was sin. I assure you that I will resolve this. I will make it right."

"Convince me." I didn't want to open my eyes and look at him, but I couldn't help myself.

"I can't. I mean not yet. But I'm convinced God will help me break through on this. The primary reason I finally agreed to come on the cruise was so I could think all this through. I've been tormented, seeking a solution without hurting *them* with the truth that—"

"Don't try to make me part of your problem."

He nodded slowly. "You're right. Forgive me." He reached for my hand. "It's just—it's just that I love you so much, and in the past we've been able to talk so freely—"

"Don't!" I stood up. "Don't. . .talk. . .that. . .way!"

He blushed—he actually blushed in embarrassment. "I apologize. Please accept my apology for doing that."

I turned away. I didn't want to look at his face. "Apology accepted."

"In the meantime, please, can we work on this—this case together?"

When he inserted the word *please*, he got to me. What's worse, he didn't do that deliberately. Manipulating people is not the way Burton thinks. Those words came from his heart. The rat! I hate it when he touches my tender emotions.

He stared at me, waiting for me to respond.

I took a deep breath and nodded.

"I loved her, too, you know," he said. "I wasn't her best friend like you, but she and I had a warm relationship. It was deeper than a pastor-parishioner relationship."

"I know." I have no idea how I hardened my voice on those two words, but I did. I struggled to stay in control of my feelings. I was afraid I wasn't going to win.

"Fine, then," he said. "Let's start with what we know, which isn't much."

"We know she left the ship," I said. "All forty-seven of us left. Zodiac one left with only eleven people. The other three left the ship full—twelve each."

"I was in the first one." He turned his head away as he added, "I wanted to get to Brown Bluff before you so I—so I wouldn't have to see you."

Instead of responding to that statement, I said, "I waited for the third one." I didn't tell him that I had watched the people line up and wanted to put space between us. I watched him get into the first Zodiac. I stood out of the way and went in the third one. "That means she was on the fourth Zodiac. We already know that, but I'm not sure that makes any difference, does it?"

He shook his head. "I don't think so." He held a small sheet of paper. "I wrote down the names of the twelve people on the fourth Zodiac, but I don't think it matters."

He read them aloud: Twila, Donny Otis, Pat Borders, Heather Wilson, Thomas Tomlinson, Mickey Brewer, Sue Downs, Jeff Adams, Betty Freeman, and

Shirley and Frank Brackett. "Number twelve, Jon Friesen, went over with them but not back. And that's beyond any question."

"I didn't pay much attention to anyone. The weather had started to turn bad. Jon was in our Zodiac, but I didn't notice he'd switched."

"He said he vomited after the Zodiac started," Burton said, "and someone—I've forgotten who—said that was true."

"Could be," I said. "I had my back to the others. I didn't look at anyone. I was doing a lot of soul-searching—"

"About?"

I wasn't going to open myself up to him on that one. Instead, I said, "I didn't pay attention to anyone; I didn't look at anyone. I was caught up in my own—well, my own thoughts."

"I think we can eliminate Friesen," he said. "He left early."

"Unless—unless he, uh, you know, did the deed first and—"

"Maybe." He paused and thought about that for a few seconds. "Yes, maybe, but I think we need to focus first on the rest of those in the fourth group."

"Someone—one of the ten people who got into the Zodiac—told Ivan that two people had gone back on the other craft."

"Exactly what I was thinking."

"Ivan didn't say so," I said, "but we all assume the person who said that also got into the Zodiac."

"What if it was someone else?"

"It doesn't make sense to me otherwise. Regardless, we know beyond doubt that Jon Friesen left on the third Zodiac."

"Yes, and your Zodiac—the third one—was already gone before the last one loaded."

I closed my eyes, trying to remember. "I'm not sure. I mean, but I have a vague sense that we left within a minute or two of each other. The weather—"

"That's right," he said. "The last two Zodiacs cut their time short and—"

"I think that's correct." I remembered then. "Yes, that's correct. I had just gotten my boots hosed, and I saw the fourth Zodiac approaching. Not that it makes a lot of difference, does it?"

"Probably not," he said. "But we definitely don't want to forget that there were thirteen people in the third Zodiac—including you—that left perhaps one or two minutes before the last Zodiac."

I didn't reply. That's the problem I have with Burton. We think so much alike. We had gotten so close we could almost finish each other's sentences.

Just then the door opened.

13

W hat are you two doing in Twila's cabin?" she asked.

I stared at Heather.

"I think we have the same question for you," Burton said.

"I don't know, exactly," she said. "I thought—oh, I suppose I think I'm Miss Marple, but you know, I thought I might find something—"

"That's why we're here," I said.

"Who could have done such a terrible, terrible thing?" Heather asked.

Neither of us answered. I wanted to learn how distraught she really was. It's not that I didn't believe her story, but she had been one of the ten in the fourth Zodiac, so that put her on the suspect list.

"She was absolutely the sweetest, kindest—"

I stopped listening to the litany. I never would have called Twila *sweet*. She wasn't that kind of person. But there was something about her that drew people to herself. She was also an absolutely no-nonsense person. She rarely used warm, cuddly words like a lot of people. She wasn't much of a hugger, either. Perhaps it was because she was a psychiatrist, but she wouldn't allow people to justify their bad behavior or wrong thinking. She wasn't rude, but she had a way of smiling, looking deeply into a person's eyes, and saying something like, "Is that what you truly believe?"

As far as I know, it always worked. People instinctively trusted her. Twice I had been standing next to her at church and saw her give that look—that's what I called it, the Twila look—and both times the other person stopped lying and opened up to her.

My mind must have wandered, because Heather Wilson was apologizing for trying to play sleuth. As she talked, her eyes darted around the room. I had the impression that she was more interested in seeing if we had discovered anything than she was in finding clues.

"You're sure you didn't notice Twila on Brown Bluff?" Burton asked.

"No, no, I didn't see her—I mean, I didn't recognize her—I mean, well, you know—"

"Yes, we all look quite a bit alike," Burton said.

As I listened to her stumble around, I knew something wasn't right. Either Heather was lying, or she was holding something back. I watched the interchange between them and tried to envision Heather Wilson as someone who carried a knife. She didn't seem to be the kind to stab someone with a literal knife, but I'll bet her words cut deeply.

It was difficult for me to be objective about that woman. I didn't like her; I didn't trust her. I didn't—all right, I was jealous. She's prettier than I am, and men's gazes follow her whenever she walks across the room. I probably secretly wished she were the killer.

With a deep sigh, I pushed aside my negative feelings about Heather.

It seemed obvious that whoever killed Twila had brought the knife—if it was a knife—hidden deeply inside checked luggage. Anything in the hand luggage would have been confiscated.

Of course, there was the possibility that someone had bought a knife at Ushuaia. For two reasons that didn't feel right to me. First, it would be easy enough to check. The business section of Ushuaia wasn't that large. Second, it would mean either that the murderer had left that part of the crime to chance or that the plan to murder Twila hadn't begun until then. I didn't know, of course, but it made sense to assume that the murderer had decided to kill her before we left Atlanta.

Planned it? Planned to kill Twila?

As repugnant as that thought was, I assumed it had been carefully thought out, and the killer waited for the opportunity. Otherwise, it probably would have happened on the first landing.

Another thought that occurred to me was that if it had been a crime of passion, it probably would have occurred aboard ship. I couldn't believe it would have started at Brown Bluff. The cold and the horrible weather didn't allow for a lot of conversation.

Yet another thought struck me: If Twila had had any kind of confrontation or argument with anyone, I'm sure I would have known. She was a professional, but she was also sensitive and easily hurt by harsh or cruel remarks. She wouldn't ever tell me who said them or what they said, but twice in the past she had opened up and talked about mean-spirited words hurled at her. She had said absolutely nothing along that line since we left Atlanta.

That forced me to conclude that someone had planned to kill her before we left Atlanta and had waited for the opportunity to do so.

I stared again at Heather as she talked to Burton. Her eyes never seemed to focus on one spot. She was nervous about the murder, I'm sure, but there was something more.

"Did you have anything in mind when you came here?" I asked her.

"Why, no—I mean, uh, what would I look for?"

"Then how would you know if you found it?"

Heather's laugh had a forced tone to it. "Yes, yes, it does seem a little silly, doesn't it?"

"A little," I said. I tried to give her the Twila look to see if it made a difference.

"I mean, what would I look for?"

"Yes, exactly," I said in my most sarcastic tone. "What *would* you look for?"

"I mean, even if I found it, I wouldn't know what I found, now, would I?"

"I don't know. Would you?" I stayed with the Twila look.

"Uh, well, uh, I suppose I ought to go back to my cabin," she said, but she didn't move.

She wasn't going to tell me, and I don't think she wanted me to stay around. And that fact had nothing to do with the death of Twila. So I said, "Burton and I have a couple of things to talk about."

"You mean you've found something?"

"Nothing," Burton said.

I tried once more. "Unless you have something specific you want to—"

"No, no—"

"We'll join the others shortly." I turned to Burton. I hoped that showed some kind of dismissal.

She still didn't move.

I stared directly at her, and dim lights seemed to turn on inside her head. I think she assumed that Burton and I were talking romance or reconciliation.

"Oh, oh yes, I understand," she said as if she had just caught on. She gave me what I assume she considered a sincere smile. It was as phony as the color of her dyed hair.

"I'm so glad," I said in a soft voice as sweetly as I knew how.

Heather glared at me, turned, and left the cabin. She didn't close the door, and I wouldn't have put it past her to stand outside and listen.

I closed the door behind her and stood there for a minute with my back against it. I then explained to Burton my thought processes about the killer.

He listened, nodded slowly. "Agreed."

"But to think someone planned—"

"Would it really matter whether it was out of sudden, uncontrollable anger or planned out of long-held anger?"

"I suppose not."

I hadn't heard any noise in the hallway, so I assumed Heather had gone. I walked over to the desk and sat on the chair. My gaze slowly swept every part of the room. I stared momentarily at the mattress. I got up to look under it, but Burton beat me to it. He lifted the mattress and found nothing.

"Let's think about this," I said. "Twila obviously had something the murderer wanted."

"Agreed."

"That person may have searched this room after killing her."

Burton pondered that one. "Agreed."

"We can also assume that whatever *it* is must be incriminating enough or important enough for someone to kill her to get it."

"Agreed."

"But Twila?" I asked. "I thought everyone trusted her. Even if she knew something—"

"As a professional—"

"She wouldn't tell."

"But what if—," Burton said and paused before adding, "the murderer either didn't know that or was afraid that Twila *would* tell."

"Agreed," I said and tried to emulate his voice.

He gave me a faint smile. "I love it when you mock me."

I chose to ignore that. "Then it would have to be something illegal. We're therapists, but the law doesn't require us to report confessions—"

"But you know Twila. If someone confessed a crime to her—especially a serious crime—she would have pushed that person to confess."

"Agreed," I said. This time I don't think he heard me.

He paced the small room several times, and all the while he seemed to scrutinize each section of the cabin.

"She once told me that one of her clients had embezzled almost a million dollars," I said, "and he confessed because he couldn't live with his crime."

"Did she report it?"

"Better than that: She convinced him to confess."

"That sounds like Twila."

"Oh, but here's the good part. His corporation—a large one, I understand—rehired him. They put him in security. He had been so good at what he did, no one ever discovered it."

"So I suppose his new job was to catch others—"

"That's what Twila told me," I said.

He smiled at me, and I looked away. When he does that, I can hardly resist him. He has those movie-star teeth and a smile that's so genuine I had to do something to keep my resolve.

"So where do we go from here?" I asked.

"I don't know," Burton said, "but I thought that by putting our minds together, we might come up with something."

This time I shut up and waited for him to speak. I knew he was thinking about the two murder cases we had worked on together. I'm sure he also knew that's what I was thinking about.

"Do you remember when—?" he asked.

"Yes, but let's focus on now."

"Agreed." This time he imitated me imitating him.

I tried to maintain a serious expression, but that made me laugh even more. I held up my hand. "Okay, let's focus."

For the next half hour we threw out ideas but came up with nothing concrete. Both of us knew all the passengers in the fourth Zodiac. To us, the ten people still seemed the most likely suspects.

"Unless—," I said.

"Unless what?"

"Unless the person who said two people were going in the other Zodiac was not only the killer but a passenger in the other boat."

"Do you mean Jon Friesen?"

"Not necessarily. That would mean it was the killer who brought the message."

"It doesn't register with me," Burton said, "but I don't want to disregard that possibility."

"The messenger had to be the killer."

"Agreed."

"The question is whether the killer was one of the ten people who went back or—"

"Yes, true," Burton said. "But let's focus on this. We can assume that whoever told Ivan about two passengers not being on his Zodiac was the killer."

"Elementary, my dear Watson," I said.

He laughed. "That's better than *agreed*."

I thought so, too, but I was creeping near the edge again, so I said, "But if we assume the killer got into Ivan's Zodiac, that means we've narrowed the suspect list. Ivan said he thought it was a man who told him that two of them went in the other boat."

"But he also said he wasn't sure. He had been distracted—"

"By the reprimand on the radio," I finished. "Makes sense."

Burton went to the closet. He took out the suitcase and ran his hands across the lining. He found nothing. He picked up each item of clothing, one at a time. He said nothing, but I watched him. He's a neatnik, too, and he carefully folded each item and laid it inside the suitcase. Frankly, Burton is more detail oriented than I am, so I knew he'd do a better job of searching.

He began to examine the three small shelves where she stored her underwear and jewelry.

I laughed. "Let me look there," I said. "I think that's more of a woman's task."

He moved out of the way, and I carefully looked at each item of jewelry without touching. They seemed to be neatly stored as if no one had disturbed them. It was the same with the underwear. The person who had been careless in the other part of the room hadn't disturbed anything.

"I'm going to assume that it was something fairly large," I said.

"Agreed—uh, elementary, Dr. Watson." He winked at me, but I turned away so he couldn't see the smile on my face.

"What do you think it was? A letter? A file folder? A book?" Burton said.

"Probably, but why would anyone want to steal something like a file unless it contained something incriminating? Maybe it was a large envelope with—" I stopped. "Wait! A book! Maybe it was a book. Look in her briefcase. She carried six books with her. I counted them."

He pulled them out. All but one of them had dust jackets. The one without a dust jacket was *Gifted Hands*. He read the other titles: "We have *When Someone You Love Abuses Alcohol or Drugs*, *90 Minutes in Heaven*, *Think Big*, *Heaven Is Real*, and *Gifted Hands*."

Again, both of us had the same thought. He snatched the *Gifted Hands* dust jacket off the last book. The title revealed definitely wasn't *Gifted Hands*.

I stood next to Burton as he opened it. It was some kind of self-published book titled *Wasted Life*. Twila's name was at the bottom.

Both of us skimmed the first few pages, and I shook my head. "It has Twila's name, but that's not Twila's voice."

"Just read it yourself," I said. "That doesn't sound like Twila."

"I thought the same thing. This sounds more—more academic—"

"More like case studies," I said. "We had tons of them during our student days."

"Case studies," he said again.

We stared at each other.

"Case studies," I echoed.

"Of course! That's what it is!" he answered.

I took the book out of his hands. "Look, it's not really bound like a regular book. It only looks that way."

"You're right." He pointed to a page where Twila had red-lined a sentence and added a full paragraph in the margin in her small, back-slanted style.

"You know what I think?" I said. "I think—"

"She had started to teach a course this semester at Clayton University." He smiled at me as if he had just figured it out. "I'll bet these are her lectures."

I started to say, "Agreed," but decided we'd worn out that joke. "That's exactly what I started to say." In spite of myself, I smiled when I spoke those words. It felt good—and familiar—to banter again with Burton.

"And this had to be important enough for her to put on a false dust jacket to disguise it," he said.

"Let's assume she did that on purpose."

"Could it have been otherwise?"

I thought about the question and tried to make a case inside my head for a mistake on her part. "You're right."

"So if she did it intentionally," he said, "she—"

"She was suspicious."

"Probably," he said.

That made sense to me. "But why?"

We skimmed the first fifty pages of the book. She had obviously written the manuscript with a scholarly approach, as we had already noted. She was careful not to use names but only initials. Because I knew Twila, I had a strong feeling that even the initials weren't the true ones.

"Where's the key?" Burton asked. "There must be some way to figure out who these people are."

358

She had twenty-one case studies. The premise of the book was that each of them had been headed toward a wasted life. The causes varied, but each of them had come to see her professionally and had become her clients.

Burton stood behind me to read over my shoulder.

I read through the introduction and went back to something I had skimmed. Her point was that too many people waste their lives instead of getting help—and not just any kind of help. She felt they needed to find the type of treatment that worked for them.

As a therapist, I was familiar with each method. Cognitive behavioral therapy worked for some, psychoanalysis for others. She talked about the value of Gestalt and RET or rational-emotive therapy. Burton had a vague idea about them, but I explained how Twila had distinguished between Freudian and Jungian analysis. I added, "Twila personally advocated psychodynamic therapy."

"What's that?" he asked.

I had hoped he'd give me a chance to say something to show off a little of my training. "Psychodynamic therapy is more long term and deals with deep-seated patterns *formed in childhood.*" I emphasized those three words, but he didn't react.

Burton skimmed the rest of the potential procedures and chuckled. "And some benefit from deep-body massage?"

"Oh yes, it has helped some."

"That's a new one to me."

"It's still around because it works for some people," I said. "It's not what I use or anything I see practiced much in Clayton County, but that doesn't make it useless."

"What is it, exactly?" he asked.

Again, I hoped I would get a response—any kind of response from him. I pointed to a paragraph where she insisted that deep-body massage had produced results for some practitioners. She also stated that it must be used only by someone who understands the body. I pointed to her reference to biogenetic analysis.

He didn't react, so I added, "Biogenetic analysis is a kind of mind-body connection. I don't hear much about it today. The expression most often used—thirty years ago—was having someone beat the ground with a stick or some angry repetitive action—"

"Why?"

"To bring emotions to the fore. The idea was that we store memories in various places in our body, especially bad memories."

I saw a flicker—quick, furtive—but I had gotten a reaction. He dropped his head and read some more.

I had tried, and I knew that was the only response I was going to get from him. He always says that Christians try to take over God's work and become the conscience for others. *I might as well surrender this to the Lord,* I thought. *I'm not making any progress with him.*

I turned back to what Twila had written. She made references to medication and stated that many of the popular drugs only masked symptoms so that clients didn't have access to their pain. She wasn't against such drugs but advocated stringent, careful prescription.

Twila devoted four pages to faith. She stated that she'd had considerable success with those who came to her about their desire for faith in their lives. She said that she wrote this with "positive prejudice toward the topic" and made a case for the transforming power of the Christian faith, "which I have followed since I was fourteen years old."

I was familiar with the various theories, of course, but I had never run across a psychiatrist who actually advocated the "different strokes for different folks" idea. Of the twenty-one case histories, before they became her patients, all of them had previously been to psychiatrists, psychics, analysts, faith healers, and counselors of every type, even exorcists.

Twila made an important note that she had changed a few details about the individuals to protect their identities. "I can say with absolute certainly that fourteen of these clients are quite healthy and no longer need any psychiatric help. Four of the cases, despite five to twelve years of care, are still symptomatic. Three of them are functional but are characterologically impaired."

"What does 'characterologically impaired' mean?" Burton asked.

"They would fall into the category of personality disorders." I enjoy playing knowledgeable occasionally. "While they appear normal in everyday social situations, they have persistent traits that aren't obvious on the surface."

"I'm not clear—"

"Try this," I said. "People with personality disorders don't think they have any problems, but those who know such people have problems with them."

"Such as?" Burton asked.

Immediately I thought of an example. "Paranoid personalities might secretly believe everyone is out to get them. If you didn't know about that secret belief, their behaviors might not make sense."

He got it, so we continued to look at her manuscript. For each case, she went through a three-to-five-page history about their condition, how long they had been aware of their symptoms, and what treatment they had received.

She wrote another section of about the same length in which she described her diagnosis (which was occasionally quite different from previous diagnoses), what she had done, and how long she had worked with the client. She also included her discharge notes. For Twila, discharge included dropping out of treatment, being referred to another therapist because she didn't feel the client had made significant progress with her, or mutually agreeing to terminate therapy.

What surprised me was her assertion that in many instances, professional interventions were no more effective than intervention by a friend, a pastor, or someone who could *listen uncritically* and *accept the other person without restriction or condition*. "Such caring individuals seem to be in great demand but short supply. Hence, the needy individuals feel they have to resort to professional help." She listed one caveat—unless there was evidence of psychosis. In that case, she would treat the person with medication.

Although she occasionally had a snappy, well-worded sentence, her writing was what I'd call turgid. If she could find a simple word, she didn't use it but threw in a lot of psychiatric jargon and never settled for five words when she could write twenty. Because her audience was primarily grad students, that made sense to me.

Burton and I stared at the book. He took it from me and leafed through the entire manuscript, which ran about 250 pages, single-spaced, in ten-point type.

"What do you think?" he asked.

"My assumption is that whoever killed her is one of those three incorrigibles," I said.

"That's logical, but—"

"I know. We can't prove it. In fact, we can't prove anything—"

"But it's as good a place to start as any," he said.

I wanted to say to him, "Please stop finishing my sentences." I didn't. He had been accurate each time. But I had to remind myself that I wasn't supposed to like him very much right now. Yet how could I remain aloof with a person like Burton who thinks the same way I do?

"We don't know the identity of any of them, especially the three that—"

"That's exactly what I started to say," I said.

He shrugged and gave me that gorgeous, heart-melting smile. "Maybe that's why we work so well together."

I chose to ignore that. "Do you suppose she left some kind of key?" I asked instead of answering him. "Surely she had some way to track and keep twenty-one identities separate."

"Of course she did," Burton said. "I assume it'll be somewhere in her office—"

"Which we don't have access to right now!" In spite of myself, I giggled. I had finished *his* sentence.

"That's what I was going to say."

"Oh, really?" I tried to act surprised. "You know, I read somewhere that if two people think the same way, one of them isn't necessary."

"Ah, but they don't know us. They obviously didn't know people who could—"

"Right, but let's focus on this situation."

I closed my eyes and thought about Twila's habits. She had a phenomenal memory. So it was possible she hadn't needed any written key.

I mentioned that to Burton, and he said, "And if she was concerned enough to use a false cover—"

"We can assume that the murderer could very well be one of the people named in her book—her lectures." I thought for a moment. "Something else," I said. "The killer must have known about the book or that she had something in writing—"

"Or he wouldn't have searched."

"Or she," I added.

"I stand corrected. It could be a woman. Anyone can plunge a knife into someone."

"Or whatever it was." Again I mentioned that someone would have had to bring the weapon inside checked luggage. I was thinking out loud. As Burton had long known, I sometimes do my best thinking when I talk.

"I don't know where anyone could have picked up a knife in Buenos Aires, because we never left the airport. In Ushuaia it doesn't seem likely, either. How many stores did you see?"

"Aside from restaurants, I'd say not more than a dozen."

"Too easy to trace and—"

"How would the person know that she or he would be able to buy a knife in Ushuaia?"

"Unless that person had an accomplice on the ship." Even as I said the words, I knew that idea seemed too far-fetched.

"Conspiracy theory?" Burton said. "Nah, I don't think so."

"I don't, either."

"I know," he said. "And I doubt that we'll find the knife or whatever it was. There is a big ocean on all sides of this ship. Too easy to get rid of."

"Agreed," I said. This time I tried hard to imitate his way of talking and cocked my head slightly, just the way he did.

He laughed. "You do me quite well."

"Yes, I know."

"You're playful and cute when you do it, too."

I think I blushed, but I had to admit to myself that I had never known anyone in my life who understood me—and especially my humor—like Burton.

"I've missed your smart mouth," he said softly. "I've missed it a lot."

"I missed someone to practice on," I said and immediately regretted it. I held up my hand. "Okay, that's the end of that road. Let's detour. I don't want to fall into our old way of talking and interacting."

He only nodded. A few seconds later, he asked, "What if we let it slip that we had found—?"

"The book?" I said. "Yes—"

"Agreed." I saw the merriment in his eyes, but I didn't give way to my feelings. Instead, I took the book from him, pulled out the first half of the pages, and gave him the rest. He had the *Gifted Hands* dust cover, and I took it from him to keep my pages together. I made a loose fold and put it inside the large pocket of my heavy jacket.

I didn't understand much, but I sensed that Twila's book of lectures would lead us to the killer.

Burton and I talked for several minutes longer in Twila's cabin. No matter where we took our thinking, it always came back to her lecture book.

Hours later and unable to think of anything new, we went to see Captain Robert. He was in the lounge, setting up a film about plant life on Antarctica. I had already read about the subject in the *Explore Antarctica* guidebook. The fact that earlier explorers found lichen meant they could classify Antarctica as a continent. By contrast, nothing grew on or around the Arctic ice cap, so it wasn't a continent.

The captain said he was finished with his work and motioned for us to sit down. Without asking, he brought each of us a bottle of cold Coca-Cola and a glass.

"You already know quite a bit about us, I assume," Burton said.

"Not really so much," he said.

In a space of twenty minutes, we told him the story of how we had been thrown together eighteen months earlier at Palm Island, off the coast of Georgia. We arrived at the island after the death of the host, Roger Harden. Because the others were already on the island when the murder was committed, and the police couldn't get to the island until the next day, we had worked together and solved the crime.

Ten months later we ran into each other at the Cartledge Inn near Stone Mountain, Georgia. Again there was a murder, and we worked together to solve that one.

"So now you are here and you will solve this murder, is that not so?" Captain Robert asked. At first I thought he was being cynical, but as I looked at his face, I knew he had asked a serious question.

"We would like to try," Burton said.

"As I told you earlier. . ." Once again without warning, my eyes clouded with tears. "Twila Belk was my best friend."

"I was her pastor," Burton said. "She was also like a second mother. I have to do what I can."

"Of course, you must do what you can," the captain said. "I cannot give you official permission to do this, but I shall assist you in any way possible."

"Will you encourage the others to cooperate with us?" I asked.

The captain pondered the question for a few minutes before he answered.

"Yes, yes, I can do that." He also said he would come to the dining room during breakfast, which was served at seven, and speak to the passengers.

We thanked the captain and left him.

I was tired but didn't know if I could sleep. I went into the room and didn't bother to undress. I was sure I would lie awake.

The next moment of awareness was when I looked at my watch. It was 5:30 a.m. Despite the rocking of the waves, I had slept an hour or two.

I wanted to stay in the room and read, but I didn't dare. Betty was likely to awaken. She's one of those people who loves to talk when she has nothing to say. Harmless enough, I suppose, but it was tiring to listen to her constant chatter. I'd tried several times to turn her off by mumbling an occasional word or nodding while my mind focused on other things. She had the most disconcerting habit of punctuating every second sentence with my name. Hearing my name snapped me back to attention, and I resented it. I enjoyed my own thoughts more.

I hurried to the bathroom for a one-handed shower. After I dressed, I put the pages I'd torn from Twila's manuscript in my shoulder bag and went to the dining room. A small light glowed so no one would knock over the furniture. I snapped on a lamp in the far corner and sat down. I laid my shoulder bag on the table, pulled out Twila's case studies, and began to read. Although I had no idea of the identity of any of the clients, the studies fascinated me. Despite the formal tone, Twila had been meticulous in her details. She clearly delineated between the objective results of tests and her own interpretations.

I must have dozed off, because I awakened to the aroma of freshly brewed coffee. I got up and poured myself a cup. As I drank, I looked around. Burton was asleep in the corner. He had probably been there the entire time.

I must have awakened him, because he looked up and stretched. "Is the coffee good?"

"Is that the masculine way of asking me to bring you a cup?"

"You catch on quickly," he said and stretched again.

I poured him a cup, added a spoon of milk, and carried it to him. As I walked toward him, I was ready to make another smart-mouthed remark, but the cad beat me to it.

"Keep it up and you'll make a macho type out of me yet and allow you to bring me coffee regularly."

"You make it; I'll pour it," I said and wished I hadn't. Once again, the language was getting too familiar.

Burton thanked me for the coffee and sipped it absently. "I've read about half of my pages. The style doesn't make for great reading—"

"Unless you like to read case studies," I said. "I read hundreds of them during my student days." I took a few sips of my coffee and added, "And I liked them, then. The style hasn't changed, but the material is fascinating."

"If you say so," he said. He went back to his reading.

Both of us focused on the manuscript. Without saying it, I think we realized that time was running out. Our ship would soon navigate the Drake Passage, and many of the passengers would stay in their rooms because of motion sickness.

He stretched and said, "I think it's time for me to clean up and shave before the others start lining up for the showers." He put his manuscript inside the book cover, took his dirty cup back to the serving table, and left.

I watched him walk away.

Instead of getting further away from the man, I'm getting closer again. That's not what I planned.

16

I had long been impressed with Twila's insight and her amazing intuition about people. But the book amazed me even more. Just from reading the first four case studies, I felt I knew the clients and understood why Twila was such an effective psychiatrist.

"Excuse me," a man's voice said.

I must have jumped. I had been so absorbed in my reading that I hadn't noticed Jon Friesen enter the room. "Sorry, but you startled me."

"May I join you?" he asked. He directed the question to me, but he wasn't looking at my face. Although he was still about eight paces away, his gaze didn't leave the pages. Instinctively, I covered them with my hand.

"Or would you prefer—?"

"No, no, that's fine," I said. "In fact, why don't we have a cup of coffee together?" I wanted to get his attention away from the manuscript. I stood up, turned over the pages, and laid my shoulder bag on top of them.

"Please, allow me to get it for you," he said.

"Thanks. No sugar, no milk. Just coffee."

While he was gone, I put the pages into my shoulder bag. For now, no one except Captain Robert knew that Burton and I had found the manuscript. I wanted to keep that information secret just a little longer.

After Jon handed me the cup, he sat across from me. He had chosen hot chocolate. He sipped the steaming beverage before he said, "That must have been absorbing reading."

I shrugged as if to minimize it.

"But you seemed so engrossed and focused on—"

"I get that way sometimes."

"I assume it's only when something commands your attention."

"Yes, that's true," I said. This conversation was headed in the wrong direction, so I decided to take charge. "Were you looking for me? Or did you just happen to come by and see me here?"

"No, I was looking for you."

"Oh, that makes me feel important. Why were you looking for me?"

"I want to tell you that I'm sorry about the death of Twila. I knew you and she were good friends." He was a tall man, thin and muscular. His face, set in strong lines, was impassive as he spoke. He wore expensive royal blue warm-up pants and a tight off-white polo shirt that made those muscular arms look even more prominent.

"We were more than close friends." I felt my voice begin to falter. Most of the time I was able to push aside my personal sense of loss, but in unexpected moments like this, the feelings overwhelmed me. I turned my face away from him and blinked several times. "I considered her my very, very special friend."

"I am sorry," he said. He reached across the table and laid his hand on mine. "This must be a painful time for you."

"Yes, it is."

"Do you want to talk about it?"

"That's what I usually say to people who hurt."

"Then perhaps we can reverse positions for now," he said. He drew back his hand and got up, came around to my side of the table, and put his arm around my shoulder.

"Please don't," I said. I pulled a tissue out of my bag and wiped my eyes.

Jon sat down and stared at me. He said nothing, as if he expected me to continue.

He won that one. A wave of grief overwhelmed me, and to avoid giving in to my tears, I began to talk. "She introduced herself to me the first time I visited the church." I closed my eyes, and memories filled my mind. The pain was deep, much deeper than I had thought. I shook my head as if the gesture would shake away my grief. "We also became friends that day."

Jon still said nothing, so I talked about the growing relationship between Twila and me. Occasionally Jon made a comment—usually a very professional one, such as "Ah, I see," or "How did you feel?"

After a few minutes, I stopped talking and stared at him. "Are you—or have you ever been—a professional therapist?"

He shook his head. "No, but I've been to a few."

"Want to talk about it?"

"No, I don't think so."

His answer shocked me. First, he didn't laugh or even smile at my quick retort. Almost anyone else would have caught the humor. Burton would have gotten it and given me a clever response. Oh, sometimes he ignored me, but I could always tell he got my meaning. I couldn't read anything from Jon's response.

"Now it's your turn," I said. "You talk and I listen, nod, or say things like 'Go on,' or 'Hmm.' "

"I don't have anything to say."

"You said you've been to a number of therapists."

"Yes, I did. Yes, I have."

I have had a few clients like Jon, and it often takes half an hour or longer to get them to start to talk. Once I get them to open up, they usually sense they can trust me. After that I sometimes have to interrupt them to get them to stop.

I didn't know Jon well. I think we met when he sat next to me in a Sunday school class. He had spoken at most five sentences to me in the months since we'd known each other. I decided to try again. Giving him my best smile and keeping my voice low and soft, I asked, "Did you know Twila well?"

He shook his head. "Not well."

"Then why did she invite you as her guest?"

"She was my therapist for a time."

"For how long a time?"

"Not too long."

"But she was no longer your therapist when you came on the cruise?"

"Correct."

To give myself time to think of a fresh approach, I took a few sips of my now-warm coffee. I studied Jon. It seemed to me that almost everyone at church knew him, and the younger girls referred to him as a hunk or a hottie. He was a couple of inches above six feet, which I liked. His almost-blond hair had a circular part, and his almond-colored eyes showed intensity. He had an incredible bod, and his pecs bulged and rippled when he made the slightest move.

The first time I saw him at church, I envisioned him behaving like a fourteen-year-old and expected him to flex his muscles and ask me to feel his arm. I had done that a few times—when I was thirteen.

"How long is *not long*?"

"A few months."

"How many months is a few? Two? Twelve?" That smart remark would have gotten a good response from Burton.

Jon stared at me. He didn't smile then, and I realized that I had only seen him smile once or twice before.

"You said not long. How long was that?" I persisted.

"Months. Less than a year. I don't remember."

"So you weren't close? I mean, she wasn't what you'd call a friend?"

"No."

"You weren't her friend?" I'm sure the shock showed on my face. "Then what are you doing on this trip?"

"I am on this trip to see Antarctica," Jon said. "Isn't that the reason all of us came?"

"But you came as a guest of Twila's."

"Correct."

"You weren't a current client and you weren't a friend?"

"True."

"That surprises me. I mean, she invited only friends and clients on this cruise. Or at least that's what I thought—"

"Perhaps she liked me."

"Perhaps." I decided to play his little game.

Silence filled the room except for faint noises coming from the galley area. A few pots clinked, and someone turned on a spigot. I was going to wait him out.

"I would like to talk to you," Jon said. He paused, lifted his hot chocolate to his mouth to finish it. But he did that muscle flexing at the same time. I suppose most women liked it.

Yes, I liked it, too. He was really quite strikingly handsome.

"I've wanted to talk to you," he said. "I've wanted to talk to you since I first saw you at church."

"Really?"

"Yes."

"But you never said anything."

"True."

This wasn't getting anywhere, so I decided to try a few more words. "So why didn't you talk to me?"

"It was obvious that your attention was focused elsewhere."

"That obvious, was it?"

"To me it was." He tried to sip his hot chocolate again but realized it was gone. He put down his cup and pushed away from the table. "The past few weeks I—I haven't seen you around much."

"You looked for me?"

Those almond-colored eyes seemed intensely focused on me. "Every Sunday."

"Oh."

"So why haven't I seen you?"

"I wasn't around much." I love those smart-mouthed answers, and they irritate Burton. Or at least he tries to make me think they do.

"Yes, I'm aware," he said. "That's why I mentioned it."

I stared at him for several seconds, and he stared back without blinking. I couldn't figure out this man. I tried to remember what I knew about him, which wasn't much. He was a day trader, and the gossip was that he had scored really big just before the dot-com bubble burst. I decided to try the question-and-answer technique.

"You're quite a handsome man. The word I heard is that you're enormously wealthy."

"Yes."

"I also know you're single," I said, "and very attractive to the unattached women at church."

He shrugged as if to say it was of no importance.

This man wasn't going to give out information easily, not even when I flattered him. "Have you ever been married?"

"Yes."

"Yes? What does that mean?"

"That I have not always been single."

In spite of myself, I laughed. His expression didn't change. *What kind of man is this? The outdoor lights shine brightly, but I'm not sure there's anyone alive inside the building.*

"How many times have you not been single?" If he has any sense of humor, that one ought to get a response.

"Three times."

"Oh, so I suppose you're one of those men who will keep trying until you get it right."

"I will get it right this time if you will marry me."

"Whoa! That's a bit fast," I said. He continued to puzzle me. He was supposed to smile—or at least make an attempt at a smile.

"I like you," he said in a soft, low voice. "Do you like me?"

"I'm not sure about a lot of my feelings right now."

"I'll wait." He stared at me as if he thought he could see inside my head.

"Enough along that line, okay? I don't want to get into anything romantic. Okay? My heart is heavy over the loss of my close friend." *Doesn't the man ever blink?*

"Yes, it is sad."

When we finally were able to talk further—beyond a few syllables at a time—he said the right words. Maybe he was too correct. He reminded me of a few college classmates. We had studied the work of Carl Rogers, who founded the client-centered therapy movement. We learned clever responses, such as "I hear you saying. . . ," and we learned to feed people back what they told us in slightly different words. That showed we focused on them. We also learned to use one-word responses—much as Jon had done with me.

The problem with most of those classmates is that they did this by rote. It was as if they had been programmed to give the orthodox response. Most of them outgrew their allegiance to pat answers, but Jon sounded as if he were still in Psych 101 or at most 201.

"Have you ever studied Carl Rogers?" I asked.

"No."

"Really?"

"Yes."

"Where did you learn all those phrases you used on me?"

"I have been in therapy."

"Many times?"

"Yes."

"Were you seeing Twila up until the time of the cruise?"

"Do you mean as a patient?"

"Yes."

"No."

"Because—?"

"Because I was no longer seeing her."

"Oh." Just then I remembered something Twila had said to me when she first began to plan the cruise. "I want to invite the people I most love from the church," she said. "I'll also invite a few others—people who need me."

I'm not sure if I responded to that statement, although at the time it struck me as odd. But then, I was so fixated on James Burton, I wasn't much interested in the rest of the people.

"That reminds me: You became sick on Brown Bluff."

"No, I got sick before I went to the island."

"Minor point. You were sick, right?"

"Correct. I had slept badly, my stomach was upset, and I was nauseated before I left. I almost vomited on the island, but I began to breathe very slowly because I didn't want to barf on that pristine land. I told someone—and before you ask, I don't know who it was—to tell Ivan that I was sick and would return on the third Zodiac. The people were climbing into it then to return."

That was the most he had spoken at one time. This came across as even stranger than his silence. The words sounded as if he had memorized a page of movie dialogue, and he spoke them like a third-rate actor.

I thought again of the way he talked. I decided his words sounded as if he had memorized a script but had forgotten to add emotions.

He didn't frighten me, but I was confused by his presence. Was he one of the people who needed Twila? When I first began to work for Clayton County Special

Services, I met a few people like him. They came across as emotional zombies. Sometimes it was the medication, such as powerful tranquilizers. Sometimes they just had a few unconnected wires inside their heads. None of them had ever been dangerous—as far as I knew—but they're not the kind of people I'd like to invite for dinner.

"Are you on any medication?"

"Sometimes," he said.

"I'm sorry, but I don't understand."

"Sometimes I take it; sometimes I don't."

"Oh."

He said nothing but kept his gaze fixed on me. *Doesn't he ever blink? Don't his eyes dry out staring like that?* I decided to play the stare game.

He won; I blinked and turned away.

I picked up my shoulder bag and got up. He pushed away his chair and stood up next to me. He held out his arms to embrace me, and he did it in such a way as if he expected me to fall into them. That gesture felt strange to me.

Instead, I took both his hands briefly. "Thank you for opening yourself so fully to me."

"It's because I like you."

"That sounds like my kind of smart-mouth speaking," I said. He didn't get it, so I added, "Thank you." I had no idea why I was thanking him, but I thought, *You figure it out, big dude.*

I walked away from him and headed back to my room. I didn't turn around, but I listened carefully. He hadn't followed me, and I relaxed.

Everything about Jon confused me. No, that's not quite accurate. I had already done a quickie professional analysis—that's one of the hazards of my occupation—and I admitted to myself that it's dangerous to make immediate judgments. But in my thinking, he fit the profile of a man with unstable personal relationships, a self-image that is not well formed, and poor impulse control. His amorous attempts were totally out of context. He had no awareness of me or of my reaction. For lack of a better label, I'd have called him a borderline personality.

He's a little creepy, I thought. *He's a handsome man, but good looks are no insurance against being creepy.* I decided to see if I could look at Twila's file on him when we returned to Georgia.

If he's so strange, Twila certainly knew it. She would have picked that up in about ten seconds. So why did Twila invite him? He must be one of those who needed her. Is he someone capable of killing her? I had no idea.

But for now, there were forty-six passengers on the ship. By eliminating Burton and me, we had forty-four possible-but-remote suspects. If we stayed with the ten who were in the fourth Zodiac, that cut down the task of finding the killer considerably. But Jon had gone to the island on the fourth Zodiac, so I decided to make him number eleven.

"He's slightly nuts," I said aloud. "He's probably not dangerous, but he's still nuts."

"Julie, no professional talks that way," I said to myself.

"Okay, he's at least a borderline personality—"

"Julie!"

"Okay, without further tests, I'd classify him as a person with a borderline personality disorder. We call that BPD."

"Now you sound professional," I said.

"I'd probably also sound crazy if anyone else heard me."

I walked along the outside deck. It was getting colder, and I pulled my heavy jacket tighter.

"He may be BPD, but that doesn't make him a killer."

18

I went back to the room and found Betty Freeman awake and in her usual chattering mood. She was nearly dressed but couldn't make up her mind whether to wear slacks or her running suit. She started to talk, and I gave her only one-word answers, but that didn't stop her.

Finally, I gave her nothing but nods. Still she persisted.

"Julie, I heard that you and Burton have received permission to act like detectives and solve this terrible—terrible thing."

That opened me up. "Who said so?"

"I don't know. Gossip among the passengers. Maybe somebody overheard—"

"Or maybe someone was eavesdropping."

She blushed. "Well, I wasn't really, Julie. I mean, I didn't intend to eavesdrop. I was only—"

"It doesn't matter," I said. I wanted her to shut up so I could have peace and quiet.

For thirty seconds, she said nothing. I stretched out on my back on my bunk and closed my eyes.

"Julie, I suppose you'd like to take a nap or something."

"Yes."

"I don't want to disturb you, Julie. I tried to read but couldn't keep my mind on it, don't you know? I get bored walking around on the deck."

I didn't reply.

"I have a question. Please, Julie, don't take offense if I ask, okay?"

"So ask." I sighed loudly, but I knew she wouldn't get the message.

"Burton. Is it over between you two? You know, romantically over?"

"Why do you ask?" That's always a safe question to find out the question behind the question.

"Uh, well, Julie, I—I'm just, uh, you know, I'm a little curious."

"And available."

"Well, yes. And he is so cute, isn't he?" Betty was about half a foot shorter than me. She was about my age, maybe a year or two older. I'm thin and willowy with almost no fat—okay, I'll translate that. I'm not rounded in the right places. Most women complain about their rear ends being too large. I'm so flat everywhere I can wear boys' clothes.

"I mean, dear Julie, if I—if I—"

"He's unattached as far as I'm concerned," I said. I hope I said it with more conviction than I felt. I also wished she'd stop using my name with almost every sentence, so I could tune her out.

She talked on and on. I think it was something about the man she almost married when she was in college. Or maybe it was one of her music professors. I didn't care, and I didn't want to hear.

Most of all, I didn't want to talk about Burton. I wanted to grieve over Twila—and I wanted to think. I finally figured out the only way to do that was to feign sleep. I turned over on my stomach and lay still.

A few minutes later, Betty said, "Well, Julie, you're sure you don't mind?"

I did mind, but I didn't answer. If she could entice him, that was fine. No, it wasn't fine, and I admitted I loved him.

"Aren't you going to breakfast?" I asked to change the subject.

"Sometimes a girl has to watch her figure," she said. "Do you think I've gotten too big in the hips? Maybe I should lose ten pounds. What do you think?"

It was much simpler to pretend to be asleep.

After that she painted her fingernails and toenails. I think I heard her brushing her hair about five hundred times. But I soon pushed her out of my mind.

I missed Twila. I didn't know how I'd function without her friendship. Even though we'd become close only within the last year, it felt as if we'd always known each other.

To distract my own grief, I thought about the book of lectures she had written. I hadn't finished reading my portion of the chapters before Jon interrupted me. I wanted to read more, but if I made the slightest move, Betty would start talking to me again. I thought of going to the lounge, but I assumed other people would be there at this time. Except for mealtime, the others could be almost anyplace on the ship.

My mind stayed on the book. That had to be the answer. Her death. The room searched. The wrong cover on the book—and because I knew Twila, I knew she had not done that mindlessly.

The killer had to be one of the people mentioned in the book. The more I played with that idea, the more sense it made. But she carefully altered the identities, so I don't see how anyone could know he or she was one of the people written about in the book. Twila would never, never knowingly hurt anyone.

As I lay in the almost-quiet room, I vaguely recalled weeks earlier when Twila talked to me about her lectures at Clayton University. She told me that she had disguised the case studies enough so that the individuals wouldn't recognize themselves. She didn't tell me she had written them in a book form.

She told me something else about the case studies. I couldn't quite remember. . . . *What was it?*

I hadn't paid much attention, because it didn't seem important then. I kept trying to replay that moment inside my head. I was actually surprised that I remembered any of it. As I lay on the bunk, I noticed the waves outside weren't yet rough. The gentleness must have rocked me to sleep.

When I awakened, I rolled over onto my back. Betty was gone. She probably decided breakfast was more important than losing ten pounds. I lay quietly for perhaps a minute, allowing my mind to go where it chose.

"What about the legal issues?" I didn't hear a voice, but the words were so loud, I sat up abruptly.

"Yes! Yes, that's what I was trying to remember," I shouted. Twila had said she'd changed enough minor facts that she could disguise the subject without distorting the truth of the case. She had assured me of this when I reminded her of a case I had read about in California. A psychologist did some weird therapy like making everyone scream like a bird or an animal. A writer who documented his practice changed names and places in her article, but the psychologist recognized his treatment style, sued her, and received a huge cash award.

"I have their signed permissions," she said that day.

I snapped my fingers. "That's it!" That's what I had been trying to remember. She told me that she had given all the subjects of the case studies a copy of their particular case study and asked them to read it and to make any changes they chose to make it more accurate. She explained that she wanted to present each one of them as a case study to grad students at the university.

Had she gotten everyone to sign? I couldn't remember if she mentioned it, but I assumed she had. Surely Twila wouldn't have gone ahead without their written agreement. If she had their signatures, why would there be a problem? Perhaps one of them may have changed his or her mind. Was that possible?

Or maybe the case studies didn't contain the story of the person who murdered her. Maybe the murder was unrelated and something totally different.

What else is there? Why else would anyone hurt that wonderful saint of a woman?

I was still lying in my bunk when Betty came back into the cabin. I tried to think of anything else about Twila and her lectures. Nothing more came to me. The subject hadn't seemed all that important at the time.

Maybe it wasn't important. But if it wasn't, why the searching in her cabin? Why had she put a different cover on her own book? That seemed strange—almost as if she suspected someone. Had she been threatened? These were people she had chosen to travel with. Surely Twila was too astute to—

A knock at the door interrupted my thoughts. Before I could sit up, Betty was at the door and opened it. "Oh, did you come to escort us to breakfast?" she asked. "I'm not quite ready." She actually posed and flipped her hair with one hand. "But it will only take a second or two."

"I thought you had breakfast," I said to Betty.

"I did have a bite," she said, "but only a little toast and black coffee." She smiled at Burton. "A girl has to watch her figure, you know. But I could sit and enjoy another cup of coffee and listen to you talk."

"I think the dining room is closed by now," I said.

"Oh no, no," she said. "It should be, but it isn't. The others have just started to come in for a late breakfast—a very late breakfast." She draped one arm over the closet door as if posing for a photo shoot. I didn't know if that was her way of being cute. No, I decided she was definitely flirting with Burton. I had watched her bat her eyes a few times at men before.

"Uh, well, you see, I came—"

"I'm ready," I said. I grabbed my bag and hurried out before Betty had a chance to say anything more.

"See you later, Betty," Burton said.

He closed the door behind me.

"Thank you for saving me," Burton whispered once we were away from the cabin.

"Oh, did you need saving?"

"You didn't see how she came on to me?"

"Did she really? Oh, surely not," I said and hid my smile.

"Okay, Ms. Smart Mouth, you almost had me there."

"She was a bit obvious," I said and walked on ahead of him.

We sat down at the far corner of the first table, where I could see everyone who entered the room. Although there were no reserved places, by the second day, most of us had established our seating preferences. I purposely moved to a different place for each meal so that I could disrupt the orderliness of always sitting in the same place. I used to love it at church when someone would say, "Excuse me, but you're sitting in my pew." I would smile as innocently as I could and say, "Oh, you're welcome to sit here with me. There's plenty of room for all of us, don't you think?" They usually declined my invitation.

Okay, maybe that wasn't the best behavior. Twila once asked, "Is that an act of kindness? You make them uncomfortable. For some people, the one place where they can come and everything is as it should be is church. They like to sit in the same pew, and they want to see the same people each time."

She could have elaborated, but that was Twila. She knew she had made her point. I embraced her and thanked her. She was right, of course. Despite my inclinations, I didn't do it again. Even so, I thought of it almost every time I went to church. My actions were a little ahead of my good intentions.

I did it other places, however, because I wasn't yet a totally nice person. I was also still new in the Christian faith. At times, I resented being a believer. When I was on my own, I could make my decisions based on how I wanted to behave. Now I had to consult the Lord on everything.

In some ways, I'm a very, very slow learner.

20

We had barely gotten seated in the dining room before the waiter brought out our meals. He was also the Zodiac driver for the first boat that went out to Brown Bluff. Most of the crew, I observed, had more than one job aboard ship.

As usual, the food was absolutely delicious. They served the usual oatmeal, cold cereal, scrambled eggs, and bacon. But they always offered something a little unusual. Today it was strawberry crepes. I wondered why some first-class restaurant hadn't hired the chef.

Something else was interesting in the dining room. Every single one of those individuals paused and bowed their heads. Their lips moved, so I assume they thanked God for their food. I had never done that on my own. At one time I lived with a religious nut of an uncle who did geographic prayers before every meal—he prayed around the world in six minutes. (I timed him, and his shortest prayer was three minutes and forty-nine seconds. He must have been hungry that day.)

———

Captain Robert walked into our dining room. "Please continue to eat," he said. "I hope you have found the cuisine to your liking."

Several people said yes. One woman clapped, and that brought about a spurt of applause.

"I wish to make one announcement. I have nothing new to report to you." I half expected him to say something obvious, such as "Someone here killed Mrs. Belk." He didn't, but he did say, "I have spoken to each of you. You are all Americans, and we have been informed that delegates from your fine country will meet us at Ushuaia. They will continue the investigation."

"Is there nothing you can tell us?" I recognized Mickey Brewer's voice.

"I can tell you nothing—"

"Or you won't?"

"—at this point," he said as if Mickey hadn't interrupted him. "However, I have given unofficial permission to the Rev. Dr. James Burton and Dr. Julie West to act on my behalf until we reach our destination. If you know anything or have any suspicions, please to talk to them."

He gave us the pep talk about how delighted he was to have us and said that in his eighteen years, this was the first time he had known of such a sad occasion. He bid us bon appétit and gave us a kind of salute before he left.

At first everyone around me whispered. Finally, Heather, who sat across from me and four seats down, asked, "Well, Julie, do you have any clues yet?"

"I'm waiting to find out what you know."

"Me? Why should I know anything?"

I smiled and focused on my eating. I had meant it as a smart-mouthed remark. As I reviewed the words in my head, I realized they hadn't come across as flip and cute.

The shock on her face made me wonder if I had spoken intuitively. *What if she does know something?*

It took about twenty minutes for us to get through the meal. Some stayed for coffee, but not many. Within another twenty minutes, only a handful of us remained in the dining room.

I got up, and Heather called my name softly. I looked up. She was sitting between Mickey Brewer and Donny Otis with Jon Friesen across from her. "Can I—can I talk to you for a second? Alone, I mean?" She turned and smiled at the three men. "Excuse me, guys."

"Sure, we can talk," I said. I stopped by Burton's chair—he sat at the other end of the same table. Betty sat across from him and was in the middle of a long story about how she had gotten lost for two hours in Amsterdam, or maybe it was Tel Aviv. Just to irritate her, I bent over and whispered in Burton's ear, "See you later."

He smiled. "Okay, I'll join you—"

Oh, now he wanted to play my game. "Give me ten minutes." I whispered in his ear, "The lounge."

"I'll be there."

"Come alone. Danger lurks."

He burst out laughing, and I hurried out of the room.

I walked slowly up a flight of stairs. Heather caught up with me and led me to her cabin. "I don't know how much good this is," she said, "but on Brown Bluff, I saw two people walking over toward a small hill or whatever you call it. It was just high enough to walk around and get out of sight. Maybe it's nothing, but. . .I thought you ought to know."

My intuition had been right, but I also sensed that wasn't everything. "What else can you tell me?"

"They both wore blue—you know, like all of us."

"Yes, of course, but anything else?"

"One was taller. I know that's not very helpful, but one was taller, and—I assume it was a man—and he wore his life jacket."

"His life jacket? Are you sure?"

"I am. I know a few of us have done that because it's too much bother to take it off and put it back on. Still, it seemed odd."

It did seem odd, although I had noticed one or two people like that. "Anything else?"

"I'm quite sure the shorter one was Twila. You know she has a kind of limp."

"Yes, the long-lasting result from the accident years ago."

"That's right. Otherwise, I doubt if I would have noticed."

"Any other detail? I don't care how trivial it may seem. Please, think. Anything— even if it's only a slight detail, it could be important."

Heather thought, and finally she said, "The taller one—and I'm not good at heights—took her arm. I think that's what caught my attention. It was almost— well, rough. You know, aggressive?"

"Why didn't you say or do something?"

"I figured that if it was something serious, she'd push away his grip or yell or something. Hey, come on now, who would have thought that any harm would have come to Twila?"

"You're right."

"Besides, the weather had already started to turn bad. Remember the wind and the first pelts of snow or sleet or whatever it was?"

I nodded and waited to see if she had anything else to add.

"That's it."

I stared at her. She really had told me nothing. "What do you mean? Surely you saw or heard—"

"No, that's it." She turned and went into her room.

"That's it?"

She said nothing more. I walked away feeling confused.

She wasn't some ditz who would just do something like that. In fact, in my limited knowledge of Heather Wilson, I would have called her a manipulator or an orchestrator. She seemed to constantly have things going on around her, but she remained in control. Maybe the term *control freak* was another apt description. Her calling me aside didn't make sense.

What is going on?

Was it possible that she wanted to talk to me for some other reason? She had very little to offer, and she could have said that in the group or at any time. Was it possible that she wanted to communicate a message to someone still in the dining room? To one of the three men? To someone else in the room?

"Stop, Julie," I said. "You've watched too many reruns of *Murder, She Wrote.*"

"But what if—?"

"You're not Jessica Fletcher, and this is no TV script."

As I slowly made my way to the lounge, I couldn't get past the idea that Heather did have some other purpose in mind. Was she trying to hint to someone? Was it possible she was trying to hint to the people around her or at another table that she had vital information? Was she merely trying to become the center of attention?

"Stop it, Julie!" I said.

"You're right. I'm becoming paranoid."

"Yes, you are."

"But still. . ."

21

He told me that no one had shown up for the first lecture on penguins. "We have already observed the chinstrap, rockhopper, gentoo—"

"Thank you for being conscientious about this, but our minds are elsewhere," I said.

"Yes, but of course, that must be so." He seemed genuinely apologetic.

"You're just being the captain. I understand."

He rewarded me with a smile. "I shall send someone to post a notice that the second lecture has been canceled."

"It's not because of you or the subject—"

"I am aware that you are correct," he said. "Would it not be difficult for anyone to sit in on a lecture about the difference between an Adélie penguin and a macaroni penguin when everyone thinks about the death of Mrs. Belk?"

Not trusting my voice, I nodded. I had another of those unexpected moments of pain rush over me, and tears stung my eyes. If I had sensed the conversation would be difficult at the beginning, I would have been able to fortify myself.

I hurried on to the lounge and reached it before Burton. I chose a table and two chairs in the far corner. No one else was in the room, and I felt relieved. I stared out the window. The weather remained extremely bad, and there was little visibility. Still, it distracted me from my grief.

I didn't hear Burton come into the room, but I sensed his presence and turned my head.

He smiled at me and sat in the second chair.

"How do we go about this?" I asked. "I'm sure you're much better at this than I am."

He didn't answer, so I said, "You're so good at this. You make people feel at ease."

Burton chuckled before he said, "You've decided to revert to the airhead again."

"Sometimes it's fun to act naive."

"Right, so what is your plan?"

"I honestly don't have one, but I want to tell you about Heather." I told him what happened. I carefully kept everything factual.

"And you think she had some ulterior purpose?"

I smiled. Yes, he caught it, too, but then, that's just one more reason I love the guy. He rarely misses anything.

"What do you think?" Again, that's a good psychological device to get the other person to talk.

"I've known Heather for about three years," he said. "She's not a bad person, and—"

"Okay, stop being the perfect Christian and sinless pastor—"

"You know I don't talk about parishioners—"

"This is murder, Burton. We both have lost—" I stopped, unable for a moment to go on. It was another unexpected stab of grief. My eyes clouded, and I bit my lip so I wouldn't cry.

He stared at me, and both of us remained silent. He clasped my right hand. "I miss her, too, you know."

I hugged him and held on. I think it was the action of a grieving parishioner, but it was probably also the action of a woman who loved the man in front of her and shared a mutual grief with him. I clung to him, and he held me tightly. He wasn't holding me as if I were a church member.

"Julie, I love you," he whispered. "I will work through this—this problem of mine. Just don't pull away from me now. I loved Twila. I'm in deep emotional pain. I feel as if I've lost two of the people I love most." He put a hand under my chin and tilted my face toward his. He kissed me once, gently.

I didn't know if I should listen to my head or my heart.

His deep, deep blue eyes bored into mine. "Would you believe me if I said I missed you?" he asked. "I've missed you more than I've ever missed anyone."

I nodded.

He pulled me closer. His hands were in my hair, caressing the nape of my neck. My heart won the battle. I lost my self-control. We held each other for a long time. His arms were over my shoulders, and I held him, as we sometimes called it, by the lower rung. I loved the smell of Burton, even the cheap aftershave he always used. It was him, and he was there to share my deep inner pain. He kissed me again, and his cheeks were as wet as mine. I didn't pull back, but I clung to him.

I'm still awkward talking to God. But hardly aware of what I was doing, I silently thanked God for this man I loved and asked Him to heal both of us.

I prayed, I thought. *I actually prayed and I didn't even think about it. It just happened.* That was a spiritual breakthrough for me, and I knew it. I had never prayed spontaneously before.

As Burton held me, calmness slowly penetrated my emotional pain. Something—something mystical—maybe miraculous—had taken place. I was at peace. In that moment, I realized how effective prayer can be. Peace slowly moved across my chest, and the overwhelming grief crept away.

He released me and took my face in both his hands and softly kissed my lips.

I didn't resist. He pulled back, and I saw the tenderness in his eyes. We stood and held each other close for a long time. We didn't need words. In fact, I feared that if I said anything, it would spoil the serene moment we shared.

22

A few minutes later, Burton and I left the lounge, walking hand in hand to the now-empty theater. We discussed our strategy. We decided to call in each of those who had been passengers on the fourth Zodiac, one at a time.

We knew each other well enough that we didn't need verbal direction. Intuitively, I knew he would observe closely when I asked questions, and I would do the same for him. Our hope was to learn something new—anything that would give us a few clues toward solving the murder.

The one thing we didn't want was to have the group of them sitting together and sharing their perspectives with each other. On an episode of *NYPD* years ago, one of the policemen said it contaminated the evidence. That made sense, and I never forgot it.

We sat and I copied his list of the passengers in the fourth Zodiac, beginning with Jon Friesen, who came back in the third Zodiac. I pointed to his name. "Let's call him first."

"That's all right with me."

"As soon as we finish with him, we'll ask him to send in the next person on our list," I said, "and in this case it will be Heather."

He said nothing, but he gave me a thumbs-up.

"By doing it that way, you and I can have a couple of minutes alone between interviews, and we'll have the opportunity to compare our insights."

"Let the show begin," he said.

Burton went to get Jon, who told Burton that he would be up within a few minutes. When he finally came to the door, he paused, and I thought he was going to go into one of those bodybuilder poses. That wasn't quite what he did. He lifted his arms to the top of the door frame (his muscles bulged), and he seemed to be doing isometric exercises. He made no noise and waited until we made eye contact.

"I'm here, babe. Whenever you need me."

I decided to ignore that overly fresh tone.

"Sit down," Burton said in that quiet, soothing voice he uses so well.

"Sure thing, Burton," Jon said, but his gaze never left my face.

"Tell us what you know about Twila's death."

"First, I didn't do it—"

"Did anyone accuse you?"

"I don't know—did they?" He had lost his swaggering pose. He turned to me. "Are you accusing me?"

"Let Burton ask the questions," I said.

"Go ahead. Ask." This time he looked at Burton. I sensed hostility in his voice.

"Tell us about you and Twila."

"She was a friend. A good friend. In fact, an exceptionally good friend."

"Really?" I interjected without thinking. "You gave me the impression that she had been your therapist for a few months, but you had no personal relationship with her."

Jon flashed me his best smile, and it probably worked on most women. He focused on my face as if nothing else in the world mattered. "I told you what you wanted to hear."

"What do you mean by that?"

"You liked me and you wanted me to talk, so I told you what you wanted to hear."

I changed my mind about him. I had first thought he was a borderline personality. Now I decided added to that he definitely had a few crossed wires. One thing to watch for in borderline personalities is how quickly they can jump from one mood to another. I wondered what medication he took—or neglected to take.

"Tell us about your friendship," Burton said.

"We were friends. We liked each other. We talked."

"About what?" Burton leaned slightly forward.

"You know, things. Movies, books, church stuff. God, sometimes."

"Did you like her?"

"Yeah, sure. Everybody liked Twila."

"Honestly, did you like her?" Burton said softly and in a quiet, intimate tone.

"Oh, she got heavy on my back about things, but yeah, she was all right."

"And you were one of her patients?"

"For a time."

"But you weren't seeing her as your therapist just prior to the cruise."

"Yeah. That's right, like I told Julie. I stopped."

"Want to tell us about it?" Burton asked.

"Not really, but I want to help, so I'll tell you anything you want." He told us that three years earlier, his wife had left him. She was his third wife, but she was the one he had really loved. He became angry and trashed his estranged wife's house. The police arrested him, and the judge said that if he'd get psychiatric help, he would let him go.

"So that's when you started to go to Twila."

"Sure, why not? I was a church member—not your church. I was a member of a small church on Highway 138 called the Holy Family of God. My parents, now both dead, had been charter members at your church. They were gone, but Twila had been part of your church since I was a teen. Everyone I talked to said she was the best, so I went to her."

"Did she help?"

"I'm supposed to say yes because everybody thinks she was a wonder-worker."

J on's response startled Burton, which was what he intended. The beginning of a smile appeared at the corners of his mouth.

"You're saying that Twila didn't help you?"

"Nah, she didn't. I mean, not much. But I got a lot of meds from her."

"Do they help?" I asked.

"When I take them, they sure do."

"Are you taking them now?" Burton asked.

Jon leaned back in his chair. "Uh, well, I started again today. See, I take Lexapro, twenty milligrams a day—"

"That's a high dose level," I said.

"That's what she said, too."

"What else do you take?" Burton asked. "I mean, *when* you take your meds?"

"I take Abilify—"

"You're bipolar?" I asked.

He shrugged. "Sometimes, I guess. I also take occasional lithium, which is supposed to make one side of my brain speak to the other." He looked straight at me and laughed as if we shared a private joke.

"Did Twila prescribe all three of them?"

"Can't remember."

"I'm sure she wouldn't have given you both Abilify and lithium—they're usually given for bipolar, but she wouldn't have prescribed both—"

"So I have more than one doctor."

Burton and I stared at each other.

He's stranger than I thought.

"Tell us about your trip to Brown Bluff," Burton said in an abrupt shift of topic.

"Do I start when I was born, or fast-forward to the day of her death, including what I ate for breakfast?"

"Just start with getting off the Zodiac when it landed."

"Sure, I can do that." He repeated what he had already told me. In fact, he repeated it almost word for word as if he had memorized his answers.

Burton kept switching from his account of the island to his medication and his feelings about Twila. Both of us became aware that when he gave us more than a smirky answer, it was the same wording each time, with almost no variation.

After perhaps fifteen minutes, Burton got up, shook Jon's hand, and thanked him for coming. He asked Jon if he would send in Heather.

"Anything for you," he said. But he looked at me.

———

While we waited, Burton put his finger to his lips and nodded toward the door. I understood and sat in silence. Burton waited another few seconds and said loudly, "We'll see what Heather says."

A few seconds later the sound of light footsteps carried through the corridor. We stared at each other. Burton smiled as if to say, "Just as I thought."

Donny Otis tapped on the door. "I know you wanted Heather next, but—well, I'd like to get in here and get it over with. If you don't mind, I mean." He had a nervous habit of rubbing his left index finger and thumb together.

"Yes, of course it's all right," Burton said.

Donny stood quietly as if waiting for direction. I knew him by name, but I don't recall that we had ever spoken to each other. He was one of those people who came early and sat in the second row. At that church they have a ritual called the passing of the peace where people get up and shake hands with each other and say, "The peace of the Lord Jesus Christ be with you." The other person is supposed to say, "And with you."

I mention that because Donny didn't participate. He sat in his pew, head down, and didn't act as if he knew anyone else was there. When we stood to sing, he opened his hymnbook, but from where I sat, and I always seemed to be several rows behind him, I don't think he opened his mouth. At the church they sometimes projected choruses on large screens. When they did that, he didn't look at the screens.

"Thanks for coming in," Burton said and extended his hand.

He shook Burton's hand. I extended mine, and he took it. His hand was about the deadest I had ever shaken.

"Tell us about you and Twila," I said. "How well did you know her?"

Donny stared blankly at me for perhaps half a minute. I guessed his age to be about forty-five or so. He had that male-pattern baldness with little hair on top, long sideburns, and a goatee. He was probably close to six feet tall, and he must have weighed 250 pounds. He was one of those men whose body was normal shaped, but he carried a watermelon-sized stomach in front of him.

"I did nothing to Twila. I wouldn't hurt her. I truly would not hurt her." For such a large man, his voice was quite high-pitched and whiny.

"Do you feel someone has accused you?"

"I don't know," he said. He leaned forward and started the index finger–thumb thing again. "You might as well know—if someone hasn't already told you.

I'm sure I'll be a suspect once we get back to the States."

"Why is that?"

"I tried to kill my wife. Twice."

"Tell us about that," I said in my most professional tone.

"The first time she made me so angry—no, Twila says—said—I shouldn't talk that way. It's my issue, not hers."

He paused, and I smiled to indicate I agreed.

"My wife touched places in me where I was vulnerable. Like we had no kids, and she always blamed me and said I wasn't man enough. That made me angry—" He looked at me imploringly. "See what I mean?"

"Go on."

"So one time I grabbed her by the throat. I probably would have killed her, but she kicked me, made me lose my grip, ran into the bedroom, and locked the door. She called the police."

"And what happened?"

"It happened twice. Both times she broke away from me, but—"

"But what?" Burton prompted.

"But the second time was the problem. I stabbed her."

"It was an act of violence," Burton said.

"That's why I'm sure I'll be a suspect."

"Go back to your situation. Did the police arrest you?"

Tears flooded his eyes. "They did. I mean, they did the second time."

"How were you charged?" I asked.

"My wife—Verna is her name—but she doesn't go to our church, which is one of our problems. That's been a big issue since—"

"I'm lost," Burton said. "You lost me between the arrest and Verna."

"It was like this. I was in the kitchen. I did all the cooking. Verna could do it, but she has defective taste buds or something. She can't even distinguish the difference between anise and oregano. I got tired of flavorless food and took over the cooking—"

"We got that part," I said. "What happened?"

"I was cooking meat loaf—that's my specialty—and ordinarily she didn't say much, but this time she started complaining about my spending money for such a good cut of meat only to have it ground into hamburger. See what I mean? Defective taste buds. She couldn't tell the difference!"

"So what happened next?" I asked. It was going to take a long time to tell a short story.

"I grabbed the butcher knife. I mean, I suppose I did." He paused briefly and said, "No, no, that's not accurate. I had finished chopping the carrots and the cucumbers for the salad. I like my cucumbers small, like—"

"Did you stab her with the knife?"

"I guess I did."

"You guess? You don't know?"

"You're right. I do know." Just as he said that, he stopped the nervous rubbing of his fingers. "I did it. I cut her arm. It wasn't bad—just a nick. She grabbed a broom and fought me off. She jumped on me, scratched my face, and bit my fingers. I collapsed on the floor, and she called the police." He went on to explain that the court-appointed attorney negotiated a plea bargain. He wouldn't have to serve time if he agreed to see a therapist.

"So they sent you to Twila?"

"Oh no, no. You see, Verna wouldn't agree to my spending money for someone as good as Twila." He told us that he went to three different counseling centers and talked to two different pastors. "I didn't go to you, Burton, because—well, I was too ashamed. Don't feel offended—"

"I'm not offended. So when did you go to Twila?"

"When Verna realized that I wasn't getting any better—I mean, I didn't get violent, but she said the anger was still in my eyes—"

"And then you went to see Twila?"

"No. Verna went to see Twila and begged her to take me but for a lower fee. She agreed, and then I went to Twila." In long, verbose statements he started to describe the counseling he had gotten from others. By the end of his second visit to Twila, she had given him an antidepressant. "I'm not on it now," he said. "She wanted me to have it until I was better."

"Did Twila help you?"

"Oh yes, yes, she certainly did. That woman is—was wonderful. She helped me see where my aggression came from. Do you want to hear about that part?"

Burton shook his head. "Do you feel you're healed?"

"Twila wouldn't say it that way. She said I'm stabilized. I guess I am. I haven't had any violent episodes in more than two years."

"Sounds cured to me," Burton said.

"I feel I am, but Twila said—"

"We understand," I said.

He told us in lengthy detail that he and his wife stayed together. Both of them taught at a school about fifteen miles south of Riverdale in Fayetteville. His wife didn't like to travel and had turned down Twila's invitation for the cruise.

If he had been one of my clients, I would have let him talk, but I felt he had told us everything he could. Burton, ever the pastor, listened without interrupting.

He said he now spoke to young people at some group called Anger Anonymous.

"Oh yes!" I said. I realized I had read his case study, even though Twila had disguised it enough that most people wouldn't have made the connection. To cover up, I asked, "Did you know that Twila prepared lectures of her case studies?"

"Oh yes, yes, indeed." He became animated. "And I'm one of the cases. She chose me as an example of someone who had been misdiagnosed by others. She showed me a list of about maybe twenty things people need to look for—"

"You mean she showed you what she was going to teach?"

"Sure she did. I signed a waiver, too."

"A waiver?" Burton asked. "What kind of waiver?"

"I gave her permission to tell my story. She said she didn't want to use real names, and I understood. I said I'd be glad to come to any of her lectures and answer questions. I want to be open about this and to help—"

"So you signed the—the waiver," Burton said. "Just one copy?"

"Oh no. Two. She kept one; I have one."

I had no questions. I wasn't surprised that Twila had asked him to sign, but I was amazed at the delight he took in being a case study.

Burton asked a number of questions, and Donny answered without hesitation. He had clearly relaxed.

Donny told us that shortly before getting off the Zodiac, Twila whispered to him, "You've remained stable. I'm proud of you."

Something about that statement didn't sound right. "Did she really say that to you? Those exact words?"

The startled look in his eyes made me know I was correct. He hung his head. "No, I told her I was doing great and that I felt the Lord had given me strength to overcome my angry impulses. She said she could tell, and then she said she was proud of me. She didn't say anything about my being stable." He apologized for lying to us.

He also said that he helped Twila get off the Zodiac. He took the life jacket from her and threw it on the ground next to his. He walked alone—which didn't surprise me. He said he noticed nothing and didn't realize that they were two people short on the return trip.

He had nothing more to add.

24

The third person to come in was Pat Borders. I knew him slightly. I remember that he wasn't a member of the church but attended regularly. He was a moderately successful real estate broker in the area. He was tall, quite thin, with sandy hair that just missed being red. He always looked malnourished to me, as if he needed a dozen good meals to make him look healthy.

"I'm surprised you came on the cruise," Burton said to him. I think those words were as much for my benefit as for Pat's.

"Yeah, well, I wanted to come. You see, Antarctica is the one place I've always wanted to visit." He explained that he was a world traveler, had been on all the other continents except this one. "This seemed like a good time to come."

"So Twila invited you for that reason?"

"Oh no, I begged her. And I insisted on paying my own way. You know Twila. She didn't like that, but I finally talked her into letting me come on the cruise."

He lied, and I couldn't figure out the reason. He was one of those people who constantly talked about what a great salesman he was—maybe that was part of being successful in his field.

"You paid your own way?" I asked.

"Okay, I didn't."

"That's what I thought."

"But I tried. I really tried." He looked away and finally said, "All right, the truth is, she didn't want me on this cruise. You know how I got on it? Only because Judson Knight broke his leg in a ski accident three weeks ago."

"So she already had the space filled and—?" I asked.

"Yeah, that's right."

"Why didn't she want you?"

He shrugged.

"Were you a patient of Twila's?" Burton asked.

"Why would you think that?"

I smiled. "That's a good evasion." I decided to flatter his ego. "Very good answer, Pat."

He smiled in return.

"So were you a patient?"

"Yeah. Well, I had been. I wasn't currently a patient."

"You felt you were cured?" Burton asked, and his eyes told me he knew the answer.

Pat shrugged a second time and looked away.

I became aware of the waves lashing against the ship. The rough waters had increased.

"No."

"Tell us about your situation."

"You can check her records when you get back. I was a patient for about three years." He held up his hands. "Okay, I play around with drugs, but I'm not an addict."

"But you use?"

"Sometimes. Yeah, now and then."

"Did Twila say you were an addict?"

"Oh yeah, sure, but she's a shrink—you know, that's how they're supposed to talk."

I smiled. "I'm a shrink."

"Yeah, but you're different, you know. You don't keep trying to make me say things like 'Hi, my name is Pat, and I'm an addict.'"

"Oh, so you mean you use, but—"

"I don't like being called an addict. It sounds demeaning, you know." He went on to say that he liked to consider himself an occasional user. "Or you can call me a recreational user."

He told us that he saw no cure for himself, and Twila had reluctantly stopped treating him.

"That's surprisingly insightful," I said. "Most ad—most users—aren't able to see that about themselves."

He shrugged and smiled. "Twila said I was bright."

"I'm sure you are."

"See, it's like this," Pat said. "I can go a full month without a fix—one time I went three months, and that was after I was with Twila. But something happens, and I do it again."

"What do you think happens?" I asked.

Pat shrugged.

"Why don't you tell me?" I said. "I'd like to understand."

"Whatever it takes for me to need to chill." He leaned forward as if he wanted to plead his case. "See, it's like this. I have this highly, highly intense job—"

"Real estate," I said. "I know, and I understand you're good at it."

"I'm the best. That's part of the problem. I am good. Last year my gross income was great—"

"But—"

"But doubts creep in, and I keep hearing myself ask, 'Can I reach that income level again? How do I keep this up?' Then after a while—"

"You turn to drugs."

"Yeah, and I can't kick them."

"Do you want to?" I asked.

He stared at me for a long time before he shook his head. "Not really. That's why Twila wouldn't see me again."

"Did you like Twila?"

He hesitated even longer before he said, "I detested her."

25

Twila said she could cure me! She promised me that I would be free, and she couldn't do that! She failed me!" Pat slammed his fist on the table. "She failed me."

"No good therapist would ever say that," I said. I moved closer so that my face was less than six inches from his. I could smell the coffee on his breath.

He blinked several times as if shocked that I would challenge his statement. "Well, not in so many words, but that's what she meant!"

"Really?"

"Okay, I *thought* she'd cure me. I—well, I want to lose the desire to—to, you know, to use. She couldn't cure me."

"So you hated her for that?"

"No, not for that."

"Not for that," I said. "But you did hate her."

"I didn't mean—no, I—"

"You hated her," Burton said in that calm voice again. "Just tell us why."

"She was so—so sanctimonious." He swore, cursed her name, and added, "She acted as if she was better than anybody else."

"You mean better than you?" Burton said.

"Okay, better than me. I detested her. Whenever she opened her mouth, it was always to talk about God. I hate God! I hated Twila!" He stood and lunged for Burton.

I grabbed his arm. He was strong, but I was able to hold him back.

Burton didn't flinch. He waited several seconds and grabbed Pat's throat. "Calm down. I'll release the pressure when you relax your body."

"What medication are you on?" I asked.

"Just a little something to raise my serotonin level, I think."

"Specifically?" I asked.

"I don't know. See, I threw a couple of handsful of, you know, prescription drugs into a vitamin bottle and brought it on the trip."

"So you don't know what you're taking?" I asked.

"No, and I'm sorry. Truly I'm sorry for what's happened to Twila. I hated her, but I didn't want to kill her."

He seemed genuinely contrite. I released his arm and sat down.

"Sorry. Most of the time it works all right for me, but sometimes I get a little—well, bizarre. Instead of chilling, I get so angry I can't control myself."

Burton released his hold, and Pat sat still. Perspiration broke out on his forehead. "She wouldn't give me anything yesterday. I asked her, but she said she had nothing with her."

"And you searched her room?"

"I would have if I'd thought of it."

"One more question I have," I said. "Did you know she was going to use your case in a series of lectures?"

"Sure, I knew. That's how I persuaded her to let me come. I said I'd tear up my agreement." He smiled at me. "She made me sign a waiver."

"You read the piece about yourself." It was a statement, not a question.

"Yeah, sure. It wasn't very good—she made me look like a loser—but yeah, I signed."

"If I take you to the ship's doctor and ask him to give you a tranquilizer, would that help?" I didn't know if the doctor had anything, but it was worth trying.

"I'd like that," he said.

I took Pat to the ship's doctor, who not only gave him a shot of Valium but said he'd keep him in the bed in what he called the sick bay. "He can stay here until we land in Ushuaia."

I thanked him and went back to the theater. Burton had already brought in Betty Freeman, the next person on our list.

She was leaning across the table and staring into his eyes when I walked in. She glanced around and saw me but ignored me. "You know, Burton, I think you have the most beautiful blue eyes I've ever seen."

"God gave them to me."

Betty laughed. "That was very good. And that dark, curly hair." She reached over and touched his curls. "So soft. Not like most men. I have a little natural curl, but nothing like what you have. Whenever I see you behind the pulpit, I want to go up there and run my hands through your hair."

Burton smiled. "God gave me the hair, as well."

"If we're through with the eyes and hair," I said, "Betty, we need to ask you a few questions."

"Anything. Oh, anything, of course."

We talked to her for perhaps seven or eight minutes. We learned nothing new. She had been on the fourth Zodiac. She didn't pay any attention to Twila. "Going over, I had a nice—really nice—conversation with Jon Friesen. He was complaining about not feeling well, but he was still nice to me. He's such a gentleman, you know. He lost his wife a few years ago, and he's so lonely—"

"Oh, right," I said.

"Did you talk to anyone else?" Burton hurriedly asked.

She couldn't remember. She didn't think so. She said she walked beside Donny and was with him most of the time.

"Most of the time?"

"Well, yes, except at one point—and I don't know where it was—he said he wanted to be alone, so I joined a group and walked around the gentoo penguins. I never get tired of looking at them. And there were two seals—"

"And you didn't talk to Donny again?"

"I did on the boat going back to the ship. Or I tried. He turned away from me and didn't say a word." She smiled before she said, "He did help me wash my boots."

I didn't think we would glean much more information from her. I made a note about Donny leaving her.

"Were you a patient of Twila's?" Burton asked.

"Client. She called us clients."

"Were you a client?" Burton asked.

She nodded.

"Do you mind telling us why she treated you?"

Betty told us a sad story about repeated sexual assault from her stepfather. She said she thought she had dealt with her issues, but her first husband beat her, and she left him. Her second husband was an alcoholic, and she divorced him. "All of that happened before my twenty-fourth birthday. I haven't been in any serious relationship since then. That was five years ago. I'm twenty-nine now—"

"Did you know Twila used you as a case study?" Burton asked. "I read the account—even though she changed your name and cleverly disguised your identity."

"Of course I knew that," Betty said. "I never would have signed the waiver without reading it first."

After Betty left, Burton shook his head. "Sad, isn't it?"

"Yes, but what about Borders? Do you think he's capable?"

"Capable, yes. But—"

"But he seems erratic. He acts on the passion of the moment."

"That's my guess," he said. "Twila's murder may have been an act of passion, but—"

"But whoever killed her had to have thought far enough in advance to take a knife—or whatever it was—to the landing site."

"I don't think we want to rule out Pat Borders."

"Agreed," I said.

Burton smiled, caught himself, and did one of those polite coughs people do to cover up emotions.

Just then Heather tapped on the door, opened it, and came inside. She sat down. Before either of us had a chance to ask her a question, she said, "Yes, I was a patient of Twila's. Yes, I have a lot of problems—and I refuse to discuss them with you."

"That's fine," I said, although it wasn't really all right. "But did you know she used you as a case study?" I didn't know if that was true, but the others had all been subjects of her book.

"Of course I knew—"

"And you signed a waiver?"

"Not at first," she said.

"Because?"

"She made me look, well, like a—a tart."

"Are you?" I asked.

"That's insulting," she said. "Anyway, after she changed a couple more of the details, I signed it."

"Earlier you told me that you saw two people walking away—"

"Sure, and that's all I know." She said it again. She was very straightforward. I didn't like her attitude, but I had no reason to doubt anything she said.

Burton asked a number of questions, and she guardedly answered them. She said she liked Twila and that she had been a client for six or seven months. "She has helped me like myself so much more." She said she had felt like damaged goods when she started therapy, but Twila had helped raise her self-esteem. "She is—uh, she was so wonderful. She helped me so much. I could never thank her enough for all she did for me."

Those words were genuine. I could read Burton's face on that one and knew he agreed.

We learned nothing from her or from Mickey Brewer, who followed. Thomas Tomlinson came after him. Both men had been patients. Brewer had suffered from post-traumatic stress disorder (PTSD). He had been an employee of an American company selling a new brand of cola called Jolt in East Africa. A group of rebels had captured him and held him for ransom. When the company didn't immediately pay, his captors beat him and sent pictures of his bruised body to the company. He had been beaten five different times before they finally paid the ransom. When he returned, he threatened to sue the company, but they gave him a generous settlement. Months later the first symptoms of PTSD showed up. He reported acute anxiety. He tightened up, went into a panic, or began to perspire profusely whenever he heard loud noises. During heavy thunderstorms, he locked himself in a bathroom or closet—any small space that was dark. The slightest noise at night awakened him, and night sweats were so bad that he often had to change the bedding.

He explained—and we seemed to have to pull out every detail—that Twila had helped him to confront his memories. She had used a technique she called childhood regression, as well as some medication (of which he didn't recall the name).

"Twila helped. She really did. It took a long time—nearly four years—but now I sleep all through the night, and I don't take any medication." He said he had a dozen Xanax in his room. He had not taken any so far.

When we asked him about the Zodiac and the walk on the island, he could add no information. He said he remembered talking with Shirley Brackett. Beyond that, he couldn't add anything.

Thomas Tomlinson was next. Before we asked, he told us, "You might as well know, I went to her because I had been arrested for DUI five times." He quickly added, "That was during my grad school days—before I began to teach." The only way he could get his license back was to go to a two-day DUI course. Afterward he also voluntarily went to see Twila. "I was determined to beat this."

She put him on Anabuse at first, but it made him sick even when he wasn't drinking. Once she prescribed Naltrexone—which was quite new at the time—it had done the trick for him.

He said his father had been an alcoholic, and so had his grandfather. He went on to say that Twila had helped him realize that he was one of those individuals who couldn't have a single drink of alcohol. "I tried cutting back to one drink, but that only started me. I couldn't stop drinking for at least two days and sometimes a full week."

Both of us listened to him. I was used to hearing such stories. That's how I make my living, but I wondered about Burton. He never showed any boredom or made any attempt to rush people. Yes, he would have made an excellent therapist.

"And did you sign a waiver so she could use your story?" I asked.

"Of course. I have no problem with that," Thomas said. "She wrote my case study objectively and correctly."

After that we interviewed Sue Downs. She was in her midthirties and had dull-looking ash blond hair and brown eyes. If it hadn't been for her sloppy posture, she could have looked attractive. Of course, she'd have to do more than let her short hair hang straight and buy something other than those amorphous black dresses and black sweaters she favored.

She had also been a patient. She'd gone through a lengthy postpartum depression. Her baby had lived only four hours. She struggled with guilt. "I kept asking if God was punishing me for something I had done."

She admitted that she had "done sinful things" before her marriage, and she was sure that God was showing her she couldn't get away with them. Twila assured her that she wasn't being punished.

"In fact, Twila taught me about a God of love—something I hadn't really understood before. Until then I believed that God was always watching the bad things I did so He could punish me."

She spoke with such tenderness and with deep gratitude for Twila, it seemed obvious to both of us that she wasn't the kind who would have hurt anyone.

As we expected, she told us that she was one of the case studies. Burton nodded and winked at me. He had already figured that out. And yes, she had signed a statement that gave Twila complete freedom to do whatever she wanted with the case study.

"There is nothing I wouldn't do for that wonderful, wonderful woman."

She was so effusive I studied her closely. Sometimes it's the bit about overdoing the explanation. But she convinced us of her innocence with the last thing she said.

I wanted to get pictures of me with a lot of penguins. Mark—that's my husband—adores studying pictures, and he makes beautiful albums for me." Sue's husband worked for the postal service and had been unable to get his vacation changed to go with her. "I don't think he really wanted to come anyway." She started telling about all the times she had begged him to travel, but he always said no. "But he's nice in that he doesn't mind my going without him."

"What about the pictures?" I asked.

"Oh yes, the pictures. Sorry," she said. "I have one of those 35mm cameras and I was having trouble getting the film threaded. It's an old camera—belonged to my father and—"

"And what about the camera?" I asked. I knew it would take an hour to get the information I wanted unless I kept intervening.

"Oh yes, that. Well, that nice Laird Hege came to my rescue. He was in the other boat, but he stayed with me until it was time for his Zodiac to start loading. Just then, Jeff walked up to where we were. He was so helpful. He stayed with me until we finished up the roll of film, and he put in a new roll for me. Wasn't that nice of him? I can hardly wait to see the pictures. He took at least one of me standing next to a sea lion. Well, of course, I don't mean next to one, but I was very quiet and stopped about five feet from the ugly old thing. He didn't make a move while I stood there. It's so funny to see them scoot across the ground when they want to go back to the sea and—"

"Was Jeff with you the whole time?" I asked.

She thought for a minute before she said, "No, actually, he wasn't. He joined Laird and me. I hadn't noticed him before because I was busy trying to get the best photo angles. And I had to step very carefully to avoid all the guano. It's so smelly and so—"

"And so Jeff just walked up to you."

"Yes, and he was so nice. I teased him because he didn't have on his life jacket—"

"No one had them on, did they?" I asked. "We all left them at the landing site."

"That's what I meant. But I had seen Jeff shortly after we got off. He had his on and started to walk away with somebody—I'm not sure who it was—and when he showed up later, without one, I teased him."

"What do you mean?"

"Jeff and I were classmates at North Clayton High School. Did you know that? I actually dated him twice, but he lost interest in me or something."

"About the teasing," I said and hoped my voice sounded soft.

"Oh, well, yes, that's why I mentioned North Clayton. We had a principal named Jim Steele, who didn't like Jeff. He was always calling him to tuck in his shirt or to tie his shoes or something."

"So?"

"Oh yes, well, he didn't have the life jacket on when he joined me, so I called out, 'Did Mr. Steele catch you and make you go back to the Zodiac and leave your life jacket?'"

"He laughed and said something like, 'No, I noticed it before anyone caught me.' And then we laughed about old cue-ball Steele. He was bald, you see, and—"

"Yes, I see," I said. I looked at Burton and met his gaze. "How long were you and Laird together before Jeff came up?"

"I really don't know. It must have been ten minutes. No, probably more like fifteen. But I don't know for sure. I know that by the time he came, the third Zodiac had started to load. Maybe someone else could be more precise about the time."

"Thanks, Sue," Burton said.

"I don't know if I had anything helpful to add. Did I?"

"Thanks," I said, not wanting to give her a direct answer. "We know how much you cared about Twila. It's nice to hear your experience. She was a wonderful woman."

"A saint," Sue said. "An absolutely true saint of God."

I got up and gave her a quick hug and guided her out the door. "Would you ask Jeff Adams to come in?"

Once Sue closed the door behind her, Burton said, "That was interesting." I knew he entertained the same thoughts that ran through my mind.

On a piece of paper I wrote Jeff's name. It wasn't that I needed to write it, but I wanted to keep notes. By the time we interviewed eleven people, I knew their stories would run together, and I wanted to keep them separate.

I wrote that he had left the Zodiac with the life preserver. When Sue saw him—which would have been at least ten to fifteen minutes later—he wasn't wearing the life jacket. I didn't know how much time Twila spent out of sight with the killer, but I figured ten minutes certainly would have been enough.

Burton said nothing, but I knew he had the same thought I had. Jeff had not been with Sue the whole time. He was no longer wearing his life jacket. That proved nothing, but it was the first significant thing we had learned.

27

Jeff Adams came in next. He was one of the half dozen or so people on the cruise I didn't know. Burton seemed to know him well and gave him an enthusiastic hug when he came into the room.

Jeff was about medium height and what I would call hefty—not fat, but what people used to call stout. He wore tight jeans, which made his legs seem even more bowed. He wore a tight T-shirt with a wool shirt slung carelessly over his right shoulder. He had thin hair, pulled severely back and tied in a ponytail. I was surprised that he wore only a T-shirt, because I thought it was always a little cool on the ship and wore either a hoodie or a sweater.

Jeff had tattoos on both arms. No words, only designs, but I didn't know what they were. From the color of them, they looked as if they had been there a long time. He wore a small gold earring in his right ear.

"I don't think I've met you," I said and extended my hand. "But I know who you are."

Jeff pumped my hand with such vigor, I felt as if I might not have circulation restored for an hour.

"I know who you are," he said. He had a wide, infectious grin. "I've seen your picture on Twila's desk."

I had forgotten about the picture. We had climbed Stone Mountain together in September. Despite her bad leg, she went all the way up to the top with me—although she was a little slow. We saw someone she knew who had a digital camera. He snapped the picture of us together and e-mailed it to both of us the next day. Twila had her copy printed and put in a frame on her desk.

"So you must have been one of Twila's clients," I said.

"Oh, absolutely. I was with her nearly three years, but she changed my life. I'm a different man today—totally, totally new and born again by the blood of the Lamb and sanctified by the atoning work of the Messiah Jesus." He had a preacher's loud voice, and I sensed he was just about ready to launch into a sermon.

"Are you a preacher?"

"A lay preacher, ma'am. How did you know?"

"Just a lucky guess." Burton's eyes said he would like to kick me, so I decided to behave.

"Yes, ma'am, I preach at the county jail every Saturday night and conduct a prayer meeting every Thursday night at the DeKalb County—"

"I see," I said in my most noncommittal voice. "You and Burton seem to know each other. Tell me a little about yourself—I mean, other than your preaching tasks."

That may have been a mistake. *A little* turned out to be nearly half an hour of lurid detail about his criminal past. He also told me that he and Sue Downs had been in high school together. If he told us the truth, however, he had done more in those years than most criminals do in a lifetime. He described four cases of armed robbery and two tales of extortion, and in one of them he broke a man's legs. He had tried to kill someone—shot her three times—but the woman lived. He also had served county jail time on minor charges. He explained that he was not in prison today only because the police had made an illegal search.

"But that's where the grace of God began to flow into my sin-filled life and utter despair and brought me into deep repentance and—"

"What about Twila? How did she come into your life?"

"*That's* when she came into my life. She knew my sister, Ev Lewis, and at my sister's urging came to see me just before they released me." He told us (in what must have taken ten minutes) that Twila talked to him with a kind voice. Just before she left, she asked, "Jeff, don't you want God's peace? Aren't you tired of being alone in this world? Don't you want a friend who will love you no matter what you do?"

Jeff went into vivid detail of the power of her words. "It wasn't just her words, either, but the blessed and most holy magnitude of God's loving Holy Spirit behind them." It took him five minutes to tell his conversion story—and despite the redundancy and over-the-top language, it was a poignant tale.

I'll admit that once I got past his preacherly tones, his story fascinated me. He spoke with deep conviction, and the intensity of his eyes convinced me of his sincerity.

When he paused, I said, "Jeff, did you kill Twila?"

"Oh no, ma'am, I couldn't do that. I am no longer capable of such degradation and violence."

That's the short version. The real one would have taken a full page to tell. Everything about him said he spoke the truth.

But I wondered. I had met people in my practice who had done really terrible things, but they were able to convince themselves they had not done anything wrong. I wondered if Jeff was one of them.

Like the others, he had seen Twila's written account of his life and had approved it. "The only thing I didn't like was that she cut out a lot of the terrible things I did BC—before Christ."

"But you signed a permission form?"

"Yes, and in fact, she used my real name. I insisted." His chest seemed to puff out with pride.

I pulled my portion of the manuscript and skimmed through the pages. His story was chapter eight. I showed it to him.

"I'll bet it's the best of them."

"I'm sure it's the most violent—"

"Oh, that, too."

Jeff Adams left shortly after that. I was weary with talking to people. We still had to talk to nearly half of them. "So far, do you have any gut reaction?" I asked Burton.

"I want to keep my mind clear until we've interviewed them all."

"Good answer, Burton. But you do have some doubts already, don't you?"

"You know me too well." He laughed and added, "But that's all right. It works both ways, doesn't it? And you're wrong about Jeff."

"How did you know I had doubts?"

"I read your mind," he said. "No, that's not true. I know you well enough that I felt you had doubts."

"How so?" That's another good way to get an answer without saying anything.

"I think he's genuine."

"Because he preaches when he talks?"

"No, I believe him because of his eyes. His eyes don't lie."

He had me there. "Agreed," I said.

This time he laughed out loud. He was mentally tired from all the interrogation, and he laughed far too much for such a stupid comment. But I'll take any kind of positive response to my smart mouth.

"Someone has to be lying," he said.

"Or maybe. . .maybe we haven't asked the right questions." I have no idea why I said that. I mean, I didn't know at that moment.

28

Shirley Brackett came in next with her older brother, Frank. I felt as if I were the big, bad wolf preying on Little Red Riding Hood. Neither of them had married. Frank had been the janitor at the Methodist church for nearly forty years. Shirley was the senior librarian at the Riverdale library.

Shirley spoke openly and candidly when we asked them anything—but Frank said nothing.

Frank was probably in his late sixties, or maybe he was just one of those people who looks old at thirty. He had thick brown hair going white at the temples, but it was the wrinkled skin that made him look old. He had clear brown eyes, a long aristocratic nose, and generally handsome features. His salt-and-pepper mustache was large but well kept.

By contrast, I guessed Shirley to be at least twenty years younger. Frank was about my height, but she was small, about five two and perhaps slightly over a hundred pounds. She had the same brown hair without the streaks of white. She had delicate features, blue eyes that seemed to whisper gentleness. Her slender shoulders, thin wrists, long-fingered hands, and tiny waist gave the impression of fragility.

She seemed to be quiet in a way that could easily be called timidity, and perhaps it was. Her voice was soft, and it was easy to see why people paid little attention to her. Maybe there was nothing much to pay attention to. She wore a soft mauve wool jacket and matching slacks with a creamy white blouse that had a simple plum-colored bow at the throat.

I liked her softness and the way she looked directly at me when she spoke. "Were both of you together the whole time after you landed at Brown Bluff?" I asked.

"Of course we were," Shirley said. She leaned forward and said, "Frank retired this year." She mouthed the word *dementia*. "He's grown quite forgetful in recent days, so I spend more time with him." She said that after their return, Frank would spend each weekday at a senior adult day-care group.

Frank smiled if I looked at him, but most of the time he said nothing. I don't know much about dementia, but I could see the deadness already starting to take over his eyes and his facial muscles. I revised my opinion of his age. His was probably closer to hers.

"Were either of you patients of Twila's?" Burton asked.

"As a matter of fact—I don't like saying that. It's such a cliché, isn't it? But yes, Frank was her patient for several years."

"What diagnosis? I mean, before—before his present condition?"

"Oh, he's schizophrenic. I keep him on his medication, and he functions fairly well. The problem, you see, is that after a few years, he has to change medication. That's where the stress comes in. He gets—well, let's say confused. When that happens, we have to change the medication. Twila was convinced that he built up an immunity to them. I believe she was correct."

Shirley offered to write a list of the medications Frank had taken, but Burton and I assured her it wasn't necessary.

"Frank never left you the whole time."

"I couldn't let him walk alone. He wants to pick up the penguins and pet them. He kneels down and tries to talk to them, and I have to remind him that he can't do that."

"Did you notice anything strange on the trip?"

"No. . .I don't think so. . . ."

"You hesitated," I said.

"*Strange* isn't exactly the word. Just something small—probably not worth mentioning."

"Try us," Burton said.

"Well, one thing that I thought was odd. I mean, it struck me as a bit peculiar."

"What was that?" This might take all night—and she might not have anything to say.

"I saw someone taking pictures—one of those digital cameras—"

"And that was odd because—?"

"I wondered what the person was photographing. I mean, there was nothing really. Two members of our group in the blue suits walking all alone. Maybe it was for perspective or something. I don't mean to—well, I used to do a lot of picture taking when Frank and I traveled. I had the distinct feeling—"

"Go on," I said. I hoped I wouldn't have to beg her for every sentence.

"It just struck me as plain odd. It was as if the person followed the couple and seemed more interested in taking pictures of them—and she was maybe fifty feet behind them. I say *she*, but I couldn't swear it was a woman. But wouldn't that strike you as odd?"

"Did the two people turn around and wave or anything?"

"Probably not—oh, I don't know, but they seemed, well, they seemed unaware. That's part of what struck me as odd. I'm sure the person with the camera didn't yell at them. You know, if they were going to pose, they would have stopped or something. But I doubt if they knew—"

"Can you tell us anything about the two people?"

"They both wore blue." She laughed. "That wasn't much of a joke, was it?" She closed her eyes as if to visualize the scene. "I didn't pay that much attention. One was taller—oh, again, I suppose that's obvious. I mean, one of them would almost have to be taller than the—"

"Did either of them have on a life jacket?"

"Oh, the taller one." She thought for a minute. "Definitely the taller. And I assume it was a man—"

"Because he was taller."

"Well, yes, I suppose, but it wasn't that. He took the other person's arm—I'm not sure how to say it, but it was, uh, well, more like the gesture of a man than a woman." She leaned forward and said, "I write cozy mysteries, and I'm always observing the way people move."

"She's published two books," Burton said. "She's a gentle soul, but she likes to kill people in print."

"Oh yes, I use a pen name, too. My pen name is Mary LaMuth. I don't know if you've read—"

"That's very interesting." I don't read cozy mysteries, and neither do any of my friends, so her achievements meant nothing to me. "Back to the couple. Anything else you can tell us?"

"They seemed to want to get away from everyone else. Maybe that's obvious. Maybe it's just the mind of Mary LaMuth working, but I had the impression—it's only an impression, mind you—I had the impression that when he took her arm—and I assume it was a man—he was, well, not forcing her, exactly. . .urging, perhaps?"

"Anything else you can tell us?"

"Not really. My curiosity was piqued—after all, I am a writer, you know—and I probably would have watched or even followed the photographer. Just curiosity."

"Why didn't you?"

"Frank had gotten ahead of me. He spotted the penguins and started calling to them as if they were chickens. And I have to watch him carefully."

"Just two more questions," I said, and already I knew the answer to the first. "Did Twila plan to use Frank as one of her case studies?"

"Oh yes. He signed the waiver or permission slip—whatever she called it. And just to be sure, I insisted on signing as a witness. You know, when he gets worse—and he will—he has—he is—I mean—"

"The other question. Can you tell us anything about who was taking the pictures?"

"I'm sorry, but I can't. As I said, I had the distinct impression that it was a woman, but I can't recall why. There was something about her. . . ." She drifted into silence for several seconds. She shook her head slowly. "I know there was something about her, but it's just not coming to me right now."

She promised she would let us know if she remembered.

As soon as she was out of the room, Burton and I stared at each other. "Who took the pictures?" he asked.

"Would the pictures tell us something?"

29

I did not kill Twila Belk!"

I looked up.

Heather slammed the door behind her. "Don't keep making everyone think I did it."

"What are you ranting about?"

"Ranting? Okay, call it what you want, but I'm angry—absolutely angry!" Her thick dark hair was parted in the middle and hung loose. She had looked beautiful before, but now she reminded me of an actress from the 1930s named Hedy Lamarr.

She slammed her purse on the table and sat down. "So let's get this clear right now. You've already questioned me once. All right? But ask whatever you want and let's get this over."

"Who thinks you killed Twila?"

"Everybody—well, I mean, several people."

"Why would they think that?"

"Because—because I got mad and said some stupid things to her, and several people heard me. That's why."

"What stupid things?" I asked before Burton could open his mouth. I'm quicker at things like that, and I love it when I jump in ahead of him. It also makes me feel bright.

"The day before, you know, before she died, I—well, I said some things."

"What?" I asked with an emphasis in my voice. "You might as well tell us. Or would you prefer we ask everyone else?"

"Oh no, no, please don't." Heather pulled a tissue from her purse and carefully wiped her eyes. She pulled out her compact and stared at herself in the mirror, brushing back a strand of raven-colored hair.

"Twila has, well, been after me for a while about something. I got tired of it."

"What did she bug you about?" Burton asked. He smiled, and I knew he jumped into the conversation to get ahead of me on that one.

"Okay, I smoke. Not a lot—"

"And—?" Burton prompted.

"She said the cigarettes affected my health." Heather looked away. "She's also a medical doctor, you know. Well, before she takes a patient, she insists they get a physical—anyplace—and have the doctor send the results to her."

413

"And—?" From the corner of my eye, I saw Burton's thumbs-up for pursuing that line. Heather didn't see it.

"Emphysema. I mean, I showed the first signs of it." She sighed. "It concerned her because, well, because I'm so young, you see."

Not that young. I didn't say the words out loud. I would have been willing to bet anyone that plastic surgery had kept that beautiful face beautiful at least ten years longer than it deserved. Or maybe I was still jealous.

"And she wanted you to quit smoking."

"She did. Like it was her own body. She was after me every time she caught me smoking."

"And—?" I said again and winked at Burton.

"Okay, the day before. Right after we came back from our first landing—"

"King George Island," I said.

"Whatever. Whatever." She waved away my words as if they didn't matter. "I stopped for a cigarette on the deck. She came by. And you know how she is—"

"Suppose you tell me," I said in that soft, professional voice. I love it when I can practice all those phrases I learned in grad school.

"She cared about me. Yes, I know that, but I still resent it when people say and do things for my good. I know that she cared about my well-being. She didn't want me to ruin my health, and I know that. She loved me—okay, I got that message, as well."

"And the problem was?"

"I resented it. Maybe I shouldn't have, but I did. I mean, I know the cigarettes may eventually kill me. Who doesn't know *that*? I didn't need her to—"

"Or did you feel guilty?" Burton asked. His voice was soft and comforting.

Heather stared at him for a few seconds and nodded. "Yes, of course, I felt guilty, so I attacked. I was angry at her, and I yelled at her and told her to mind her own business. And she said I was really angry at myself."

"Was she correct?" I asked. "Were you?"

"Yes. And that made me even angrier. I have tried to quit. Eight times I've tried during the past three months. Honest, I've tried and—and I am going to get free. I mean, as soon as we get back—"

"So what did Twila say?"

"She saw me smoking and looked at me. Just that. Just a look. If she'd said something, I might have gotten really, really mad—"

"So if she didn't say anything," I asked, "why were you upset?"

"Because she *didn't* say anything, that's why!" She looked around to make sure both of us got it. We nodded, and she said, "So I yelled at her. I told her that if she didn't stay out of my personal life, I'd make her sorry."

"What did you mean by 'make her sorry'?" Burton asked.

"How should I know? I was upset. I didn't know she was coming up behind me, or I would have waited until she was gone before I lit up."

"And other people heard you? Is that the problem?" I asked.

"Yes, and they whisper among themselves."

"What do they say?"

"It's not so much what they say. It's—well, it's the way they look at me. I can tell what they're saying behind my back. I just know."

"You know because—?"

"Because they act odd. They act extremely innocent as if they haven't said anything, but I know they've been talking about me." She brushed back her dark hair with her right hand. "Oh, I wish I had a cigarette now. It would calm my nerves."

She obviously showed signs of paranoia, but I waited to see if she had anything else to tell us.

"As a patient of Twila's, did you know she was going to use you as a case study?"

She sighed deeply. "We've been through this before, but okay, yes, I knew. Why wouldn't I know that?" I heard the anger in her voice.

"And you signed the consent form, didn't you?"

"No, I did not—not right then."

"Why?"

"She didn't think I was—well, curable. That's not the word she used, but that's what she meant."

"So that was the end?"

She shook her head, took out her compact, and carefully applied lipstick— which she didn't need—to those already bright red lips. "No, she disguised my identity and said no one could ever recognize me."

"Did you object then?"

"No, but after I signed, I decided not to see her again." Before either of us asked, she told us she had been a patient for a few months. Her company refused to keep paying, so Twila took her at five dollars a visit. She said she had been raped as a teenager. "Twila never believed that. She always thought I made it up."

I wanted to ask, "Did you make it up?" but I restrained myself and got a nice smile from Burton.

She started to ramble about her treatments, and I was ready to cut her off until she said something about being involved with Jon Friesen.

"Really?" I asked.

"Oh yes. We had appointments right after each other. Every Tuesday and Thursday I came out of Twila's office at ten minutes to six. Twila always liked to have ten minutes between appointments to compose herself before the next client. Jon followed me at six. Almost every time when I came out, he was there, waiting for me, and we talked until she called him into her office."

"And what about you and Jon? Do you have a good relationship?" As I asked the question, I thought about his heavy-handed come-on to me.

"Oh, now, and that's—well, that's probably the reason I was really ticked off at Twila."

"You lost me there," Burton said.

"Well, Jon and I became, uh, I mean, *intimate*." She smiled demurely. "We fell in love. We were going to get married in April. But he broke it off. He broke it off, but she put him up to it."

"How did she do that?" That's another question I learned in grad school.

"She told him I wasn't healthy enough for a mature relationship."

"Did she say that to you?" I asked. Such a statement didn't seem like anything Twila would say.

"Well, naturally, not to me. She wouldn't dare."

"What did she say?"

"I mean, she didn't say it in those words, but I knew what she meant. And then—can you believe this?—she said I should tell him, tell Jon. Can you believe that? I was supposed to tell him that I was too messed up in my head."

"And naturally you resisted?" Burton used exactly the right tone, and she almost purred. "Did you?"

She shook her head. "Three days before we came on the cruise—three lousy days—he broke up with me. He just said we didn't have a healthy relationship. Now he won't talk to me—I mean, alone. When there are other people around— you know, like in the dining room—he's okay. But even then, sometimes he moves to the other side of the room when I come near him. No, I know what happened. Twila! She told him to break up with me because I'm—well, I'm emotionally delicate."

"Emotionally delicate?"

"So you honestly think Twila told him?" Burton jumped in with that soft tone.

"How else would Jon have found out?"

"You were a patient," Burton said.

"Client. Did you know she liked to call us clients?"

"Yes, he knows," I said, "but he forgets."

"So you hated Twila for that?" Burton asked.

"Hated her? I told her that if I owned a gun, I would shoot her fifty times."

"Did you stab her once?" I asked.

"Look, Twila may have thought I was on the wrong side of normal—and sometimes she might have been right—I don't know. But look at her files when you get back. I'm not violent. I yell and get mad, but my violence comes out in words."

"Oh?" That's always a safe word to use.

"If I were going to kill someone, I'd probably kill Jon!"

30

"I'm not clear on something," I said to Heather. "If Jon avoided you, how was it that you were on the Zodiac together?"

She smiled brightly. "Oh, that. Well, you see, when we prepared to land at Brown Bluff, I stood aside so no one paid any attention to me. I was there when the first Zodiac went out."

"And you waited for him to get into the fourth Zodiac?"

"At first I wondered if he had decided not to. Twila was the tenth person, and he was right behind her. So I took the last spot."

"Did you and Jon talk?"

"I tried. He turned his back on me."

"Did you talk to him at any time on the Zodiac or after you landed?"

"No, of course not. I decided to wipe that jerk out of my life—you know, Jon."

"So you didn't see Jon or Twila after the wet landing?"

"No, I don't know who got off first or last, and I didn't care. I didn't want to have anything to do with him again. Or with her, either."

Heather was lying. I knew it, but I couldn't figure out what she lied about. It didn't make sense. I stared at her.

"Okay, I did say something to Twila on the Zodiac."

"And—?" Burton beat me to that one.

She began to play with invisible lint on her turquoise sweater. "I, uh, well, okay, okay, I asked her to get Jon and me back together."

"What did she say?"

"She only laughed, shook her head, and turned and started to talk to someone else. Jeff, I think, but I can't remember now. It was something about the pristine blue of the icebergs. Something like that."

"Twila laughed at you?" I knew that was a lie. "Twila laughed at you?"

"Laughed? Hmm, all right, maybe she didn't actually laugh, but I heard the mockery in her voice."

"Mockery?" I asked.

"Go on," Burton said and frowned at me.

"Twila said I don't always have a clear picture of reality—as if she knows everything. Okay, so I asked her to get Jon and me back together. Maybe it wasn't a laugh. Maybe it—maybe she didn't. I *felt* like it was a laugh anyway. She said,

'It's out of my hands.' Out of her hands, huh? She made Jon break up with me, and it's out of her hands?"

"So what did you do?" Burton jumped in again before I could challenge her.

"We were almost at the landing. I waited for Twila. She seemed to be in no hurry and was the last one to get off the Zodiac. As soon as she was ashore, I helped her take off her life jacket. I dropped hers and mine with the others on the shore. 'Please,' I whispered to her.

"'If Jon doesn't want to marry you, that's his decision.' Just that and she walked away from me."

"And—?" I said it first this time.

"I joined a group—Shirley and Frank and maybe Thomas—I don't remember exactly."

"That was it?"

"I called her a. . .well, let's just say they were a lot of terrible names. Words I can't say with a preacher being present and all."

But you can say them to me, I thought.

She recounted her movements to us for a couple of minutes before she stood up and said, "I think Jon and I are going to get back together. You know, mutual grief and all that."

"Really?"

"Truly and really," she said and smiled. "He really does like me after all."

"Oh?" I asked, but she didn't respond.

We stared at each other, and she said, "I really have nothing more I want to say, so I think I'll leave."

Burton smiled and thanked her for coming.

Once I was sure she was gone, I turned to Burton. "She said one thing that bothered me—"

"The bit about the life jackets?"

"You picked it up, too?"

"I felt as if she wanted to give us a coded message," he said. "I didn't think it would do any good to ask her."

"I felt the same way," I said. "It was as if she threw a grenade at us and wanted to see if it would go off. There was something about the life jacket that she could tell us if—"

"But she won't."

"I know." That was part of her strange personality.

———

I had so many notes and much confusion going on inside my head. I knew—with that intuitive inner knowing—someone had lied. Maybe more than one.

"Someone knows who killed Twila," I said, more to myself than to Burton.

Burton looked quizzically at me and said, "Why would someone know and not tell?"

"I don't know the answer."

"But I agree with you." Burton's fingers drummed the table, and I knew he was trying to sort through everything we had heard. "Yes, someone is lying."

"One of them is Heather. But why? And about what?"

We decided to take a break for twenty minutes or so. I had a splitting headache. Maybe some of it was grief for Twila. I don't know. I decided to go back to my cabin for a Tylenol.

I had missed something. What was it? Something kept bothering me that I couldn't remember. It was some detail—something I had noticed, but I couldn't place it.

31

I walked slowly to my cabin, quite unaware of anything except my headache and trying to figure out what to do next. Somewhere there had to be an answer.

I sneaked into my cabin. And to my delighted surprise, Betty had fallen asleep with a book on her lap. I grabbed the Tylenol bottle and sneaked back out of the room. I walked down the hallway into the dining room where I could get water. I poured myself a glass of water and downed two pills.

"Need anything stronger?"

I turned around and saw that Jon Friesen stood in the doorway.

I smiled. I wondered if he would offer me an illegal drug. I put the small bottle in the pocket of my slacks and started to move past him, but I thought of Heather's comments.

"By the way, Jon, you came on to me pretty strong."

"And I hope you're reconsidering."

"Why would I do that?"

He leaned closer to me. "Because I like you. I like you a lot."

"Really?"

"You know I do." He smiled, and I'd swear he flexed those biceps, but maybe I only imagined it.

"But I understand that you and Heather planned to get married."

"Not quite accurate. Heather planned to get married. I didn't."

"You mean you led her on?"

"No, I loved her, I truly did. Or maybe I only thought I did. She's very, very affectionate." He smiled, and this time I did see him flex his muscles. "I doubt that she's as affectionate as you would be—if you really tried."

I had gone as far down that strange path as I wanted. "But you broke off the relationship, right?"

Jon walked past me, picked up two cups, and poured coffee for himself and for me. I started to decline but thought better of it. I took the cup, and we sat at the first table.

"You want the story? Okay, it goes like this. I did love her—or maybe I only thought I loved her—I'm not sure. But she drove me crazy."

"In what way?"

"You want a list? That's easy. To begin with, she phoned me five or six times every day. I finally turned my cell on vibrate. I'd be in the middle of something, and the phone would ring. It would be that schizoid, and she'd say, 'I've been thinking about you. I've missed you.' She'd talk like that when she had called me only an hour earlier."

"Did you hang up?"

"No. I mean I didn't for a long time. When she called, she'd tell me how much she loved me and how much brightness I brought into her dark night. You know, heavy-duty gunk like that."

"And obviously you didn't like it."

"It was a burden. She constantly told me she loved me, and she would pout or cry if I didn't say I loved her."

"So you broke up?"

"Yeah, and that's why I'm available." He put his hand on mine. With my left hand I picked his up and moved it.

"I like the feel of your hand. Soft. Warm. I'll bet your heart is the same way: soft and warm."

"So, Jon, you broke up but you still came on the cruise?"

"I thought she would cancel. She said she would. She'd go into all that melodrama about how life had no meaning without me."

"So that's why you came? You thought she wouldn't?"

"That and something else."

"What?"

"Do you really want to know?" He leaned forward so that our faces were only inches apart.

I didn't answer; I didn't blink; I waited.

"I knew you would be on the cruise. I like you—I think I love you—"

I laughed. "I believe you knew I would be on the cruise. I never made that a secret. But you didn't come because of me."

"You don't believe me?"

"Not for a fraction of a nanosecond."

"I'm not good enough for you?"

I didn't flinch, and I wasn't going to show him he made me uncomfortable, although he did. "It's my understanding that you and Heather have gotten back together again."

"Did she say that?"

"Yes."

He shrugged. "Okay, that's true. We're being discreet, but if you'd open up to me, I'd dump her—"

"Don't dump her for me."

I saw his fisted hands and the swollen veins in his neck. "I'm not good enough for you, am I? You think I'm trash because—"

"I'm in love with somebody else."

He stared at me for a long time before he said, "I thought that was over—you and Burton."

"Ask him." I got up and walked out of the room. He had frightened me. I didn't realize he was so capable of blowing up like that. But bipolars' emotions can jump from one extreme to another in seconds.

I decided I didn't want to be alone again with Jon.

As I hurried from the dining room, I tried to force myself to breathe slowly and deeply. I didn't accomplish that very well. Just then the ship rocked in the seas, and I had to grab the handrail to walk along the passageway. We were definitely in the Drake Passage.

For several seconds, a tiny spasm of dizziness came over me. *I can't get seasick now. Dear Lord, please don't let me get seasick.*

The dizziness left me, but the lurching of the ship didn't stop. It seemed to get worse.

Burton was in the theater when I arrived. His head was bent over. He was in such deep concentration that he didn't hear me come in. When I sat down, I startled him.

"I feel we're close—so close," he said, "and yet nothing makes any sense."

"Close to solving this?" I asked. "You're a lot more confident than I am."

"If only we could just get something concrete about the person—probably a man—who walked off with Twila. We know he was wearing his life jacket then. We can only assume he came back alone."

"Except that no one saw him come back."

"Surely someone must have," Burton said. Unconsciously he pushed back that gorgeous shock of dark curls. He smiled, but it was a tired expression.

"Let's call it a night," I said.

"It's not even noon yet," he said.

I looked at my watch. It was exactly 11:45.

We stood up and faced each other. I know he wanted to kiss me. Okay, I wanted him to kiss me, but I couldn't. If he took me in his arms, I'd lose my resolve about having him make things right first.

He must have read my face, because he said, "I won't kiss you—not this time." We walked down the passageway together, then he went up a flight of stairs to his room and I started down one flight to reach mine.

I went into the room, and the ship rocked wildly in the waves. Betty had left the room, and I was glad that I wouldn't have to mumble answers. I got into bed—still dressed. I pulled my luggage inside the bunk, made my body the shape of a banana, and put books and luggage on both sides of me. I had learned that as a trick when I had gone on a cruise with my late husband, Dana Macie.

EVERYBODY'S SUSPECT IN GEORGIA

I don't remember going to sleep, so I must have dozed off pretty fast. But I also awakened with a start. I have no idea what awakened me, but I was fully alert. I know myself well enough to realize that when I'm that alert, there is no going back to sleep.

I lay in my banana position for several minutes. I prayed. I honestly prayed for divine guidance. It's not supposed to be difficult to pray—or at least the books I've read seem to say that. But it was for me. *Who am I that the God of the universe wants to listen to my petty cries?*

I smiled to myself. I had asked Twila that question. She said that was how God's grace worked. And God cares about every single person. I believed her and I had started to pray—not as much as I knew Burton did. I had decided that I would set aside a few minutes when I first awakened and talk to God. I still planned to but had never felt good enough, despite what Twila had said.

But then—right then—I *knew* I could pray and that God would hear me. It was almost a giddy experience. *God will listen! To me!* I talked to God right then. I poured out my concern about finding the killer. I asked God to show me or Burton or both of us what to do.

I had no answer, but I had peace.

I stuck my arm out of the covers and held it toward the light. It was 2:37 p.m. I had slept through lunch. The sea felt even more ferocious than before.

Betty moaned. If she was following the same pattern going across the Drake Passage as she had before, then she had taken two seasick tablets. I suspected she still was feeling somewhat queasy.

Finally, I got out of bed, put my shoes back on, and tiptoed out of the room. I thought perhaps a cup of tea would help. According to my British friends, tea is the cure for everything.

If the trip back was anything like our trip going to Antarctica, we'd have a number of seasick people, including some of those who had taken medication.

I held on to the railings because of the pitch of the ship. Even though I was holding on, a sudden rocking of the ship threw off my center of balance.

Just then I heard a voice. It was a woman's voice, and she was shouting. I couldn't make out most of what she yelled, but I heard the word *camera* several times, as well as the word *picture*.

The other voice, a man's, was too low for me to be sure of, but I think I heard the word *observant*.

A shrill scream filled my ears. Despite the noise of the waves striking the hull of the ship, I heard that scream.

Foolishly, I raced forward and left the handrail.

I reached the top of the stairs, but in my haste, my clasp on the railing wasn't strong enough. Another wave hit. I lost my balance and pitched forward. I screamed—it just came out. I tumbled all the way down to the bottom of the passageway, perhaps ten or twelve steps.

Once the shock was over, I got up slowly. I had landed on my right arm and right side. I had probably bruised my arm, but nothing was broken. I got up cautiously and moved as quickly as I could to the area where I had heard the voices.

"Listen, Julie," I said aloud to myself, "just because you heard a few words, don't go jumping to conclusions."

"You're right," I said. "But still—"

"Still, what?"

"Something about the tone of her voice. She sounded afraid. Maybe almost hysterical—"

"Oh sure, so that means the conversation has relevance to this situation. You think everything that's spoken by anyone refers to this—"

"Right," I said and added, "but still. . ."

I kept going. I wasn't sure where I was going, but I knew the general direction.

Then I saw her.

My initial impression, of course, was that she had fallen. She lay facedown on the carpeted floor. Blood was already beginning to seep from her body. I knew immediately who it was.

33

I recognized Heather's turquoise sweater and that inky black hair. She had fallen forward. A pool of blood had seeped onto the carpeted floor.

I touched her gently and tried to turn her over. Her eyes fluttered, and she tried to say something, but I couldn't hear it. Her eyes glazed and all life was gone.

Stab wounds around her neck made my stomach roil.

"Oh, dear God, not another life taken." As I held her, not knowing what to do, I thought of the two times Burton and I had been involved in murder cases. Both had started with a murder, and there was a second one—someone who had witnessed the killing or who held a vital clue toward solving it.

I hadn't liked Heather very much, but a wave of sadness came over me, and tears filled my eyes. Perhaps I was really mourning for Twila. I know only that I hugged the lifeless body and sobbed.

———

I was too distraught to be fully aware of what happened during the next few minutes. Sue Downs came out of her cabin—she later said it was to get more seasick medicine. She saw me holding Heather's body and screamed.

I calmed her down by talking slowly and softly and told her to go to the navigation bridge and tell the captain. Minutes later, two of the seamen came. They gently lifted Heather's body, covered her in some kind of tarp, and took her away. A stewardess came and wiped away as much blood as possible and covered the blood with a small rug, which was almost the same color as the carpet. Heather's blood had streaked the front of my clothes.

It's fuzzy in my mind, but I know that I asked someone who came by—maybe it was Jon or Mickey—to call Burton. He came soon after that. I had been so caught up in the trauma of the situation that my mind had been unable to function properly.

Burton put his arm around my shoulders and led me to the dining room. He sat down next to me. He held my hand. "We've been through this kind of thing before," he said. "People see something, and the killer takes them out of the way."

Then I remembered what had been lurking in the back of my mind. "I know why she was killed—I mean, I think I do." Before he asked anything, I said, "There was something tickling the back of my memory. Now—maybe too late—I know what it was."

I stared at him. "A camera. Heather had one of those tiny digital cameras and snapped pictures all the time."

"You know, I do remember that."

He told me to wait, and he ran to her room. Minutes later, he returned. "No camera. Sue is her roommate and she'll look more carefully, but neither of us found her digital camera. Sue said she never left the cabin without it." He said he had also checked with the ship's doctor, who confirmed there was no camera on her person.

It was obvious to both of us what that meant. Heather had seen someone walk away with Twila and had probably photographed them.

"Remember what Shirley said? That's what bothered me. She referred to the woman who watched them—and who took pictures. That had to have been Heather."

"We can't prove it, of course," he said, "but it makes sense to me."

"So Twila's killer was probably being blackmailed." I told him about hearing the voices and the scream.

"That fits." He began to ponder the time frame. "By then the first two Zodiacs had gone, and maybe ten minutes afterward, the third one left."

"Let's not even think along that line," I said. "Too many suspects again."

Burton stared into my eyes. "I haven't napped. I've spent the whole time in prayer. I don't know anything, but I sense, I truly sense, that God will help us find the killer before we dock at Ushuaia."

Please God, I prayed silently. *Please hear his prayer. And mine, too, if You don't mind.*

Burton and I met shortly after dinner. He said he had finished his half of the book. I had also finished mine. He walked me to my cabin, and we exchanged halves.

"Two of the accounts are extremely interesting. I don't know if it means anything, but if we knew who they were, it might help. But without any identity—"

"I'm sure we can get the key from Twila's file once we get back to Atlanta."

"But we may also lose the impetus and any chance to find who killed both of them."

He didn't have to say it. Both of us assumed the same person who killed Twila had also killed Heather.

"I had a thought—" I was a little embarrassed. "Do you think God sometimes puts thoughts into our heads? Please don't laugh. You know I'm still new at this Christianity—"

Burton took my hand. "I'm not laughing. And yes, I believe the Lord speaks to us. If not, why do we ask for guidance?"

"I mean, it's not a solution or anything—"

"It's all right." This time he gave me what I call the sideways embrace—like two friends who stand next to each other. His arm around my shoulder comforted me.

"Well, it's just that I keep thinking about the book—the lectures—"

"And—?"

I laughed this time. "And—to repeat your word—maybe the killer isn't in the book but doesn't know he isn't. So he still tried to steal it—"

"Unless that person already has what he wanted."

"That's a possibility," I said. "Okay, I prayed, and here's what came to me, whether it's my subconscious working overtime or—"

"It's all right."

"But, darling—"

"You called me darling," he said.

"Yes, I did."

"Did you—were you aware—?"

"I'm aware of my words, but, you know, sometimes words just slip out."

"Let them slip out as often as you like. *Darling.*"

"Meanwhile, back in Antarctica, let's assume that the person didn't find what

428

he wanted—that is, he wanted the manuscript—he may not have known what it looked like."

"He wouldn't have known what it looked like," Burton said. "That is, assuming the book is what he wanted."

"You're probably right. If he had known it was a book, he would have riffled through the six books in Twila's briefcase."

Burton thought for a few seconds before he said, "So he probably doesn't know Twila had the case studies bound."

"I feel—oh, Burton, is it okay to say that? I feel God is going to help us figure this out."

"Yes, yes, it's fine. And I hope you're correct."

Burton and I talked for almost an hour, going over our notes and our impressions. We were more convinced than ever that the killer was one of the people on the fourth Zodiac.

At breakfast the next morning, Captain Robert announced the death of Heather Wilson. Everyone seemed shocked.

"Oh dear, is it something we should fear?" Shirley asked. "Is there a killer loose who—?" She stopped and said quietly to me, "There I go in my Mary LaMuth mind-set."

"Doesn't anyone know anything?" asked Mickey. "How many more people will die before we get back to Ushuaia?"

"Do you suppose we ought to, you know, stay in twos?" Betty Freeman asked. "If one of you nice gentlemen wanted to guard us defenseless females, I, at least, would appreciate it."

"After all, both people who died were women," Sue Downs said.

"I'll be your escort," Donny said.

Several other men echoed his words.

Burton stood up and waited until everyone stopped talking. "I don't think anyone else needs to be afraid. I'm quite sure there will be no more deaths."

I stood next to him and said, "I think it's time we told you what little we know."

Burton stared at me as if to ask, "Are you out of your mind?"

I stared back and shrugged just the way he does. I love communicating with him when we don't have to use words.

"The captain gave Burton and me unofficial permission to work on finding the killer—"

"And you've brought about a second murder," Donny said.

"That's not fair!" Jeff yelled. "They didn't kill Heather."

"You're right, Jeff," I said. "Heather would have been killed even if we hadn't gotten involved."

Now I had their attention.

"We know one thing we can tell you: Twila planned to do a series of lectures at Clayton University, and she had written twenty-one case studies. We think the killer wanted to get the material and destroy it."

"And did the person succeed?" Thomas asked.

"No," Burton said. He held up his pages. "This is half of the manuscript on which she worked."

"I have the other half," I said.

"We're still reading it," Burton said.

"What kind of case studies?" someone asked. I don't know who asked, because it came from behind me.

"I can only say this much—and I'm sure it's obvious to all of you. We have good reason to believe these pages will implicate someone on this cruise." As I said the words, I could hear Jessica Fletcher on *Murder, She Wrote* say the same thing. In fact, I could probably go back to those old black-and-white Perry Mason cases where he often said something just as silly.

"Is that all you're going to tell us?" Jon Friesen asked.

"For now." I have no idea why I answered that way. I think I was trying to imply that we had information we weren't ready to divulge.

Despite all the questions people wanted us to answer, Burton and I left the room. "This is beginning to sound like some TV plot," I said. "We announce the evidence and set a trap for the killer to come and try to steal the book, and we've got him."

Burton laughed.

"Do people really think that way?" I asked.

"Only in movies and books. Only in fiction."

35

I decided to go to the lounge. A lecture was scheduled for ten o'clock in the theater. I couldn't have concentrated on it anyway. I wasn't sure where Burton went.

After getting a glass of water, I sat in the corner and read through the chapters. In spite of my PhD in psychology, I have to admit I learned from Twila. She was insightful and obviously saw things that I probably wouldn't have picked up.

I felt my eyes starting to water again, and I resolutely fought the tears. I could grieve later. This was our last full day on board.

Perhaps twenty minutes later, I heard whistling and looked up. Larry Dean Yoke came into the room. I knew him slightly, and he usually gave me a cheerful salute.

"I finally feel good," he said. "I had a good night. I took a seasick pill and slept fine." Larry Dean, maybe fifty years old, looked like a big farm boy who had awakened inside the wrong house and been forced to clothe himself in Yves Saint Laurent gear. His brown hair was combed straight back, and he had long gray sideburns. Despite his expensive clothes—and they shouted money—his square face and plain features looked out of place.

Larry Dean said he had decided to bypass the lecture and find something to read instead. He spotted a book called *With Byrd at the Bottom of the World* by Norman Vaughan. He picked it up and started telling me what a fan he had been of Byrd and his historic air flight over the South Pole in 1929. He admitted he had read the book years ago, but he liked it, and since it was here, he decided he would read it again.

He came over and started to sit down but saw I was busy. "Oh, guess you don't want company."

I shook my head.

He leaned over and read enough to see what I was reading. "I'm in that book. I suppose you know that."

"You're one of the twenty-one?"

"Absolutely. I'm the male with the multiple-personality disorder." He beamed as if proud of his past condition. "I'm fine now. Occasionally, I get slightly, well, strange, but not often."

"Do you know anything about Twila's death?"

"Nope. Sorry. I liked her. I really did. It's because of her that I first went to church and eventually became a serious Christian." For another minute or two, he went into the details of his conversion story. He paused abruptly and said, "Sorry. You didn't ask about all that, did you?"

Rather than answer, I asked, "Do you know anything that would shed any light on this?"

He shook his head. "I was on the first Zodiac. We left maybe ten minutes after the fourth one landed. I never went near the fourth one or talked to anyone." He went to great length to tell me the people he had been talking to. And he took a lot of pictures of the Zodiacs as they came in. "I like those little things."

"So you read what Twila said about you?"

"She didn't have anything to hide from us. She talked to each of us and explained what she was going to do. She said that by telling our story and the way she had intervened, she could help professionals treat others."

"Yes, yes, that's excellent," I said.

"I feel honored to have been in the book. In fact, I was one of the last ones to go into it." He took my copy and turned to the last chapter. "See, that's me." He pointed to MEZ.

"But she doesn't identify the people—"

"Well, not really. I mean, she does in her own coded way."

"What do you mean?"

"I gave her a simple system—I mean, really simple. She called it a great memory retrieval system."

I must have looked totally puzzled, because I had no idea what he meant.

"It's easy and obvious. My name is Larry Dean Yoke. That makes my initials LDY. Right?"

"Of course."

"So instead of using those initials, she took the *next* letter in the alphabet. Instead of *L* for Larry she used *M*. Simple, huh?"

"Yes, it is. So MEZ moved back one letter makes it LDY."

"That's it. You still can't identify everyone, but those of us who were patients could identify each other. And that was part of the permission form."

"What do you mean?"

"Well, Twila didn't think it ought to be a secret among her patients—her clients. She had a party every couple of months for all of us—if we wanted to come. Nice party. Good food."

"You mean like an AA meeting or—?"

"Not that formal. But we talked a little about ourselves. So we pretty well knew each other. Most of us thought it was fun." He abruptly stopped and pointed to the chapter I was reading. "That's Pat Borders. He's Pat Robert Borders and that becomes RSC. We used to laugh about each other's problems."

"And everyone was cool with that?" I asked.

432

"Cool? We loved it. She also had a contract with one of the university presses—University of Iowa. Or maybe it was Illinois."

"By any chance, do you know if all twenty-one people in the book are on this cruise?"

"Absolutely. That's one of the reasons we came. It was her way to thank us. She said she learned so much from treating us."

"And the rest of us on the cruise are friends, right?"

"Yeah, maybe seven or eight like you."

I stared at Larry Dean for quite a while. I had made a list of the three-letter codes of my half of the manuscript. I went down the list. Larry Dean was quick. He called out their names before I did.

I had the names of all twenty-one.

"Thanks, Larry Dean. Twila would have loved you for what you just told me."

"You mean I helped? I don't see how, but I'm glad if I could do anything." He started into a story in which he told me how Twila had saved his sanity and had made him a more solid believer in God.

"Forgive me for interrupting you—"

"Oh, that's all right," he said. "You have something more important to do than listen to me."

"It's not that I don't want to hear," I said as I gathered up my materials. "I have to see Burton."

He winked. "Naturally."

I hurried out of the lounge.

Now I know.

A t first I couldn't find Burton. He wasn't in his cabin, and I knew he wouldn't have gone to the theater. I went back to the dining room and didn't see him.

"Julie."

I whirled around. He had been sitting in a corner with no light on.

"I know, Burton! I know who did it."

He listened to my long explanation of the conversation with Larry Dean. I did that on purpose and strung out the explanation as long as I could. I love to make him eager and expected him to say wearily, "And what's the point?" The rat! He never did. I looked at his face, and I understood. He knew what I was doing, and he was willing to wait me out.

"So do you want to know?" I asked.

"Yes, and I will as soon as you decide to share your information."

Impulsively I pecked him on the cheek. Only after I had done that did I realize what I had done. I felt my face flush.

"It's okay, Julie," he said. "I won't take the kiss personally." He said the words with no facial expression, but I knew he was laughing at me.

"Okay, here it is." I showed him my list of four columns. Their names were listed first; then their initials in Twila's code; and third, their true initials, which matched the first column. My final column was a brief note of the problem the person faced.

"So now at least we know the identities of all twenty-one people," I said.

He studied the list carefully. "And, of course, each one is on the cruise."

"That was part of Twila's way of thanking them for their help."

"And you think you know who did it?"

"Absolutely," I said with a little hint of pride. I felt great. Burton is usually a step ahead of me, but not on this one. "Of course, I can't prove it—"

"So now you want my help to bring out the evidence to convict the guilty one."

He's bright, and I never have to explain anything to him twice.

"So tell me."

"First, the killer isn't one of the people in the book of lectures."

"He's not? Then why—?" I loved the look of confusion on his face. It was worth stringing out the story just to see that.

I didn't answer, but I did smirk. I love doing that.

"So you want the great dramatic ending to this, do you?" he said. "We get them all in the dining room. You make your grand explanation, point to the guilty one, and proclaim, 'You did it.' And that person cries out a confession—"

"Not quite that simple," I said.

"Life rarely is."

"Let me try this," I said. I still hadn't told him who the guilty person was, and I wanted to wait until he begged me.

"At last," he said and smiled. He had figured out my game.

"He was one of those who never made progress in therapy. Don't you get it?"

"He wasn't in the book because—?"

"Because he was *too* sick—*too* mentally ill. He wasn't a good case study." I didn't need to explain to Burton that she chose the twenty-one clients because she felt her students could learn from the cases. Not all of the subjects ended up normal or cured (a word we professionals don't use). But she wouldn't have made a case study of someone who remained stuck for years and hadn't moved on.

"I hate to admit it, but this time you're way ahead of me." He scratched the back of his head as he skimmed the list. "You'll have to convince me that the killer isn't on the list."

"The best argument," I said, "is the most obvious. Every one of the people— all twenty-one of them—gave their consent."

"Have you asked all of them?"

"No, and I don't need to do that. I can if you like, but you're missing the obvious."

"No, you're missing the obvious. Until you know—"

"Try this, then. I've spoken to everyone on the fourth Zodiac. All of them have said they signed off—"

"Right. Okay, for now. I agree with you that—"

"That they had nothing to be afraid of. She gave each of them a copy of the chapter in which their case is discussed."

"Oh, I get it!"

I smiled. All right, I smirked again. I could get good at that expression.

"So the killer *assumed* she had written—"

"You were a little slow on this one, Burton, but that's exactly right."

"It makes perfect sense," he said. "So the killer didn't sign—"

"And—" I paused for dramatic effect and just one more smirk. "He didn't know he wasn't in the book, so—"

"So he searched the room to find it—"

"Now that makes sense, doesn't it?"

"It's worth exploring." I knew he agreed with me completely, but he wasn't going to let me score too many points. "Let's be really sure," he said. "Let's compare the list to the eleven other people in the Zodiac with Twila."

I had already done that, but I wanted him convinced. All of those who came back on the Zodiac were on the list.

"No, no, I'm sure who killed Twila, and he also killed Heather—"

"Because she saw him do it?"

"No, but she knew."

He stared at me for a long time. "You lead," he said. "I'm with you all the way."

As we both stood up, I said, "I can't prove this yet, but there is a chance I can later."

"We have nothing to lose, do we?"

"Only that we'll enrage the wrong person and let the guilty one get away."

We started to walk, and I put my hand against his chest. "Uh, I, uh, want you to do something. Please."

Burton stared quizzically at me.

"Will you pray for God to help us? I mean, that's all right, isn't it?"

"Here's my rule," he said. "If anything is big enough to concern you, it's big enough to concern God."

"I like that," I said. "That's a good rule."

Burton took both of my hands in his and prayed. The words flowed so easily from him. My uncle's prayers had sounded more like commands or sermons. I loved to listen to the way Burton prayed.

When he finished, I said, "You talk—well, as if you're conversing with a friend. It sounds so natural."

Burton beamed. "Jesus Christ *is* a friend. My best and truest friend."

Burton and I went to find Captain Robert. It took about ten minutes for me to explain everything to him. He didn't understand about Twila's lectures and why permission was important, but he didn't demand any further explanation. I finished and Burton clarified a few minor points for him. I didn't explain to him and I hadn't told Burton, but I was positive I knew the killer's identity. It simply made sense to me.

"You are convinced that you know the killer's identity?" Burton asked.

"No," I said. "I'm not positive, but I think so." I turned to the captain and said, "If you'll help us, we'll soon find out if I'm correct."

He pondered the situation for perhaps half a minute. "I have no objections whatsoever. My concern must always be about the comfort of our passengers."

I started to say, "I read that in your brochure." Instead, I saw the frown on Burton's face and said, "I'm sure that's true."

"We live in—what do you call it—a litigious world?"

"We certainly do," I said. "But I don't think that is a problem."

"You see, Captain, I know every passenger on this ship," Burton said. "Except for eight of them, the rest are members of our congregation. I don't think we'll have any problem."

"You *think*?" the captain asked. "How strongly is that?"

"I can assure you," Burton said.

I looked at his face. He meant it.

"Besides, you never gave us official permission," I said. "And if there is any litigation, Burton and I will assume full responsibility."

"Then we shall do it," he said. He turned on the loudspeaker that connected to every room on the ship. "This is Captain Robert speaking. All passengers are please asked to assemble in the theater in ten minutes." He repeated the announcement twice.

His voice carried well. In my cabin I heard it every day five minutes before each meal. No one could miss it anywhere on the ship.

⌐

To my amazement, everyone was present before the expiration of the ten minutes. I wondered if they had all been sitting in their cabins waiting for something to

437

happen. Probably not, but I sensed a tension among them.

Burton counted to make sure no one was missing. "There were forty-seven passengers, because Twila did not have a roommate. We have lost two people, so that should be forty-five." He finished and said, "All accounted for."

As soon as Burton assured him that we had forty-five passengers in the room, Captain Robert stood up. "Ladies and gentlemen, thank you for coming." He made about a thirty-second speech to apologize for our having to return to South America, saying, "In view of the sad circumstances, I am most certain each of you understands." He concluded by saying, "As you know, Dr. Burton and Dr. West have investigated this deplorable situation as a personal favor to me. They now have something to report to you."

He turned toward us and waved at me to come forward. I had previously asked to sit near the door. "It may not be necessary, but as a precaution," I had said.

I explained to the entire group about Twila's book of lectures. On a whim, I asked, "Is there anyone here who doesn't know about the lectures and the book she was writing?"

"Everybody knows," Jeff said. "The gossip mill has spread it everywhere."

"You didn't specifically ask us not to say anything," Sue said, "but common sense would say we should hold everything in confidence."

"I, for one, did not say a word." Jeff stared at Betty.

"I didn't realize it wasn't—"

"It doesn't matter," Burton said. "In fact, it saves us explanation." He smiled at Betty.

"So someone killed Twila because he or she didn't want to be in the book?" Mickey asked. "That's strange, because all that person had to do was say, 'Take me out,' and she would have done it."

"That's not exactly the reason," I said.

"What is the reason?" Jon asked.

"I'll answer that later," I said.

"I'll bet all of us, or at least most of us," Pat said, "were Twila's patients—"

"Clients! We're clients. It's a kinder word," Betty yelled.

"Okay, clients. Whatever!" Pat said. "And for everyone's information, I would never kill Twila or anyone."

"I'm in her book, but I would never, never, never kill her!" Jeff yelled.

I heard a couple of other voices say the same thing. I waited. *Oh God,* I silently prayed, *please, please help me right now.*

"Are you going to accuse me of killing Twila just because I'm in her book?" shouted Jon.

"We're making no accusation just yet," Burton said.

"But we expect to be able to have some concrete evidence to show who killed

Twila and Heather," I added. "Before we reach Ushuaia tomorrow."

"And this is also to tell you," I said, "that none of you needs to be afraid. I assure you: There is no danger of any further deaths."

Burton stared at me, and our gazes locked. I saw the beginning of a smile escape his lips. He nodded slightly.

"There's one more person we need to talk to, isn't there?" Burton whispered. "I think I finally got it."

I'm not sure what the Cheshire-cat smile is, but I think that's what I gave him.

I turned to Captain Robert and said, "I think we can dismiss everyone." He looked at me strangely, and I said sotto voce, "Stay here. We have one person with whom we need to speak."

"What? You call us down here just to tell us *nothing*?" Donny said. "What is going on?"

"I resent this kind of strange behavior," Shirley said. "If you have some vital clue or urgent information—"

"Why did you call all of us here?" Jon asked.

"All right," Burton said. "Please forgive any inconvenience. I'll explain later why we did things this way."

We both heard grumbling, but Burton tried to assure everyone. "Trust us," he said several times.

Captain Robert talked to several people, and so did Burton and I. However, I watched the one person I wanted to stay. I realized Burton was doing the same thing. Burton had figured it out. As soon as that person reached the door, I leaned over and said, "Can you wait until the others leave?"

"Oh, I can wait for you anytime," he said and gave me a full grin.

It took perhaps three minutes before everyone left the room. Once they were all gone, I walked over to where Jon Friesen was seated. "Jon, I asked you to stay because I have a question for you."

"Anything. Or I could ask you a few questions—a few very personal questions."

"Ah, but I'm first," I said and smiled.

"Go right ahead."

"I'm curious about something. How did you know Twila was writing about you?"

"Word got around that she was going to write about all her patients—her clients."

"You mean you heard that on board the ship?"

"Nah! I knew before we left. The word had circulated, so we knew."

"Everyone knew? All of you?"

"Probably not all, but the word got around that she was going to use us in her lectures, and afterward she'd polish it and have it published."

"How did you know?"

He shrugged. "All of us knew. It wasn't any big secret." He shook his head.

"Can you believe it? Some of them were delighted to have her spread their names all over the world."

"Some people like publicity of any kind," Burton said. I knew he was making conversation and waiting for me to take the lead.

"But how did you know?" I asked. "Did Twila tell you? About the book?"

"I don't remember the details, except—"

"Did she tell you that you were one of the people in her lectures?"

"Maybe not directly, I mean, I *know* I'm one of those she chose. Why wouldn't she want me in her lectures and her book?"

"Good question," Burton said. "I assume you have rare qualities and presented a unique case for her."

"Unique. Yes, that's true." He seemed to preen as he answered.

"Did she ask you to sign a permission slip?" I asked.

He blinked, and the easygoing manner seemed to slide away from him. "I don't remember signing one, but I may have. I signed a number of papers. Twila was always shoving a paper in front of me to sign."

"Who told you—the first one who told you—what Twila was doing?" I asked.

"Hmm. Will I get someone in trouble if I tell you?"

"*You* may get into trouble if you don't tell me." I thought that was a brilliant response. "We think we know who killed Twila and Heather, but we need your help."

"Of course I'll help you." The smile was in place again.

"And—?" Burton asked.

"Betty Freeman. Please. I don't want to get her into trouble. You see, she had a long talk with Twila and asked her to make some changes."

"Because Twila painted her too—too dark?"

Jon roared. "Too dark. No, she didn't think it was dark enough. She felt she had been in far worse shape before she started treatment. So, yeah, that's how I found out."

"Anything you can tell us about Betty and the lectures—the book?"

"She told me she had second thoughts and wasn't sure she wanted to be in Twila's book."

"When was that? When did she tell you?" Burton asked.

Jon stared into space for a few seconds. "That first landing. King George Island. Yeah, that's when it was. On the Zodiac going over."

"Was she upset? I mean, really upset?"

Jon eyed me cautiously. "I'm not going to get Betty into any serious trouble, am I?"

"I don't think so," I answered.

"In that case, she was really ticked. She didn't explain why, but she kept saying she needed to talk to Twila and straighten something out." He looked into my eyes and said, "You don't think Betty would—?"

"People react strangely when they're angry or upset," Burton said.

"Yeah, yeah, they do."

Just to keep him off balance, the way good lawyers and detectives work, I asked, "Did Twila ever say specifically that you were in the book?"

"No, I mean, not in so many words, but I knew."

"How did you know?"

"I just knew."

"But Twila didn't say so." I kept my voice calm and I hoped conversational, so he wouldn't know how important his answers were.

"Not in so many words." He looked at me, and just then it seemed as if the lights came on inside his brain. "You knew I didn't sign a permission form, didn't you?"

"It was a good guess."

"Did you ask Twila if you were in the book?" Burton stepped closer. He handled the question well and in such a casual way he might have asked about the weather.

"Yes, as a matter of fact, I did. That made me angry—not angry enough to—to hurt her or anything like—"

"But angry."

"It's my life, isn't it? If she was going to teach and write about me, didn't I have the right to know?"

"Of course you did," Burton said in a smooth, quiet voice. "It's a normal question. Why wasn't she open with you?"

"I don't know. Honest. I don't know. But I asked."

"What did she say?" Burton was a trifle too eager, but I didn't think Jon picked up on it.

"She said, 'That is none of your business.' Can you imagine that? None of my business. It was *my life*."

Neither of us said anything to Jon. The captain, as an objective observer, sat silently and listened to everything. For several minutes Jon ranted. He called Twila unprofessional, unfeeling, uncaring. He said she only wanted to make money from her clients and report their cases so she could become a big star in her field. His voice grew louder. He slammed my chair twice with his fist.

I interrupted with the pseudo Carl Rogers approach that first-year students at the university used. "You're really quite angry now, aren't you?"

"Wouldn't you be upset? Of course I was upset. I had planned to talk to her about it, but—well, you know, someone else must have been even more ticked off than I was."

Burton said nothing, but his facial expression was such that Jon felt secure enough to continue ranting.

Jon used a lot of profanity before he stopped abruptly. "I'm sorry, Pastor. You're a man of God and all, and—"

"I've heard those words before," Burton said.

Good for you, darling, I thought. *That was a perfect answer.*

I wasn't aware how long Jon yelled, but his anger increased instead of diminishing. That's typical of a person in his condition. After a while, even the profanity became repetitive, so I said, "You are so angry, Jon. Her actions really upset you."

He stopped in midsentence and slumped in a chair.

Now I knew.

His extreme anger made it clear that he hadn't benefited from his therapy.

Excuse me just a second, will you?" I said to Jon.

"If I must—but don't go too far."

"Oh, I'm not going far," I said. Despite my anger, I gave him a fairly decent smile. "I need to speak with the captain about something."

I walked across the room and tried to sound as if I were whispering to him. "He's the one. We think Jon Friesen killed Twila and Heather."

"I heard that! You are crazy! You're the one who needs a psychiatrist. You're crazy, you know!"

Burton moved right in front of Jon and put his arm on the man's shoulder. "I certainly hear your protests. She's made a strong assertion about you."

Jon swore and called me the worst names that seemed to rush into his head. "I thought you loved me," he said. "I thought—well, I thought we had something going for us!"

I thought he was going to spit at me.

"I'm glad I found out now about who you really are."

"I think we can settle this," Burton said. "It's very easy, you know. And if Julie is wrong, I shall insist that she apologize to you."

"Thank you, Burton. You are a friend. A true friend."

I thought Jon was going to hug him. Instead, he extended his hand and shook Burton's.

I wanted to smile. Burton had gotten my message even though I had not said one word to him. "So how does Jon prove that you've falsely accused him?"

"Simple," I said. "We can search his room."

"Would I kill a couple of people and keep the weapon?" Jon leered at me.

"Let's search his room anyway," I said.

"Search my body first," Jon said. "I might have some weapon on me."

I nodded to Captain Robert to do just that. I was sure Jon didn't have the evidence on his person, or he wouldn't have been so insistent that we search him.

But I wasn't looking for the murder weapon. I was sure he had disposed of that.

The captain patted him down. I wondered if that was something they taught sea captains or if he had seen the same movies I had.

"Let's go to your room." I said the words in a commanding tone. "If I'm wrong, I'll get down on my knees and apologize."

Jon snickered like a ten-year-old boy. "I'd really like to see that!"

"Then let's go," I said.

Burton led the way, and Jon swaggered behind him. I say *swaggered*, but both had to hold on to the railing because the ship was really heaving and rocking wildly.

"Do you think he has the knife—or whatever it was—in his room?" the captain asked me softly.

"No, I don't," I said. "I think we need to assume that he threw it overboard."

"Or I didn't have any weapon," Jon said. "I heard that. So if I threw a knife overboard, why would you search my room?"

"There is something else—something that I think we will find inside your room."

"Oh, and what would that be?"

"A camera," Burton said. "Unless you've thrown that away." He winked at me.

I frowned at Burton, but I thought, *You really don't miss much.*

"You think you're so brilliant!" Jon shouted. "You won't find a camera in my room. I didn't kill anybody."

"Wow, that sounds just like the dialogue on a TV series called *The Closer* that had reruns just before we left."

Jon dropped his head. It was obvious he had watched the same episode, and I'd caught him.

"The man on that show was innocent," I said. "Remember?"

"And so am I."

"Prove me wrong!" I didn't wait for an answer but moved ahead of him and Burton. "Which cabin?"

"Twelve," he said.

I walked in first, and Jon came in right behind me. "I gotta see this. I gotta see you find something that *isn't* in my cabin."

Burton and the captain flanked each other and followed. The sea was still rough, so I held on to the guardrail. Jon saw me turn my head and look at him, so he tried to tough it out, but about the fifth step, he lurched forward and grabbed the railing just before he fell. Burton hugged the rail without trying to prove anything. The captain must have had what the sailors call sea legs. I looked back and saw that his body made the slightest weight adjustment with each step he took. It wasn't a conscious shift, but I assume it had come after years of sailing across the Weddell Sea.

The captain opened the door to cabin twelve. Jeff Adams lay on his back in his bunk. He had a book in his hand, but I think he had been asleep. "Please let us have the room for a few minutes," the captain said.

Jeff's gaze shifted from one of us to the other before he got out of bed. He grabbed his book and left without saying anything.

"Let the captain search," I told Burton. "If he finds the evidence, Jon can never say we planted it."

"There is nothing to find! Nothing to find! Nothing to find!" Jon yelled. "All this accusation and there's nothing to find!"

"Sit on Jeff's bunk." Burton's strong voice implied that it was not a matter for discussion.

Jon sat quietly with an expression somewhere between a smirk and a grin as the captain searched. I had the utmost certainty that the evidence was in Jon's cabin. The camera was small, but I was sure we would find it.

Without his being aware, from the corner of my eye, I followed Jon's gaze. His eyes flared briefly when the captain picked up the shaving kit, opened it, saw nothing, and put it down.

Jon relaxed. "Keep looking. Do you plan to spend the night?"

"Captain, empty everything from the shaving kit onto the bunk," I said.

Without asking the reason, the captain did so. He began to sort through everything. Then I saw *it*.

Now it was my turn to smirk.

Jon didn't have a camera. I assumed he had thrown Heather's away. That had been a smart move. In a small plastic bag was a black object about the size of a postage stamp.

"That's the evidence," I said and pointed to the object.

"What is it?" asked the captain.

Jon closed his eyes.

"It is the camera's memory card," Burton said.

"It's so small," I said, "Jon wouldn't have had any trouble getting ashore with that."

"Thank you, Captain," Burton said. "We had expected to find Heather's camera, but I'm sure we can find someone on the ship with a digital camera that this memory card will fit."

"They're fairly universal," I said. "So you shouldn't have a problem."

"I'll make an announcement and ask anyone with a digital camera to bring it to the theater." The captain turned to Jon. "Sit. You can't run away, so just sit on this bunk until I return."

Jon sat in a hunched position, his eyes closed.

The captain left the room.

Less than two minutes later, the captain made the announcement over the intercom. Perhaps another ten minutes passed before he came back to the cabin with four digital cameras. The memory card fit in the third one.

We turned on the camera and stared at what we saw. Heather had taken perhaps a dozen pictures at Brown Bluff. We were particularly interested in six of them. The first showed two figures, dressed in blue, walking toward the hillock. One of them was taller and wore his life jacket. The next picture was about the same, but in the third one, Jon had grabbed Twila's arm, and we could see his profile and hers.

The fourth picture showed them walking over the rise. In the fifth picture, Jon had turned his face, and we clearly saw him. He was coming back alone. He wasn't wearing a life jacket. In the sixth frame, we had a clearer view of his face. The time frame at the bottom told us that the entire ordeal had taken slightly under seven minutes.

"Do you wish to tell us what happened?" The captain asked.

Jon hugged his body and pulled his legs in tightly on the bunk. He rolled

447

over and lay in the fetal position.

"I'll explain it, then," I said and turned to Captain Robert. "You have the right to correct me, Jon, if I'm wrong."

He remained in the fetal position with his eyes closed.

"I have to guess about a few things—I mean, up until the killing. That much we can prove."

"No question about that," Captain Robert said. "I shall be most happy to write a deposition for you."

I thanked him and said, "Here's what happened." I smiled because I was sure I must have sounded exactly like Jessica Fletcher as she explained how she put the clues together to catch the culprit.

"It began with a simple assumption: Jon wrongly assumed that Twila had included him in the book." I paused and said, "I'm not sure why—maybe he was angry because he didn't like the way he *assumed* she portrayed him."

"You have no idea, do you?" Jon said, but he didn't move.

"No, but I'm sure it was something trivial." I gazed at Burton. The shocked look on his face made me feel good. "Something more normal people wouldn't have thought twice about."

"Trivial? If only you knew," Jon said.

"Maybe we're not bright enough to figure it out," Burton said, "but nothing is important enough to kill for."

I wanted to see if I could make a Jessica Fletcher script actually happen, so I said, "After all, you are a mental patient."

"I was. I'm cured."

"Oh, that's what the nutcases say?"

Burton's mouth opened, but he caught on and said nothing.

"You think you know just about everything, don't you?" Jon sat up in bed. "You have no idea why I killed her."

"The book—your mistaken assumption—"

"That's not what I meant," he said.

"What did you mean?"

"She knew. I thought she would tell."

"Knew what?" I feigned indifference. "It couldn't have been much—"

"I loved you, did you know that?" Jon yelled. "I loved you. I was willing to marry you!"

Now I knew he really was a borderline personality. I sat down on the bunk beside him. "And I'm not worthy of your love. Right?"

"Just like the others," he said, and he focused on me with that unblinking stare.

I heard something—something ominous—in the way he said, "Just like the others." Any good therapist automatically listens to the tone of the voice, perhaps even more than the words. "What about the others?" I said in my quiet, professional voice. "Twila found out, didn't she?"

He nodded.

"How did she find out?"

"I did something stupid—I mean, really, really stupid."

"You told her? Is that it?"

"How did you know?"

I didn't know, but I was trusting my intuitive sense on this one. "She was your doctor, and you felt you could trust her. . .that she'd never tell. . .and you were safe."

"That's exactly right! She led me on! She made me feel I could say anything, and I would be safe."

"But weren't you safe? Did she betray you in some way?"

"Worse."

I must have frowned, because I was momentarily lost.

"So you don't know everything, do you?"

"She may not be as bright as you are," Burton said. He spoke with exactly the right tone that invited trust.

"I told her—about the others—about my first three wives—"

"That you killed them?" Those words just slipped out of my mouth, but as I said them, I knew they were right.

"Yes, I killed them. Do you want to know how I did it? No one suspected me. I was far, far more clever than the police."

I didn't want to know, but Burton said, still in that calm voice, "Yes, tell us how you outwitted everyone."

Jon got up and paced the small cabin. *Paced* may not be the correct word, but his movement reminded me of the way a lion walks around in a cage. He spoke faster and faster, and at times Burton calmly asked him to say something again.

"Fascinating, isn't it?" Jon said.

"Oh, that it is," I said perhaps a little too skeptically, but he didn't catch the sarcasm in my voice.

He had married three times and in three different parts of the country. The marriages started fine, but (in his words) in each case his wife became difficult and constantly nagged him. They fought. He beat up the first one, and she called the police. He knew he had to be careful. So he made up with her. "She believed me." They lived in Colorado and decided to sell everything and move to Florida.

He killed her along the way, weighted down her body, and dropped her off a bridge along the Mississippi River. He moved, instead of to Florida, to Kentucky. The second wife he dumped in the Ohio River. For the third wife, he rented a motorboat at St. Petersburg and pushed her off into the Gulf of Mexico.

He went into vivid detail about what he had done, explaining that no one had ever tracked him down. He wrote to friends in various places and told them that his wife had met someone else and left him.

"But I made one big, big, stupid, stupid mistake: I trusted Twila."

"Did she threaten to turn you in?" I asked.

"No, she couldn't do that." He winked. "Doctor-client privilege."

"Oh," I said.

"But she bugged me again and again. 'You need to make this right,' she would say to me. Almost every time she saw me, she said something like that. But I fixed her—"

I was ready to say, "So you killed her?" but I hesitated.

"No, see, I planned to take care of her. I smuggled a knife in the bottom of my luggage. I was going to kill her and toss her overboard, but she never walked on the deck alone. When I tried to talk to her, she insisted on sitting in the lounge."

He said that after he saw how they did landings on the *Vaschenko*, it was easy to lure her. On the Zodiac, he whispered to her that he was ready to turn himself in when they got back, but he needed to talk to her about something first.

He got her away from the others. As they walked along, she began to resist him and said she didn't believe him. He grabbed her and told her he wouldn't hurt her. "She believed me then," he said with a satisfied smile.

After that it was simple. He stabbed Twila six times to be sure she was gone. He dropped his life jacket next to her body so there wouldn't be an extra one on the beach and made his way back to the others.

He saw Heather, but at the time he didn't realize she had taken his picture. "Or there might have been two bodies left on Brown Bluff."

"So you waited until Ivan was distracted on the VHF radio to the ship, got behind him, and said that two passengers were sick and were going back on the third Zodiac." I stopped and turned to Jon. "How am I doing so far?"

"You make it sound easy. It worked because I was clever. I had vomited on board the ship before we went. Three people saw me. That was clever, wasn't it?"

"Oh yes," I said. "I would say that showed how cleverly you planned everything."

"Ivan was the only weak part of the plan. But it worked easier than I thought."

"Obviously," I said.

"You got into the other boat and probably induced your own vomiting again so there would be no question about your being sick," Burton said.

"I want to be clear about one thing." The captain spoke for the first time. "You killed the woman—Ms. Wilson—because of the pictures? Is that not so?"

"You might as well admit it," I said. "We have enough circumstantial evidence."

"We have everything but an actual picture of the murders taking place,"

Burton said.

"But that's good enough," the captain said.

"So the reason for killing Heather—"

"Don't go stupid on me now," Jon said.

We stood silently around the bunk. I wasn't sure what to do next. We had him—I knew that, and so did Burton and the captain.

"You are saying, then, are you not, that you also took the life of Ms. Wilson?" Captain Robert said.

He shrugged. "What is it they say about if you're going to hang for a chicken, you might as well hang for a cow?"

I had never heard that before and wasn't sure it made sense. But it didn't have to make sense to me.

"All right, I did it," Jon said in a faint voice. He sounded like a child. "Twila wanted to ruin my life. She was going to put everything about me in her book."

"You're wrong," I said.

"You're not in the book," Burton added.

"How do you know that?" His eyes popped open wide, and he stared at me. "What do you mean? Not in the book? How can that be?"

"Because we have identified all twenty-one people. You're not one of them."

"That is a lie!"

"I'll show you." I poked my hand into my shoulder bag and pulled out the list and held it out to him.

He snatched the paper from me. His whole head moved as he read down the list.

"My assumption is that Twila thought you were either too far beyond her help, or—"

I watched the movement of Jon's eyes as he read down the page, reached the bottom, and went through the list again. He screamed and wadded up the paper with his left hand and struck out at me with his right.

Burton grabbed his left hand and twisted his wrist. "Let go of the paper."

It didn't take much pressure before he dropped the single sheet. I folded it. "We know all the information," I said, "so you couldn't have destroyed anything significant."

41

I might as well tell you the rest of Jon Friesen's story. I hesitated because this honestly sounds like the conclusion of *Diagnosis: Murder* or *Murder, She Wrote* where they corner a criminal and he cries out something like "You have to believe me because I didn't mean. . . ," or some silly babble. It's a clear, neat ending for a TV script that has a forty-eight-minute time length for each episode.

Life isn't usually that clean; however, in this case Jon finally said he wanted to talk to me. Alone.

I told Burton it was all right, and the other two went outside the cabin and closed the door.

"You know I love you, don't you?" he asked. "I saw the way you looked at me at church."

This was true paranoia speaking, and I sat down on the bunk across from him. He confessed his love to me several times. When I mentioned his affair with Heather, he said, "She meant nothing to me. It was you—only you that I wanted."

I believed that he believed his own words right then. In an hour he probably wouldn't.

He began to ramble about not trusting people, especially shrinks. "She didn't turn me in and said she wouldn't, but she begged me to give myself up. I told her I wasn't ever going to do it again—you know, hurt anyone." He rambled then about forgiveness because he had asked God to forgive him, and if what Burton preached was true, he was forgiven.

I wanted to say that I was sure Burton also pointed out that we have to take responsibility for our wrongdoing and pay the penalty.

I didn't.

He seemed to calm down and said, "You know what she told me?"

I shook my head.

"She said I have no conscience!" His voice began to rise again. "Who did she think she was to say that?"

"Is it true?" I hadn't meant to say that, but the words popped out.

He stared blankly at first before he said, "I guess that's true. I don't regret killing any of them."

"So you killed your former wives—"

"They were an inconvenience—"

"I'm sure of that."

"If only Heather hadn't been so underhanded and scheming. And demanding. That was the worst part: her demands."

"Demands?" I echoed.

"Yes, she wanted to marry me or—"

"Oh." I had no idea what else to say.

Jon went into another tirade about Heather, and I let him talk. This time it must have gone on for twenty minutes. I didn't understand it all, but I think he mixed up Heather with his mother and a sister and someone else. Or maybe I just couldn't follow his nonlinear ranting.

He finally shut up and sat quietly on his bunk for a few seconds. Then, as if he had flipped the switch, he said, "So that's over. What's next?" His voice was as casual as if he asked, "What's next on the menu?"

"I know you don't get it, but this is an extremely sad and painful time for me," I said. "Twila had only a short time to live, and you killed her."

I told him about her cancer.

He giggled. He actually giggled. "Then I saved her a lot of pain, didn't I?"

Burton opened the door just then. The captain and two crewmen were behind him.

I wouldn't have killed Jon, but I would have hit him. As it was, I burst into tears and couldn't stop sobbing for a long time. Burton's warm, comforting arms finally calmed me. He led me to my cabin. He had Betty bring the doctor, who offered me a tranquilizer. I refused it and lay on my bunk and sobbed as if I could cry out all the pain.

I cried for peace, but none came.

After what seemed like hours, exhaustion set in and I felt myself drift slowly to sleep.

42

When the ship docked at Ushuaia, the Argentinean police stood at the foot of the gangplank, ready to arrest Jon. An American official, who I assumed was the ambassador, was with them. Even though the murder took place in international waters, Thomas said Argentina claimed ownership of that part of the world. "They must decide whether to try him in South America or in North America." He spat over the side of the ship and added, "For two killings, does it make any difference where the trial happens?"

I didn't want to hear any more of his speculation, so I walked away.

We stood on the deck but couldn't leave the ship until they took Jon away. No one told us anything.

As soon as he was off the ship, Jon stopped and waved to all of us. Despite his handcuffs, his arms waved wildly. To their credit, no one waved back. No one spoke. He said something to the police and looked back at us. He yelled something at us. I was glad we couldn't hear what he said.

On the return flight from Ushuaia to Buenos Aires, Burton sat next to me in Twila's vacant seat. Neither of us said a word until we were airborne.

"How are you feeling?" He turned to me with those soft, pastoral-looking eyes, and I had to look away.

"How do you think I feel?" I realized I had an edge to my voice. "I've lost the dearest friend in my life."

To his credit, he didn't say, "I know just how you feel," or some inane remark. Instead, he took both my hands before I could pull them away. He prayed for me and asked God to grant me peace and to soften my sense of loss.

I cried again, but this time the pain wasn't as deep. I missed Twila—and I knew I would miss her for a long time—but his prayer brought solace. I don't know how it's possible to be at peace and to cry at the same time, but that's what I did.

"Thank you." As soon as I was aware that he still held my hands, I pulled them away. A flicker of pain crossed his face.

"Julie, I—"

"Don't," I said. "I love you. You have done so much for me. I'm a serious Christian today—maybe not a good one, but I'm learning."

"There is definitely a *but* at the end of that sentence," he said softly.

"And you know what it is." I turned my face away from him. "Please leave my life. I don't want to see you again until—"

"You did say *until*?"

"Yes, of course."

"I'll call you," he said.

He didn't change seats but remained next to me for the rest of the flight. Our plane was late pulling into the gate, but I didn't say a word to him for the three hours we were together.

On the flight to Atlanta, he changed seats again and sat beside me. I watched movies and he listened to music. We sat as if we were total strangers. Once his leg brushed mine and he apologized.

The plane landed in Atlanta, and we still hadn't spoken. I wished he had stayed in his own assigned seat. I couldn't help but look at him. He needed a haircut, and after all those hours on the plane, his dark facial hair made it look as if he had started to grow a beard.

He was on the aisle and stood up. He looked at me and said, "May I get your bag from the overhead compartment?"

I shook my head. "Please, I don't want to see you or hear from you until."

He nodded and went forward with the crowd. I waited until the aisle was empty before I got up and retrieved my bag. A couple of minutes later, I spotted him in a line at customs, but he was quite a distance ahead of me. By the time I had my luggage and got to the taxi stand, he was gone. I shared a cab with Betty Freeman.

Betty gurgled over the wonderful trip, and I smiled whenever she paused. I didn't hear anything she said. My mind flitted between my grief for Twila and my love for Burton.

Dear God, if You don't mind listening to me, please help Burton. He really needs You.

My cell rang on Friday morning, which was the third day after our return from Antarctica.

"It is Until Day," he said.

"You're sure?"

"You said I couldn't call until. Remember?"

I started to cry softly. I couldn't help it. Two or three times he tried to explain, but my sobbing increased.

"I can't talk—" Fresh tears stopped me from saying anything else. I hung up.

Afterward I wondered if Burton understood my tears.

43

Saturday morning the doorbell rang just before seven o'clock. I knew who it was just by the three short rings.

I had barely gotten in from my morning run and was perspiring, but I opened the door.

"I know, I know," he said. "You just got in." Before I could answer, he said, "I parked across the street and waited for you to come back." He held a bag from Starbucks. "Vanilla latte and a chocolate bagel for you," he said. "Black with a spoon of milk and a raisin bagel for me."

I had spotted his car across the street but pretended I hadn't.

"You'll have to sit at the breakfast table while I shower."

He sat down, and I hurried to my bedroom. I closed the door, and fresh tears came. But this time, I prayed. I prayed out loud. It was the first time in my life that I had ever done that.

"Thank you, God." I said the words several times.

And something else happened: I knew God heard me. I didn't know where this would end, but I knew God had heard me pray. And I knew I had a true talking-praying relationship with the Lord.

"So that's what people mean when they talk about touching heaven," I said to myself.

For once, I had no smart remark to make to myself.

⌒

"I think it's time I talked to my parents," Burton said. He set down his cup of unfinished coffee and stared at me. Those blue eyes showed such sorrow that my maternal instincts wanted to grab him and soothe him. This wasn't the time to soothe him.

"With me? Without me?" I asked.

"I can't do it unless you're there. You know everything anyway."

"You're sure? Really sure that you're ready?"

He didn't answer. The grim set of his jaw was the only response I needed.

"As soon as you can get dressed, we'll drive there."

"I am dressed," I said. I wore my only pair of Donna Karan jeans that flattered my amorphous figure better than anything I'd ever owned. They were topped by a

456

simple pale green sweater with kelly green piping. I had hesitated about earrings and finally wore tiny gold ones. And sandals, of course. With Burton always flat shoes.

He smiled and embraced me. "You know, the few times I was able to hold you in Antarctica, I missed the fragrance of your perfume."

"Why waste it?" I said. "Besides, I didn't know I'd let you hold me."

He smiled. "I knew."

"Oh, and how did you know?"

"Twila told me. She assured me—no, she actually promised me as if she had been able to look into some kind of magic fortune cookie—"

"That's because she loved us both," I said. "I don't think she saw it. I think she wanted it to happen."

He kissed my cheek. "So did God."

―

The Burtons live in Woodstock, which was close to an hour's drive for us from Clayton County on the Southside of Atlanta.

Burton had finished his coffee and swallowed the last of his bagel. "Whenever," he said.

"I'm ready. I'll finish my latte in the car."

By the time we left Riverdale and headed up the east side of I-285, I had drunk the rest of my coffee and decided I was too nervous to finish the bagel. I put it in the bag for garbage.

Burton handed me his cell. He refuses to talk while he's driving, and I like that about him. I opened the cell and thumbed down until I found their number. "Hi, this is Julie West—you know, Burton's friend—"

That was all I needed to say. His mother, Marianne, was a warm, talkative soul. "So when are you coming to see us?" she asked.

"Strange you should ask. I'm in Burton's car right now. We're on the way. I estimate about thirty-five minutes."

"Thank you for coming with him," she said and asked me questions about the cruise. I promised we'd tell her details after we arrived.

That satisfied Marianne. Before she hung up, she said, "I'll have coffee and fresh muffins ready for you."

That was Burton's mom. I had liked her the first time we met. She was slender, maybe five three. I'm sure most people looked at the family and assumed that he had gotten the smile and those blue eyes from her. The elder James Burton had dark, curly hair. He was about an inch taller than I was. On the few occasions I had been with him, I always said, "You're a man to whom I can look up."

He liked that.

James Burton was quiet—and he'd have to be with a lively wife like Marianne.

But one thing I liked about him: When he did speak, he always had something to say.

Nearly forty minutes later, we arrived at his parents' house. I knew Burton had kept the speed down, and I told him, "You drive as if you want to prolong the time until the moment of truth."

"Moment of truth? From which TV show did you pick that one up?"

"I don't remember, but it has a nice ring to it."

If his face hadn't been so grimly set, I think he would have smiled.

His father was James Burton Jr., and Burton hadn't wanted to be called the Third or Trip, so he asked everyone to call him Burton. James and Marianne had called their son Burton from the time he was about three years old.

———

Burton hadn't said more than three or four sentences on the drive. I knew he was lost in his own tortured soul.

We pulled up to the main entrance of a gated community with a guardhouse and two security guards staffing it. Even though both of us had been there before and Burton recognized one of the guards, we still had to show them our IDs. One guard scrutinized our drivers' licenses while the other guard phoned the Burtons' house.

He handed us back our licenses. "You take a left at the top—"

"I know where it is," Burton said.

"—of the hill. That's Twelve Oaks. Go two streets and take the next left on Tara Trace. It's the second house, number 107." He held out a clipboard for Burton to sign. After the signature, he saluted us. "Sorry, Burton, but I got reprimanded a month ago for being friendly."

"It's okay," I said. "We understand."

The house on Tara Trace was not only large but also two stories high, and I think it must have had six bedrooms. (I never asked.) It looked like something out of *Gone with the Wind*. But then, that was the idea. It had four immense white columns in front, and the building was made of weathered red brick. As we pulled up, I saw the open garage and a Mercedes parked next to a sleek-looking sports car.

We walked up the eight steps to the immense front porch that went halfway around the house. The front door was made of thick dark cherrywood and flanked on each side by narrow leaded windows.

We had barely gotten to the door before it flew open and Marianne Burton rushed forward and hugged both of us. She wore a simple pale pink pantsuit that probably cost more than everything I wore. She wore one thin, scalloped gold necklace with matching earrings. I liked the simplicity of her clothes. I had no doubt that everything she wore was expensive, but her clothes were what I call subtly elegant.

James Burton Jr. stood at the door and waited his turn so he could embrace us both.

"You're the finest woman he's ever brought here," he whispered and chuckled. "Come to think of it, you're the only one." He wore a blue blazer, white trousers, and a silk shirt with an ascot tied at the neck. On most men it would have look pretentious; on James Burton Jr., it looked natural.

James brought us immediately into the living room, which was a cluster of huge English Chippendale wing chairs and Irish Chippendale side tables in front of the fireplace. I don't know much about furniture, but I know my Chippendales.

After we sat down, Marianne brought coffee and hot bran muffins on a tray. She and her husband had tea, but they served us coffee.

"So you went to Antarctica?" Marianne said. "I'm sure it was lovely—I mean, what you saw of it."

I knew she and James had been there a decade earlier, so I added, "I don't imagine anything has changed."

"Not there."

Burton sat quietly. He gave one- or two-word answers if asked, but otherwise he sipped his coffee slowly. He left his muffin untouched.

For perhaps twenty minutes, Marianne and I talked about everything that had happened in Antarctica. They had gone from Australia and seen the larger, emperor penguins but admitted they hadn't seen nearly as much wildlife as we had.

After a few minutes, the conversation lagged. To her credit, Marianne stayed cheerful. She asked about Twila, expressed sympathy, and then asked about Jon Friesen. CNN had said he was being sent back to Atlanta for trial. "We also read about it in the papers. Terrible, terrible."

"Yes, it was," Burton said.

That time he spoke three words. But it was obvious he wasn't going to say more.

Marianne cleared away the coffee and muffin crumbs and came back to the table. "Okay, son, what is it? Something's bothering you very, very much." She smiled and said, "I don't have to be a mother to detect the sad face."

Burton looked at her and then at his father. The love those eyes showed toward him touched me. I wished I had grown up in a family with that kind of warmth.

"I have something to tell you," he said. "Something that's not easy for me to talk about—but I have to say it."

Ordinarily I would have immediately made some smart remark to relieve the tension, but this time Burton didn't need any distraction.

"Let's sit in the den," James said. "It's more intimate." We followed him into the room. The furniture was every bit as expensive—or at least it looked expensive to me, but it had a warmth about it. Two walls were lined with bookcases, a third wall was mostly window, and the fourth wall housed another fireplace. It wasn't cold enough for a fire, but it felt cheery sitting in a semicircle.

For at least a full minute, no one said anything. I heard the ticking of the grandfather clock from the room we had just left.

"Do you remember Dan Rosenberry?" Burton asked.

"How could we ever forget him?" Marianne said. She turned to me. "Burton and Dan were inseparable friends. I mean, like twins—"

I knew that, but I smiled and asked, "That close?"

"Oh yes, they did everything together. Burton never had a sibling, so we welcomed Dan."

"I think he slept here more than he slept at home," James said.

Marianne leaned forward. "Just to fill you in, Julie, Dan had a terrible childhood. His dad was an alcoholic, and I think his mother drank a little—"

"She drank about as much as he did," Burton said in a soft but unemotional voice.

"The boys were about the same size," Marianne said. "They shared each other's clothes constantly—"

"Primarily, Dan shared Burton's," his father said. "Most of Dan's clothes weren't very good." He smiled and said, "I don't mean that to sound snobbish. His clothes were faded, small holes in his sweaters; sometimes his shirts lacked buttons—that sort of thing."

"That's right," she said. "I had forgotten. We loved the boy. We truly did. In fact, by the time they were in fourth grade when we bought new clothes for Burton, we frequently bought clothes for Dan. But his mother just couldn't seem to keep them in good condition. Despite all of that, he was a sweet kid."

"His parents," James said, "were rather strange. Both parents worked—that is, both worked some of the time—"

"They had a special ability to get fired," Burton said. I was surprised at the lack of emotion in his voice. "She couldn't get to work sober, and he argued with everyone."

"But Dan was special. Yes, he was very, very special," Marianne said. "He was also bright—in fact, he was probably a little smarter than our Burton."

"That's true," Burton said, "but most of all, I loved him, you know. He was—" His voice broke, and he pulled out a handkerchief and wiped his eyes.

"That's what made the loss so bad for you." Marianne patted his hand. "The accident was such a terrible, terrible blow for you. I wasn't sure you'd ever recover. And all those months you spent in the hospital—"

"That's what I want to talk about," Burton said. "I need to tell you about the accident."

44

Are you sure you want to?" the elder Burton asked. "We'll listen, of course, but we know how much you loved him, and it hurts us to see you in pain."

"You don't have to tell us anything," Marianne said. The tone of her voice sounded odd, and I couldn't figure out what she meant. "Sometimes it's best to leave the past behind and to move on."

"Yes, son," James said, "it's all right not to go into the accident."

"I have to tell you. I have to explain—explain things no one else knows—I mean, except Julie. There's something—something I did. Something wrong—really wrong—and I've carried it all these years. I need to tell *you*, most of all."

James walked over, pulled Burton to his feet, and hugged him. That didn't seem characteristic of him, so it was obvious James sensed that this was a terrible confession Burton had to make. "I hope you know we love you, son. No matter what you have to tell us."

Burton held James's shoulders, and I thought Burton's heart had broken. I suppose it had. Many people have come to my office over the years and cried, and some of them reminded me of wounded animals, wailing in despair. I had never heard such convulsive crying from a man before.

As I watched, and despite my resolve, tears cascaded down my face. I was so proud of Burton. At last he was going to tell the truth. I thought of a verse in the Bible—although I had no idea where it was—that said the truth would set people free.

Marianne clasped my hand. Her grip was so tight I finally had to pull it away to get the circulation going again.

I don't know how long Burton cried on his dad's shoulder. It was probably only four or five minutes. I didn't think about time; I thought about Burton's pain, something he had carried for almost twenty years.

Burton sat on the sofa next to me and took my hand. "I have to tell you this. It's hard on me, and I know it will be harder on you, but I owe you the truth."

"You're sure?" Marianne said.

"I have to tell you."

45

Both boys were ten years old, although Burton was younger by four months. A few days before Christmas, Dan Rosenberry's father decided he wanted to put up a live Christmas tree. His father told him that they had not been able to afford one since Dan was a baby. Things were different now. He had a good job and had been with the same company ten months, which was the longest Dan ever remembered his dad keeping a job.

His mother had worked steadily at a convenience store for a couple of months and had been sober when she went to work.

Instead of buying a tree, Randolph, Dan's father, decided it would look nicer (and save money) to drive north of Atlanta to the mountains near Dawsonville. Dan's father had heard that there were many good trees of the right size less than a mile off the road. "They're just waiting for someone to claim them."

"But that's stealing—"

"Shut your mouth," Wanda Maxine Rosenberry said.

"I don't plan to pay for no tree while they're just standing alongside the road, begging for someone to take them."

Dan knew better than to argue.

They took both Dan and his best friend for the big tree-hunting event. They also carried a large supply of beer and popped open one bottle after another.

Randolph drove his ten-year-old Honda Accord about twenty miles over the speed limit. Once in a while he'd get so caught up in his beer, the speed would drop down, but then he would abruptly speed up again.

Both boys knew it wasn't wise to say anything. Dan had once commented on the speed, and Randolph slapped his son and sped up more. Dan never said anything again about it. Burton whispered that he felt better not looking at the speedometer.

Shortly after they left the Southside of Atlanta, the first raindrops landed softly on the windshield and ran downward in hesitant streams. The farther north they drove, the more intense the rain became. Before long, hard spikes of rain made tuneless music against the top of the Honda. From the distant mountains came the ominous, rhythmic booming of a storm. It was getting worse.

"Heavy rain ain't no big deal," Randolph said. "Only sissies are afraid of a little wet stuff."

The air had grown colder, and the rain turned into sleet. They were going steadily uphill and around tight curves, but Randolph didn't slow down. Soon the barren trees were jacketed in glittering ice. Bare, black branches poked from beneath the outer layers like shattered bones.

"Honey, you might be going a little fast for the curves," his wife said.

"Just shut up. Hand me another beer and leave the driving to me!"

The two boys sat in the backseat. Dan hugged himself and bunched into a corner.

"You cold?" Burton asked.

"A little." His jacket was hardly warm enough for the temperature that hovered just above freezing. Randolph refused to use heat in the car. "Suck it in, boys!" he yelled back at them. "Cold weather makes you strong."

"If I had a hundred extra pounds on my body, I'd feel the same way," Burton whispered to his friend.

Dan's teeth began to chatter.

Burton took off his heavy, hooded jacket. "Here, put this on. It's plenty warm."

"But you'll get cold."

"When I do, I'll ask for it back," Burton said.

Dan smiled gratefully, and they exchanged jackets.

A little later, Randolph stopped on private property that was far enough from the main road or from any house so that no one would see them. He walked around and seemed not to notice the stinging sleet. The boys wanted to stay in the car, but he wouldn't let them. "See how a real man works," Randolph said. He grabbed his gas-powered chain saw and paced an area of about fifty feet until he found exactly the tree he wanted. He circled the tree several times. Wanda Rosenberry pulled her cotton coat tighter. "Yeah, fine. Just get it."

"This is some beauty," he said and started the saw going. The sleet had not let up and a few snow flurries mingled with the sleet. The boys wanted to go back to the car. "Just stand there and see how a man works!" he repeated.

It took less than a minute for the tree to fall, and its icy blanket shattered on the ground.

He made the boys grab the top and help him carry the tree back to the car. "Don't want to drag it on the ground," he said. Burton had gloves and Dan didn't. "Keep your hands in your pocket," Burton whispered. "I'll do it." By then, he was also wearing the hooded jacket again.

Randolph tied the tree across the top of the car with the ropes through the two front windows. The trip going back was even colder with half an inch of space for the sleet to come into the vehicle.

Dan's teeth began to chatter. The boys decided they would alternate wearing Burton's jacket every ten minutes. Burton handed him his watch (Dan had none). "Put it on and you watch the time. When the ten minutes are up, you give me back the jacket and the watch."

Dan smiled gratefully and said, "This makes a good game."

Before they got back on the main road, both of Dan's parents drank four more bottles of beer, and his mother opened a new case. They started driving south.

The flurries grew heavier. The windshield wipers could barely keep up with the white flakes. The more beer Dan's parents put away, the more erratic the driving became. Several times Randolph swerved across the road into the other lane.

Burton opened his mouth to say something, but Dan put his hand on his sleeve and whispered, "Don't. It will make it worse."

"So what do we do?"

"Pray, I guess," Dan said. He scrunched down in the seat behind his father, hoping that being out of the path of the wind and wearing the hooded jacket would help him warm up before he had to return it.

Events after that weren't clear. The police report said that Randolph Rosenberry, age forty-nine, driving south on Georgia Highway 400, attempted to pass a slow-moving Ford pickup on an upward curve. He crossed the double yellow lines to make the pass. He barely passed the truck and reached the top of the incline when a school bus appeared heading north. Rosenberry pressed his foot on the brake. Either the car skidded on the icy road or he turned the wheel too far to the right to get back into his lane. No one was sure about that part.

The car ran off the road and down an embankment. The police records stated the drop was ninety-eight feet. When the vehicle hit bottom, the speedometer stopped at eighty-six miles per hour. The Honda landed on its side with the passenger side smashed on the ground and glass spattered all through the car.

Both of Dan's parents had been smoking. The report said that as far as they could tell, one or both of the cigarettes ignited their clothes or their upholstery. Within minutes after the car hit the bottom of the ravine, the entire interior of the car was aflame.

The driver of the bus stopped his vehicle and started to rush down the embankment. It was dangerous getting to the car. He fell twice. When he finally reached the burning car, the door behind the driver was partially open, so he reached inside and grabbed the first body he saw and carried it about twenty feet away. By then, two other men had also stopped and raced down to the scene.

Someone pulled out a second body—the driver. He was breathing and his arms flailed.

Because of the spread of the flames, the three men weren't able to get to the other two people still inside the car. Someone rushed down to them with a fire extinguisher. It didn't matter; their bodies were so badly burned that no one would have been able to recognize them.

The first survivor, a boy, was unconscious. His face was smashed from the impact, and heavy shards of glass were wedged into his face and skull. Third-degree burns covered both legs and later required grafting. On his arms were first- and second-degree burns. His right arm was broken, and he had contusions and minor lacerations all over his body.

—

The boy awakened in the hospital. His face was wrapped in bandages and his arm in a sling. Every part of his body cried out in pain.

"Good afternoon," the nurse said. "Are you ready to stay awake now?"

He nodded. "I—I don't know what—"

"Shh, be quiet," she said. "Your parents are in the waiting room. I'll call them. They've been here almost around the clock."

"Am I going to die?"

"No, you're going to be fine."

"My friend—"

"Shh, you rest now." She checked his IV, flicked it with her finger. "Relax. You're going to be fine, but you need to rest."

He wanted to cry out and ask what happened, but he fell asleep.

When he awakened, the doctor was examining him. The nurse pulled the thermometer from his mouth. "Normal," she said and smiled. "First time."

"Well, you've had quite a journey, haven't you?" the doctor asked.

"What happened?"

The doctor turned, and the boy saw the Burtons holding each other. "You tell him," James Burton said.

"The car ran off the road," the doctor said. "Your friend Dan died instantly; so did his mother. His father survived about two hours, and we couldn't save him."

"Just me?"

"Yes, only you," the doctor said. "And we weren't sure about you at first. Your injuries were quite substantial—"

The doctor patted the edge of the bed. "But you'll be fine now. You'll have to stay with us for a while, but I think we can fix you up."

"Just me?" the boy asked again.

"Just you." The doctor's voice cracked as he added, "Your parents identified you because of your jacket and your watch with your name engraved on the backside. Your face was so badly damaged, no one would have been able to recognize you. By using pictures from your parents, we've tried to reconstruct your face. We can't make you quite as pretty as—"

"When? When did it happen?" the boy asked.

"Six days ago," the nurse said. "You've been unconscious most of the time."

"Six days?" The boy heard the words, but the meaning eluded him. "I don't understand."

"Your parents tell us they call you Burton. Just rest, son. You're alive."

"But what about—?"

"Your friend died, and so did his parents."

"Dead? Dead?" the boy asked again.

He remembered nothing after that. He must have drifted off again. When he awakened, his room was dark. Only lights of the city shone into his room.

As the boy lay there, the meaning of the words sunk in. He was the only survivor. The doctor said that all three Rosenberrys were dead.

All three?

They think I'm Burton.

He lay quietly as that thought filled his mind. "They think I'm Burton," he said aloud.

Sleep eluded Dan for the rest of the night. "This isn't right," he kept saying to himself. "I'm Dan. I'm the only survivor. I can't let them think I'm Burton."

He was too worn out to do anything. In the morning he would tell them the truth. He had lost his parents; they had lost their son.

But as he drifted into sleep, he thought of what it would be like to be James Burton III.

He knew his parents hadn't been good parents. He had seen too many examples of happy families, normal people like the Burtons. So many times he had yearned to have a family like that. He used to daydream that he had been adopted or stolen and his real parents found him. They would love him, and he'd never have to worry about having decent clothes or enough food to eat.

He was almost asleep before he asked himself, "Why can't I? Why can't I become Burton? By the time they fix my face, no one will ever know." They were about the same size, same color hair and eyes. People had sometimes called them brothers or even twins.

"No one will ever know."

He said those words aloud several times.

"Besides, I don't have anyplace to go." Tears seeped out of his eyes. He felt he had never really had anyplace to go except the Burtons'. They lived in a big house only four streets away from the run-down apartment his parents rented. "They wouldn't want me if they thought I was Dan."

The two had been close friends since they met in first grade. Burton had no brothers or sisters. Dan was an only child. There had been a sister, but she died when he was three or four. If he had other relatives, he didn't know about them.

"And the Burtons have nobody," he said.

Again and again he thought about the situation. *I don't have anyone in the world who knows me. My parents are dead. And my old man was nothing but a drunk anyway. Mom was a little nicer, but she was just as bad a drunk.*

"What do I have to go home to?" he asked aloud. "I don't even have a place to go. Who would want me?"

He became suddenly alert and thought about the situation. If they believed he was Burton, he could have parents—real parents—people who would love him. He wouldn't have to lie to the apartment manager about why they couldn't pay the rent. He wouldn't have to beg the owner of the liquor store to let his parents have just one more six-pack.

"I'm Burton," he said aloud. "I'm James Burton the III."

For the next three hours he tried to think of everything Burton had told him and what he had observed in the home. "I'll be Burton."

—

His face was in such bad shape that it took four surgeries before Dan resembled the pictures of James Burton III. Nearly six weeks passed before he went "home."

For a long time he tried not to think about what he had done. He became extremely quiet for several weeks. He tried to absorb as much information as he could about the family and especially about Burton. He didn't want to make a mistake.

His "parents" took him to their church. After he became a believer, he went through a communicants' class. The pastor assured him that if he confessed his sins, God had forgiven him.

"All my sins?" the boy asked. "Even the worst, worst sins in the whole world?"

"Yes, Burton, even the worst of the worst."

It was the first time he had felt at peace since the surgery.

After that, the new Burton blossomed. His grades at school were near the top. Burton hadn't been as good a student as Dan, so he emphasized how hard he studied so he could bring home better grades.

The Burtons never questioned his identity. They showered the same warmth and love on him that he had seen them display toward Burton.

He became a better listener, and for several years, he remained afraid that he would be exposed. But the pastor's words slowly eased themselves into his heart. "I am forgiven," he said. "Jesus Christ has forgiven every sin."

Those words brought deep peace.

For a long time the pastor's assurance had been enough. It wasn't until he was in seminary that he began to think of the consequences. He had lied. He had deceived the Burtons.

He hadn't told anyone except Roger Harden, who was dead. And then Julie, whom he loved.

—

Roger Harden had seen Burton's grades. He had the eleventh highest grade-point average in his graduating class. Eleventh. He could have been number one, but he was afraid that would expose him.

Too late he realized that if he had made only a slightly better GPA, he would have received a full scholarship to Yale, something Roger Harden offered to only one student each year.

Harden sought him out, and they talked for a long time. He was a man in his midfifties, and he had a way of listening to people that immediately enabled them to trust him. Burton liked Roger, and the older man offered him a scholarship to any school he wanted to attend. He chose Wheaton College, which is in a western suburb of Chicago.

Over the next two years, Dan-now-Burton felt a kinship with Roger. At Christmas after his first year, the student came home to Woodstock, where the Burtons now lived. But the first opportunity he had, he visited Roger at his office in midtown Atlanta.

Roger spent nearly three hours with the young man.

"What's wrong with you, son?" the man asked. "You look so sad."

"I did something bad—really bad."

It was the first time Dan felt he could trust someone with the truth. With tears streaming down his face, he told Roger Harden the truth.

"That's not so bad. You want my suggestion?"

"Of course. It's been a big burden all these years."

"Say nothing. You can't hurt anybody but your new parents, right?"

"But it's not right. I lied. I stole their son's identity."

"So you want to tell them now? After all these years? As far as they are concerned, you're their son. Don't hurt them."

Roger Harden needed almost an hour to persuade Burton not to tell.

With his head in his hands, Burton finished the story. "I love Julie, and I want to marry her. I need to make this right with God and with you. She said she wouldn't marry me until I do. She pushed me to do the right thing."

"I don't want to marry him with this on his conscience," I said. "I love him, and—and I know it hurts you—"

Burton paused and pulled out a handkerchief. "I'm sorry. So sorry. I love you, and I didn't mean to hurt you or to deceive you—"

James pulled Burton to his feet. "We love you. We've always loved you. That can't change." He kissed Burton's cheek. "Of course we forgive you."

"But I've deceived you for nearly twenty years. I know this must hurt you—but I can't—can't live with the lie any longer."

"We forgive you, son. We love you. It makes no difference to us," James said. "You have been our son. You are our son."

Burton nodded slowly, and tears fell again. When he was able to talk again, he knelt in front of Marianne. "Please forgive—"

"I love you. You have been a wonderful son to us," she said.

"How can you be so—so kind and forgiving when I've been so deceitful?"

Marianne looked at her husband, and he nodded.

She hugged Dan tightly. "We knew, *son*. We always knew."

With a dazed look on his face, Burton stared at her. He tried several times to speak, but the words seemed stuck in his throat. His lips trembled, and tears filled his dark blue eyes.

"Parents just have a sixth sense about their own child," James said.

"You had been so close to Burton, and we loved you, too," Marianne said. "You know that, don't you?"

Burton nodded twice, and more tears flowed down his cheeks.

"You had no one to take care of you." Her voice cracked before she added, "And we had lost our only child."

James cleared his throat before he said, "It seemed to us that's what Burton would have wanted us to do."

Epilogue

Everybody likes a happy ending.

And this story also has a happy ending.

First, we consulted the Burtons' family lawyer about the Dan Rosenberry–James Burton III thing. Although he agreed with us that there would probably never be any legal or ethical repercussions, Dan-cum-James should officially change his name. He did.

He also recommended that Marianne and James officially adopt James "to forestall any further legal problems."

They did.

By then, we had been back from Antarctica for six months, and my grief over Twila had begun to heal. I still miss Twila—and I think there is a hole in my heart that will never heal.

Burton asked me to marry him, and I said yes with three tonal variations and in five languages.

Burton thanked me in all five languages.

I wanted the formal Episcopal wedding ceremony, and Burton was all right with that—he's amazingly agreeable about most things. He said no only to one thing. I wanted to have three bridesmaids—which wasn't a problem, but I wanted to have two of them and leave the middle space open in memory of Twila.

"Twila is not here. You may miss her," Burton said, "but she is not here. Theologically, I wouldn't be comfortable with that."

That's Burton. When he says he wouldn't be comfortable, that's his soft way of saying no. So we compromised when I said, "We'll name our first girl Twila."

"I would be comfortable with that."

On March 23, we had our wedding. Burton contacted his best friend from his seminary days, Dr. James Martin, and he agreed to perform the ceremony.

I loved the language of the vows so much I memorized them.

Dr. Martin told Burton to face me and take my right hand before he repeated these words: "I, James Burton III, take thee, Julie West, to be my wedded wife, to have and to hold from this day forward, for better or for worse, for richer or for poorer, in sickness and in health, to love and to cherish, till death do us part, according to God's ordinance; and thereto I pledge thee my troth."

Burton released my hand. We still faced each other, and I took his right hand in mine and repeated these words: "I, Julie West, take thee, James Burton III, to be my wedded husband, to have and to hold from this day forward, for better or for worse, for richer or for poorer, in sickness and in health, to love and to cherish, till death do us part, according to God's ordinance; and thereto I pledge thee my troth."

During the rest of the ceremony, right up until the kiss, our eyes focused on each other. Never in my life had I felt so loved. I felt as if I were the most blessed person in the world: I had Burton's love, and I knew God loved me.

Surely nothing would mar our happiness—not even another murder.

When **Cecil Murphey** isn't plotting murder, he writes or cowrites books such as *90 Minutes in Heaven* (written for Don Piper), which has sold five million copies. His more than 100 published books include *When Someone You Love Has Cancer*. He speaks nationwide and enjoys meeting his readers wherever he goes. Please visit his Web site at www.the manbehindthewords.com.

You may correspond with this author by writing:
Cecil Murphey
Author Relations
PO Box 721
Uhrichsville, OH 44683

ALIBIS IN ARKANSAS

THREE ROMANCE MYSTERIES

CHRISTINE LYNXWILER
JAN REYNOLDS
SANDY GASKIN

Two sisters find mystery and love in small-town Arkansas. No matter where southern sisters Jenna and Carly go, murder turns up like a bad penny. When the local newspaper editor is killed and Carly's son is a suspect, Jenna decides to go undercover to get the scoop on the murder. A vacation in Branson, Missouri, sounds like fun, but Jenna and Carly are surprised to find that the glittering lights and twanging tunes make a perfect backdrop for. . .murder! Back home in Lakeview, Carly's new diner is really cooking. But last time he looked, murder was *not* on the menu.

ISBN 978-1-60260-229-8
$7.97

Available wherever books are sold.

COZY IN KANSAS

THREE ROMANCE MYSTERIES

NANCY MEHL

Mystery, love, and inspiration in a small-town bookstore. College student Ivy Towers has definite plans for her future. But when her great-aunt Betty is found dead inside her rare-book store, Ivy must travel back to a place and a past she thought she'd left behind. She discovers that Bitty's supposed fall from her library ladder seems quite suspicious. Ivy's decision to poke her nose into things changes her destiny and propels her into uncovering carefully hidden secrets buried deep below the surface in the small town of Winter Break, Kansas. Along the way, she will discover that love can be found where you least expect it—and in the most mysterious of circumstances.

ISBN 978-1-60260-228-1
$7.97

Available wherever books are sold.